STAR SUMMIT

THE DEBT COLLECTION
BOOK 3

ANDREW GIVLER

STAR SUMMIT
Book Three of The Debt Collection
Copyright © 2023 by Sad Seagull Publishing. All rights reserved.

Editor: Laura Jorstad
Cover Illustration: Chris McGrath
Cover Design and Interior Layout: STK·Kreations

Hardcover ISBN: 978-1-958204-09-2
Trade paperback ISBN: 978-1-958204-08-5
eBook ISBN: 978-1-958204-07-8
Worldwide Rights

THE DEBT COLLECTION SERIES:

Soul Fraud

Dandelion Audit

Star Summit

Death Tax

STAY UP TO DATE

Scan the code or find me on these social media platforms to stay up
to date on my upcoming projects and book releases!

Sign Up for my Newsletter by visiting andrewgivler.com

Book YouTube Channel: @GivReads

Instagram: @sigils

Twitter: @Sigils

Facebook: @andrewgivler

*This one's for all my friends who read the terrible books
I wrote when I was in college and told me I could be an author.
(Aki, Molly, and Caleb, I'm looking at you.)
This is definitely a little their fault.*

STAR SUMMIT

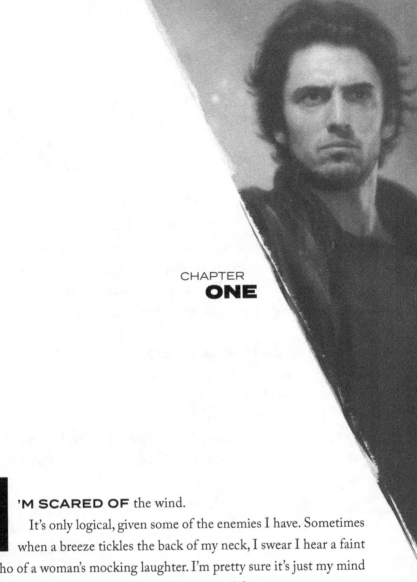

I'M SCARED OF the wind.

It's only logical, given some of the enemies I have. Sometimes when a breeze tickles the back of my neck, I swear I hear a faint echo of a woman's mocking laughter. I'm pretty sure it's just my mind playing tricks on me. But I wouldn't bet my life on it.

It was the ninth day of October, and even the eternally temperate Los Angeles winds had a cool edge to them, slicing through my thin T-shirt as I panted, trying to catch my breath. A lean Nephilim named Nika stared at me from across the arena. We were facing off in a children's playground. The ground was made of bouncy rubber, and a two-story wooden castle dominated the center, fortified with slides and all manner of monkey bars.

"Sixty seconds," called Orion from the edge of the jungle gym. The rest of the class stood next to him, watching us intensely. More than one of them looked annoyed that I was the last man standing. They had good reason: I was the only mortal in the group, and Nika was Orion's best student.

"You got this, Matt," Alex called from the sidelines, the only member of my fan club. Although from the wry smile on his face, I knew he was irritated that he had been tagged already too.

I deepened my crouch, tensing as I waited for Nika to make a move. Her body twitched before she exploded forward, which was enough warning for me. I cut to the right, running up the metal slide as smoothly as I could.

The entire structure shook as Nika leapt onto the slide behind me. I ducked through the low opening to the top of the playground and raced along one of the wooden bridges, intending to loop around the monkey bars to put some space between us.

In my head I was counting Mississippis as I sprinted; there should only be about forty seconds left. All I needed to do was be smart with my pathing, and *wham*—

The entire bridge shook like a flag in a hurricane as Nika landed in front of me. The Nephilim had used her superior strength to simply vault to the top of one of the playground's triangle roofs and leap ahead of me. The blond warrior gave me a tight, cocky smile as she blocked my path.

About thirty seconds to go. I was so close!

I leapt backward, spinning. Nika was faster than I am; the demon DNA in her blood gave her too much of an advantage for me to outrun her. But I've been chased by a minotaur. Comparatively speaking, this was a walk in the park.

Back on the main structure, I leapt off the side, grabbing the fireman's pole and using it to swing out and around as I crashed down to the earth. I could hear my pursuer's feet pounding on the rubber ground as she closed the distance between us.

I cut under the bridge Nika had trapped me on, leaping up to grab the monkey bars and wrenched my whole body up like a pole vaulter. My feet landed on top of the swing set next to the structure, and I released my grip on the metal, letting my momentum carry me up to land on the thick wooden beam.

Scrambling for my balance, I raced along the top of the swings, waiting for the structure to shake as Nika followed me up. The second I felt her land, I would jump across to the—

An iron grip settled around my shoe, causing me to stumble. My arms windmilled as I tried to catch myself. I caught sight of a smirking Nika, dangling from the wooden beam. Instead of following me, she had simply run underneath and leapt up to grab me.

Must be nice to be able to dunk on a regulation hoop. With a sigh, I stopped trying to catch my balance and dropped down to the rubber ground, landing in a crouch next to Nika.

"Time," Orion called, his tone ice-cold. My head whipped up at the displeasure in my teacher's voice. Alex and I were squires of the Hunt, and he held us to higher standards than most of his students. I knew he wouldn't be happy with how I had been caught. Then I realized the Hunter wasn't looking at me; his black eyes were fixed over my shoulder, and they moved with a dark heat.

A slow, arrogant clapping came from behind me. I turned to find myself staring at a full Nephilim. The tall man was dressed in black leathers, and golden hair fell to his shoulders in a flowing mane. His face was covered with scars, which tugged his lips back, making his sneer even more severe. He and three other Nephilim all carried naked black blades.

"Is this what the Hunter has become?" The interloper chuckled. "A babysitter teaching children to play games?" I sensed Nika shift uncomfortably next to me, as if embarrassed.

Officially, Orion makes a living teaching mixed martial arts out of a small, run-down studio in Van Nuys, because of course he does. I say "officially" because the only classes I have ever seen being held in those rooms are ones in which I'm getting my butt kicked by a bunch of overeager junior Nephilim, and there's no way they pay him enough to afford rent, let alone all the leather jackets he's always wearing.

Rumor has it he runs private training for some A-list action heroes. I'm not saying that's true, but some of the moves in my favorite movies definitely look a little familiar. Something to think about.

"What do you want, Bellerophon?" Orion replied, his tone dark and soft. The two Nephilim stared at each other for a long moment before the scarred man broke away from his group and stalked toward the Hunter. My eyes tracked his drawn sword, and I tensed, bracing for an explosion of violence. The ruby hilt of Orion's blade twinkled over his shoulder.

Bellerophon paused just out of Orion's range. "A Constellation Congregation has been called. Polaris and the Auroras have summoned you to stand before it," he said, reaching into his back pocket for a manila envelope and tossing it to Orion. "Even the mighty Hunter has masters he must obey."

I tried to picture anyone telling Orion what to do, but I couldn't. Smart people do their best not to get in his way. Not even the Queen of All Fae had dared to order around the Hunter. Whoever this guy worked for sure had a lot of confidence.

Orion glanced down at the envelope. For a moment he was completely still, the immortal way of displaying shock, but after a couple of heartbeats, he raised his head and fixed his target with a dark glare.

"You have delivered your message, Bellerophon. Now stop disrupting my students." Orion's voice was empty of any emotion, as flat and hard as a smooth marble countertop. The air around us was motionless, the calm before a storm.

The other Nephilim laughed, a cruel sound better fitting a bird of prey than a man. He turned to go, that same smirk plastered on his lips. "I've been waiting for you to get what you deserve for centuries. This is even sweeter than I imagined."

Without another look, he walked away from the Hunter, collecting his troop of minions as he went. My eyes followed the four of them until they disappeared down the street. Turning to Orion, I watched him open the envelope and pull the contents out, brows furrowed.

"Dark Abyss," the Hunter swore under his breath as he read.

"Bad news, boss?" Alex called from behind me.

"What was that?" Nika demanded from next to me, tucking a strand of blond hair behind her ear.

Orion glanced up, as if suddenly remembering his students were still there. "Class is over for today," he murmured. "Everyone who is not a member of the Hunt should go."

"You want us to just forget that a Congregation has been called?" she protested. "What if you need more help? I can—"

"Nika, go home," Orion interrupted, his black brows furrowing as he stared at his best student. She glowered at him before shooting me a nasty glare and storming off the playground in the direction of the parking lot.

The rest of Orion's students followed, and although none dared to complain like Nika, I could tell from their longing gazes they wanted to. Orion stood silently, watching them leave, the manila envelope in his hands fluttering in the light breeze. Only when the last of the junior Nephilim was gone did he turn back to us, his expression grim.

He fished out several plastic badges with lanyards and tossed one to me. The card was white with a purple border. The name CONSTEL-

LATIONCON ran vertically down the side from top to bottom. In the center it read:

MATTHEW CARVER

THE HUNT

INDUSTRY

A quick glance at his hand revealed a badge for each of us—although Orion's read PANELIST instead of INDUSTRY, which made sense. He had been a living legend for several millennia, and a year ago I was bumming rent off my best friend because I couldn't hold down a job. We are not the same.

"This doesn't seem so bad. It's just some dumb convention?" I said, looking back at my badge. "I've never been to one. Is this a nerdy or a normal one?" I didn't get why the big Nephilim was being so dramatic about Bellerophon bringing us some badges.

"It is definitely far from normal," Orion growled, glaring at the credentials as if he could intimidate the ink into running off and leaving them blank.

"Is this really happening?" Alex breathed, accepting the one with his name on it. "I never thought I would get invited to one."

"It seems a Constellation Congregation been called," Orion confirmed darkly.

"Okay, I'm starting to feel a little left out," I complained. "What is a Constellation *Congregation*? Because the badge says Constellation Convention. Also, will there be any *Star Trek* people there?"

"It's not really a convention. Well, not the kind you usually think of," Alex said.

"It is a meeting of the council of the Nephilim," Orion grumbled, reading through a sheet of paper he had found in the envelope. "All the Constellations will be there to vote on policies for the future."

"Hang on, are you some sort of senator?" I asked in mock horror. "All this time we've been working together, and you didn't tell me you were a *politician*?"

Orion ignored me and crumpled up the sheet of paper, tossing it over his shoulder and sinking it in a trash can behind him without even a glance. Some people just have too many talents, I swear.

"This is the first Constellation Congregation in almost two hundred and fifty years," Alex offered. "They're usually only called when something major is happening, or someone is in trouble."

I had just enough time for a bad feeling to creepy-crawl its way down my spine. Maybe it's my ego talking, but I've noticed in my life when "someone" is in trouble, more often than not it's me, I'm the one in trouble.

"I am being called in front of the other Constellations to be censured," Orion announced.

"I don't know what that means," I replied.

Orion let out a small, defeated sigh. "The Constellation Congregation considers itself to be the government over all Nephilim," he began. "They make the rules they expect all of us to follow."

I could already see where this was going. Somehow, I just knew Orion didn't have a great relationship with these Nephilim authority figures. I don't know what ever might have given me that idea, call it a flash of intuition.

"Let me guess," I interrupted. "You have a reputation for going rogue, coloring outside the lines, and usually they let it fly because you're the freaking Hunter, and you get results, but something has changed, and now they want to bring you in?"

"Oh no—they literally gave him a badge," Alex groaned.

"They claim," Orion murmured, "that I do not have permission to rebuild the Hunt or to choose mortals as squires."

"Well, that seems kind of discriminatory," I huffed. "Besides, I'm only mostly mortal. Technically my dad's a Faerie, so I'm practically a cousin or something."

"Furthermore," the Hunter continued, ignoring my commentary, "it seems the Dragon Dons have taken their grievances with us to the North Star directly." A year and a half ago, the Hunt had smashed our way into a laboratory owned by a man named Lazarus, mistakenly believing that he had kidnapped my sister. During the course of it, I sort of accidentally burned the whole place down. It could have happened to anyone whose hands were full of magic fire.

We had patched things up with Lazarus, but he had been paying protection to the so-called Dragon Dons, which made my little fire an invasion of their territory. Despite the fact that the dragons were another enemy, I must admit I was a little excited we might get a chance to see one. I mean, dragons are real? How cool is that?

"Oh," Alex said quietly, staring at the badge in his hand with something like horror.

"You burn down one measly lab, and it's all anyone wants to talk about," I grumbled to no one in particular.

"I suspect there will be more than just talking in the days to come," Orion promised grimly.

The wind's mocking laughter echoed in my ears as we left.

OF ALL THE places I ever expected to be fighting for my life, a candlelit dinner at Balsamic, a Michelin-starred Italian restaurant in the middle of Hollywood, was not on my bingo card. Also not on the list was sitting across from my betrothed, a bombshell Faerie-princess-in-exile with red hair and a devious smirk that had to be inherited from her father.

Her name was Ash, and we were "courting," which is an olde word from when the English language was full of extra -*e*s tacked on the end of words, and peasants like me weren't allowed to own property. "Courtship" in this case meant we were contractually obligated to be married to bind our bloodlines together—it was functionally an arranged marriage with a business emphasis.

If that doesn't sound sexy, it's because it isn't. It's mostly awkward.

It's also dangerous. Since our escape from the Faerie Lands on my birthday, the Dandelion Throne has been oppressively *silent*. If there's one thing I've learned from my dealings with supernatural beings, it's that just because they're quiet doesn't mean they've forgotten—or forgiven. Immortals hold grudges like nobody's business.

So even though I was doing everything I could to keep my half of the bargain I made with Ash's mother, I was stressed about what Dawn and her court were planning for when they inevitably showed up to ruin my day.

Despite the corporate origins of our relationship, I would be lying if I said I was completely bummed with how it was working out. I knew for a fact that I could have made worse choices. Ash's younger sister literally murdered her mother shortly after my decision was finalized. Her older sisters were pieces of work too.

This might be hubris, but I got the sense Ash felt the same about me. If I was wrong, she sure laughed at a lot of my jokes for a miserable prisoner. Maybe that was just to lull me into a false sense of security.

"You're telling me mortal women find this charming?" she asked, glancing around the room with an imperiously arched eyebrow. "We're in a dim room being served dinner. What am I missing?" She fixed her green eyes on me with a bemused air.

Even though Ash spoke fluent English and half a dozen other languages to boot, I had spent most of the last six months acting as her mortal translator. Her mother had kept her trapped in the Faerie Lands for her entire life. I'm sure Rapunzel had a bit of an adjustment period too when she finally got out of that tower.

"Well," I said, around a mouthful of delicious fresh bread I had just dipped in olive oil and balsamic vinegar, "most mortals don't have a world-class kitchen staffed with indentured chefs of the highest caliber cooking their every meal."

Ash's eyes glinted dangerously in the low light. She might look human, but that did not mean she understood the human experience. For all her wonderful traits, and there truly were many, she was still Fae—and something more. Her mother had been Gloriana, once Queen of All Fae, now ashes and dust. Her father, however, was still alive and kicking. I don't even like *thinking* his real name, let alone saying it out loud. He has many nicknames, and all of them make me feel itchy. But if I have to use one, I usually go with el Diablo, because it makes it sound like I might know some Spanish. Yes, *that* el Diablo.

I know.

I know.

"So, it is charming because it is novel," Ash mused, sipping at her glass of red wine. The wine guy, the someli-whosie-whatsit, had recommended it, and Ash had agreed instantly. From the smug grin on his face as he walked away, I knew it wasn't cheap.

Pro tip: If you're trying to impress a royal lady, don't try to do it with luxury unless you own your own country. You're better off trying to give her the moon as a necklace.

"Novelty is part of it," I said, trying to figure out how to explain the concept of going on a date to an Immortal. "But it's only one of the ingredients. It's also about spending time with someone special and experiencing something new with them."

Ash was silent for a moment, her glass hovering a few inches above the table and her head cocked slightly to one side as she studied me. If I was her humanities tutor, then she was a very diligent student. The mortal world fascinated her, even if she didn't understand it.

"Spending time together with someone special," she repeated softly. "You value the time you share because you will run out of it. Like those two." Her gaze tracked to her right, where an elderly couple sat at a different table in a future echo of our date. Although if she and I made it that far, we would look different. I would be old and wrinkled, but my Immortal betrothed would look the same as she did now.

"Well, that's depressing," I said, setting down the rest of my bread with a sour twist in my gut. "But you're probably right on an instinctual level. I'd be willing to bet mortals value time differently than someone who isn't on Father Time's hit list. But there's more to it than that. Most of us aren't always thinking about how our time is slipping out of the bottom of the hourglass."

I mean, I assume most mortals aren't. I remember a time in my life when I wasn't tracking my days like a reverse Christmas countdown. At midnight tonight, it would be 3,101 days until my expiration date. Sometime after midnight on the fifth day of April eight years from now, my date's father would pull up and shuttle me directly downstairs to The Bad Place™. Given the history between me and old Lucypoo, I was certain he would be there at 12:01 on the dot. Last I heard, His Evilness was busy renovating the Pit with a brand-new circle just for me. At least I would have a chance to finally achieve the American Dream and own some property.

All because an idiot demon named Dan had forged my signature and stolen my soul.

Some of my dark thoughts must have shown in my eyes, because Ash's face changed from thoughtful to concerned. When I reached for more bread, she placed a comforting hand on my wrist, which was a nice gesture, but I really wanted some more of the bread.

"I'm sorry," she murmured. "That was a stupid question."

"Most mortals aren't playing the same game that I am," I said with a small smile, letting my gaze be torn away from the warm, delicious bread to meet the scrutiny of my betrothed. When she was channeling her Fae powers, her eyes would be a golden mirror to Orion's black ones. Tonight they were just green. I still haven't figured out exactly how that works. I think it has something to do with her unique heritage. "My life has different rules," I added. Ash gave my forearm a gentle squeeze and pulled her hand back, freeing me to plunder the breadbasket.

"Excuse me, sir, ma'am." Our sommelier interrupted, approaching our table holding a champagne bottle and a pair of flutes. "I come bearing a gift, a congratulations on the anniversary."

I felt my heart lurch in sudden panic. Was it our anniversary? Did we have an anniversary? Ash had been here in the mortal world just over six months, but that meant the anniversary of our betrothal should have been earlier this month. Did she plan this? I glanced at her, only to see an equally confused look on her face. That made me feel a little better but also a little worse. I don't like surprises. I didn't like them before my soul was stolen, and I *definitely* don't now. Supernatural creatures tend to produce surprises that are no fun and have way too many teeth.

"This is a nineteen seventy-seven brut from the Champagne region of France," he continued, giving the cork a practiced wrench, holding it firmly as a loud *pop* echoed around the room. "It should give you notes of vanilla and gooseberries. Please enjoy with compliments from your friends at table thirteen." He gestured across the room as he poured a serving into Ash's flute.

I turned to look in the direction he pointed, and a low note of fear began to hum deep in my chest. There were four individuals seated at lucky table thirteen. Three of them stared at us with the professional disinterest of warriors. I didn't recognize them, but that didn't matter.

The fourth woman at the table made identifying the rest of the assembled Fae easy. She had long blond hair that fell to her shoulders in rolling waves. A white gauzy dress grew on her like moss on a boulder. The blue eyes of Dawn, the current Queen of All Fae, sparkled with mischief as she raised her own champagne flute in a toast to us.

The wind's laughter rang in my ears, mocking me.

Wordlessly, I accepted my flute and followed suit with my betrothed as we returned her older sister's salute. The last six months of my life had been pleasantly Dawn-free. Well, I guess there had technically been *dawns*, the sun was still operating on its normal schedule, but other than that.

"Darlings," she purred, strolling over from her table, glass in hand. "It has been far too long." She gave both of us an appraising glance with an arched eyebrow. The former Lady of Summer didn't seem close to violence, in her dress and stilettos, sipping from her flute like a proper LA socialite. But appearances can be deceiving—doubly so when it came to the newly crowned Queen.

"Hello, Dawn," Ash replied in a tone so neutral it was room temperature.

"Oh please, don't get up." The elder sister rolled her eyes after neither of us even twitched. The Queen of All Fae looked between us with an amused smile plastered across her face. "You know, Matthew, maybe you did make the right choice," she mused.

Before choosing which of Gloriana's daughters to marry, I had been forced to audition in what felt like some sort of supernatural dating show. Ash had won—or lost, depending on how you looked at it. But that didn't mean that her sister hadn't tried to win in her own way.

"Hello, Dawn," I said softly, testing the waters. There are at least two Dawns. One is crueler than a high school cheerleading captain and just as vapid. The other is as sharp as iron, with a wicked sense of humor. One is a mask worn to make people underestimate her, a weapon in her arsenal. The other is the real her—or an even deadlier weapon. I'm never quite sure which.

There was no spark of anger in her eyes as she glanced at me, only a flash of amusement, like a parent watching a toddler break the rules. This was the real Dawn then, the one that only surfaced when her subjects weren't there to see. "What brings you to the mortal realm?" I asked. "I thought you Faerie royals liked to stay in your bunker."

"Mother was a bit of a recluse, it's true." Dawn sniffed. "But the winds begin to shift, Squire Carver, the winds begin to shift."

"Shift how?" Ash asked, suspicion heavy in her voice.

"Both of you are members of my court and have responsibilities you must attend to," Dawn said, ignoring her sister's question. "I have been more than gracious in allowing you this vacation, but now it is time for you both to stop taking advantage of my generosity and Earn. Your. Keep." Her blue eyes settled on me with a predatory gaze, and I felt my stomach lurch again. I had a funny feeling I was not going to enjoy where this was going.

Part of my deal with the Dandelion Throne, and therefore now with Dawn, was that I would be a member of the court, serving its needs and helping to rebuild their fallen empire. If I didn't fulfill those duties, then I assumed she would be free to kick me to the curb and leave me all alone in the struggle to get my soul back.

"Here." The Queen of All Fae produced two familiar-looking badges with lanyards and tossed them on the table. I saw my name on one and pulled it closer. It read simply:

MATTHEW CARVER
DANDELION COURT
VIP

Just like the card Orion had handed me earlier today, CONSTEL-LATIONCON was printed in giant letters running vertically down the side. My funny feeling now had a funny feeling of its own. I stared at the flimsy piece of plastic in my hands for a long moment before looking back up at Dawn. I could practically feel the badge from earlier burning a hole in my pocket. Metaphorically, I mean. I didn't actually have it with me, it was in my other pants, I had changed for my date. Besides, the event wasn't until this weekend.

"This is a convention badge," I said, stalling for time as I tried to figure out how to handle this development. Before today I had never heard of it, despite living in LA my whole life. Now I had two different badges with my name on them.

"Very good, Matthew," Dawn replied dryly, a hint of her meaner alter ego lurking under the surface. "I'm so glad to see the reading lessons have been worth every penny."

"What do you want us to do with them?" I asked, ignoring her barb. Orion had made it seem like this convention was more of a front for the Nephilim UN. I didn't know why the Fae would want anything to do with that.

"Polaris has invited the Dandelion Court to attend the Congregation for the first time in almost five hundred years," Dawn replied with a hint of a pleased smile. "We are basically cousins after all," she continued. "I require my sister's counsel and the attendance of *all* of my Lords of Fire."

Dawn's smile only grew as she saw the expression on my face. The term "all" implied that there were more than two Lords of Fire. There weren't. There were, in fact, exactly two, if you didn't count the Lady of Autumn herself. I was one, good old Matthew Carver, playing for the home team. The other was my father, Damien Carver. I don't know what team he plays for, but so far, it's never been the one I'm on.

"There's a problem with this plan," I said, feeling like I had somehow just gotten supernatural jury duty twice in one day. "I'm already attending as a member of the Hunt."

"That *is* a problem," Dawn agreed, something deep sparkling in her eyes. "But I don't think it is my problem. You know what they say about serving two masters, don't you?"

"It's actually become quite common for people in the middle class to have to work two jobs in order to make ends meet in large cities," I said with a shrug. "Have you seen the price of rent in this part of town?"

Ash snorted quietly to herself across the table. I beamed at her with pride—not in my comedic skills, but more in my role as teacher. Only six months and I already had her laughing at rent jokes. Give it a year and you'd never know Ash wasn't an Angeleno herself.

With a roll of her eyes, Dawn opened her mouth to put me in my place, but whatever caustic comment she had prepared never emerged. Outside, a car's tires squealed, and the glass of the window on the wall next to our table exploded inward as gunmen opened fire.

MY TRAINING FROM Orion kicked into overdrive before my brain even fully processed the sound of automatic gunfire. Quicker than a rumor, I leapt out of my chair and dove across the table, arms wide to catch both Faerie women. My dive carried them to the floor with me as the bullets ripped into the restaurant like a swarm of furious wasps.

I lay on the floor holding them down as the gunfire continued for another ten seconds, sweeping around the room, searching for us. Dawn grabbed my right arm and pulled me off her.

The Queen of All Fae rose to her feet, golden eyes blazing with murderous fury. She twitched as a bullet struck her, red blood blooming on her shoulder, staining her white dress. She raised both of her hands, and the air pressure of the room bent to her will. My instincts had forgotten a few facts when I tried to knock everyone out of the gunmen's line of sight.

Dawn and Ash were Immortals, with the capital letter and everything. Bullets were more than capable of turning me into bloody scraps, but they didn't have the authority to kill someone like the daughters of Gloriana.

Dawn gestured, and an invisible wall of air suddenly filled the gap in the ruined window. I couldn't see it, but the bullets slamming into her will slowed to a crawl as if they were traveling through gelatin. After a few heartbeats, the gunfire came to an abrupt halt as our attackers realized their shots were being stopped.

"You okay?" I asked Ash in the deafening silence. My ears were ringing like I had just been in the front row of a rock concert. I scrambled to my feet and offered her a hand up.

"I've been better," she replied dryly. "But this is one of the most eventful dates I've ever been on." I'm not sure I wanted to know what date she thought came close for excitement. Maybe it was the time we played laser tag.

Around the room, diners hunkered down beneath their tables or scrambled for safety. I saw several still forms on the floor that did neither. My jaw clenched at the sight of innocent mortals caught in the crossfire.

"Who dares?" I snarled, turning back to face the shattered window.

"Quiet!" hissed Dawn, her hands still up, holding the wall in place. "Something is wrong..."

Her warning was eclipsed as a brilliant orange glow enveloped the ruined window like the rising sun. I could feel the inferno's heat from twenty feet away. Fire is a friend to me, but even I took a step back from the fury of the flame.

Dawn isn't the only one with a cool party trick. With a grunt, I set

Willow free, and my clenched fists burst into a cherry-golden fire of their own. I raised my right hand and sent a dismissive gesture at the wall of fire trying to gnaw its way through the wall of the restaurant.

"Shhhh," I scolded the fire.

The flames dimmed for a second, fading to an angry red before the heat swept back in a fierce orange wave. Was it just me or did the room feel even hotter now?

Ash strode to my side, her own hands aflame, and offered me a small smile. "Together?" she asked, which was very polite since she both was a princess and had a far more powerful connection to Willow. I should have been asking for permission to help her.

"Together," I said, returning her smile.

As one we raised our hands and repeated my flippant gesture, using our connection to the Flame to order the fire to dismiss itself. With a dull *whump* the fire winked out, like a closing eye. After a moment, Dawn lowered her hands, releasing a hundred bullets to fall to the ground in a metal rain.

Clenching my fists, I took an angry step toward the gaping ruin of a window. They wanted to play with Fire? That was my favorite game.

I made it only a few feet before a massive figure leapt through the bullet-riddled glass. Two more followed, landing behind the first. The backup dancers carried what looked like Tommy guns right out of a mobster movie, complete with large round drums full of bullets. The matching three-piece suits really sold the mafia connection.

As I tore my eyes away from what large machine guns they had, the better to shoot me with, I noticed they weren't human—and I don't mean in the fun Nephilim or Fae way of not being human, with pointy ears and unfairly strong jawlines.

These were monsters.

Although they had two legs and two arms, any resemblance to us *Homo sapiens* ended there. Leathery claws hovered over the triggers of their weapons. Their bodies were covered with metallic scales. Instead of hair, they had ridges of triangle-shaped spikes running back like hardcore mohawks. They had snouts full of sharp teeth in place of mouths, and their reptilian eyes twinkled in the ambient lighting. They looked like some mad scientist had successfully blended man and alligator into a living, breathing nightmare.

I suddenly had a very bad feeling about where the fire had been coming from.

The green-scaled leader opened its mouth in a draconic smile, and a red forked tongue slithered out to taste the air.

"Maffew Carver," the dragon hissed in sibilant pleasure. "At long last."

"Sorry, my name is Matthew Carver," I replied without even blinking. "I think you're looking for a different guy. Don't worry about it, it happens all the time."

The creature's snout curled into a snarl. Maybe I should learn to think twice before I make fun of monsters with speech impediments. One of these days it's going to get me killed.

"Don Doyle sends his regards," the beast bellowed, slashing his clawed hand at me. His two drag-goons raised their weapons, making my insides wobble with fear.

I leapt to the side, slinging a fireball from my right hand, not waiting for them to turn me into a Swiss-cheese version of myself. Bullets whizzed by me as I dove behind a table, pulling it down to form a wall. Angry little slugs whined in frustration as they slammed into the thick wooden table, showering me with splinters.

I channeled Willow into my right hand and lobbed the flames over the top of the table like a hand grenade. "Danger close!" I screamed. A small explosion rocked the room as the fire spirit detonated its essence, sending hungry flames hunting my enemies.

The flames on my hand dimmed as the firebomb went off.

I had been afraid of that.

Willow was a creature of the Faerie Lands; they didn't get whatever essential vitamins and minerals they needed from the mortal realm to keep their flames fueled forever. Once they ran out of juice, I would have to revisit the Fae homeland in order to recharge.

That meant I only had a few more hits I could get in. I needed to make them count.

One of the gundragon's weapons clicked empty. A moment later so did the second's. I leapt up in the echoing silence as I heard the metallic snaps of them swapping out the heavy drums on their rifles.

"Let's make it count!" I yelled to my faithful fire spirit. The two gunmen had been stalking toward me, no doubt trying to find an angle where their bullets could reach me behind my makeshift barrier.

No matter. Now they were in my range.

"Burn!" I cried, sending all my will out in flames. A jet of fire swept from my hands and slammed into the lead dragon like a geyser from a fire hydrant. The monster vanished in the beam as the hungry flames consumed him.

After a few heartbeats, my flame began to dip, like I was running out of whatever the equivalent of water pressure is for fire. Fire pressure, I guess. I gritted my teeth and poured on the gas for as long as I could, until with a hiss the fires on my hands vanished.

Panting with exertion, I looked to see what damage my fiery wrath had wrought on the lizards. Dread filled me as I saw the lead dragon still standing, its suit mostly gone. It swatted at the remnants of its shirt, which was burning in patches, in an amused manner. Its clothes extinguished, the dragon looked up from slapping itself and gave me an openmouthed smile, full of teeth.

"Oh no... fire," it said with a dark chuckle.

I guess Faerie fire doesn't trump a creature that can handle dragonfire.

"Enough!" A harsh gale of wind cut through the room, throwing the three dragons back a half step. Dawn, Queen of All Fae, stepped up next to me, her perfectly manicured fingers curled into claws of her own. Ash followed, her Willow burning brightly. Dawn's bodyguards from the other table formed up behind us like an immortal phalanx. I appreciated the solidarity from Team Fae, but seeing as I was the only one whose weaknesses included bullets, it would have meant a little more if they'd stood between me and the gunmen.

Just saying.

"Out of the way, Faerie," the lead dragon hissed. "This mortal has offended our master and we're here to collect." I felt my jaw drop a little as I realized they had no idea who they were talking to. A wicked little laugh bubbled out of my throat when I saw Dawn's shoulder tense.

Power is a tricky thing. It has more rules than it appears to someone who has none and is watching from the sidelines. A lot of the rules fall under what I call the Law of Predators. I'm no Isaac Newton, but it goes something like this: An Immortal in power remains in power by crushing anyone who dares make them look weak.

I was technically a member of Dawn's court *and* of her family. The Dragon Dons sending hitmen after me was already toeing a few lines. But disrespecting the *Queen* to her face, in front of her court? Oh no no no, that puts the Law into motion! There was no turning back now. Things were about to get political.

"You dare speak to the Queen of All Fae like that?" Ash demanded from my right, picking up on the same thread.

The lead dragon paused, reptilian jaws hanging open slightly in what I assumed was the lizard form of shock. I could practically see the cog wheels turning in its cold-blooded brain. This was supposed to have been a simple hit and run, a whack and pack if you will. All they had to do was kill one mortal and call it good. Instead, they had accidentally ambushed the Faerie Queen.

Dawn was still for a moment, letting the tension build. Slowly, she raised her right hand, which she had been holding against her shoulder, revealing the deep red circle on her dress centered on a dark bullet hole.

The silence was beyond pregnant, it had several children already in college. The dragoons gulped at her like three stooges, their forked little tongues flickering in and out rapidly. What did they taste on the air, I wondered. Was it the blood of an Immortal? Or maybe a premonition of just how screwed they were.

"We're here for the human," the blue one hissed uncertainly, breaking the fragile peace.

"Tell Doyle and the rest of your Dons I take offense," Dawn snarled, lifting her right hand, red with her own blood. "The mortal is mine. You cannot have him."

"Yeah, get in line," I muttered. Ash gave me a subtle whack on my thigh with the back of her hand. Okay, sure, now might not be the moment for the Matthew Carver commentary. It's not like I can just turn it off, but I can admit when it's not needed.

"We're here for the mortal," the leader repeated in a slower, more puzzled tone, as if it couldn't quite believe what was happening. I could relate.

"You cannot have the mortal," Dawn replied in the same methodical cadence.

The dragon took a step toward me, and then a gale whipped up in the room and threw him backward against the wall, shattering plaster with the force behind it. "You have *offended* me, little snake," Dawn hissed. "Tell your masters to expect the Dandelion Court's wrath. Now flee."

All around the room, dishes, chairs, and everything else not bolted down began to hover, borne into the sky on invisible strings of air. With a vicious slash of her hand, Dawn sent her arsenal of everything flying at the dragons. I saw forks and knives sticking out of their scaled flesh like little flagpoles.

The dragons retreated under the barrage. I hunkered down as the vicious winds whipped past me, chasing the dragons out the hole they had smashed and into the LA night. Car tires squealed as they sped away, driven off by the natural force that was the Queen of All Fae.

With a wave, Dawn banished her miniature hurricane. The debris dropped to the floor, released from the angry wind that had kidnapped it.

In the distance, sirens sang as emergency services raced toward us. I glanced around the ruined restaurant, at the still bodies and cowering survivors, unsure what to do.

Dawn swept past me, boiling with anger. "Tell the Hunter I want an alliance," she snarled.

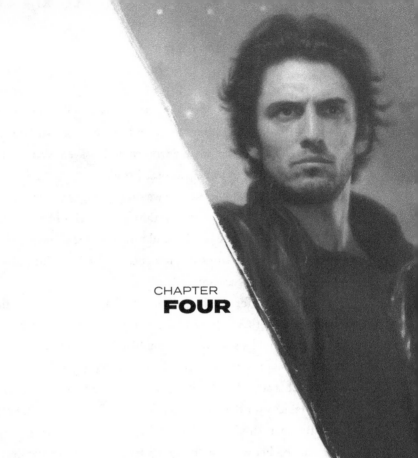

THE SIRENS GREW closer, so I used my phone call preemptively. No matter what happened next, I knew Ash and I would need the services of our lawyer, Robin Goodfellow. Robin was a member of the Dandelion Court and had been the right hand of Gloriana herself before her untimely death. Since then, he had served a similar function for Ash. I paid him a million of my demonic dollars to be on retainer, which was turning out to be a killer investment.

"Goodfellow Law," he answered in a warm tone.

"I need you to get here now," I told him.

"Where exactly is here?" I could feel the Faerie narrowing his eyes as he heard my tone. I gave him the sixty-second story while Ash rushed to the nearest body on the floor, checking for a pulse. Unhappy with what she found, she moved to the next one, working through the room, looking for anyone who could be saved. When I hung up on Robin, I dove in to help as best I could.

The first man I checked on was gone, caught in the spray of bullets meant for me. Guilt coursed through my veins like a thick sludge. I left him lying where he died and turned to the woman he had been eating with. Hope surged in my chest as I felt a faint pulse on her neck. I could still save one.

Scrabbling for anything to use as a bandage, I grabbed the cloth napkins from their table and pressed them to the bullet holes in her chest. If I could just slow down her bleeding for a few moments until the EMTs got here, she would be fine, I told myself.

With a start, I realized this was the couple that had been sitting a few tables over that Ash had pointed to. The woman was older, her chestnut hair streaked with gray. She let out a faint whimper as I put pressure on her wounds. "It's going to be okay," I told her desperately. "Help is on the way, just stay with me, ma'am."

Her brown eyes flickered open, but they seemed to stare past me, at something else in the room. "Hello," she whispered softly.

"I'm right here," I said fervently, reaching to grip her hand with my free one. Panic flared in my chest. She was going to make it. She had to make it. This was my fault, but that didn't mean she had to die.

"Is it time?" she asked, still staring over my shoulder.

"Time for what?" I replied. The blood loss must be affecting her. I'm sure it would mess with me too. "The paramedics are almost here. Just stay with me for a few more minutes, okay?"

"I did so want to see my granddaughter's recital," she murmured. Her eyes were open and focused now, but she did not seem to see me. "Are you sure I can't wait a little while?"

Goose bumps flared up my arms as I realized she was not talking to me. Still applying pressure to her wounds, I looked over my shoulder, terrified of what I might find.

Somehow the empty room behind me made me more nervous.

"I understand," she said breathily, her voice fading like it was going down a long tunnel.

"No, no!" I cried, squeezing her hand as if I could somehow pump life back into her veins. "Don't understand. Whatever it is you understand, forget it!"

The old woman continued talking, deaf to my pleas. "Earl is waiting? We'd better hurry. He hates it when I make him late…"

Her body gave a great sigh, an exhale that seemed to empty her entire being into the ether, and then was still. With a shaking hand, I reached to feel for a pulse. There was none. A loud sob burst out of my mouth as I let go of her hand and knelt beside her cooling corpse. The world had gone fuzzy. This wasn't my first time seeing death, but I had only seen it visit combatants—beings who were living by the sword and therefore dying by the sword. I'd never watched someone's grandmother die before.

I was still kneeling over her when the SWAT team burst in.

"Down!" screamed a harsh voice as three different doors shattered at the same time. Dimly I was aware of strong hands forcing me to the floor, of pressure on my back as my hands were zip-tied behind me. But that all seemed so small, a part of normal life, insignificant before the end that I had just witnessed.

Those same hands wrenched me to my feet, pulling me away from the grandmother. I saw EMTs rushing to her side, and I almost told them not to bother, but the words wouldn't form on my lips. They'd find out soon enough.

The officers marched me toward the exit, and as we walked I felt my shock begin to fade, replaced by my own survival instincts. How in the world was I going to explain this to the mortal police? Two officers marched Ash in front of me, similarly restrained. Something about the way they aggressively held her arms stoked a fire deep in my belly. If my connection to Willow had any juice left in the tank, I'm certain my hands would have been burning with a fiery rage.

I forced myself to exhale. Ash could take care of herself. I was pretty sure she still had enough fire left to turn the two men holding her into her namesake in the blink of an eye. If the daughter of the Devil could control her anger, then so could I. For once in my life, I managed to keep my mouth shut. I'd like to think that counts as emotional growth.

The SWAT officers hustled us out of the restaurant, and my jaw dropped at the sheer number of cop cars waiting outside. The entire street was filled with first responders, from tactical vans and patrol cars to EMTs and fire engines. They'd sent everyone. I glanced over my shoulder and got my first good look at the exterior of the smoldering restaurant. As I watched, a jet of water shot up from one the fire trucks to douse the roof. I wondered if the Michelin judges factored in mob hit frequency when they were awarding stars. If so, Balsamic might be in trouble next year.

We marched past the line of trucks, through the sea of milling officers who parted for us, eyeing us suspiciously. I've been in a few firefights, but my butt cheeks still clenched when I saw the number of guns pointed in my general direction. I doubted even Dawn's winds could stop their angry swarm if they chose to open fire. The officers escorted us through the battle line to a long mobile command center, like the ones in the movies.

"Stay," grunted one of the SWAT members, shoving me into a seated position against the outside wall. Ash joined me on the ground a moment later, although they were gentler with her. My shoulders began to pull painfully in their sockets as my bound wrists refused to let me sit at a comfortable angle.

One of the officers rapped on the door of the trailer before opening it and sticking his head in. "Next batch is here, sir."

I heard a vague shout of assent, and the leader retreated, waving to two of the SWAT members with us. The three of them trotted back toward the restaurant, leaving us under the watchful eye of the fourth.

For a heart-racing second, I thought about trying to escape. All it would take was a little flame to free our hands. I could sweep the legs of the guard and we could make a break for it... through the entire active-duty LAPD roster. I leaned my head back against the wall with a frustrated sigh. There was no getting out of this one.

That didn't mean staying here was a good option. Outside of the fact that mortal authorities were not really equipped to handle a draconic mafia-style shoot-out, Ash wasn't *from here*. She was born in another world. She did not have a Social Security number, driver's license, passport, or library card. Her fingerprints were not in the system. The second they started looking into us, we were going to set off all kinds of alarms.

"You gotta be kidding me," a stern voice drawled, interrupting me counting the ways that this could go wrong. My blood ran cold. I did not have him on my list. I could only stare in horror as Detective Jones stepped out into the street and put his hand on his hips. The big man wore a gray suit jacket over black slacks, with his badge hanging around his neck like a pendant. Absent his usual aviator sunglasses, his blue eyes were cold and unfriendly as he stared at me.

"Look, Rodgers, it's our old friend Mr. Carver," Jones said in a delighted tone. "We haven't caught up with him in a long time."

His partner, Detective Rodgers, stepped out into the night and fixed me with a piercing look. She wore a black suit; her dark hair was bound in a tight bun that made her look even more severe than usual.

"Hola," she said in a flat, unamused tone.

Ash's lack of documentation was suddenly the least of our problems. I had met these two detectives before, several times in fact. When my sister had been kidnapped by Lilith, I had filed a police report with them. Over the course of their investigation, they had decided I wasn't telling them the whole truth—because, well, duh, I wasn't.

That had made me their favorite suspect in Megan's disappearance. Truth be told, I think I was the only suspect. They weren't exactly prepared to look for a VP of Hell. The last time I saw them, they had dragged me in for an aggressive questioning session that Robin had rescued me from. I guess time really is a flat circle.

"Hello, Detectives," I said as somberly as I could, as if I weren't horrified to see them. "Hell of a night for a reunion."

"Yup, don't worry, I got a feeling we're getting the band back together," Jones remarked smugly, bending down to grab my arm and pull me to my feet. Rodgers did the same to Ash.

"Come on inside, let's get comfy," Jones continued, ushering me up the steps into the command center. "I'm sure we got a lot to catch up on."

THE INSIDE OF the command center was packed with screens, radios, and other technical equipment, but it was empty of people. A cheap-looking table was bolted to the center of the floor with a handful of metal chairs scattered around it.

Rodgers snipped our restraints and gestured for us to sit. I took my seat, rubbing my wrists, trying to get some feeling back into them. Ash tossed me a nervous glance as she took the chair next to me. The two detectives settled across from us, their eyes glinting with suspicion.

This was turning into a terrible scene of déjà vu.

"I hope you both had dessert," Jones chuckled. "Our buffet menus are much more limited here in the field."

"I'm not hungry," I said. Ash murmured in agreement. Slowly, so as not to be obvious, I moved one of my hands under the table, looking for hers. After a moment of searching, I brushed her fingertips. Her hand instantly moved to mine, clasping it tightly. I struggled not to wince at the raw strength of her grip. I wasn't the only one who was nervous. However Ash felt on the inside, though, none of that tension made it to her face. She gazed at the two detectives with an unreadable expression, looking more like her mother than I had ever seen.

I couldn't help but be impressed. If I was mostly alone in a world that was not my own, had barely survived an assassination attempt, and then was nabbed by the authorities, I'd be a wreck. As I stared into the hungry faces of the detectives, I realized I was in danger of becoming a wreck myself, despite being from here.

"Let's start with the basics," Jones said amicably, plopping a small notebook on the table. "We have one Matthew Carver." He paused and leaned over the table conspiratorially. "You are still Matthew Carver, right?" Something dark twinkled in those icy eyes, making me swallow before I could answer.

Jones was intimidating, but Rodgers always scared me more than he did. Every time she looked at me, it felt like she was dissecting me with those cold scalpels she called eyes. No matter how subtle I had been moving my hand under the table, I had no doubt she caught everything.

"Sure am," I said as cheerfully as I could. Technically I did have another name now, and a title. I suppose it would be more correct to call me Squire Matthew Fireheart, but Mr. Fireheart was my dad, and I didn't want anything to do with him. Carver was the name my mother had given me, and that was good enough for me.

Besides, Fireheart is a stupid name.

"And you, young lady?" Jones asked, turning his attention to Ash. "I do not believe we've had the pleasure." I found myself holding my breath, hoping my mortal lessons had stuck. We needed to seem as normal as possible.

"I am Ash-ley... Flowers," she replied. I gave her hand a reassuring squeeze. It took everything in me not to let out a relieved sigh. The Fae can't lie, which could be a very big problem for us right now. It had been Alex's idea to give the Lady of Autumn a mortal name and use it enough that she could count it as *one* of her names. I had assumed we would use it for to-go orders at restaurants, not this.

Definitely not this.

"Lovely to meet you, Ms. Flowers," Jones said, scribbling something in his notebook. Rodgers stared at me, unblinking as a predatory owl. "And how do you know this rapscallion?"

"We're seeing each other," Ash replied, getting more comfortable in her character. That one wasn't a lie. We were seeing each other. Technically we were seeing each other at this very moment.

"My condolences," Jones remarked dryly. Rodgers let out a dark chuckle, still staring. I gave her a weak smile, as if I appreciated her trying to cheer me up after the traumatic event I had just survived. She did not return it.

"Okay, Ms. Flowers, if you could, just give me a rundown of what happened in there tonight. You're out on a date, you go to the restaurant, you sit down, and what happens?"

Ash's hand squeezed mine tighter as she straightened her posture. "We arrived a little after eight thirty," she began.

"And is this a first date, second date?" Jones interrupted.

"No—we've been seeing each other for a while." I squeezed her hand back, proud at how well she was handling this situation.

"Of course." Jones gave her a warm smile and motioned for her to continue.

"We were seated and got drinks. An old friend was leaving and stopped by our table to say hello."

"LA is such a small town," Jones said understandingly. "You saw a friend, what kind of friend?"

"One of her old… sorority sisters," I offered, giving her hand another reassuring squeeze, belying the panic that was making my own heart race.

"Not your turn yet, Mr. Carver," Jones scolded, pointing an admonishing finger at me. "We'll get to you, I promise." The fear in my heart doubled at the steel in those blue eyes. Something told me Robin's hypnotism hadn't been designed to protect me from this situation.

"Yes, it was one of my… sisters," Ash confirmed with only a slight hitch in her voice.

"And what is your friend's name in case we need to look her up?" Jones asked, still scribbling away. My guts clenched as I imagined the look on the detective's face when they couldn't find Dawn to corroborate our story. Maybe we could get one of Orion's Nephilim students to play the role.

"Dawn Rose," Ash told him confidently. I wondered if that was real, or if Ash had given her sister a nickname to let her dance around the truth.

"Sororities really like their themes, don't they?" Jones observed to no one in particular. "Okay, you said hello to a friend, then what?"

"Suddenly there were bullets flying, people were screaming. Windows were breaking, someone jumped through the window. We dropped to the floor to hide. It was terrifying!" A single tear began to roll down her cheek. I tried to make my face look concerned, impressed by her acting.

"Then," she sobbed, "we couldn't see what was going on. The restaurant started burning. I thought Matt might die!" I freed my hand from her grip and put it over her shoulder, trying to play the role of consoling boyfriend. Not that I wouldn't comfort her if she was upset, but Ash had shed fewer tears when her mother was murdered right in front of her. It would take more than a few disappointing dragons to rattle her. I noticed she was only worried about me dying, which was sweet, but also a little rude.

"I know this must have been very traumatic for you," Jones said in a flat tone, "but we've got to keep going through this, okay?"

Ash nodded once, tears free-falling down her face now. I was pretty sure she was acting. Pretty sure. "There was shooting, some people in the restaurant started fighting back. Then the ones who smashed through the window jumped back out the window, and the rest ran off."

"Did you get a good look at any of them?" Jones asked.

"I think there was one man and two women who were the targets. I know at least one of them left after the attackers ran off."

I had to stifle a grin when I realized what she was doing. Most of the survivors had fled, but if any other eyewitness told them they saw some diners standing up to the attackers, Ash was doing her best to make her story line up while still implying that it wasn't us doing the fighting. I don't know what I was worried about; the Fae are masters of the half-truth.

"We've been hearing reports of men wearing masks—some sort of Halloween monster mash attacking the restaurant? Does that ring any bells?"

"They certainly didn't look like men," Ash agreed.

"What does this have to do with your sister?" Rodgers spoke for the first time, her voice cold and accusatory. Her brown eyes bored into me, as if she were trying to pin me to the wall. Caught off guard, I blinked at the two detectives, leaning away from Ash to sit up in my seat.

Now would be a lovely time for my lawyer to arrive.

"I'm sorry, what?" I demanded, not needing to fake the shock filling my voice. "What do you mean?"

"Ms. Flowers, are you aware Mr. Carver's sister disappeared under mysterious circumstances?" Jones asked, still as cool as a cucumber.

"He's told me the story, yes," Ash said, "although I'm not entirely sure how that's relevant...?"

"The night after his sister went missing, there was a shoot-out much like this, and a very expensive building burned down." He gestured vaguely at the restaurant through the wall of the command center. "I'm just glad we got here before it was completely on fire this time."

That was so unfair. I didn't even start this fire; in fact, I put part of it out. Besides, that incident was totally different... Actually, now that I thought about it, they were kind of related. The Dragon Dons were trying to whack me because I burned down a building under their protection. But there was no way the detectives could know that.

"I would hope you could tell me," I said as the two detectives stared at me, waiting for an answer. "I was a victim tonight. If you think they're connected, *please* tell me how."

"Here's the kicker," Jones commented. "The guys who kidnapped his sister? They were wearing monster masks, just like the perps tonight." I froze mid-objection, my mouth hanging open. My sister had been kidnapped by *ghouls*, not dragons. But how in the world was I supposed to explain that difference to a guy who thought they were masks, not monsters?

"You know Rodgers always thought you were dirty," Jones remarked conversationally. "I wasn't so sure—but you know what changed my mind? You stopped calling."

"What do you mean?" I asked, an icy feeling running down my spine.

"Families of missing victims, they don't just accept that a case has gone cold. They call the department weekly, daily. They make internet campaigns or put up flyers."

"You did none of those things," Rodgers said, leaning forward like a hyena on the hunt.

"Sometimes people don't go looking. You know why? They don't need to look for someone if they already know where she is."

I felt my eyes go wide at the detectives' calm accusation. They were really good at this. I *did* stop calling. I *did* know where my sister was. She was in a medically induced coma in the care of a billionaire named Lazarus with a supernatural medical facility.

It seemed I had been hoisted on my own petard, as they say.

"Do you know how many people died tonight?" Jones asked softly, a note of anger finally entering his voice.

I knew of at least two. My shoulders suddenly felt heavier, weighed down by the burden of souls lost that weren't mine.

The door to the command center burst open, and Robin Goodfellow strode in, his eyes blazing with rage.

"Sir, you can't go in there!" a distressed officer's voice called from outside, but Robin made a dismissive gesture in their direction. Our lawyer wore an immaculate gray suit, and his black hair was coiffed in perfect waves. He looked ready to stand before the Supreme Court.

I felt hope rise in my chest. Best million dollars I've ever spent.

"I think that is enough," Robin said, taking in the scene with a single glance. "I seem to recall making it clear to both of you to leave my client alone."

"We are merely taking witness statements," Jones protested. "It's not our fault your client was hanging out at the scene of the biggest shoot-out since the OK Corral."

"Clients," Robin corrected him firmly, moving to stand behind Ash's chair like a golden shadow.

"You represent them both?" Rodgers asked, her tone thick with disbelief.

"He, uh, introduced us actually," I offered with a shrug.

"You're welcome by the way," Robin told me with a smug smile.

"I don't care if your lawyer is also the mayor, neither of you is getting out of here until we finish taking your statements," Jones declared, pointing an aggressive finger at Robin.

"Hmmm." Robin began to hum, his golden eyes twinkling as bright as Orion's were black. "I seem to recall we've done this dance before, Detective." I watched in wonder as the two detectives' jaws went slack, the tension rushing out of their bodies. I glanced at the golden ring on Robin's right hand, identical to mine except it had no precious stone, where mine was set with a ruby. I wasn't sure which Path my lawyer followed, but wherever Robin's tricks came from, they were quite useful.

"My clients have been model citizens," Robin offered soothingly.

"Yes, they have," Jones agreed. Rodgers nodded begrudgingly. Even under the mental control of Robin's Pied Piper, she was a tough sell. Part of me was glad she was on the streets hunting down criminals—the ones that weren't me, anyway.

"If you have any more questions, refer to your report. It should tell you everything you need to know."

"Yes, I have it right here," Jones confirmed, his eyes almost completely unfocused.

"We have the report," Rodgers grunted, still not happy about it.

"Lovely!" Robin shouted, clapping his hands together. The sound jolted the two detectives out of their stupor. I watched as Jones shook his head like a dog, trying to clear whatever fog Robin had poured into his brain. "I assume my clients are free to go then?"

"Yes…" Jones said slowly, turning to look at Rodgers as if he couldn't quite believe that was right. "We have everything we need in our report." Rodgers didn't say anything, but she made no move to stop us as Ash and I stood up and walked out with Robin. I could feel their heavy gazes boring into my shoulder blades as we exited the command center, like two guard dogs at the edge of their leashes.

The officer on duty outside blinked in surprise as Robin came out leading the two of us. "All done!" Robin announced cheerfully, nodding back at the room where we had left Jones and Rodgers sitting in stunned silence. "Thank you for your assistance!" He patted the cop on the shoulder and kept walking. Ash and I followed in his wake. I was so tense I could barely breathe. Any second now, the two detectives would snap out of it and come running. But Robin led us through the current of officers, medics, firefighters, and civilians milling around in the street. Ash's hand slid into mine, and I curled my fingers in hers. I wasn't sure if I was comforting her or if she was comforting me. Either way—it felt nice.

Robin's bright-gold Mustang convertible was parked just on the other side of the police line. The front door was sitting open, its engine still running. Who would dare try to steal it in front of this crowd?

"That's enough fun for one evening," Robin said, gesturing for us to get in. "Sorry, Matthew, you'll have to sit in the back. A princess must have legroom."

I let out a little sigh, but I got in the back.

M Y TENSION DIDN'T begin to lessen until Robin pulled away from the curb, and we put the crime scene in the rearview mirror. It didn't completely go away, but faded to a dull hum that seemed to be coming from somewhere below my stomach.

"Tell me everything," Robin commanded as he roared out onto the 101 Highway away from Hollywood and back toward home.

So we did. From Dawn's surprise appearance to the Dragon Dons' ill-timed ambush and the interrogation we went through after. Being a Faerie and a lawyer, he demanded we give an *exact* accounting of all that had been said, especially by the Queen. It was like going through a second interrogation. When we finished, Robin was silent for a few moments. I could only assume he was lost in the mental gymnastics that legalese requires.

I'm not nearly as smart or educated as Mr. Goodfellow, so I spent the silence thinking about how my knees were being crushed in the tiny half-seat space and watching the night's traffic whiz by. Los Angeles has a reputation for terrible traffic. To be fair, we do have terrible traffic. That is one of the foundational truths of the world, right up there with the sun rising in the east and setting in the west.

But most people don't know the secret to avoiding LA traffic is just to be a weirdo. Los Angeles works like a body, its highways the veins that move blood, oxygen, and whatever else it needs to function around.

Those fortunate enough to have a schedule that goes against the flow will find themselves much freer to get around. At this time of night on a Tuesday, everyone was headed inward to places like Hollywood or K-Town to eat and party. No one was heading out to Northridge. Between that and Robin's psychopathic lane switching, we were making great time.

Ash broke the silence by turning around in her seat to fix me with her green eyes. "Thanks for trying to take me on a date," she said with a straight face. "It was a nice thought. Maybe next time we do something a little less invigorating so we can actually talk?" A hint of a smile tugged at the corner of her mouth.

"I'm sorry if tonight was too much," I replied, matching her serious tone. "Next time we'll just sit on the beach."

"I'd like that." She favored me with a real smile this time. My stomach did a weird little flip-flop, and I felt my face try to bend itself into a warm smile back. Our relationship might not be *organic*; it certainly wasn't following the path of a traditional romance. Originally, I had picked Ash because all her sisters seemed way worse. I'm no dating expert, but I don't think that's one of those rom-com "meet-cutes" I hear so much about. It would be more than fair to say we both came into this with a few walls up.

Despite how we started, over the last six months there had been moments that made me feel like the foundations of my walls were not up to code. They were starting to feel a little wobbly, and I'm still not sure how I feel about that. Good and bad, excited and terrified, all wrapped up in one giant burrito.

I was spared spending any more time trying to untangle the riddle of my love life when we pulled up at my house. I say my house, but it's my *rental house*. A million dollars in cash and no credit to speak of won't buy you a home in Los Angeles—it will barely buy you a condo. Plus, I felt a little weird about spending Hell's dollars on nice things for myself.

Still, this place wasn't just a luxury; it was a practical decision. Not living with Connor made hiding from Violet much easier—although not perfect. Somehow my friend's demonically infatuated fiancée still managed to find me with unerring accuracy. But at least now she had to work for it. Also, when the things that go bump in the night come to kill me, there's a much lower chance of my normal friends getting caught in the crossfire like that poor grandmother at the restaurant tonight.

My home is one of those modern three-story houses that are built vertically on tiny LA plots. They look like they've been made out of Lego bricks, full of squares and hard edges. I know they're probably tacky, because it's the flavor of the decade for new homes, but I kind of love it. It's one step short of being a fortress, it just needs some buttresses, or murder holes, and maybe some crenellations. I'm not sure what any of those things are specifically, but I know they're all essential pieces of the castle pie. Toss in a moat, and I would be set. I wonder if digging one myself would void my security deposit.

Leading my two companions, I walked to the front door and punched my keycode into the door. It opened with a click, and I stepped across the threshold before turning back and gesturing for the two Fae to enter. "Please come in, be a guest in my home," I said formally.

There is something about mortal homes that restricts supernatural beings from coming in. The more power someone has, the harder it is for them to cross over the barrier. I'm not entirely sure how or why it works, only that it does. Sometimes I think my home is my own mini domain, powered by my soul, the same way the Faerie Lands run off souls like batteries. All I know is even Orion has to be invited in every time he comes over or he gets grumpy—well, grumpier.

On the other hand, Ash and Robin do not have to invite me into their luxury townhome—which my demon money pays for. I'm not sure if that's due to the soul thing or because I'm on the lease for their place. I'm technically half Fae myself, but that doesn't seem to be enough to trigger the special rules.

"Thank you for your hospitality," Robin said with a smirk as he followed Ash into my home. I led them down the hallway, past the kitchen, and into the living room, only to stop dead in my tracks.

My new roommate, Alex, sat on our giant, white L-shaped couch next to Nika, the female Nephilim who had tagged me earlier today. I'd never gotten the impression she was a fan of either of us. But glancing at the wineglasses they both held and the open bottle sitting on the coffee table, maybe it was more of a me thing. Technically, my date and I shouldn't have made it through the main course yet, so Alex had clearly been expecting to have the place to himself.

Whoopsie.

"You're back early!" Alex said with forced enthusiasm. His painfully amused smile vanished as he spotted Robin behind me. "What happened?" he asked, setting his wine cup on the table and leaning forward.

I gave his guest a pointed look. Nika placed her cup down with a sigh and rose, brushing her hair behind pointed ears. The Nephilim's vibrant blue eyes glimmered with a hint of annoyance as she glanced at me.

"That seems like my cue," she said dryly. Alex stood with her, but she turned, placing a hand on his chest to stop him from following her. "I'm a big girl, I think I can find my way down one hallway on my own." She leaned up and placed a kiss on his cheek. "Thanks for the wine," she said sweetly.

"Nice to see you, Nika!" I called as she strode out of the room. Faintly I heard the door close behind her as she slipped out into the night. I turned back to Alex, a dozen remarks fighting to the death for the right to be first out of my mouth.

"Not a word," he hissed, holding up a hand to stop me. "Now tell me what happened."

With a sigh, I filed the winner of my comedic cage match away for later use. There were more important fires to deal with. "The Dragon Dons dropped by to say hello. They shot the restaurant to pieces with Tommy guns and then set it on fire."

Alex let out a little squeak of surprise, his eyes going wide.

"It gets better," I said, giving him a tight smile. "They decided to send their regards while Dawn was interrupting our date, demanding we attend the Constellation Congregation on behalf of the Dandelion Court."

Alex sat down on the couch and ran one hand through his perfectly swooshed blond hair.

"One of the dragons shot her, and she took that personally. She wants to talk to Orion about teaming up against the Dragon Dons and has ordered me to make that happen. Then we had the pleasure of being interviewed by Detectives Jones and Rodgers, who think I was involved in tonight's events and that they're related to the reason I kidnapped my own sister."

Alex picked his wineglass up from the table and drained it in a single gulp. After swallowing, he eyed the remnants of Nika's glass and, with a shrug, drained that one too. I understood the feeling. I could have used some more wine myself.

"I told you that restaurant had bad reviews," he said after he finished his second glass.

The rest of us filed into the room and commandeered sitting spaces. Robin snagged a chair, leaving Ash and I to take the other side of the L couch from Alex. Despite the intensity of the situation, I couldn't help but feel a little thrill at the warmth of her knee against mine. Hormones just never take a day off, apparently.

"On the plus side, Orion probably won't be hard to convince," Alex mused wryly. "The only thing he hates more than everyone is dragons."

"One dragon more than the others," Robin offered from the chair.

"One dragon more than the others," Alex agreed.

I don't know the full story. I don't know if anyone who wasn't there does. But I do know the original Hunt, the one whose shadow Alex and I live in, was wiped out by the dragons. If I had a million dollars to bet, it would be that the dragon responsible was at the top of Orion's list.

"I have a question," I said into the heavy silence. "I sort of expected the dragons to be more... dragony? The dragoons they sent looked like science experiments gone horribly wrong."

"Dragoons?" Alex asked, raising an eyebrow.

"You know, they're like goons for the Dragon Dons, so they're dragoons."

"You are aware that dragoons were a cavalry unit in seventeenth- and eighteenth-century Europe?" Robin interjected.

"That was a long time ago, I don't think they're using the name anymore," I said snidely.

"They're cursed," Robin answered softly. "The entire race is cursed."

"With gingivitis? What do you mean they're cursed?"

"Dragons are shapeshifters. They used to look more 'dragony' as you so eloquently put it. That is their original form. But the curse limits their power, preventing them from becoming their true selves. Instead, they are stuck in these tortured half-human, half-beast bodies."

It took me a moment to absorb that information. "How did they get cursed?" I asked, feeling a little stunned. Curses still fell on the side of the supernatural that I wasn't comfortable with. Nephilim, Faerie, and demons were old news now, but so far, we had really avoided getting into the whole "magic" thing. Curses risked crossing the line into truly weird. Orion used a cell phone, for Pete's sake, which made him *almost* normal—I tended to think of him as "Normal Plus."

"No one quite agrees on how the curse came about," Robin told me with a small smile. "But its efficacy is undeniable."

"Okay, so mystery curse makes them weaker, got it," I said, giving them a thumbs-up. "It's nice not to be the one with the disadvantage for once."

"Don't get too ahead of yourself," Ash interjected. "If that was a weak dragon, I have no interest in seeing how strong their flames could be."

I remembered how the fire refused to go out until both of us bent our will and our Willows to the task and shuddered in agreement. I had used all of Willow's stored energy and hadn't even inconvenienced the dragon I had tried to burn.

"Yup, that's a good point," I agreed. I'm fond of living. As much as my dream had been to see a real dragon, I would rather live with the disappointment of never seeing that fulfilled than die immediately after it was.

"Oh boy," Alex sighed, leaning back on the couch. "I guess it's time for another adventure of the Hunt." He didn't sound too excited. "At least there are no demons this time."

"Now you did it," I muttered under my breath.

"With the advent of the Constellation Congregation, now seems like the time to speak to you about what you pay me for," Robin interjected, shifting in his seat, crossing one leg across his knee. "Another way out of your contract has opened up."

A wild hope shot through me. The primary reason I kept Robin on a retainer wasn't to get me out of legal trouble with the mortal authorities, but to help me find another way out of the fraudulent contract Dan the Demon had signed in my name.

The first loophole he had found was a simple one: Hell had to pay me five million dollars a year or the contract was in breach, which is a fancy word that means it would be broken. The only problem with that way out was it left my undead sister firmly in the Devil's clutches. I hadn't been willing to sacrifice her for my own survival, which was why I was now a millionaire.

The night that Hell's CFO, Zagan, had handed me the bags of cash, Robin had promised me there was still hope but had refused to share what he'd found, claiming he needed more time to "research." As if I didn't know he loved to be dramatic.

"Now?" I asked, my earlier longing beginning to fade as I wondered what had prompted him to start talking. "You couldn't have done it when we were less busy?"

Robin gave me a guileless smile and clasped his hands together over his knee. "The Constellation Congregation has created some new opportunities for all of us. But there are rules that must be observed. This information falls under client–attorney privilege. Are you comfortable with me sharing it with everyone here, or would you rather we meet in private?"

Caught off guard, I glanced at Alex and Ash. What might he have to say that I wouldn't want them to hear? There was no point in asking Alex to leave; I'd just tell him everything anyway. As for Ash, well, that got a little complicated. Technically this whole thing was a contract dispute between me and her father, although she didn't know the guy. Still, there's something to be said for playing your cards close to your chest. How much could I trust her?

"It's all right," Ash said with a tight smile, starting to stand.

"No, no." My hand shot out and gently grabbed her upper arm before she got more than a few inches. "You can stay." I gave her a warm smile. I'm not sure if I really thought that all the way through, but it was too late now. My body had acted on instinct, without bothering to check in with the reason department.

"Hit me," I said, leaning forward to stare at Robin.

"As we've discussed, your friend Dan took it upon himself to customize your contract, which makes working through it exponentially more difficult," Robin began. "However, I believe that there is another way to end it."

"Perfect. What do I have to do?"

"There's a legal term, force majeure."

"Force major?" I asked.

"No, majeure. It's French, you uneducated swine." Robin sighed. "It means something like 'greater force.'"

"So, I just need to become stronger than… the Devil."

"Not everything needs a wisecrack, Matt." Ash patted me chidingly on the shoulder. I held up my hands in surrender. I don't mean to be obnoxious—most of the time. It's how I compensate for being nervous. Given the stakes, I think I'm allowed to be feeling a little tense.

"Force majeure is a section of a contract that explains why it might no longer be enforceable in the future. If something bigger than the contract happens that interferes with the fulfilling of the terms, both parties agree to walk away. Usually this part contains phrases like *acts of God*, *armed conflict*, or *natural disasters*."

"So hypothetically if an earthquake destroyed the house I'm renting, the lease would end because of force majeure?" My lips stumbled over the new word. My almost legitimate college degree had not covered any French.

"If that was specified in the clause, then you would be off the hook," Robin agreed.

"So we just need an act of God, armed conflict, or natural disaster to affect the contract? That seems like a tall order, even for us." My mind was racing. An act of God seemed pretty out of my reach. So did a natural disaster. But armed conflict—I get shot at all time. Surely that had to count for something.

"Imagine my joy," Robin said, a giant smirk spreading across his face, "to learn Dan the Demon also chose to rewrite the force majeure clause and make some truly interesting additions."

Hope soared. If there's one thing you could count on Dan to do, it was mess everything up.

"'Neither Party shall be liable for any failure to perform its obligations where such failure results from any cause beyond such Party's reasonable control,'" recited Robin, utilizing his photographic memory. "'Including, without limitation: Armageddons, Apocalypses, Cataclysms, Decimations, or Endings of any sort. Furthermore, if the receiving party should become: Assimilated, Absorbed, Conquered, Overthrown, or Subjugated, they will therefore be ineligible. Likewise, if the signatory mortal: Ascends, is Unmade, or Completes an Impossible Task, they will be rendered ineligible.'"

Silence reigned after Robin finished his delivery. Scratching my head, I glanced across the couch at Alex, who shrugged, a confused look on his face.

"You're kidding," Ash breathed in horrified wonder. My head snapped around to stare at her. Whatever Robin had just said might as well have been in French for all that I followed it. But it seemed my betrothed had understood just fine. If Ash was the smart and attractive one in our relationship, what did that make me? I hope it was the funny one.

"Okay, uh, there was a lot there." I scrunched my forehead as if that would encourage the hamster that powered my brain to run faster on its little wheel. "I heard a lot about being conquered. If Hell is conquered, then they don't get to collect my soul? That seems unlikely to me."

"Not that one," Robin sighed. "I mean, technically yes, that would be a way out of your contract. If Hell were to no longer exist under its current regime, the contract would be void. But if I were you, I wouldn't hold my breath. There are very few Powers left that could even think about taking the field against the Dark Star and his legions."

"Okay, let's call that Plan C then," I said, a little relieved. I'm all for overthrowing literally the evilest country in the universe, but I suspected I was unequipped for such a task. "Please tell me it's not the Armageddon one."

"That too would technically be a way out, but Endings are also a bit out of our collective pay grades," Robin agreed somberly.

"Okay, let's call that one Plan D. Somehow it sounds worse than trying to invade and conquer Hell."

"It is no surprise that it didn't leap out to you as it did to the Lady of Autumn." Robin inclined his head respectfully to the princess. "You were not raised as a Fae despite your father's heritage, so you would not know the history of an Impossible Task."

Across from me, Alex gasped softly.

"What?" I asked him.

"An Impossible Task is how a Nephilim becomes a Constellation," he replied, a strange stiffness running through his body. "But that isn't an option for you—you're Faerie, not Nephilim. The Fae were kicked out of the Constellation Congregation centuries ago..." His voice trailed off as his eyes went wide with realization.

"Dawn told us tonight the Fae have been invited to attend for the first time in five hundred years," Ash said, finishing his thought for him.

"You begin to see." Robin laughed, clapping his hands gleefully and rubbing them together. "A new door has the chance to open."

"I see nothing," I interrupted, raising my hand for attention. "Are you saying in order to get out of the contract, I need to complete an Impossible Task that usually takes an Orion-level hero, a demigod, to finish?"

"Technically it's three tasks that are impossible that make up the Impossible Task," Alex muttered.

"That's Plan B?" I shouted in horror. I have made great strides in my martial training. I'm way better with a sword and gun than most normal mortals are. But I am but a toddler in his first year of walking compared with an immortal like the Hunter. All of a sudden, I felt very small and insignificant in this world I lived in. "Also, even if I do complete all *three* of these impossible tasks, they might not count because I'm not Nephilim?"

"Polaris and the other leaders kicked the Dandelion Court out during the peak of the fighting between the Hunt and the Fae," Alex said ruefully. "The Fae somehow betrayed the Hunter."

"Allegedly," Robin murmured to no one in particular.

"Sure. For whatever reason, there was constant fighting between the two groups, and after the fall of the Hunt, I think everyone was afraid to get in Orion's way. So they kicked the Fae out of the Constellation Congregation, and he was free to do his thing without waging war on another member."

"But now there's the treaty between the Hunt and the Fae," I breathed. It felt like my view of the world had suddenly zoomed out and I could see more of the puzzle that I was trapped in the center of.

Gloriana had been obsessed with keeping the treaty alive. It had been part of the deal we made for her to help me get my soul back. Her ambition had been to restore the Fae to their former glory. How could they if they couldn't take their place among the stars?

"So, all we need to do…" I said, pinching the bridge of my nose between my thumb and forefinger. I could feel a stress headache coming on. It had been a spicier night than I had planned for. "…is help Dawn get the Fae accepted back into the Constellation Congregation and *then* have me complete an impossible trifecta."

"I told you, there was still a way," Robin said cheerfully. "I haven't told you the best part—if a contract is broken through force majeure, the parties walk away as is."

"What do you mean, 'as is'?" I asked.

"It means you keep whatever you have possession of at the time—or whomever. No questions asked."

He was talking about my sister Megan. If this major was forced, or whatever, Megan would be free. I glanced at Alex, whose face was oddly still. Why did I have a feeling this was just going to get me killed and sent to Hell even faster?

CHAPTER
SEVEN

WHISTLING TUNELESSLY TO myself,
I strolled down the faded gray carpet of the
Between. I tossed the key of good old Portunus,
the forgotten god of portals, into the air once before catching it and
tucking it safely away in my jeans pocket.

Gloriana had given me the god's key as my birthday present, right
before her daughter Tania had murdered her. Any door I unlocked
with the key would bring me here. On first glance, the hallway looked
like it belonged in an office building that had been built in the 1970s
and forgotten. Cobwebs dangled from the ceiling, illuminated by
horrific incandescent lightbulbs that hummed faintly while casting
their diseased light on the mustard-yellow wallpaper. The ceiling was

made out of those white spackled tiles that exist in every building ever built. Even the air tasted stale, as if the building had been sealed for a long time.

The hallway stretched before me as far as I could see. Both sides were dotted with white doors every few feet. I knew from prior investigation each had frosted glass windows hinting at the world waiting behind. Some doors featured bright lights with shadowy figures moving on the other side. Others were empty, dead worlds fallen to the Nothing, the endless dark that devoured all things.

Each door was labeled with the name of a realm out of myth and legend. I have walked past the doors for Olympus, Asgard, even Atlantis, although that last one had been moist and rotten, and I did not think it was safe to open. Others were chained shut with thick, black irons. As I walked past one, whose placard had long since faded into unreadability, the door popped open a few inches, straining against its bonds like a rabid dog.

I let out a very dignified squeak and leapt to the far side of the hallway, glaring at the offending door, now open a hair. A cold, whispering wind blew through the crack, and it took me a second to get ahold of myself. I still hadn't gotten used to them doing that.

With an annoyed snarl, I kicked the door with my toe, shoving it closed, sealing off the world that had been devoured by the Nothing once more.

Whoever had placed these chains must have done so to keep them shut. As far as I knew, you're supposed to need the Key of Portunus to open anything in here. I've been too much of a chicken to try any door other than the Faerie Lands, but I've noticed the fallen worlds seemed to have loose latches. The racket from them opening and closing adds a little spooky ambience to the whole place that I don't appreciate.

The mystery caretaker was long gone. I've never seen another soul when I sneak down the halls. As far as I know, I'm the only person in the universe with a key. Let the building cry and moan, I'm its master now—or at least the current tenant.

When the gang and I fled Dawn and her new regime change, I hadn't realized what a hindrance returning to the mortal world would be for me personally. My main advantage when it came to supernatural combat was my access to Willow's flames. Which, like all fire, required fuel.

Living in the Faerie Lands had been the magical equivalent of being plugged right into the power source. I could draw on as much of the fire spirit's power as I could handle. Since coming back to good old Mother Earth, I was practically on starvation rations.

When I first bonded with Willow, taking its essence from the minotaur, the spirit had been stuck on earth for a long time; its reserves were almost depleted. I burned through them in just a few minutes with all the fighting. On a full tank, Willow and I can go much longer, assuming I don't spend everything we have on a creature that's immune to fire.

The first time I entered the Faerie Lands, Willow had equated being in that realm to being able to breathe again. Magic fire needs magic oxygen, apparently. Since then I had discovered that every time I went back to help the spirit take another breath, we could hold more magic oxygen than the last time. If a swimmer can train his lungs to hold more air, then Willow and I were learning to hold more fuel.

Regardless of how ineffective Willow appeared to be on dragons, I was not willing to set foot into the games that were afoot without refilling their battery. That would be like bringing a gun with no bullets. I'm plenty dumb, but I ain't stupid. Or maybe it's the other way around—I forget which is which.

Finally, I found the entrance I was looking for. For some reason, the doors are never in the same place twice. I strongly suspect if you walk down the hallway long enough, it eventually loops back into itself, but I'm too lazy to test my theory. Usually, I just pick a direction and walk until the door I want pops up.

It's never where I saw it last, but it always looks the same. The white paint on the door was peeling, and the sign read FAERIE LANDS—NO TRESPASSING. I always figured that didn't mean me. I was courting one of the princesses after all.

Still whistling to myself, I fished out the key and held it up against the door handle, just outside the lock. For a moment I paused, trying to make sense of the shadowy figures I saw moving behind the frosted glass. Sometimes they stirred unbelievably fast; other times they were practically frozen. As usual, the choreography gave me no clue what might be waiting on the other side.

Organizing my thoughts, I tried to focus on where I needed the door to open to. It would be somewhere in the Faerie Lands, but I could help it choose where I came out. As far as I could tell, the key read my intentions and then did its best to find an entrance that matched what I wanted.

So far, I had entered via a broom closet, a bathroom, and an abandoned apartment. That last one had been the most convenient. I didn't actually need to go anywhere or do anything special once I was inside the Faerie Lands. I just recharged Willow then popped right back home before anyone even knew I'd visited.

Trying to remember the exact instructions I gave it last time, I muttered under my breath, "Out of the way, private, and comfortable." I slid the key into the lock with a click and gave it a twist. For a second, I hesitated. I always got a little nervous right before I took the plunge.

Steeling myself, I turned the knob and pushed into the Faerie Lands. The moment I set foot on Fae ground, my hands burst into flame.

"*Took you long enough!*" the fire spirit cheered gleefully into my head.

There was a loud clatter as the doorway I had just walked through collapsed on itself behind me. My head whipped around—it had been some sort of temporary door, rigged up on two-by-fours and held together with spit and a little bit of gravity. The force of my entrance had shaken it into pieces, closing that exit. The only way I was going to be able to leave was if I found a new, working door—or if I got really good at carpentry all of a sudden.

The room was brightly lit and heavily furnished, featuring several large couches. It was even fully catered—there was food everywhere. I even saw a plate of cookies. Someone had gone to a lot of effort to make sure this space was out of the way, private, and comfortable, with a feast thrown in for good measure.

There was a normal door waiting for me on the other side, I realized.

All I had to do to get to it was go through my father.

I shouldn't have been surprised to see him. If anyone could have guessed how I was keeping Willow charged, it would have been him. I just figured he wouldn't care. A familiar numbness spread through me at the sight of him. I knew how to weather his kind of storm.

I gritted my teeth and began drawing Willow's flame. The spirit was entirely capable of recharging their own batteries, but they had taught me how to speed up the process, which also seemed to increase my body's capacity to hold magic oxygen. It was a bit like inhaling two breaths at once. Power flowed into me, like a burning breeze.

Damien Carver, aka Damien Fireheart, rolled his golden eyes as he watched me try to suck down all the power that Willow and I could carry. "Don't be so dramatic," he snapped, waving his own flaming hands in a dismissive gesture. "You and I need to talk. Stop that ridiculous attempt at cycling and sit down."

Shocked, I practically choked on my spicy breathing, forcing me to stop. "We can talk," I said stiffly, "but I'm good standing."

My father sighed and sat down in one of the large dining chairs. He helped himself to a cluster of purple grapes and began to pop them off and into his mouth one by one. His golden eyes stared at me, his face the picture of boredom. I know I can be a little stubborn, but I never stood a chance with only half of his genes in my DNA. If I didn't give in a little, I was going to be here until The End.

Matching his sigh, I sat down at the table, in the farthest seat away from him. Eyeing the spread, I helped myself to a pair of green grapes and began copying his eating. A shadow of something crossed his face, and he put his fruit down. I kept eating mine. They were delicious. They may not pay their mortal servants or let them leave, but the Fae have killer produce.

"If your mother could see what you have become, she would die all over again, I think," Damien mused after a few moments.

Yeah, Dad's not one for small talk. I wish I could say I was used to it and that it didn't sting, but his opening salvo hit harder than any Nephilim I had ever sparred with—except maybe Orion.

"Oh, I'm sure she'd be real thrilled with you, Mr. Secret Faerie," I shot back.

"She knew." My father's quiet assertion rocked me in my seat a little. I had been assuming my mother was a vanilla mortal, completely unaware of the world that her husband had left behind. Maybe I had judged him a little too harshly.

"You. Sold. Your. Soul," Damien accused. "I smelled the stench of your infernal deal the moment I saw you outside your sister's hospital."

I had assumed now that he was back and working for the Faerie home office, he'd be up to speed on the whole soul fraud situation. That was literally the cornerstone of my deal with them.

"Not only that, but you mixed your sister's soul up in your greed, and now she is trapped in Limbo, being tortured, because of *you*. You got her killed once, and you seem Hell-bent on getting her killed a second time."

"I didn't sell my soul," I snapped, feeling a flush of anger burning in my cheeks. He was wrong, but his judgment got under my skin. I was angrier with myself than with him. I knew better than to rise to his bait. "A demon forged my signature. I didn't ask for Megan to be brought back. I didn't ask for any of this!"

"Yes, I've heard all about your allegations," Damien sneered, a cruel twist to his mouth. "Spare me the sob story. Even as a little boy, you didn't have an ounce of self-control. Which is more likely? Satan and his demons have violated one of the fundamental laws of this world, or you gave in to temptation?"

I don't know if hearing my father's low opinion of my moral fiber was really a surprise, but it still hurt. I was not a perfect kid. I got in trouble, stole cookies from the cookie jar, and lied about doing my homework. But there was a difference between being thirteen years old and wanting some sugar and selling your soul to the Devil.

Maybe Dan was just that bad a salesman—a more talented agent of Hell might have had me signing on the dotted line before you could blink. But somehow, I doubted it.

"Okay, Father," I sneered back at him, matching his tone. "Then why was I accepted into the Hunt? Why are the Fae helping me get my soul back?"

"Because you are my son," he said with absolute certainty.

I sat there for a second, stunned by his casual arrogance.

"Orion has long sought powerful, naïve disciples. Idiots like you are much more willing to die for him than the rest of us. Just look at the last Hunt."

My anger, bubbling just beneath the surface, broke into a full-on boil. The Hunter was always the first to put himself in danger. How many times had he stood up against a terrifying enemy to shield Alex and me? I opened my mouth to object, but he cut me off.

"Gloriana saw you as a stud, fit for pasture to give her a new brood of Fae capable of bonding with the Flame. She would have promised you the moon to have your genes, and you walked right into her trap."

Okay, that one was a little more accurate. Gloriana had straight up admitted to it, *but* she had also believed that my soul had been stolen and had accomplished more to help me get it back than anyone else. Her death had been a blow to my chances of getting out of this.

For the first time in this conversation, it clicked for me that my father was a Faerie. This whole time I had been reacting like a mortal teenager standing up to his dad. But I had forgotten there were other rules at play here.

The Fae cannot lie.

I forced myself to take another deep, cycling breath and fed my anger to the flames. I don't know if it worked, but I felt myself becoming more rational as I gazed at my father with new eyes. Everything he had just said was true—at least to him. He really believed I took the deal. He really thought so little of Orion. I finished my cycling breath and accepted that.

It was time to stop letting him push my buttons and use the one advantage I had.

"What do you want?" I asked with a tired sigh.

"Vengeance." The word sounded almost reverent as he spoke it.

The last time I had seen my father, moments after becoming betrothed to Ash, he had hit me with a bombshell: Gloriana had been responsible for the death of my mother and sisters. Another one of her daughters, Mav, the Lady of Winter, had controlled the waters that swept them off the road, ensuring they drowned.

It would be a bold-faced lie if I said the concept of vengeance on the frigid Faerie wasn't appealing—but it was sure complicated. "Haven't you given your oath to serve Dawn?" I asked, suspicious. "Seems like that might get in the way of killing her sister."

Dawn had welcomed my father back with open arms, giving him Robin's old position of right-hand man. There was probably some sort of fancy title like Hand of the Queen, or Vice Regent, but I had no idea what it was. The new ruler had insisted that her elder sister was too useful to give to my father.

"I swore to protect her and serve her interests," Damien shrugged, as if his oath was as restrictive as a spider's web. "The Lady of Winter has actively sought to exterminate Willow and the followers of the Path of the Flame. If she succeeds, it will be the end of our people. The success she has already seen has been catastrophic. Removing her is the only logical outcome of my duty."

It occurred to me for the first time that Mav might have made a point of killing my sisters when Gloriana had sent her to kill my mother. The former queen had wanted my father to be the sire of the Lady of Autumn. He refused, and their falling-out had led to him vanishing from the Dandelion Court. Gloriana eventually got good old Lucifer to be her baby daddy instead, but she had never forgiven my father for cutting off her access to Willow's fire as he left.

For Gloriana, it had been petty rivalry that made her send her headsman after my mother. But unbeknownst to her, Mav had been killing off all the Lords and Lady of Flame, trying to exterminate the fire of Willow. Had she killed my siblings to prevent them from ever becoming bound to the Fire? Would the Lady of Winter have found me in a dark alley one night too? My hands curled into fists as a new pulse of anger toward Mav ran through my bones.

"Let's say for a moment that I'm interested," I said through gritted teeth. "What would you need me to do?"

"Dawn has kept Mav locked away since she ascended to the throne," my father said, rising to pace, his hands clasped at the small of his back. "In part because she cannot trust Mav, but also to keep her out of my reach." My father glanced sideways at me, his golden eyes gleaming. "Dawn is wise enough to know I cannot permit Mav to live. She is stalling for time while she seeks another solution."

"That sounds like Dawn," I agreed. Dawn had been her mother's director of what I call the FIA, which is basically our Central Intelligence Agency, but for the Fae instead. They don't call it that, but they should. The idea that Dawn was managing the murderous tension between my father and her sister didn't surprise me in the slightest. "What do you want me to do about it?"

"The Constellation Congregation has been called," my father said simply. "The Fae have been invited for the first time in five hundred years. Dawn wishes to attend but will require bodyguards. Convince her to include Mav on the list, and then get out of my way."

My eyes widened as I realized the depths of my father's plan. Not only would it bring Mav out into the open, but it would also bring her out of the Faerie Lands, leaving her more exposed for him to strike. Dawn would not have as many Fae with her to separate them if a fight broke out.

"About that," I replied, realizing he must not be up to date on last night's events. "We might actually need all hands on deck for bodyguard duty."

"There will doubtless be factions unhappy to see us return to our rightful place," Damien shrugged, nonplussed. "We will deal with them."

"Well, one of those groups has already caused some problems. The Dragon Dons sent some dragoons to kill me last night, and they caught Dawn in the crossfire."

My father broke his pacing and froze, turning his head to stare at me quizzically. "Dragoons? Oh, I see it, dragon—goons, yes, yes." He really must be my father. There's no other explanation than shared DNA to explain his brain instinctually understanding my nonsense.

"And why... are the Dragon Dons trying to kill you, Matthew?" My father's voice was as crisp as a brand-new hundred-dollar bill.

"When I first bound to Willow, I had no idea what was happening for some reason," I said wryly. Taking a small amount of delight at the faint trace of an embarrassed shadow that passed across his face. "I might have burned down a laboratory that was under their protection."

"What were you doing in a laboratory under the Dons' protection?" he asked incredulously.

"I thought they had Megan, so I went to get her back." I raised my chin to give him a defiant stare. Something in the corner of his eyes softened for a moment. I think that might have been one of the first times he understood me. I just wished it had been about something normal like baseball or whiskey.

Something deep in my chest, the lurking child that is present in all of us, demanded to speak in this rare opportunity. "Dad," I said, without even processing my thoughts. "I'm sorry about Mom and the girls."

Damien Carver—for in that moment he was Damien Carver and not Damien Fireheart—was silent for several beats, a host of emotions playing across his face as he stared at me. "I knew," he croaked after an eternity.

"You knew what?" I asked, my heart racing.

"I knew Mav was in LA to kill your mother. I told your mother it was dangerous and to stay home."

"But I convinced her to come see me..." I trailed off as I finally understood all of my father's anger with me. I had understood part of it before. It had been raining, and I convinced her to drive. But my father had *known* that someone would try to kill her, and I had been the bait that lured my family out.

"If you knew, where were you?" I demanded, feeling a pang of anger like an echo of his own. "Why didn't you protect them, Lord of Fire?"

"She didn't tell me they were leaving!" my father roared, turning away from me to stare at the wall. Both of his hands were at his sides, balled into white-knuckled fists. Not for the first time, I wondered if two people bound to Willow would be able to burn each other.

"They're dead because you guilted her until she disobeyed me!" Damien Fireheart spun back to me, the flames dancing in his golden eyes matching the ones swirling around his fists. "She disobeyed my command after *you* tempted her."

"They're dead because of both of us," I said, taking a step back and raising my own hands. It took all of my self-control not to summon my own Willow's flames. I knew if I did, this conversation would be burned to ash. "But they're also dead because Mav killed them."

"Then let's make it right," my father snapped, "or get as close as we can."

"I will see what I can do with Dawn," I agreed cautiously. My father gave me a slow nod and turned toward the exit, apparently satisfied with the level of therapy we had just gone through.

"But in exchange you have to help me with something," I called after him.

"What do you want?" He turned his head to look at me, eyes narrowed in suspicion.

I held up my hands and summoned my flames. "How the hell are you supposed to fight dragons with fire?" I asked.

"It's simple," my father called over his shoulder as he walked out the door. "Don't fight their flames, *feed* off them."

AFTER MY FATHER left me, I wasted no time using Portunus's key and getting the hell out of Dodge. That painful conversation had been more than enough time for Willow to charge, and I didn't want to spend any more time than I had to in Dawn's domain. I had a sneaking suspicion she would be happy to throw me in a gilded cage next to Mav's to have on hand when she needed me for something.

Popping out of my closet like it was a wardrobe, I closed the door behind me and leaned against it, letting out a long exhale, as if purging my body of every single ounce of carbon dioxide would fix all my problems.

It didn't. As my lungs began to protest the lack of incoming oxygen,

I caved and inhaled, heading downstairs. My little fortress is tall and narrow, more like a single tower than a whole castle I suppose. My room took up the entire third floor, with a descending concrete staircase that wound its way down through the open air above the living room.

Alex occupied both bedrooms on the second floor. He used one as his room and the other as an office. I clomped past his floor and headed down to the main level, where I collapsed into the couches, exhausted. Even though I hadn't physically fought my father, between the battle last night and the emotional one today, my gas tank was running on empty.

Somehow this stupid convention-congregation thing I had never heard of had upended my life in just twenty-four hours. The Hunt was in trouble, Dawn was trying to get her hooks into me, dragons wanted to eat my face, and my dad wanted me to help him kill one of the Faerie princesses.

I'm sure there was more trouble I was forgetting, but it was only Wednesday, and the convention didn't start until Friday. There was plenty of time for more things to go wrong. If I was smart, I would have gone looking for Orion and started convincing him about Dawn's plan to team up.

But I had just spent the last hour fighting with my father about who was responsible for getting my mother and sisters killed. What I needed to survive right now was cartoons, the dumber the better. Maybe the fight had woken my inner child, and I was regressing. I think most people would argue that it's hard to regress when you haven't made any progress. I still watch cartoons, sue me.

As I fired up the TV, Alex trotted into the room, dressed in a pair of gray sweatpants and a black shirt. I nodded at him as he flopped down on the couch. As much as I wanted some mindless entertainment, there was no way I was going to be able to think about anything other than the fact that he had been having a nice, quiet little bottle of wine with Nika while I was out.

You could practically feel the tension of unasked questions in the air as we both pretended to watch the show. "Do you remember when the TV was invented?" I asked, breaking the silence.

"Dude, I'm over two hundred years old," Alex scoffed. "I remember when they invented the telephone."

"How weird is it to go from those days to seeing the talking sea creatures hit each other on the head with bug nets?" I gestured at the screen to make my point.

"They used to put leeches on people as medicine," Alex observed loftily, arching an eyebrow at the screen. "Honestly, I've seen weirder."

"Speaking of weird," I began, turning from the TV to stare at my best friend. "I saw something *super weird* last night. You know, the kind of thing you wouldn't expect to happen—"

"Do we have to do this?" Alex complained, draping an elbow over his eyes as if blocking the sight of me would block my questions.

"Oh, we have to do this," I responded cheerfully, my earlier exhaustion fading at the prospect of torturing my friend. "I've had to put up with six months of this from you. I don't care what they say, payback is a dish best served immediately and often."

"Haven't you heard of turning the other cheek?" He groaned.

"Tried it. Terrible at it."

"Fine. Let's get this over with." Alex sat up and fixed me with a blue-eyed stare. "What's it gonna take for you to let this go? What juicy morsel will sate your insatiable thirst for gossip?"

"Let's start with how whatever this is started and see if that's enough to curb my appetite," I replied, feeling a wicked smirk spreading across my face. "Last time I checked, Nika didn't really associate with grunts like you and me."

Part of what went into her status as one of Orion's better students was the unfortunate calculus that her ancestry had a larger ratio of demon to human DNA than most. She wasn't on Orion's level; her eyes were still human and not the empty black of a demigod or demon. But she was noticeably stronger and faster than Alex or I, and she knew it.

"It's not like that," Alex said quietly, his usual playful expression replaced by an earnest one. "I think it's hard for her to open up to people, having as much strength as she does and being as famous as she is."

Oh yeah, that was the other thing about Nika. If it wasn't enough to be the however-many-generations-removed grandchild of a demon, she was also about as LA as you could be. She was an *influencer*. I guess I couldn't blame her; if I had supernatural genes that made me more attractive, athletic, and kept me from aging, maybe I'd be famous too. Still, it seemed a little shady to me to post pictures of her workouts as if she didn't have an inhuman metabolism that was the real secret to her six-pack.

But I don't think it was the fame or the money that bothered me. Rent in LA is *expensive*. I'd done plenty of sketchy things to keep a roof over my head and that was before a demon gave me five million dollars. The thing that really got under my skin was how Nika acted like she worked hard for it.

"Ah, is she worried everyone is just trying to use her to get more social status?" I asked, arching a skeptical eyebrow.

"That's what I suspect," Alex said with a shrug, "but after I beat her in training one night, she struck up a conversation with me, and we got to talking, then we got a drink, and that turned into dinner."

"This has happened more than once?" I gasped in mock horror.

"Only a few times." Alex gave me a rueful grin. "I'm beginning to see how annoying this is."

"Don't think acting all sorry will get you out of your punishment," I replied sagely. "So what's going on, are you guys talking, are you dating, what are we calling this?"

"We're calling it nice."

"How boring."

"It is nice. All my life, my heritage has left me an outsider on both sides of the fence. I've lived long enough to see two different generations of my mortal friends die of old age, but among the Nephilim I'm an afterthought."

I gave Alex a slow blink as I processed that. I had never thought about the downside of straddling two worlds like he did. It occurred to me that immortality could be bone-crushingly lonely. It gave me a new appreciation for the plucky Nephilim who came up to me at the Mount Olympus Bar and Grille and offered to help me.

At the time, the whole room had been hostile to me because every supernatural with a pinch of power could smell the stench of sulfur from the demonic deal I didn't sign. It was hard to make any new friends, even as I was being driven away from my mortal ones because of my new life. But the outcast, the one who knew what it was like to not fit in, had welcomed me.

Friends like that are priceless.

"I think I can understand a little," I said over a lump forming in my throat.

"Nika has just been nice to me. I enjoy talking to her and spending time with her. For once in my life, I truly feel an equal." He looked down at his hands, embarrassed. "It's part of what I've been struggling with in our friendship lately."

"What do you mean?" I asked, caught completely off guard.

"You have no idea how far you've come in such a short time, do you?" Alex replied, shaking his head. "It's quite embarrassing to be passed up by a mortal who is barely a quarter century old."

"How have I passed you?" I demanded. "I occasionally sneak a victory in the practice ring, but I am light-years behind you."

"In the practice ring, sure," Alex snorted. "But they don't put people in the stars for how well they perform in *practice*. It's the real moments that matter. You slew an Immortal."

"Which was a terrible idea," I interjected.

"You defied a fallen angel that almost killed me," he continued as if I hadn't spoken.

"And only survived because I ran away through a magical dandelion highway."

"You have a magic fire spirit strong enough to burn Immortals."

"You do realize Willow is severely weaker here in the mortal realm, right? I have access to a fraction of the power that I could use when we were in the Faerie Lands."

"And now Robin wants you to complete an Impossible Task and become a Constellation… I know you don't have any perspective on what that means, but that's like every Nephilim child's dream."

I thought I understood. It was as if Alex had studied his whole life to be a musician but had never made it past the garage band phase. Then along comes Matt Carver, who has no idea how music even works, let alone how to make it, and after a year I get a record deal. He might be happy for me, but it still had to sting a little.

"I don't mean that I don't want you to get your soul back or that I won't help or anything," Alex said after a long moment.

"No, no, I know, never doubted you for a second. But you're right, I have almost no idea what an Impossible Task is. I know Jason and the Argonauts had to complete one, and I think there was something about a golden sheep?"

"Yeah," Alex chuckled dryly, "there was a golden sheep."

"That's all I got."

"There are at least two ways to become a Constellation. The most common one is to become so iconic with an attribute that you almost become it."

"Orion is the idea of the Hunter," I said.

"Exactly—it's a weird blend of fame and success. You have to have piled up so many deeds that people think of you when they think of that aspect and vice versa."

"I can't believe there isn't a Michael Phelps Constellation of the Swimmer yet."

"It's harder to become one that way now," Alex said, ignoring my joke. "There are a lot more people you have to influence than there used to be."

"It's like a percent thing? You need to convince a certain portion of the entire human race?"

"I don't know the exact rules, but something like that."

"What's the other way you become a Constellation?" I asked.

"The whole Impossible Task process, but that's much rarer."

"Why?"

"You have to convince someone who is qualified to *give* you an Impossible Task, and then you have to survive it. Few do the first part—fewer still the second."

"That's what Orion is for," I chuckled.

We were both silent for a moment, the weight of the conversation holding us down. I probably should have been overwhelmed with questions about what Alex had just told me, but I found thoughts gravitating toward concern for my friend. It felt like a flashlight's beam had illuminated him and solved a mystery I had been trying to crack.

"Is that why you took the mask?" I asked into the silence.

"Part of it," he agreed, not meeting my eyes. During my birthday party, traitorous Faerie from the Court of Spring attacked, wearing black masks filled with demonic power that left them even stronger and faster than usual.

Alex had taken one of the masks from a defeated Faerie, but as far as I knew he had never put it on. Orion had been unhappy but hadn't ordered him to get rid of it. It was not his way to take decisions away from his squires.

"After Zagan sliced me up, I just felt so useless, like all I ever did was slow down the Hunt. I won't be a victim ever again."

"Are you sure using a weapon made by demons is the way to go about that?" I asked as gently as I could. As far as I was concerned, I was the weakest link on the team, but I didn't think he wanted to hear that right now.

"Why not? I am part demon. Orion has a magic sword, why should I not have a magic mask?"

I didn't have a good answer.

DAWN HAS MANY strengths, none of them are patience. I had only made it through a few episodes of my cartoons before the Queen of All Fae demanded my attention. In fact she demanded all of the misplaced Fae in our group—whom Robin called Dandelions in the Wind—attend her.

That was how I found myself jammed back into Robin's Mustang's tiny rear seats for the second time in two days, my knees pressing into my chest with enough force that I worried they might shatter my rib cage like kindling.

For once, the golden convertible's hood was up, and Robin wasn't driving like a lunatic, switching lanes at every possible moment. If I didn't know any better, I'd say the Faerie was stalling. The mood inside was dour; an echoing silence hung over the three of us as we headed toward Beverly Hills, where Dawn apparently owned a home, because of course she did.

If Robin was stalling, I wouldn't mind if he decided to go a few miles under the speed limit, just to give me a little longer to think. While technically I knew where I stood with Dawn thanks to the deal I had made with her mother, it was never that simple with a Faerie. There's a big difference between following the spirit of the agreement versus the letter of it. I'm sure there was a way she could hang me out to dry without ever breaking her word.

To make things even murkier, it wasn't long ago that the new Queen had tried to place Ash under arrest while she consolidated her power. For all I knew, that was still her plan.

"Remind me why we're doing this again?" I sighed into the silence of the car. "How do we know she's not going to toss us in some cage the moment we get there?"

"Dawn made assurances," Robin grumbled, not sounding any happier than I did.

"Besides, she told us she wanted us at the convention," Ash supplied. "We have to be alive and free to do that."

"So you don't think it's a trap?" I asked incredulously.

"No, it's a test," Ash replied tersely. "Everything Dawn does is a test."

"Are we sure attending is going to give us the grade we want?"

"It's a failure if we don't show up at all," Robin explained.

I took a moment to think about that. I'm no Faerie—well, that's not completely true, but I wasn't raised like one. They take to politics like a fish to water, it just makes sense to them. I had spent the last six months hanging out with a Faerie princess and lawyer and had been doing my best to learn.

Dawn was still a new Queen. Her reign was clearly more stable than it had been the night that Gloriana was murdered, but that didn't mean it was rock-solid. Since Ash was the only one of her sisters who had left the Faerie Lands, she had the most potential to be a rallying point for anyone opposed to the new order.

I was pretty sure the test was to see if we were going to fall into line and respect Dawn's authority or be problems. She'd chosen to put us to this test here, away from the majority of the Dandelion Court. If we did defy her, almost no one would be around to see it.

"She wants to know if we're going to play nice or not," I breathed to the car full of people who already knew that.

"Well done," Robin affirmed.

"What happens if we spit in her Cheerios instead of following her lead?" I asked.

"I'm sure she'll tell us," Ash murmured from the front seat.

The Dandelion Court apparently owned a Beverly property that would be the jewel in any Hollywood star's eye. It sat toward the top of one the rolling hills, with a perfectly manicured lawn and a three-story mansion looked like it was modeled after the homes of English nobility. I guess that made sense for a Faerie.

The wrought-iron gate was worked with real gold, and there was plenty more to be seen throughout the property. I was pretty sure I saw a fountain made entirely of the stuff in the garden as we pulled up the drive.

My least favorite butler from all the worlds that I have visited, Dawson, answered the door when Robin knocked. His immortal face was set in a permanent scowl, which impossibly deepened as he saw me among the guests on his Queen's doorstep. I gave him a little wave. He didn't bother saying anything, just sniffed once and stepped to the side, allowing us inside. With another huff, he led us across the ornate dark wood floors of the Beverly Hills mansion.

Dawn was waiting for us in the dining room. She sat at the head of a long mahogany table that would have fit in any boardroom. Her bright-yellow sweatsuit had clearly come directly from some designer shop on Rodeo Drive. Dawson ushered us in and pulled the large doors to the room shut behind us with an aggressive thud.

The Queen of All Fae was alone. I had been right: If this went poorly, she didn't want any of the other members of her court to get any ideas. For a moment we just stared at one another, like a pack of cats trying to see who would blink first.

"Well?" Dawn demanded after the silence stretched well beyond awkward territory. She arched a cool eyebrow as her gaze flicked among the three of us.

"Well, what?" Ash mimicked her tone effortlessly. "You summoned us, dear sister."

"I suppose I did," Dawn agreed languidly, a faint smirk quirking the corner of her mouth. It seemed reasonable Dawn was out to play today. "Are you two ready to come home?"

"Just like that?" Robin mused; his eyes narrowed as he studied the Queen from Ash's side.

"Just like that," Dawn promised.

"What happened to consolidating your rule?" I asked.

"Darling, I have been quite busy over the past six months," Dawn purred. "The Ladies of Winter and Spring have declared their support for my rule. So have the lords and ladies of all the Paths, including Fire." She tossed Ash and me a wink at that. "I'd say it's pretty consolidated."

I don't know what the normal turnaround for the dust to settle after a new administration takes over post-coup is, but that seemed more than a little impressive to me. I still had boxes in my new place that weren't unpacked.

"So now it is our turn?" Ash pushed quietly.

"Consolidated, not complete." Dawn leaned back in her chair and gave her sister a frank glance. "While our sisters have agreed to my rule, they are both traitors and practically worthless. Mav did more damage to the Dandelion Court than I dare to admit, but she was not successful in stomping out the flame. I need the Lady of Autumn, now more than ever."

It was not lost on me that she no longer called it the House of Fall. From the surprised look on Ash's face, she noticed too.

Robin looked skeptical but arched a single, perfectly trimmed eyebrow. "Need her for what?" he asked, evidently still serving as the official Autumnal lawyer.

"To rebuild our species," Dawn snapped, irritation passing across her face for the first time. "Our mother was a lunatic, but she wasn't wrong. The Fae sun has begun to set, but I would see it rise again on a new day."

No wonder Dawn had orchestrated this meeting to take place without any other Fae present. There's no way she would ever speak so bluntly about her mother in front of the rest of her court. It struck me how clever this approach was for her. Ash was very grounded—for a Faerie princess. She wouldn't be won over by flowery speeches or presents. She'd want to know the truth of what Dawn was planning.

"And if I reject your offer?" Ash inquired, her face unreadable.

Dawn sighed and ran a hand across her face, as if she could scrub her irritation away. "Then you force me to do something drastic. I need a head of the Autumn House, Ash, and whoever it is has to have a bond with Willow, which doesn't leave me with a lot of options, does it?"

My heart skipped a beat: The only two other candidates in the world were my father and me. Given Damien was currently operating as her right hand, I had a guess which was her top pick. I mean, I wasn't even technically a full Faerie.

"You'd give one of the seasonal houses to someone outside the royal family?" Robin gasped in shock.

"No, no, that would be too far," Dawn agreed sagely. "Someone would have to marry him. Someone who isn't already head of their own house…"

The three of us stared at the Queen in horror. My brain had no idea how to process all of the layers to that threat, so it just gave up, leaving all the new information scattered around the floor of my mind like a deck of cards. If Ash didn't resume her duties as the Lady of Autumn, Dawn would make my father the new Lord of Autumn. But because he wasn't a royal, she would marry him to Ash, leaving me without a betrothed.

Also—just ew.

Ew on so many levels.

He was at least a couple hundred years older than her, which means almost nothing to an Immortal but still made me feel slimy. Plus, he was my *father*. My mother had only been dead for a little over two years; I wasn't sure I was ready for him to move on yet. The whole her-being-my-betrothed thing made it even weirder.

Ash glared at Dawn, who had the grace to at least look embarrassed. "It's not my first choice," the Queen murmured softly, a faint blush creeping on her cheeks. "Don't put me in a corner I can't get out of."

"If I agree to come back, what is expected of me?" Ash pressed, her voice deceptively cool.

"Do your job," Dawn snarled. "Rebuild your court, rekindle the flame, make it strong again."

I found myself conflicted on Ash's choice. On the one hand, being free of Dawn's games had been nice for the last six months. I had no doubt rejoining the everyday activities of the Dandelion Court would ruin that. But selfishly, I liked the arrangement we had going—I needed it. If Ash walked away from her sister, I would understand, but I had a feeling I would end up out in the cold too.

Ash glanced at Robin as if asking his opinion. Ever so slightly he inclined his head, with a tiny shrug as if to say, *What else can you do?*

"Very well," Ash said after a long moment. "I will resume my duties, but I require Robin to remain as my counselor." I breathed out a small sigh of relief.

"As you wish, my lady," Robin replied, bowing deeply to Ash in a more formal gesture than I had seen him make in the last six months. There was no playful smile on his face, no twinkle in his golden eyes. I might have said he was angry, but I wasn't quite sure why.

"See? Look at us, reunited, just like Mother would have wanted." Dawn beamed, clapping her hands once in approval. "I knew I could count on you."

The Queen's gaze left the Fae and fell on me with a physical force, her smile fading behind a cold mask. "Now, as for you, Matthew Carver, Lord of Fire, I seem to recall asking for an alliance with the Hunter," she drawled. "But I do not seem to have one. Are my commands so easily forgotten? Or do you not serve me?"

"I'm... still working on that," I replied, wincing a little. I hadn't even told Orion what had happened yet. Which seemed like a mistake now that I was standing in front of Dawn.

"There must be some fundamental misunderstanding about your relationship to the Dandelion Throne." Dawn leaned forward and placed her elbows on the table. "If you still wish to be a part of *my* family and benefit from the resources of *my* court in your quest to regain your soul, then you will behave as a loyal member of my court or will you face down Hell on your own."

A chill settled on my spine as I saw where this was going. Gloriana had been happy to use a carrot to lead me around, but it seemed Dawn wasn't afraid of showing me the stick.

"Sorry, which resources of the court have been working on my behalf since your reign began?" I asked, my eyes narrowing. "From my point of view, it's been rather quiet on your side for the last six months."

Expressionlessly, Dawn gestured at the two Fae standing next to me. "You've been with members of my court the entire time."

"Estranged members," I protested.

"Nonsense," Dawn said, dismissing my argument with an annoyed wave of her hand. "You know how family is. We squabble, but we never stop being family." I glanced over at Ash and Robin; their faces were both very still. I guess that was the price of their new peace.

"Surely there has been *some* work accomplished by my vassals on your behalf?" She turned to my lawyer, an amused smirk on her face. "Robin, are you expecting me to believe you have not made any progress on Matthew's case?"

Robin froze, his golden eyes tracking over to me with a look of despair. I knew what was coming. Dawn was about to know everything. Damn, but she was too good at this.

"There has been one recent breakthrough, Your Majesty," Robin admitted after a brief pause.

"See?" Dawn demanded brightly, gesturing at Robin as if his service hadn't cost me a million dollars. "That is excellent news. Tell me about this breakthrough."

Robin shot me an apologetic look before obeying. "It appears that if Matthew is able to complete an Impossible Task, he will be free and clear of the deal."

Dawn's smile grew wicked horns as she heard Robin's news, like a cat that has found a mouse stuck in a trap. My palms grew sweaty as the Queen of All Fae leaned forward, golden eyes boring into mine. I could feel her hunger from across the table. I knew she understood all the layers of what Robin was saying, that I needed the Fae more than ever.

"It seems it is now doubly in your best interest to show me you are a loyal and useful member of my court. Get. Me. That. Alliance." She glanced at Ash, a hint of her cruelty coming back to the surface.

"This is the task I set before the Autumn House for this convention, in order to prove their worth to the Dandelion Throne: Protect me from our enemies, punish those who have made us look weak, and guarantee our return to the Constellation Congregation, or be cast out into the dark."

I swallowed once but nodded, not trusting myself to speak. The Queen of All Fae eyed the three of us for a moment before raising her hands and clapping them once. "Tick-tock," she sang as Dawson came to retrieve us.

As we exited Dawn's mansion, I pulled out my phone and dialed Orion. "Hey, so you're going to hate this," I said as he picked up. "But I think we have to make another deal with the Fae."

CHAPTER
TEN

ORION AGREED TO meet with Dawn.

It wasn't as hard as I'd expected to convince him.
The Hunter hates dragons above all things, even Fae.
When he found out that the Dragon Dons had tried to kill me, he was
quite wroth, which is another olde word for "angry," and I can think
of no better term to describe the fury in those black eyes. The Hunter
is ancient, and his anger is a primal thing from the dark before-times.

So, acting as intermediary for the two groups, I proposed a meeting
place as the Hunt, which I then agreed to on behalf of the Fae. It was
a remarkably pleasant experience, working with myself. I really felt
like I was on the same page as me. It made everything very efficient.

If I thought Orion had been upset when he heard about the

dragons, I was wholly unprepared for his response to Robin's discovery about the major clause thing.

We were in Alex's minivan, zooming in the carpool lane to the meeting site when I finally broke the news to him. I don't know why, but I felt more nervous about bringing up the Constellation situation than I did about the dragons. Still, I didn't have a choice. I was positive Dawn would bring up the Fae rejoining the Congregation in this meeting. I was equally sure Orion would be opposed to it, but he didn't have the latest update. When I finished telling him the story, the big Nephilim was silent for a long time.

He always rode in the captain's seats in the middle row, both as a weird power thing and because they had more legroom for his giant frame. This meant I couldn't see the expression on his face as I white-knuckled my way through the silence.

After a few moments, he murmured, "Finally, many things begin to become clear," which was both obtuse and not very encouraging.

"What do you mean things are becoming clear?" I demanded. "They seem murkier than ever!"

"If you do this, there will be consequences," Orion said slowly, sounding like he did not want to talk about it. "You must understand—I cannot help you with it."

"Why not?" I craned my head around to stare back at the Hunter. His stony face was even stonier than usual, hiding its emotions under its thick crust.

"I have already been granted a Constellation in the night sky," Orion explained. "I cannot earn a second. I can advise you. I can watch over you. But I am forbidden from participating."

Alex let out a low whistle.

The coals of excitement that had begun to burn in my heart hissed out as if they had suddenly been doused in water. I had assumed Orion would be my get-out-of-jail-free card. What kind of Impossible Task could stop the Hunter and his magical blade? An impossible one, I guess, but unless there was a horde of fallen angels guarding a treasure at the bottom of the sea, I had a hard time imagining it.

Without the Hunter's backup, my chances were a lot worse. I'm pretty sure Jason had some deities lurking in his corner when he finished his task. All I wanted to bring was one measly demigod.

But I shoved that worry into the back closet of my mind for later, with all the other secondary problems. I didn't even know how to get an Impossible Task to fail at, and I had a dragon issue to deal with.

The historic meeting between the Hunt and Dandelion Court took place on the roof of a mostly empty car park in downtown LA. The Hunt arrived first, five minutes early, just how Orion liked it. Alex eased the minivan into a spot and killed the engine. A minute later, a golden Suburban with tinted windows parked across from us, followed by Robin's golden Mustang, carrying my lawyer and Ash.

My anxiety rose as I tried to finalize a plan for bringing these two groups together after millennia of bloodshed. I probably should have this figured out by now, but I was stumped.

"It's not quite an Impossible Task," Alex said, giving me a clap on the shoulder. "But it's pretty close—maybe it's a semi-impossible task. Do they have those?"

"You still suck at pep talks," I replied, getting out of the car. Time to see if I could work a miracle.

The doors of the SUV opened, and Dawn emerged, flanked by a pair of serious-looking bodyguards, each with a sword strapped over the back of their suit. The Queen of All Fae wore an elegant white pantsuit, with a thin golden tiara sparkling in her blond hair. Her blue eyes flashed in an amused hello, as if she was surprised and delighted to find me waiting for her here.

Despite my glib comments to Dawn, I had a kernel of dread growing in the fertile soil of my imagination about this meeting.

I worked for two different groups, and they did not see eye-to-eye. I wanted my priority to be the Hunt. Orion was my friend and mentor. I owed him in ways that cannot be repaid in gold, only in loyalty. But without the Dandelion Court's blessing, my chance to complete an Impossible Task would be gone.

The two parties stopped a handful of feet apart, eyeing each other across the blacktop. As the host of this gathering, I stepped into the no-man's-land between them, my heart already beating faster than usual.

"Be welcome, my friends," I said, invoking the ritual of parley. "We come together as guests to speak for our mutual benefit. Swear to bear no weapons other than words, to spill not a single drop of one another's blood, and to defend this solemn meeting from all outsiders."

"I swear on the Dandelion Throne," Dawn replied instantly, binding not only herself but all the Fae with her.

Orion measured Dawn calmly for a long moment with his black-eyed gaze. A tiny bead of sweat gathered near my eyebrow. I did not need this from him right now. "I swear by my stars in the sky," he agreed at last.

With his oath, the palaver was officially agreed to. Some of the tension vanished, but there was still plenty to go around. The Hunt and the Fae had a long and bloody history. One nice meeting wouldn't make all of that go away. But it could be a good start.

Dawn marched to stand next to me. Orion strolled languidly to meet her, his every move casual and relaxed, as if he didn't consider himself to be in the slightest danger. Alex followed in his wake, doing his best to mimic that posture, like a younger brother copying his older sibling. I stayed right in the middle, a wishbone ready to be pulled in two different directions until it snapped.

"The Dragon Dons go too far," the Queen of All Fae said without preamble. "The serpents have forgotten their place, and it is time they are taught how to fear again." It seemed that Business Dawn was the mask she was wearing today. No drama, no games, just straight to the point. I thought that was the right choice for dealing with the Hunter. I noticed she was being way less pushy with him than she had been with me. As always, there were at least two Dawns, probably more.

"What do you propose?" Orion asked. I was shocked to hear an eager undertone to his voice.

"You have to know what they are planning," Dawn replied, arching an imperious eyebrow. "The complaint to the Congregation is only part of their game. Even if Polaris stripped you of your titles, you would still be Orion." Her voice had a fierce passion as she gazed unblinking into Orion's eyes.

"That's an unexpected position from a Faerie," Alex observed from Orion's right shoulder.

"My mother may have been your enemy at times," she said, smirking at the slightly surprised look on the Hunter's face, "but do not think she did not learn to respect who you are."

"Draco," Orion breathed in horror, his voice thick with barely restrained anger. "They seek to free Draco." Alex paled visibly.

"Of course they do! The snakes only crave power, and you took some from them. This Congregation is an opportunity for them to reclaim it." Dawn snapped her finger for emphasis.

"Sorry, who exactly is Draco?" I interjected, looking between the two leaders for some answers.

"The Dragon Constellation," Dawn replied, not looking away from Orion's eyes. "He's as close to a god as the dragons have, the master that all the Dons answer to. He was imprisoned and put to sleep by the Congregation for his crimes."

"What were his crimes?" I asked, although something told me I already knew the answer.

"The slaughter of the Hunt," Dawn confirmed, her voice unusually gentle, expression softer than I had ever seen it.

Orion's face by contrast could have been made of bedrock. The only clue to his anger was the fell light dancing in his dark eyes. A coldness seemed to permeate the area around us, and even Dawn crossed her arms against the icy fury radiating from him.

"His sentence still has more than three centuries to run," Orion growled, one of his hands crumpling into a fist. "Polaris would never allow—"

"Think for a second, Hunter!" Dawn interrupted—a pretty ballsy move for anyone, even a Queen. "There are plenty of Constellations among the Congregation who do not wish to see the return of the Hunt. Do know how many celebrated your downfall behind closed doors? Even now, they entertain motions to prevent your return. You truly think your enemies would not gladly set Draco free to stop you? You underestimate how much they fear you. You would not be the first of their strong arms they left out to dry when they weren't needed anymore."

Orion was silent, completely still, as if every molecule that made up his body suddenly hit absolute zero. It's an immortal trick; I don't know how it works. My favorite theory is that when the rest of their body turns off, they can devote extra power to their brain, but I have absolutely zero science to back this theory up. It's just a Matt Carver Hunch™.

"What do you propose?" he asked at last.

"An alliance against the Dragon Dons," Dawn replied without hesitation. "We remind the stars why the Dandelion Court and the Hunt are to be feared. Neither of us will make peace with them without the other, and we crush their heads until they crawl back into their caves."

Goose bumps crept up my arm as I heard Dawn's proposal. She had definitely brought the right version of herself to this meeting, for she was speaking the Hunter's language fluently. Orion has no patience for smoke and mirrors, but vengeance and action are part of his DNA.

"What are the terms?" Orion asked, wrinkling his forehead in thought.

"You support the restoration of the Dandelion Court to the Congregation, and you do not stop Matthew from speaking or acting on our behalf at the assembly," Dawn replied without hesitation. "In exchange, the Dandelion Court will stand with the Hunt when you face the dragons."

It took most of my self-control not to squeak in surprise. Not that I have a surplus of self-control lying around in the first place. I had been expecting something along the lines of the first part of her request. That was why I'd briefed Orion on the way here on how letting them back in also benefited me. All we needed was for him to give the okay, and we were one step closer.

But I couldn't begin to imagine what I would need to speak to the Congregation about. Why would they want to hear from me? I was a Squire of the Hunt and a Lord of Fire, but in the grand scheme of things, that's little better than being middle management at a Fortune 500 company. I was not interesting.

"I cannot agree to this," Orion said slowly, glancing at me and giving me an apologetic frown. "You ask too much." My heart fell as the Hunter turned and began to walk away from the meeting, taking my chances at getting my soul back with him.

Dawn stared daggers into the big Nephilim's back as he left, then turned her icy gaze on me. Her expression shouted, *Do something!* I glanced at Alex, who gave me a depressed shrug. Thanks, bud.

I raced to Orion's side and fell in step with him. "What are you doing?" I hissed, trying to keep my voice low enough that all the freaking supernatural creatures couldn't hear me with their super hearing.

"She's using the situation to her advantage," Orion said with an irritated shake of his head.

"You do remember the Fae getting back into the Congregation

is a good thing for me, right?" I reminded him. "Not that it's all about me, but I can't take on an Impossible Task without a membership card."

"She seeks to wipe the slate clean of so much blood," Orion grunted. "The scales between us are out of balance. You cannot simply make oceans vanish because they are inconvenient."

"Have you met Dawn? Because if anyone could, it might be her."

"Maybe," he replied with a shrug.

"I think the imbalanced scales died with her mother," I tried, desperate. "Can you not start a new account with the daughter?"

Orion didn't respond, only kept trudging toward the van. It occurred to me then that he wasn't walking as fast as he normally did. In fact, it almost felt like he was taking his sweet time...

"You sly bastard," I whispered, searching his black eyes for a clue. "You're waiting for something, aren't you?" A hint of a smile tugged at his mouth, but he kept walking.

Hope flaring in my chest, I looked over my shoulder at Dawn, who was still staring us, and made a furious gesture with my hands for her to say something. An irritated frown built on her face, and she crossed her arms again.

"I'll give you the lance," she called, her tone tinged with annoyance.

Glancing at Orion, I was just in time to see the wicked grin growing before it vanished behind the stone mask he called a face. Clearly Dawn wasn't the only one with tricks up their sleeve. Slowly, the Hunter turned and fixed her with his full stare.

"What lance?" he asked mildly.

"You know exactly which lance," Dawn muttered, rolling her eyes. "Ascalon. That which belonged to Saint George."

My eyes went wide with shock. The tale of Saint George the Dragon Slayer is one of the few I remember my grandmother telling me when I was a boy. Probably because it had dragons in it. I had no idea what the lance could do, but I had a couple of guesses I felt good about.

"You have it?" Orion demanded, striding back to the meeting center, so quickly I had to trot to keep up.

"Oh, spare me the dramatics," Dawn snapped, her good humor gone. "You knew I had it and that I was desperate enough to part with it. I'll give you the lance, but only if you promise to shove it down one of those smug dragons' throats."

"Agreed," the Hunter said with a primal grin. He stepped up to Dawn and held out his hand to shake. His smile's twin slithered across her face as she reached out and clasped his hand. A faint wind of pride stirred in my chest as I watched them shake hands. Behind them, Ash beamed at me, and I smiled back, that weird tingly feeling running down my spine once again.

But it wasn't done yet. There was still one more puzzle piece that I had to pull into place. My promise to my father burned in my heart hotter than dragonfire. "Dawn?" I called, seeking her attention as I took two steps away from the rest of the group. I took a deep breath to try to calm my nerves before I lied to an Immortal's face.

The Queen of All Fae walked toward me, a rare, satisfied expression on her face as she stopped in front of me. "Sometimes Mother still absolutely surprises me with her wisdom," she murmured, gazing at me as if I were her favorite pet.

"If we're going to face down dragons, we're going to need help," I said, ignoring her underhanded praise. "The dragons in the restaurant were pretty fireproof. It might be wise to bring more firepower than just Lords of Fire."

Her blue eyes narrowed in suspicion. "Surely you are not about to say what I think you are about to say."

"Dawn, I hit that dragoon with every ounce of fire I could summon with Willow. It didn't even blink. Ash and I can help control their flames, but I don't know if we can quench them."

Her gaze stabbed into me like a shovel trying to dig out my secrets.

I tried to look serious rather than guilty. "Are you suggesting I include Mav as part of my bodyguard?"

"I am bringing you my concerns about how effective fire is against dragons," I replied, matching her stare. "Any conclusions you wish to make, I leave to you."

Dawn was silent for a moment, pondering my words. "You expect me to believe that you would tolerate her presence? I've kept her locked away for a reason, Matthew. I know what she did. I know what your father would like to do to her."

I closed my eyes as if the memory was too painful, but in reality, I was hiding the fear that she had guessed Damien's plan. When had I become such a good liar? "Let me ask you something. If we fail to protect you and you die—who becomes Queen next?"

Dawn turned to give Ash a measuring gaze before turning back to me. "That's difficult to predict," she admitted after a moment, "but there's a chance it goes *very* poorly for you."

"My math comes out the same," I agreed grimly. "Which means it's in my best interest for you to remain Queen." Despite my deception, I actually believed that. Dawn was complicated and not afraid to threaten me to get what she wanted. But in a lot of ways, she was her mother's daughter. She would honor the deal between us because it helped strengthen the Fae as a whole. If she died and Mav became the Queen, things could only get worse for me.

"I will consider it," Dawn said with a stiff nod. Without another word she turned and strode back to her SUV. Feeling like the parlay had gone as well as it could have, I watched her go.

If that was a semi-impossible task, how bad could an Impossible one be?

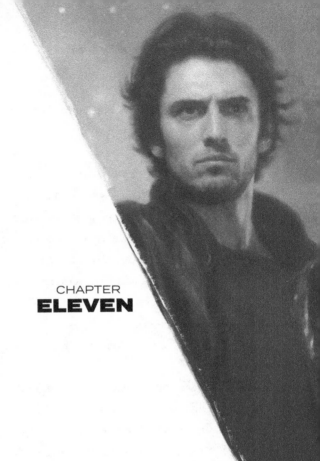

I'D NEVER BEEN to a convention before, so I mistakenly assumed that they started on the official starting date. It turned out those are more guidelines than hard rules. If you're important enough, you might get invited to events before the convention even starts.

Alex and I were in Orion's dojo cleaning and prepping our gear for the weekend to come when the boss walked in carrying a small piece of card stock and a frown. "Do you both own suits?" he grumbled, looking up.

"Why?" Alex asked, suspicion thick in his voice.

"We've been invited to a party tonight," Orion replied, holding up the card for us to see.

It was solid black, worked with silver embossing that read:

MONSTERS & MEN MIXER:
YOU ARE CORDIALLY INVITED TO A NIGHT OF
SOCIALIZATION AND FRATERNIZATION BETWEEN THE
VIP MEMBERS OF THE CONGREGATION & FRIENDS.
JOIN US FOR DRINKS AND HORS D'OEUVRES.
INVITATION ONLY.
BLACK-TIE ATTIRE ENCOURAGED.
SPONSORED BY: THE LAZARUS GROUP

"You have to be kidding me," I groaned after I read it. "I gotta wear a tie?"

"That's your takeaway?" Alex asked, arching a blond eyebrow at me. "Did you see who is sponsoring it?"

"One piece of terrible news at a time, please." I really hate ties. While technically Lazarus, the leader of the group with the same name, had no beef with us, he also was one of the reasons the Dragon Dons were currently crashing my dates. Just because I accidentally burned down *one* building.

"Dawn has informed me the Dandelion Court will be attending, so we will join them," Orion announced, ignoring the groans of the peanut gallery. "Go get your suits."

I've said the traffic in LA isn't that bad when you move against the grain, but this surprise party made it impossible for us to avoid the slog that is rush hour. The party was in Downtown, near the convention center. We were in Orion's Van Nuys dojo when we found out about it, and our suits were in our Northridge home.

I could spout a bunch of famous highway numbers that we had to battle through in order to make the journey happen, like the 5 and the dreaded 405, but that doesn't really mean much. All I know is that it was about 4 p.m. when Orion dispatched us to get ready and well after 5 p.m. by the time we got to our house. After we changed and met back up with Orion, we barely managed to arrive at the venue by eight thirty. A whole day ruined, just to go get a pair of suits. Society was a mistake.

Our rideshare, a black SUV, dropped us off right at the front. Appearance matters at these sorts of things, so showing up in Alex's beat-up white minivan wasn't an option. The driver had clearly been picking up weirdos in LA for too long. He didn't even blink at Orion carrying a sheathed sword in his hand as we slid into the vehicle.

The Nephilim of the Hunt looked sharp as a knife. Orion wore a black suit perfectly tailored to his Olympic frame, complete with a skinny black tie and cuff links with rubies that matched his sword's hilt. Alex's was slate gray and equally as custom. He wore a light-pink tie that he called puce.

I wore the black suit I had bought at a big-box store for my family's funeral. Yeah, not as cool.

The Lazarus Group had taken over the Swallow, a bar perched on the rooftop of one of the historic tall buildings that fill the Los Angeles skyline. Downtown LA is a study in extremes. It has some of the city's nicest restaurants, most beautiful homes, and harshest poverty. The towers of the rich and famous reach as high as they can so they don't have to see the war zone right outside their door. Swallow continued that tradition. It took up the entire top floor of the fifteen-story building with a breezy, open-air venue.

A check-in desk waited in the bronze-filled lobby, staffed by two models in black cocktail dresses. Three beefy linebackers in suits lurked in the back, their arms crossed. I recognized Bruno, who usually worked the check-in desk at the facility where they kept my sister. I gave him a little wave, but the big guard didn't react. And I thought we were becoming friends.

We stood behind the couple checking in, whose ears were suspiciously pointed, when the Dandelion Court burst onto the scene like a hurricane. Three golden SUVs pulled up, their doors swinging open. Dawn stepped out of the middle one, looking stunning in a long white dress with a bejeweled crown nestled in her blond curls. I had just enough time to notice that her eyes were the solid gold of an elder Fae before my attention was ripped away.

Ash emerged from the rear SUV in a black cocktail dress that sharply contrasted with her red hair. Don't get me wrong, my betrothed *always* looks good, but there's a difference when someone is good looking and trying to look good.

She was stunning.

Her eyes found mine, and she must have seen some of my shock, because her mouth opened in a small laugh that I was too far away to hear. Her eyes were still green, and they sparkled at me in genuine amusement.

"Close your mouth before something flies into it," Orion muttered darkly behind me. I snapped my teeth shut with a click, shaking my head slightly to free it from the spell that must have been cast on it. Even if Ash and I were only technically dating, she was so out my league. I felt like the nerd who ended up with the cheer captain in one of those high school rom-coms.

"Excellent! You waited for us," Dawn called, leading her retinue of bodyguards and court members up to us. Without hesitation, she continued to the desk, going around the couple that was still trying to find their name on the list.

"Dandelion Court and the Hunt," she informed one of the girls working the desk without giving her a moment to object. I guess when you're a Queen, you're not so good at waiting your turn. Otherwise, how would you ever get to be Queen?

A warm hand slid onto my biceps as someone linked arms with me, and I turned to find Ash standing next to me. "You clean up pretty good for a mortal," she said with a wink. "Why is this the first time I'm seeing you in a suit? You couldn't break it out for our fancy dinner?"

"I probably should have," I admitted, feeling stupid. "I don't like wearing it. It reminds me of dark days. I guess I didn't want any of that bleeding over onto our night."

Her hand squeezed my arm, a soft look on her face. "I'm so sorry, I didn't think of that," she whispered.

"It's fine." I patted her hand. "Maybe it's time to make some better memories in a suit."

"That sounds like a good plan." Ash's smile was back, and I felt my own leap to join it.

"Okay, you two," grumbled Alex, "do your weird dating-not-dating thing on your own time. On company time we do our best to not die horribly." He mimed checking an imaginary watch on his wrist. "And it is currently… company time."

Dawn beckoned to us with one imperious finger, and one by one we stepped up to the check-in desk. The hostess slipped green paper bracelets saying GUEST around our wrists, secured with self-adhesive ends. I suspected the bracelets had more meaning in the supernatural world than the mortal one.

"ID, please," the hostess said with a smile, picking up a different black band. This one had the number 21 plastered over it again and again. Amused, I pulled out my license and waited for her to check it. I guess even supernatural parties have to card you if you look underage in LA.

We managed to pile the entire party into the fancy elevator. There was only one button, and it took us to the roof. As we ascended, Dawn gave Orion an appraising glance out of the corner of her eye. The Hunter had slid his sword back over his shoulder now that we were out of the car and looked like a cross between a spy and a gladiator, only cooler.

His black eyes stared back into her gold ones, face unreadable.

Dawn's smile only grew wider. The longer she stared into his abyss, the more she seemed thrilled by what she saw.

"We're going to be so dangerous," she murmured in amused tones as the elevator doors opened onto the rooftop bar, ushering us into a new world.

Ash and I followed Dawn and Orion out into the night, letting the bosses go first. I cannot overemphasize this point: The supernatural world is full of predators. It's very primal, eat or be eaten. If you want to be feared, you must be terrifying, and to be terrifying, you have to be strong. You can show no weakness.

If Dawn waited until an army of bodyguards and attendants went before her, it would imply she was afraid, that she needed others to see if it was safe for her to enter. That's not what apex predators do. Anywhere they go is safe because they are the danger.

The rooftop was full but not crowded. As advertised, I saw monsters, men, and everything in between scattered all around. In the center of everything stood an old man with a cane.

Lazarus looked far more like some English literature professor than the head of a billion-dollar empire. He wore a brown tweed jacket with a yellow pocket square. In the corner of his mouth hung a horn pipe, which matched his horn-rimmed glasses. Seeing Dawn and Orion, he made a beeline for them, offsetting his limp with a short, golden-topped cane.

"Your Majesty," he said warmly, approaching Dawn and giving her one of those European greetings, kissing the air near both of her cheeks. "It is an honor to officially meet you for the first time."

"And I am delighted to be welcomed," Dawn replied warmly. "It has been far too long since we Fae made our presence felt at one of these events."

"I couldn't agree more," Lazarus chuckled. "Although this is the first Congregation in my lifetime, I see tonight as almost a reunion of sorts. A chance for old friends and acquaintances to see one another before the madness begins."

"Speaking of acquaintances." Dawn pivoted, gesturing at the human mountain of muscle and violence standing next to her. "Have you met my companion Orion, of the Constellation fame?"

I blinked in surprise at "companion." I guess we had arrived together and had negotiated an alliance. But I had thought that was more a business-partner thing. How in the world had that turned into an—I felt Ash's hand shift where it was still threaded through my arm—oh. I knew firsthand supernatural creatures took the *relationship* part of the term *business relationship* seriously. I just hadn't considered what that might mean for Orion.

From the look on Orion's face, I thought he might not have realized it either. The Hunter froze in the immortal way, his very atoms seeming to pause for a moment. It seemed Dawn was taking some liberties with the plan.

Shocker.

Lazarus's eyes narrowed as he took in Orion, with Alex and me standing behind him. He turned back to Dawn and arched a fuzzy white eyebrow that could have doubled as a caterpillar. "Your companion? He and I have met once or twice."

"Lovely," Dawn said, walking past Lazarus into the party, leaving him with a dazzling smile. Like a dutiful herd, we began to plod along in her wake. I had to prod Orion once on the back of his shoulder to get him moving.

As I passed the philanthropist billionaire, he turned his watery blue eyes on me and reached out a hand to grab my free arm. "We should chat soon, Mr. Carver," he said in a somber tone. "I fear you have some bills that are coming due."

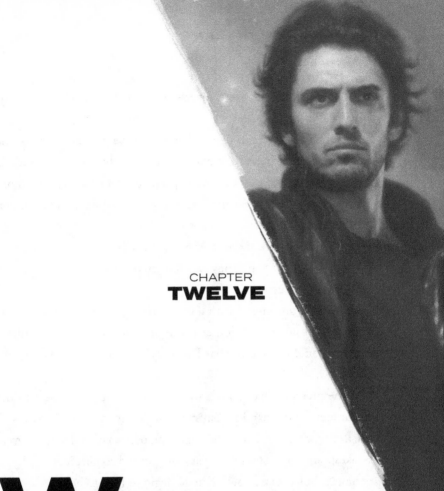

CHAPTER
TWELVE

WHAT WAS HE talking about?" Ash whispered as we left Lazarus to rejoin the Fae herd. I shrugged mutely, terrified to think too much about his cryptic message. Mom always said there was no point crying about the milk you hadn't spilled yet, so I squared my shoulders and shoved those concerns into the back broom closet of my mind, right next to the rest of my worries. The door could barely close, and it bulged a bit in the middle, but I managed.

Fortunately for that overworked door, there were plenty of worries at this party to keep me from going back in there and opening it again. The first person I saw among the suited-and-tied mortals, Fae, Nephilim, and more, was a familiar face. She was short and pale, with porcelain features and raven-dark hair that matched the inky blackness of her eyes.

Her name was Samael—not Sam—and she was the Devil's Dark Whisper. She has been given many names over the centuries: Seducer, Poisoned One, and other similarly positive monikers. Samael's most recent crime was convincing Tania, the Lady of Spring, to kill her mother and giving her the means to do it.

The demon's black eyes met mine easily, her expression blank as a slate. I felt Ash's grip on my arm tighten like vise clamps as she saw who I was staring at.

"Easy," I murmured with a grunt, trying to keep my voice low enough that none of the other partygoers with freaky supernatural hearing could make out what I was saying. "I only have two arms, you know."

The pressure abated instantly, but I could still feel the tension thrumming in her hand as Ash stared at the creature that had caused the death of her mother at the command of her father. I suspect even Shakespeare would struggle to put that pain and conflict into words—I certainly didn't even know where to begin or how to help.

I had half a mind to lead Ash over to the Seducer and see if we could rattle her cages a little—but that half-baked plan was interrupted when the next guests arrived behind us. A hush swept through the room as the elevator dinged and four of those walking nightmares stepped out into the bar.

The dragons were here.

The man in the lead had bright-red hair and was the most normal looking of his kin. He wore an expensive suit and obnoxious little round sunglasses that covered his eyes. He looked almost human except for the clusters of red scales along his jaw and on the backs of his hands. Several of his fingers ended in wicked claws instead of fingernails.

His gaze swept across the room and paused on me, a faint sneer crossing his face, revealing sharp teeth no dentist would ever feel comfortable cleaning. The three dragoons in his wake looked exactly like the ones that had attacked us at Balsamic—suspiciously so, I thought, complete with horrific alligator snouts grafted onto their faces.

Lazarus went to greet the lounge of dragons (which is apparently the correct term for a herd of lizards), and the conversation slowly resumed its previous cadence, like an old lawn mower's engine stuttering to life.

I glanced back to where Samael had been, but the Poisoned One had disappeared. Growling in irritation, I looked around and spotted a buffet line, which I guess was the next best thing.

"Snack?" I offered to Ash, gesturing toward the row of silver shells with my head.

"I could use a drink, but we can get you a bite on the way," she replied, pointing at the open bar beyond the food.

"Who says arranged relationships aren't fun?" I asked, setting us off in that direction.

"Did someone say that?" she inquired sweetly. I glanced at her to see her green eyes sparkling with a mischievous fire.

"No, no, no," I backpedaled, panicking a little. "I think I read it somewhere."

"I'm sure." She gave my arm a condescending pat as she released it so I could help myself to a buffet plate.

"Excuse me," I said, stepping past a tall gaunt man who was staring at the food line with a look of profound longing. He turned to face me, a deep contempt lurking in his flat brown eyes. His long, sour features made me think of the word *sallow*.

"What?" he demanded, as if I had interrupted him from something of vital importance.

"Sorry, I was just trying to get to the plates." I pointed at the stack of dishes he had been blocking.

"Be my guest," he said bitterly, waving a dismissive hand at the plates and stepping aside. He wore a giant gold ring on his right hand, with a large, yellow stone that reflected the lamps around us with a murky light.

"Thanks!" I said, eagerly slipping through the gap and working my way down the buffet line. This was my first time going to one of these fancy VIP events, and I fully intended to cash in on the free bougie food.

By the time I joined Ash in the short line at the bar, my plate was loaded down: prime rib sliced right off the bone, some sort of baked chicken, and two rolls. I had even gotten a scoop of Caesar salad, because a fresh Caesar is out of this world, and I won't be told otherwise.

"Did you leave enough for the rest of the guests?" Ash asked, eyeing my meal with a raised brow.

"I think they should be fine, unless there's some sort of buffet famine going on that I don't know about," I replied, chomping down on one of those fresh rolls. I'll say this for him, Lazarus knows how to cater a party. The rolls were heavenly; they practically fell apart in my mouth. I could get used to going to conventions if there were more rolls like this.

I managed to keep a straight face as Alex joined us in line, Nika hovering over his right shoulder. She wore a little black cocktail dress that was clearly from some designer, I just had no way of knowing which. I'm pretty sure it's bad form to ask to check the tag. She was rocking a tight updo, held by a net made of sparkly stones, like her own personal Constellation twinkling in her hair. I'm sure that wasn't deliberate at all.

"So those are dragons, huh?" Alex said, skipping over any awkward attempt to integrate his companion with us.

"In the flesh," I said, eyeing them over the rim of the drink Ash handed me. It smelled of bourbon and class, two things I'm not good at. "I'm pretty sure the green ones in the back tried to dine with us at Balsamic."

"I don't believe it," Nika murmured.

"You better believe it. Here there be dragons," I replied.

"Not the *reptiles*," she said with a note of disgust. "That's Carina of Argos." She gestured at a broad-shouldered Nephilim woman dressed in black leather and spikes speaking with another of her kind, brow furrowed in concentration. I didn't recognize her, but I certainly remembered the beautiful and dangerous Cassiopeia she conversed with. I hadn't seen Cassie since she'd fought against Lilith to protect me. I should probably thank her for that, if I got the chance. My mother would want me to.

"I don't think I'm familiar with any of her movies," I mused, rubbing my jaw. You know you've lived in LA too long when that's your polite way of saying you don't recognize someone.

"No, you mortal fool, that is the Constellation Carina, who was once known as Atalanta."

"That's really not helping me either. I went to public school."

"She was one of the Argonauts; she helped Jason complete his Impossible Task and was elevated into the Constellation Argos before being renamed to Carina."

Alex and I traded knowing glances. Now, that meant something to me—it wouldn't have a week ago, but thanks to Robin's education, I had taken a keen interest in the story of Jason and his Argonauts. I needed to acquire one of these Impossible Tasks for myself. What were the odds that Carina had one on her? Maybe in her pockets or something? I didn't know if they were a verbal thing or if they came on a scroll.

"You know, it's rude to stare," Dawn cut in, inserting herself boldly into our little huddle, Orion in her wake. I glanced around our crowded little pack, feeling almost claustrophobic. I was used to there being only three of us, not six. What was happening? Orion nodded a greeting to his student but didn't comment on her presence.

"You're new," the Queen of All Fae said, eyeing Nika with distaste. "Our runt is aiming above himself I see."

"He's got a pretty good aim," Nika replied with a tight smile, looping her arm through Alex's. "I'm Nika."

"She's Nika," Dawn said to Ash as if that explained everything. "She's Nika, and she's somewhere she shouldn't be." Nika's face tightened in the corners, but she didn't let go of Alex's arm. "Did I whisper too quietly for your pointy little ears, *Nephilim*," Dawn hissed after she did not move. "You are not Hunt. You are not Fae. Get. Out."

Nika cast one pleading glance at her teacher, but Orion's face was as implacable as a mountain. Seeing no help there, she turned to Alex, who could only give her an embarrassed shrug. Stiffly, Nika drew her arm out of his and raised her glass to Dawn.

"To your health," she murmured and then poured the drink into a potted plant to her right. A couple of Dawn's attaché Fae gasped in horror from somewhere behind us. Dawn gave her a wry smile and the faintest of salutes with her own glass as Nika left.

"Well, I like her," she said, looking at Alex. "But talk to pretty things on your own time, okay?" Alex was wise enough not to rise to Dawn's bait. He merely gave her a slight shrug, his cocky smile matching the Queen's.

"You doing okay?" I asked Orion, who seemed even stiffer than usual. The Hunter is not someone I would generally consider laid-back, but tonight he was practically vibrating with restrained violence. He rested his black eyes on the dragons in the center of the venue, unable to look away even as he answered me.

"I'm fine."

Real convincing stuff there.

As if they could feel the pressure of Orion's malevolent gaze, the leader of the dragons turned from his conversation with Lazarus to gaze at our group with a flat-eyed, reptilian stare. After a few more words, he stepped away from the old literature professor and made his way directly to us. The leader's face twisted into something resembling a smile as his dragoons followed behind him like a pack of scaly hounds.

"The Hunter and the Queen of All Fae in the same corner!" he declared cheerfully. "I have truly lived long enough to see everything." He had a strong Irish accent to match his bright-red hair, which was... not what I was expecting? When I think dragon, the first thing that comes to mind is not Irish.

"Don Doyle," Dawn replied coolly, transformed in the blink of an eye from playful cheerleader into a cold, marble shadow of her mother.

"Crom." Orion's voice was as hard as diamonds.

A twitch of irritation rippled across the Don's face, and I fancied I could hear the creak of his sharp teeth as he clenched his jaw. "Haven't you heard, Hunter? They call me Doyle now."

"They can call you whatever they please," Orion replied, unfazed.

Dragon and dragon slayer stared at each other for a moment that stretched longer than it should have, two gunslingers in the middle of a dusty western street, hands hovering over their shooting irons. I shifted my feet under me, tensing to spring the moment either of them drew.

But the Irish dragon snorted dismissively after a few more heartbeats and turned to Dawn. "Still the same old Hunter, I see. Wouldn't have it any other way." A forked tongue flicked out of his too-human mouth, tasting the air before it slipped back inside like a groundhog hiding from winter.

"I understand some of my idiot wing has offended you," he said to Dawn, clasping his hands in front of him. "I wish to offer an apology and make amends."

Her gold eyes sharpened, a dark delight shining in them. "Interesting. They did offend me. They shot me. I found that to be offensive."

"You have my most sincere apologies on behalf of the Dragon Dons. I feel right terrible about it myself," Doyle told her, bowing gently from the waist up. "Please allow us to make this right."

"What do you have in mind?" she asked, a note of genuine interest in her tone. Concern began to grow in my belly. Dawn had wanted an alliance with us against the dragons, but she was ever the opportunist. If Don Doyle's offer was good enough, could we trust her?

"These worms are the ones responsible for such a grave offense." Doyle gestured at the three dragons escorting him. "They are yours, the lot of them. Do with them as you will." The Queen of All Fae's right eyebrow grew an evil-looking arch. "Furthermore, the Dons are prepared to give the Dandelion Court an offering of ten thousand souls as an *éraic* on account of all your pain and suffering."

Judging from the wide eyes on all the faces in our group, everyone felt like they had just been hit by a train, not just me. *Ten thousand souls?* As in the souls of ten thousand mortals casually exchanged like a few bars of gold? How could that be possible?

I remembered the Nothing, the endless dark that was devouring the Faerie Lands like a cancer. I wondered how long ten thousand souls could keep it at bay. How much lost land such a sum could reclaim from the abyss. It was a terrifying gift, but a wise one. Judging from the dumbfounded look on Dawn's face, I knew it had hit the mark.

But she had sworn an oath, and Fae can't lie, even if they might want to.

"Where did you get ten thousand souls?" Orion demanded, taking a half step forward. Dawn raised her right hand and placed it on his chest without even looking at him, the gesture stopping him in his tracks. Orion stared down at her hand as if it were a spear that had suddenly sprouted from his heart.

"Oh, we have plenty of vendors and suppliers." Doyle's hungry, inhuman smile curled up at the corners.

"Stolen souls—" Alex choked next to me. "Are you insane?"

"Accidents happen, crates fall off of wagons. Accountants everywhere are happy to ignore the occasional rounding error. Chasing them all down would be murder if you take my meaning." As a rounding error of Hell myself, I was only too willing to believe that. My mind was reeling at the thought of souls being *stolen* and sold on the black market. No, that term was nowhere near shady enough for a place that would sell mortal souls.

The Fell Market. That's the one.

"How about it, Your Majesty? Let's let bygones be bygones, eh?"

"And what of the Hunt?" Dawn asked, clasping her arms behind her. "Surely I was not the only insult your wing handed out."

"Ah well, that's another matter entirely, I'm afraid. It seems some fool thought it a good idea to burn down one of our buildings." The Dragon Don's sunglasses turned to fix me with a direct stare. My what big teeth he had. I had never understood Red Riding Hood more than in that moment.

Despite the fear squirming in my guts, I gave him a small smile and a wave. "So, any offense that might have been given there was quite intended, I assure you."

"I see," Dawn said in her marble tones. I'm sure she was wondering if there was a way to have her souls and eat them too. She glanced over her shoulder at Orion, her golden eyes meeting his black ones with an amused question lurking in them.

The Hunter gave an almost imperceptible shake of his head. The exact oath Dawn had made with Orion said that neither of them could make peace with the dragons without permission from the other. I wonder if she regretted that wording now.

"Sorry, Crommy," she said, her real personality shining through the shadow of her mother like a beacon. "No can do." There was a dangerous glint in her eye that made me think I had been wrong to doubt her. The mark she was looking to leave was much bigger than accepting a bribe and a pat on the head. Her mother had presided over the setting of the Fae sun, but Dawn was striving to see the sun claw its way above the horizon the next day.

"So be it," Doyle sneered, his Irish accent growing thicker with anger. He raised his hand and pointed an accusing finger at Dawn. I blinked as the human hand shifted, flowing like sand to become a scaled monstrosity with razor-sharp talons. "When the ash settles, remember we offered you mercy, but you were too busy acting the fool. You seem to have forgotten how much we dragons love gold." With one last glare, the Dragon Don turned away and led his wing to the far side of the venue, where they clustered together like a middle school gossip ring.

"Circle the wagons, Hunter," Dawn said, staring after the retreating dragons with a serious look on her face. "It begins in earnest now."

"I'll need that lance," Orion agreed.

AFTER OUR HUDDLE, Dawn, Ash, and Orion wandered off to schmooze more Constellations while Alex went looking for his banished date, leaving me to my own devices. It must be a testament to how stressed everyone was that none of them noticed I was unattended.

Now that I had a drink in hand and had been fed, there was nothing to distract me from looking for Samael. I'd never had the chance to confront her after I found out who she really was, and this seemed like the perfect moment to me. I was a guest, so I was pretty sure she wasn't allowed to murder me at the party, so that was a plus.

I worked the outer edges of the rooftop, scanning the milling supernatural beings for the missing demon. I didn't recognize many of the hundred or so partygoers. Some species were easy to identify—Nephilim and Fae have pretty distinct markings—but there were other lineages there I could only guess at. It made me realize how little I still understood the world I was in the middle of.

I managed to keep my brain focused on the task at hand, ignoring the mysteries of the gathering around me. But no matter how hard I looked, Samael was nowhere to be found. I began to wonder if she had fled the party after seeing us. Maybe the thought of having to face Dawn and Ash looking for revenge was enough to send her scampering back into the shadows.

Or maybe it wasn't.

Just as I was about to give up, I caught a flash of pale skin and black hair disappearing around a corner across the room. *Aha*, I chuckled to myself, cutting across the party like a hound with a scent in his nose. My prey was on the run; what self-respecting member of the Hunt wouldn't give chase?

As I approached the corner she had vanished behind, I realized it was a stairway to a lower balcony that wrapped around the building, below the level of the rooftop. I paused for a moment listening, but I couldn't hear anything over the buzz of so many conversations behind me. Unable to restrain my curiosity, I risked a peek around the corner, but it was empty.

With a shrug, I placed my drink on a table and made my way down the first flight, doing my best not to let my dress shoes click with each stride. The stairs wrapped around another corner, and I peeked again, but there was no one there. Starting to feel a little stupid, I picked up my pace, hoping not to lose the demon.

The stairs turned a final time, and when I leaned around the corner, I found what I was looking for. A balcony ran the length of the building, full of plants like an urban garden terrace. This part of the venue must not have been rented for the party, because the lights were off, but I could make out two figures standing close together, illuminated by the light pollution from the building around us.

"How do I know it will work?" a familiar Irish voice hissed.

Head halfway around the corner, I froze, not even daring to breathe. Eavesdropping on a shady conversation between a demon and a Dragon Don was an even better treat than getting to be sassy to one of Lucifer's pets.

"My master has given you his word," Samael responded calmly, her tone pointedly neutral. "Do you doubt him?"

"Relax, lass, I'm not calling *him* a liar," Doyle replied placatingly. "But from a practical perspective we don't even know if it works—"

"You have been given a promise," the demoness interrupted, a hint of dark anger entering her tone. "It is enough for you to know that it will do as *he* promised."

"But we haven't been able to test it, which makes me a mite worried."

"It has been tested."

A stony silence stretched between demon and dragon. The hairs on the back of my arms stood up as I felt the two ancient beings shift in their stances aggressively. Being here suddenly felt stupid, like hiding next to a power station during a lightning storm.

"What did you test this on—a dragon?" Doyle's voice was hard and full of fury.

"It works, Doyle," Samael replied in equally hard tones.

"Who?" the Don demanded.

"No one you missed, apparently."

The demon's reply seemed to take a little of the wind out of the dragon's sails. The silence held, but the tension retreated. Heart racing, I leaned on the corner, doing my best to not draw their attention. Whatever they were discussing seemed like something I absolutely should not know, which made me want to know all about it—especially if Samael's boss was involved. That guy had it out for me.

"Doyle, it *works*," Samael pressed.

The Dragon Don was silent for a long moment, composing himself. "How many can you give me?"

"You are only being trusted with one, for now."

"One? What am I supposed to do with only one?"

"You know what you're supposed to do." Samael's voice was cruel. "And you know the price of failure."

"I know," the dragon said eventually, puffing out a small sigh. "I know," he repeated as if trying to convince himself. "Is it permanent?"

"One way or another," Samael replied darkly.

The Don was silent for a moment, digesting that. "All great works require sacrifice," he sighed heavily after a moment.

"But also bring glory," the Seducer said.

"That they do," Doyle agreed, his earlier anger already faded and forgotten. "I meant no disrespect or insult to your master."

"Of course not."

"It's just that this didn't go so well for us the last time, lass."

"And this time will be different," the demoness assured him in clipped tones. "You have what you were promised. Now use it to kill *him* this time."

"I'll see it done," the Irish dragon promised. "Where is it?"

"It arrives in two days. One of my master's associates will contact you to arrange an exchange."

I missed Don Doyle's reply, distracted by the sound of feet crunching down the stairs behind me. Fear bloomed in my stomach like a mushroom cloud. There was nowhere for me to go; I had trapped myself rather efficiently on this straight path. For a wild moment, I debated throwing myself over the railing and dangling off the side of the building before I remembered this wasn't a corny action movie.

Maybe whoever was coming down the stairs was a waiter who

wouldn't know I was eavesdropping on a dragon and a demon. Slowly, I pulled my head back around the corner and started trotting up the stairs.

Just act casual, I told myself. All I needed to do was look like I belonged, and no one would question me. It really wasn't hard, all I had to do was—my train of thought derailed as I turned the corner of the stairs and practically bounced off the chest of a freaking dragoon.

You gotta be kidding me.

"Oh, excuse me," I said, giving him a friendly smile and dodging to the side. "I didn't see you there." With a polite nod, I resumed walking up the stairs as if I was a normal guy out for a normal walk. I resisted the urge to whistle.

I didn't even see the dragoon move. One second, I was fine, the next I was smashed up against the wall and pinned like I was in middle school all over again. My shout of protest was muffled when a leathery claw clamped over my mouth.

The dragoon let out a long hiss as it leaned into my face, a forked tongue slipping out of its mouth. "What are you doing here, Huntling?" it snarled.

I heard the Don and the demon coming up the stairs behind us. The dragoon turned to Doyle. "I found thissss one lurking on the stairsssss."

"The Hunter's squire snooping around all alone where he shouldn't be? Isn't that fascinating?" Doyle drawled. "The idiot should know better than to wander out into the dark."

I tried to lie and say that I had only been looking for the little mortal boys' room, but the dragoon's hand still covered my face. None of my protests were understandable, and it tasted like I was licking the heel of someone's expensive boot.

"Fair is fair," Doyle said after a moment's thought. "Kill him and let's be done with it."

The claw gripping my head tightened with incredible force. The only reason no one heard my terrified squeak was because of the lizard leather filling my mouth. The pressure mounted, and I could imagine my skull exploding like a watermelon. At least my horrific end would leave the villains with a large dry-cleaning bill.

"Stop," Samael commanded.

The pressure paused, but did not lessen, as the dragon looked to its boss for instruction.

"What do you mean? He heard too much; we should kill him."

"My master has plans for Matthew Carver," the Seducer said. "His death will come at the appointed hour, which is fast approaching."

The thought of the Devil having my death planned out made me wish that the dragon would keep crushing, just to spite him. But then I remembered I would still be dead, and my soul was forfeit, so I decided living was better than petty revenge.

Doyle was quiet for a moment as he digested Samael's information. At last, he grunted, and his dragoon released its crushing grip on my head. "What about what he heard?" the Don demanded. "Are you just going to let him go?"

"Let him tell whoever he wants," Samael replied, her black eyes reflecting the streetlights below us. "They will all know soon enough." The cold hand of doom settled over my heart as she spoke. If she was that confident, part of me believed it was too late to stop her. I had seen her handiwork up close. If she thought I couldn't do anything about it, she was probably right.

"Now go back to the party, mingle, and make the rest of the guests uncomfortable," Samael instructed Doyle and his dragoon.

"What about you?"

"I'll be along presently." Samael's lips quirked up in a vicious little smile. "But my master has given me some words for Matthew Carver." Somehow that was more terrifying than having my head crushed. Was it too late to go back to that option instead? The two dragons let out grim chuckles but did not move.

"Are you sure it's safe to be alone with him?" Doyle asked in a more serious tone. "He did kill Lilith." Now it was my turn to flash a threatening grin. The dragon was right, the little mortal had a few teeth.

"That's sweet of you." Samael clicked her tongue in an amused way, pursing her lips into a pout. "Lilith did try her best, but she wasn't really *family* if you know what I mean. I think I'll take my chances." Her black eyes glittered in the darkness. I did my best not to gulp in terror. What if the appointed time for my death was the next thirty seconds?

That would suck.

"Fine," Doyle grunted after a moment. "Keep your secrets, demon, but if the mortal sticks you like a pig don't come crying to me."

"I would never," Samael replied, amused.

"Pleasure doing business," he grunted. He jerked his head at his dragoon and the two of them slithered up the stairs, leaving me alone with one of the most terrifying individuals I have ever met.

An awful silence fell as the Seducer stared at me. The first time I encountered her, she had been wearing a bathing suit and lounging by a pool with a bunch of Fae royals, going by the name Sam. That was about as nonthreatening as a demon could possibly get. Tonight she wasn't playing her cards as close to her chest, and it reflected in every aspect of her being, from her posture to the aura of power that seemed to radiate from her just as it did from Zagan, the only other fallen angel I knew.

"Lovely to see you," I said after a moment. The silence was starting to feel like it had teeth and was eating away at my sanity.

"Aren't you going to ask me?" she prompted, arching one dark eyebrow.

"Ask you what?"

"When the appointed hour is?"

"Would you tell me if I did?"

"You never know, I might." Another wicked smirk crossed her lips. I don't know if it's possible for demons to smile any other way. I think it comes with the territory.

I stared at her, mind racing. This was a test of some sort—I was sure of it. Demons are a tricksy lot, and Samael by all accounts was one of the tricksiest. If she was asking me, there was something else she wanted.

Maybe she just wanted to get under my skin. The Seducer was one of the scariest beings I have ever met, but she wasn't *the* scariest—a year and a half in the Hunt had put a little bit of steel in my spine. I wasn't so easily frightened anymore. The more I thought about it, the more indignant I became. The Devil and his ilk had an appointed hour for my death?

I think not.

I had not been consulted, I had not agreed to a time or date. Something told me we would also have different ideas on the method of my passing. If it wasn't in my sleep with a belly full of cookies, I wasn't really interested.

"Nah," I said, turning away from Samael and starting my way up the stairs. "I'm good."

I left the demon alone in the dark.

CON DAY DAWNED like most Los Angeles mornings, with bright-blue skies, puffy white clouds, and a hellish traffic jam en route to Downtown. Any sane resident would do anything possible to avoid driving into the city during work commute hours, but we were on our way to attend the opening ceremony of something called the Constellation Convention. Sanity had gotten off this road a few exits ago.

Before we left the party, I'd briefed my friends and allies on what I had overheard between Samael and Doyle. We went back and forth on what the demon and dragon might be collaborating on, but it was a futile exercise. We didn't have enough information to make any sort of reasonable guess who they wanted to kill or how they wanted to do it. Which meant the only way to play the game was to keep going and keep our eyes open.

Alex and I were piled in his faithful white minivan, which was loaded for bear. Under the cover of night, we had emptied the armory in Orion's dojo into the vehicle. We had pistols, rifles, something that looked suspiciously like a rocket launcher, and more.

The Hunt had been summoned, and the Hunt was coming.

Orion led our convoy on the back of his sleek black motorcycle, his short dark hair practically unruffled by the wind, as if the air itself knew to get out of his way. I wouldn't have been at all surprised to learn he experienced less drag than the rest of us.

"Okay, so we're going to the opening ceremony of the Constellation UN," I said, trying to wrap my head around what I was being pulled into. "Because Orion is in trouble for re-forming the Hunt, and there's going to be some sort of hearing."

"Yup."

"And this whole event is going to happen out in the open in front of everyone, by posing as a convention?"

"Just you wait," Alex laughed. "You're going to be so mad."

An hour and twenty-seven minutes later, my jaw was hanging open as we slowly fought our way through the traffic outside the LA Convention Center. The center is right next to the basketball stadium where the Lakers have played since time immemorial. For sportspeople it's practically hallowed ground. Still, it was one of the strangest buildings I'd ever seen. It curved in a half-moon, with a structure hanging off the front towering up another story or two. The whole monstrosity was painted teal and white, which made it somehow ugly and boring at the same time.

Huge lines of people stretched out of the doors like snakes. Giant banners hung from the two-story front announcing the Constellation Convention and telling people where to get tickets. This wasn't some dinky event. This was a major operation.

Alex laughed so hard at the expression on my face, he almost ran into the car in front of us when it stopped. I almost wished he had hit them, just to wipe that smug look off him.

"It's an actual convention?" I demanded, turning to glare at him. "Those can't all be Nephilim or other supernatural beings."

"Oh no, those are mortals," Alex agreed cheerfully. "Are you kidding—you know your people love this stuff."

"But this is a very serious meeting…" I protested weakly. My eyes didn't want to believe what I was looking at. Several thousand suckers lined up like cattle, excited to check out the booths, while the supernatural community moved around them, and they were none the wiser. "You told me this wasn't a *real* convention."

"There's a difference between the Constellation Convention and the Constellation Congregation," Alex said, relenting. "The convention is a cover. They have a convention every year. Makes it easy to do the meeting right out in the open without anyone noticing all the monsters. Plus, I think events like this make a pretty penny."

"They charge the mortals to pay for their Congregations," I said, aghast as I watched several modelesque cosplayers make their way through a crosswalk, wearing armor and carrying weapons. "Holy crap, you're hiding among the nerds."

"Bingo." Alex laughed again. "Camouflage."

"Even that scaly freak Doyle will look normal," I breathed. I was stunned at the brazen ingenuity of the Constellation organization. The more I learn about the supernatural world, the more offended I get at how they dangle things right in front of our faces, like parents spelling out "I-C-E C-R-E-A-M" in front of toddlers so the kids won't realize they're missing dessert.

"What happens if someone blows it and the mortals figure it out?"

"Humans don't want to," Alex said with a shrug. "Apathy is a hell of a drug. Plus, it's a pretty serious no-no to expose mortals to this side of things."

"How serious are we talking?"

"I heard about one werewolf that started biting people in public and got sent straight to Tartarus, and they threw away the key."

"Isn't that the sauce you put on fish?"

"You're thinking of tartar," Alex sighed in frustration. I managed to keep most of my grin off my face.

"Should we have come earlier?" I asked. "If the ceremony is at noon, I don't know if we're gonna get through that line in time."

"That's what industry badges are for." Alex grinned. "Those lines are the normies."

I rolled my eyes.

We managed to fight our way into one of the mega parking structures surrounding the center and pulled into a spot next to Orion and his bike on the top level, which was mostly empty but—judging by the line of cars waiting to get in—wouldn't be for long.

"Surely they haven't been calling it ConstellationCon for hundreds of years," I protested as another thought occurred to me. "Conventions are a modern thing."

"It's had other names, but the idea hasn't changed," Alex called over his shoulder. "Council, fair, or circus, it's the same thing wearing a different hat."

Orion walked over to the van and popped the back door open. After a moment of rustling through the duffel bags, he pulled out his infamous sword and threw it over his shoulder, bandolier-style.

He reached into the duffel again and produced a black Desert Eagle nestled in a cloth holster. I felt a flash of recognition at the sight of the giant pistol. The last time I had seen it, I had used it to shoot a fallen angel. It didn't kill him, but it still was pretty satisfying. I didn't know Orion had kept it.

Alex fell in beside the boss and started pulling weapons out of the van too, strapping a pair of pistols underneath his jacket in shoulder holsters. For a moment I just stood there, unsure what I was supposed to be doing.

"You geared up already?" Alex asked as he got his second weapon situated.

"Nope, just a little confused."

"Confused about what?"

"Don't they have metal detectors down there? There's no way they let us walk in with"—I made a vague gesture toward the weapons—"everything."

"I told you," Alex said with a grin, "industry badges."

I let out a frustrated sigh and rubbed my face with my hands. "We don't go through a security check, do we?" I muttered. No one bothered to answer what was obviously a rhetorical question.

"He figured it out," Alex told Orion.

"Was he upset?" Orion asked, amused.

"It was beautiful. Total meltdown." The two Nephilim chuckled at my ignorance as they continued strapping on enough weapons to make Neo proud.

"Give me some of those," I snapped, reaching past Alex to grab a pair of 9mm pistols with a holstered belt to match. I slid them to hang behind my back, hidden under my light jacket. Muttering under my breath about stupid Nephilim, I stuffed a few extra magazines in a pocket. When in Rome, I guess.

As we finished, a familiar golden SUV pulled up and parked nearby. The front passenger door opened, and Robin hopped out. He was dressed in a more spartan style than I was used to. If I hadn't already been nervous after strapping enough weapons on my person to invade a small country, seeing my lawyer in combat boots and black cargo pants would have done the trick.

Giving us a friendly nod, he walked to the back of the vehicle and reached inside to grab an oversized black duffel bag, like something you might use to carry ski poles, only longer. He carried it over, the giant bag cradled in his arms.

"As promised," Robin declared as he stood before us, "from Her Majesty Dawn, Queen of All Fae, a gift to the Hunter and the Hunt."

I moved out of the way to let him slide it into the open back of the van. It ran all the way up the middle. Orion grunted and slid the zipper partway, revealing a polished wooden bar and the glint of something that looked like brass.

Something dark and terrible filled the air around us like an ominous, low note from a cello. My teeth immediately went on edge as the hairs on my arm began to rise. It felt like I was alone in the woods, but something was watching me from the dark. I glanced at the other members of the Hunt, wondering if they felt it too. Alex's face was drawn tightly, as if he was holding back genuine terror. Orion was glaring black daggers at Robin.

"Well," the Faerie offered, a mildly surprised look on his own face, "it seems that it is not thrilled to be here."

That made me realize where I had felt this kind of low, burning anger before. It was the same irritation that Orion's sword had sent my way seconds before I killed Lilith, and it branded my palm. Orion reached a hand toward the weapon, and the fury in the air spiked, like a feral dog growling in warning. The Hunter paused before withdrawing his hand and staring at the lance lying in the back of our van in frustration.

"Well, it seems real," Alex grumbled, a haunted expression still on his face.

Orion hmphed in agreement, staring at Ascalon as if he could glare it into submission.

"It is real," Robin promised. "I did not know about its temperament, but I assume you have some experience with that, Hunter?"

Orion grunted neutrally.

Anything that could kill a dragon was a welcome addition to the armory in my book, no matter how grumpy it seemed at the moment. Maybe it just wasn't a morning lance and would be in a better mood later. I had no idea how to use it—besides the obvious. I assumed the pointy end goes into the other guy, but the steps to get to that stage were a little lost on me. We were also lacking in the horse department, which seemed like an important piece of the puzzle. Too bad Saint George didn't use a machine gun.

I had a sneaking suspicion, after seeing a dragoon shrug off Willow's fiery attacks, that the reptiles were immortals, if not Immortals. The capital *I* is important there. An immortal is ageless, but they can still bleed out if you put enough holes in them. An Immortal, on the other hand, takes a little extra killing. I hoped Ascalon had enough power to make them hurt.

"Nicely done, by the way," Robin said to Orion as he stepped back from the van. "I was wondering if you had forgotten about this old thing."

"Do you know the story?" Orion asked him.

"I do," Robin replied neutrally.

"You know the story, and you thought I might have forgotten?"

"No, but I wondered if you had the same priorities now that you did then." Robin's eyes held a hint of sadness as he began to head toward his golden SUV. "Tame it and use it well, Hunter—for all our sakes. The Queen and her retinue will arrive shortly before the convention begins. She urged me to remind you of your agreement to stand for the reinstatement of the Fae to the Constellation Congregation."

"I have given my word, Robin," Orion grunted in irritation. "I will do as I have promised."

"Never doubted it for a second," my lawyer replied, with a hint of his usual cheer. "See you on the flip side." With a wave, he hopped into his vehicle, and they peeled away.

In almost reverent silence, the three of us stared at the legendary lance in its duffel bag in the back of Alex's van. My brain tried to comprehend the priceless piece of history that had fallen into our possession. I pictured some museum curator's horrified face as they realized we meant to use it as a weapon.

"I assume we can't bring that with us?" I said, trying to imagine carrying it through any sort of crowded convention. Although plenty of cosplayers probably had similar items, I doubted any of them had some sort of holy rage that made all of us afraid to touch it.

"No," Orion murmured, a dark satisfaction in his voice despite the weapon's issues, as he slammed the van's hatch closed. "That's a problem for later."

CHAPTER
FIFTEEN

WE LEFT SAINT George's lance unattended in the back of Alex's van in Downtown LA—which seems like one of the most irresponsible things you can do with an ancient relic, but what do I know? Orion led us out of the parking garage and into the sea of humanity that swirled around the convention center, jockeying for a place in line.

I felt my mind sharpen as that special blend of adrenaline that comes before a fight coursed through my veins. My stomach had an excited flutter; my legs suddenly felt like they propelled me farther with each step. It was as if my body was drawing strength into itself, preparing for what was to come.

"You good?" Alex asked, walking next to me. "You look a little stressed."

I grunted noncommittally.

Orion didn't seem too bothered about being called in front of the Constellation Congregation for restarting the Hunt without permission, but I've seen him stare down fallen angels without breaking a sweat. Orion's morale levels aren't a reliable road marker for me. The man has confidence in spades. Plus, my life just never gets to be easy. I had a huge, vested interest in the Dandelion Court being accepted back into the Congregation. If they were, then in theory I would be eligible to get an Impossible Task, which brought me one step closer to getting my soul back. Best-case scenario, this was going to be annoying. Worst-case: We all died. Could it be something in between? Who knew!

So yeah, I was a little stressed.

"That sword looks sick!" someone yelled at the Hunter as he stalked through the crowd, dragging us along in his wake.

I rolled my eyes. Of course it was sick. It was *real*. The rest of our trek to the front door of the convention was much the same. I saw people wearing fake pointed ears to make them look like elves, while Nephilim walked right past them. I saw two girls with contacts that turned their entire eyes black.

It was a little mind-blowing, standing amid the people who most wanted the stories to be real, watching them walk right past the very thing they were looking for. I'm sure there's no life lesson to be learned in that at all.

"There has to be a better name for this thing," I mused, eyeing the giant banners hanging off the front of the building that read CONSTEL-LATION CONVENTION in bold letters.

"What do you mean?" Alex asked, "it dates back to—"

"It's just so *long*," I pressed, interrupting him before he could get into full-blown lecture mode. "They could go with something snappier, like *Star Summit* or something. The name doesn't even fit on the freaking badge."

"That's offensive," Alex replied, glowering at me for talking over him.

"How is that offensive?"

"There is not one star in my constellation," Orion answered, without turning back to look at us. "There are seven."

"Okay," I surrendered, raising my hands. "I get it, you are represented by a plurality of lights in the night sky. My suggestion would fit on the page better."

Orion ignored me as he led us around the long line snaking along the edge of the building and walked right up to the front. The Hunter pulled his badge out of his pocket and slid the lanyard over his head. I dug both of mine out of my jacket and fumbled around until I found the one with my Hunt credentials on it. I stuck my head through the loop and stuffed the other back in my pocket for later.

Given how anal-retentive supernatural creatures could be, I had a feeling I needed to be careful to wear the right one at the right time. Matthew Carver, Squire of the Hunt, and Matthew Carver, Lord of Fire, were not always invited to the same parties. I've heard of wearing multiple hats before, but this was ridiculous.

The front of the convention center was fenced off with event barriers watched over by a dozen security officers, directing the crowd through metal detectors one at a time. The two pistols holstered on my belt felt heavier all of a sudden, special badge or no.

"The line starts that way," a bored guard said as we approached the metal fence she was leaning on.

"Where can I find the industry entrance?" Orion replied, tapping his badge.

The guard gave his badge a casual glance to verify it and then pointed the opposite direction to a gap in the fences that was otherwise empty. "Go around the detectors, first door on your left," she said in the same bored tone.

"Thank you." Orion turned away and led us through the gap. I clocked a guard or two check our badges to confirm they said INDUSTRY, but no one said a word to us as we strode past the security checkpoint armed to the teeth. I had mixed feelings about that.

The interior of the LA Convention Center has two different halls, their entrances situated on each end of the building's half-moon curve. We entered at Hall A, which according to the banners was where the booths and things you would expect to find at a mortal nerd convention were.

My heart skipped a beat as I saw signs pointing toward HALL B for the CONSTELLATION CONGREGATION. It didn't take a genius to figure out where we were supposed to go. We hooked a right and walked down a long hall around the edge of the convention center that eventually dumped us out at the entrance to Hall B. I know it doesn't matter, but why have hallways leading to Halls? It's just confusing.

The row of doors that led to Hall B were closed, except for a single pair, guarded by a familiar, nephilic face. Bellerophon, the scarred antagonist who had brought Orion his summons to the Constellation Congregation, sneered at us as we approached. I gave him a little wave and was rewarded with seeing his scowl deepen. I love hitting immortal beings with sarcasm—most of them don't know how to process it. It's not their fault. They might have an eight-pack of abs, but they're old. My grandparents can barely keep up with my generation's sense of humor. What chance does someone whose birth year has only three digits in it have?

"Cutting it a little close, aren't you?" Bellerophon called as we drew closer. "I half expected you not to show up."

"I thought about it," Orion replied offhandedly as we walked past the other Nephilim.

"Why did you then?" Bellerophon asked with a twist of his mouth.

"I decided seeing Polaris's face when I walked in was worth it," the Hunter replied. Squaring his shoulders like a bullfighter entering the ring, he led us into the Constellation Congregation. What waited for us on the other side of the doors was truly a marvel of engineering. Hall B had been filled with a portable arena.

The structure was three-quarters of a bowl, enclosed on all sides but open facing us. Stadium seats ascended the interior of the bowl into the very rafters of the ceiling. Many of them were already filled. At the bottom in the center was a stage with a simple podium.

The rest of the hall was cavernously empty. No lights were on except for the ones shining down on the arena. I felt like I'd stepped into another plane of existence.

"Ah, Hunter," a skinny Nephilim holding a clipboard remarked as we entered. "One of the last to arrive. I will need you to sign the attendance book. Just a moment please." She jotted something down.

"Excuse me, where's the nearest restroom?" I asked, realizing this might be my last chance before things got really long and boring. It probably wouldn't be a good look for Orion's squires to walk out during the event.

"Around the corner." She gestured with her pencil.

"I'll be right back." I left Orion to his paperwork and dashed down the hall, around the edge of the giant bowl. The back side of the stadium was clearly not intended for official use. The lighting was low and full of shadows. It looked like a staging area, pallets stacked with chairs and tables waiting to be deployed. A pair of women stood among the equipment outside the restrooms, getting a little socializing out of the way before the shindig started.

The woman facing away from me threw back her head and laughed, golden tresses glinting in the low light. I knew that cruel sound too well. Who was Dawn talking to out here in the dark?

Curious, I adjusted my path to get a look at her partner. When I saw her companion's face, I dropped to a crouch and slunk toward the nearest pallet, heart pounding.

Why was Dawn with Samael?

Staying low, I crept closer, straining to hear their conversation.

"—was so much fun," Dawn agreed, chuckling softly.

"You have ever been a hospitable host," Samael replied in a similarly friendly tone. "Sometimes I miss living my life by your pool."

"I suppose it does offer a different sort of atmosphere than you get in the office."

"Not many forest glades in my line of work," Samael agreed. "Perhaps I should come visit sometime. I'm sure we have *plenty* to talk about." My eyes narrowed in suspicion. I had first met the Seducer when she had been staying at the Lady of Summer's house participating in the endless pool party. Now that I thought about it, Dawn had benefited from the demon's machinations—they had made her Queen.

"Wouldn't that be lovely?" the Queen of All Fae murmured in agreement. "I'll have to check my calendar. Maybe if we find the time we can finally discuss—"

Whatever Dawn wanted to talk to Samael about was lost to a cracking sound as the temperature around me plummeted. Even in the dim light I could see my own breath as a cloud, and a thin layer of frost formed on all the chairs stacked in front of me.

I rose to my feet and turned to face Mav. My family's killer stood a dozen paces behind me. I don't know how I'd missed her, she must have been lurking in the deep shadows. She wore a black and blue gauzy dress that ended just above the tops of her combat boots. Around her neck she bore a golden collar that gleamed in the low light.

I guess Dawn had taken my advice. For a moment, we stared at each other, Lady of Water and Lord of Fire. A terrible anger burned in my chest, a temptation to start Damien's task without him. She must have felt the tug of a similar thread of violence because she snarled, and a gleaming spear of ice, formed by her Faerie spirit Undi, grew in her grip. My hands burst into fire as I gathered myself, preparing to dodge when she sent it hurtling toward me.

Mav's whole body twitched, and the ice spear fell to the carpeted floor, breaking into pieces. The Lady of Winter hissed and held a hand up to her golden collar. Her eyes burned with murderous rage, but she made no move to attack me.

Warily, I lowered my hands, banishing Willow with a thought. Now wasn't the time, and we both knew it. I risked a glance over my shoulder, but the two women were gone. I'd missed the ending. Irritated, I gave Mav my best scowl.

"Be seeing you," I promised before I stomped toward the restroom.

Mav was nowhere to be seen when I exited the bathroom, and that was fine with me. The Hunter was waiting impatiently, his arms crossed. "Stay together," he growled, striding onto the red carpet that led to the center of the bowl. A faint hum of conversation filled the room, like a classroom before the teacher arrives.

As we drew closer, the sound began to die out. A hundred pairs of immortal eyes stared down at us as we walked. I wasn't even their focus, but I could feel their attention as a physical weight just by being near the splash zone.

As I've said, Orion isn't a good barometer for how tense a situation might be. He might as well have been taking a stroll along the beach for all that he appeared to notice. His footsteps did not falter, his shoulders did not slump. He looked back at the sea of staring Nephilim with a stony face. I did my best to copy his posture as I followed, as I imagine squires have done with their knights since the Middle Ages. The only emotion I saw Orion display was a nod he gave to Cassiopeia, who returned it in kind.

Orion led us up the stairs, past the first row of silent immortals, and up to the fourth row. With the same unbothered movements, he slid into a seat right next to the aisle. Alex and I piled in next to him, like little boys sneaking into an R-rated movie with their older brother.

Slowly, the conversation around us began to resume, although it felt muted, as if everyone was speaking at a fraction of the volume they had been before. I kept almost catching people staring at me, but every time I checked, no one was looking *at* me. Everything seemed completely normal but felt completely wrong.

I glanced at my phone to check the time: eleven fifty-seven. Three minutes until things got started. Putting it back in my pocket, I leaned over Alex to be able to speak to my two companions softly.

"You good?" I asked Orion, echoing Alex's earlier question to me.

The elder Nephilim gave me a small smirk and a wink as he reclined in his chair. It was gone so quickly I wasn't sure I hadn't imagined it. I leaned back myself, trying to process that.

"He lives for these moments, doesn't he?" I whispered to Alex.

"They're like catnip to the big guy," Alex agreed somberly. "It's a miracle he hasn't gotten us killed yet."

"The day is young," Orion grumbled from his seat.

"Oh no," I gasped.

"He told a joke." Alex's voice echoed my horror.

"We're dead," we said in unison.

The Hunter snorted softly.

Somewhere below us, a single bell rang a mournful note, beautifully clear and strong. Silence fell in an instant. After a few heartbeats, the bell rang again, somehow even more mournful as it echoed in the silence. When it rang a third time, I felt moisture gather in the corner of my eye, attempting to coalesce into a tear, like wisps of clouds threatening to become rain.

As the peal faded, the seated Nephilim stood in unprompted unison, even the Hunter. Alex and I scrambled to our feet, following suit. As we rose, three figures approached the bowl's opening on the red carpet.

A man and woman wore a matching set of diamond diadems in their hair, but otherwise could not have been more different. The crowned woman was average height and slender, with luxurious brown hair that spilled down to the shoulders of her dark-blue dress. In her right hand she carried a large scroll.

Her counterpart was tall, possibly taller than Orion, his broad frame packed with tight muscle like a bodybuilder. His dark head was shaved and polished, reflecting the light that danced off the diamonds in his crown. He carried a long staff in his right hand that gave a dull thud every time he tapped it against the carpet in time with his steps. Both of their eyes were black as night.

Between them strode another man, who was beginning to show the faintest hints of age. I'd never seen a Nephilim with wrinkles before, even if they were sparse. His hair was gray at the temples but still dark toward the top of his head. Around his neck he wore a silver necklace worked into the shape of a giant star that seemed to shine with an inner light, or maybe just a ton of diamonds.

"Who's that?" I whispered to Alex, standing next to me.

"Corona Borealis and Corona Australis," he murmured back. "The Northern Crown and Southern Crown."

"And the old guy?" I nodded toward the man in the middle, although I had a good guess.

"That's Polaris, the North Star himself."

Polaris led their little retinue up onto the dais and turned his gaze across the assembled members of the Congregation, the corners of his mouth turned into a frown. Was it my imagination, or had he paused when his black gaze landed on the Hunt?

After a few long moments, he rapped his staff three times on the stage, and the assembly sank back into our chairs. Which—despite the ostentatiousness of the bowl—felt like cheap movie theater seats. The last time I'd sat in one of those, things did not go well for me.

"The Constellation Congregation is officially called to order," the Corona Borealis—or maybe Australis, I wasn't sure which was which yet—intoned from his position hovering behind Polaris. "Let all Congregants be welcome and be made Guests in their own right, according to the law."

I thought I felt the tension levels drop by a notch or two in the room. Being a Guest has big connotations in these circles. You aren't supposed to kill a Guest. I wouldn't say being one meant you were completely safe—I've been hurt before—but it meant you were *safer*.

"Let the attendance of the heavens be called," the woman cried, unfurling the scroll she had been carrying with both hands and holding it before her.

"Polaris, North Star," she intoned.

"Present," the old Nephilim said dryly, his eyes still scanning the crowd.

"Ariadne, Corona Borealis," she read next. "Present," she answered herself with a small smile.

Roll call continued for another ten minutes, Corona Borealis called out names from myth and legend and the holders of those names replied.

Alex gave me a pointed nudge when Carina's came up. I felt a rush of excitement as I spotted the broad woman a few rows back to our right standing up to affirm her presence. Following her were Puppis and Vela, the two other Argonauts who had been awarded their place in the stars. Together they once formed the keel of the legendary ship *Argos*, but that Constellation had been broken up. Now each of them had their own constellation. I'm not educated, but I looked them up after Nika pointed Carina out at the party. None of the former Argonauts were sitting together. I wondered if their breakup was both metaphorical and literal.

I was so lost in the moment of the roll call that I forgot I wasn't here as a spectator. I flinched in surprise when Ariadne read, "Orion, the Hunter," from her scroll.

The room had been respectfully silent, allowing the Constellations to answer, but the silence abruptly felt sharper, like the edge of a knife.

Into that brutal stillness Orion rose, his gaze fixed on the North Star below. "Present," he rumbled with a voice like thunder. For a moment, everything remained quiet. The Crown did not read another name, instead looking to the man standing in the center of the room.

The North Star and the Hunter stared at each other, unblinking, unyielding. Polaris might be the only old Nephilim I have ever seen, but there was no frailty in him. Whatever steel ran through his bones was the same stuff they mined to make Orion.

Polaris pursed his lips but finally gave a single nod. Orion returned to his seat. The two of them kept staring at each other, locked in a quiet battle of wills.

"Octantis, South Star," Ariadne called out at last. No answer came from the seats. The silence stretched from a moment to something just short of an eternity.

For the first time, Polaris looked surprised. He turned away from his staring contest with Orion, his dark gaze sweeping through the assembled Constellations, searching for someone. Octantis was nowhere to be found. Eventually he gestured to the woman. For the first time, Ariadne answered for another Constellation, rolling up her giant scroll as she did.

"Absent."

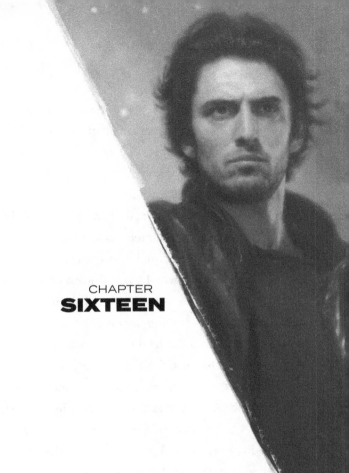

THE NORTH STAR stepped up to the podium in the silence that followed and gazed out at the assembled denizens of the night sky, his face once again placid.

"It has been almost two hundred and fifty years since the last Constellation Congregation," he began, his voice bold without giving the impression he was shouting. "In that time much has changed—the mortal world has entered a new era and us with it."

As if to emphasize his point, someone's phone went off in the audience. A low murmur of amusement ran through the room. Polaris gave a tiny smile that didn't reach his eyes as the offending Nephilim rushed to silence the ringing.

"Our agenda for this Congregation is quite full. Starting tomorrow we will move at a brisk pace. Today, however, I thought it important to highlight two matters to all of you." He placed both his hands on the podium and gripped the sides. "The first is the Coronas and I have seen fit to invite two external sovereign nations to this Congregation."

A rumble of surprise echoed from the audience this time.

"We welcome Dawn, the new Queen of All Fae, and the Dandelion Court as candidates for reinstated membership." As he spoke, the doors behind him opened, and in swept Dawn surrounded by her sisters.

All four of them. I guess Tania wasn't dead after all.

Dawn strode at the head of their little diamond formation, with Mav and Ash flanking her on either side. Tania followed a few steps behind them, head held high. Dawn must have raided her mother's wardrobe because the Dandelion Crown twinkled in her hair. The surprised murmurs broke out into open conversation as people commented on the Faerie Court's arrival to their neighbors.

"Oh sure, let the Fae in, they have a *pedigree*," sneered the man sitting next to me. I glanced at him. His name hadn't been on Ariadne's list, I realized. Now that I looked closely, it was clear he wasn't a Nephilim—or at least that he didn't have enough demon DNA to turn his eyes black or make his ears pointy. In fact, his eyes seemed to have myriad colors in human-looking irises. On a driver's license, the section for his eye color would have just said "Yes." Long-limbed like a runner, with a narrow, bitter face, he glanced at me and gave a frustrated gesture at the scene below.

"Can you believe this crap?" he hissed at us, giving me the opportunity to observe that all of his teeth were dagger-sharp. "Surely you're not going to just *sit there* and let the Fae waltz back in here?"

The Hunter was as silent as a stone.

Dawn led her retinue to the dais and left them standing beside it before joining Polaris at the podium. Again, I felt the attention of the silent room settle on Orion. Everyone was clearly well aware that the Fae's war with the Hunt had led to their expulsion. The Constellations were tensed for an explosion of anger from Orion. Polaris and Dawn openly stared at him from below.

I glanced at him and felt a tiny flutter of fear. Orion Allslayer had made a deal and given his word, but I could tell there was a struggle raging inside his stone exterior. I held my breath, internally begging him to follow through on his promise. It was selfish, but I couldn't help it. I wanted my soul back.

Polaris stared up at Orion like a dog daring a squirrel to come down the tree, but the Hunter didn't rise to the bait. Whatever battle was being fought behind his black eyes ended, and he squared his jaw, still silent as the grave.

The North Star flashed another of those tiny smiles that didn't change anything other than the shape of his lips. "The second delegation comes to us from the Dragon Dons, who bring a petition before the Congregation. We welcome Don Doyle as their representative."

Again, the doors behind him opened. Doyle stepped through, his red hair distinguishing him from the three dull-colored dragoons that shadowed him.

The silence was absolute.

All eyes were on Orion, no one even bothering to hide it now. Everyone knew what this was. During the course of this Congregation, Orion was going to be on trial for re-forming the Hunt without permission. Still, this was a congress of sorts, not a dictatorship—as far as I understood. Polaris couldn't just wave his hand and declare Orion guilty. He needed the support of his peers.

Parading all of Orion's enemies in front of him and daring him to throw a fit was politically brilliant. If Orion exploded and embarrassed himself in front of the entire assembly, more of them might be inclined to condemn him.

The Hunter had passed the first test with flying colors. But this second one was cruel. Both his hands were balled into white-knuckled fists as he stared at the lounge of dragons below.

"It's a trap," I muttered under my breath. "He wants you to get mad."

Tension flowed out of my friend as he saw in a heartbeat what had taken me minutes to put together. A cocky smile tugged at the corner of his mouth, and he leaned back in his chair, eyeing Don Doyle as if he were thrilled that the dragon was here.

It was somehow more terrifying than when he broods.

Doyle and his dragoons stopped on the opposite side of the dais from the Dandelion Court, and the red dragon stepped up to stand on Polaris's other side.

"Thank you, North Star," he said, with his Irish brogue. "I bear greetings from the Seven Dragon Dons, who sent me to bring our petition before this august body. We believe that the punishment against our kin has more than surpassed the crime. We request Draco's sentence be lifted, and our Constellation be woken from his slumber to be returned to us—immediately."

Pandemonium erupted. All around us Nephilim leapt to their feet, screaming and shaking their fists. I felt the portable stadium creak beneath our feet under the combined force of so many bodies moving. For a native Angeleno like me, this felt too much like an earthquake for me to be comfortable.

The Hunter remained in his seat, and Alex and I followed his lead. Orion's smirk only grew as he stared down at Polaris, who looked properly annoyed now.

Dawn made eye contact with me from beside the irritated North Star and half arched an eyebrow as if to say, *I told you so*. I gave her a tiny gracious nod. She had told us, and I was grateful. The wisdom of a tricky Faerie had kept us from being caught flat-footed. Polaris had planned this convocation as a series of sucker punches for the Hunter, but they were bouncing right off him like water off a duck.

I wondered what Orion had done to make the North Star hate him so.

As I looked around the room, I realized not everything was sunshine and roses. I saw pockets of Constellations arguing, gesturing at the dragons or at us. Maybe the idea of releasing Draco was more polarizing than I thought.

"Enough!" Polaris called after a few moments when the furious debates did not burn themselves out like little trash fires. "Enough!" An uneasy, oily silence spread over the room as the Constellations sat down one by one and looked at the North Star. "We are not debating the Don's request at present. There will be *ample* time for discussion and voting on their request, as well as the reinstatement of the Dandelion Court to the Congregation. However, before we—"

"North Star, I demand to be heard!" the strange man next to me shouted, leaping to his feet. Polaris's black eyes slid up and settled onto him, his displeasure evident. A scowl crept across his face, and his gray eyebrows tilted downward until they formed a V.

"I demand to be heard!" the man repeated. Sitting as close to him as I was, I could hear the ragged breaths he took between shouts. He sounded one or two choppy breaths away from full-on hyperventilation. "The Forgotten Agency again puts their name forward for membership in the—"

"Don't push it, mutt," Polaris interrupted, glaring at the man. "You're lucky to even be allowed to attend a meeting of your betters."

"You'll take the Fae back and kowtow to dragons' demands but leave the rest of us out in the dark?" he shouted, ignoring the threatening faces all around him. "Why should we suffer and be excluded? What gives you the right to deny us?"

I watched as the rage melted off Polaris's face, replaced by emptiness. "Sit. Down. Or you will be sat down." The North Star's voice was beyond anger, an icy void as blank as his black eyes. Even the other Nephilim were still, as if they were afraid to move and attract Polaris's wrath.

My neighbor stood defiant for a moment, breath still ragged. This close, I could see he was shaking. I didn't blame him. The fury on Polaris's face was awful to behold. But eventually he crumbled under the weight of that stare and dropped back into his chair.

The North Star cast his baleful gaze around the bowl, as if daring anyone else to interrupt him. When no one did, he clenched his jaw and spoke one final time.

"We are adjourned until the first general session."

FREED FROM THEIR seats, the members of the Constellation Congregation streamed out of the bowl into a fully catered event. I suppose it would technically be called a happy hour, but I got the feeling it was neither happy nor going to last only an hour.

A liveried waiter approached us as we emerged from the stadium, holding a tray of bread and tiny mugs of beer. Orion paused, accepting both before nodding for Alex and me to do the same.

Following his lead, I tossed the piece of bread in my mouth and washed it down with a double shot of beer. It reminded me of going to church with my grandmother, but I knew that couldn't be right.

"In ye olden days you invited a *Guest* to break bread and drink beer with you," Alex leaned in to explain, seeing my quizzical expression. "It's all part of the show."

I nodded and finished chewing my little hunk of bread. It was kinda stale. I guess you don't have to offer Guests your best bread; any old loaf will do. I hoped the rest of the catering was better quality because it was past lunchtime, and I was a growing young man.

Glancing around the room, I saw the Constellations had spread out among the little standing tables, many talking with serious expressions, casting furtive glances at their peers. It might have been my imagination, but the edges of the party seemed to shrink away from Orion like a school of fish parting for a predator swimming through their ranks. "How do you think that went?" I murmured to Alex as we followed in Orion's wake.

"Honestly, better than I thought it was going to, but also worse."

"That's not an answer," I complained.

"I think Orion not trying to strangle Polaris with his left hand while he stabbed all the dragons with his right during the speech was better than I'd expected."

"True," I agreed. "That part went well."

"But this whole event seemed geared to piss him off."

"I thought so too," I muttered. "What happens if he is censured or whatever? Do they have real power?"

"It's complicated," Alex admitted, half his attention clearly on a roaster filled to the brim with macaroni and cheese. "They could tell him to disband the Hunt, but he would probably ignore that."

"Then what happens?"

Alex shrugged. "Not really sure, it doesn't happen often. The Congregation is somehow both ceremonial and very serious. They don't have a lot of power to enforce things, but if someone pisses off enough of the Constellations, sometimes they work together to administer their justice."

"I assume Draco would fall into that category?"

"The way I heard it, he was reprimanded several times, and he laughed at the Congregation, and no one did anything about it. But when he led the slaughter of the Hunt, that was too far, and many of the Constellations formed a joint task force to take him down."

"So as long as you don't stray too far outside the lines, they slap you on the wrist and let you go," I said, struck once again by how similar this felt to mortal politics. "But if you become a big enough problem, everyone comes together and deals with you."

"Yup, and it seems to me that the entire agenda of this convention is geared to give Orion an opportunity to be a problem."

"I noticed."

Alex gave me a tiny grin as he slipped into the buffet line. I was about to follow his lead when I spotted the only thing more interesting to me than free food—a way to free my soul. Carina of Argos stood by herself at one of the cocktail tables on the edge of the gathering, her black-eyed gaze sweeping the room distrustfully.

Telling my stomach that it would have to wait its turn, I gave Alex a wave and headed toward the former Argonaut. She noticed my approach and her brunette eyebrows came together to form a V as her eyes narrowed.

"Where do you think you're sneaking off to?" a cold voice called behind me. All my nerves and social anxiety faded in a heartbeat, swallowed by the hollow anger of loss.

Mav was behind me again. Her barbed obsidian sword still hung from her belt, and I eyed it with distaste. For a moment we just stared at each other, picking up our standoff from where we'd left off, neither willing to breathe or blink.

Finally, she looked away with a small, unimpressed huff. I felt a cruel little grin tug at the corner of my mouth, and I gave it free rein. There was no use in pretending to get along with Mav. We both knew what we were.

"You have been summoned," the Lady of Winter told me. "With haste."

With a furtive glance over my shoulder at Carina, I sighed in acknowledgment and turned to follow Mav. I stayed a few paces behind her, making it clear she was leading me as if I were a servant. Plus, I hoped it would make her shoulder blades itch, knowing I was lurking in her blind spot.

As we walked, my mind raced. Had Dawn spotted me when I spied on her meeting with Samael? Had Mav told her? I hadn't stopped to think about the consequences of being caught snooping, but would it be enough for Dawn to kick me out of the Dandelion Court?

Even if it wasn't, could I trust someone that cozy with demons?

The Lady of Winter brought me to the opposite side of the room, where the Fae contingent had hunkered down. With a grunt, I remembered my second badge and made a hot swap, officially changing from MATTHEW CARVER, SQUIRE OF THE HUNT to MATTHEW CARVER, LORD OF FIRE before we reached Dawn.

The Queen of All Fae was holding court, drinking champagne from a flute and nodding as several of her advisors spoke. I couldn't hear a word anyone was saying, which meant Dawn was using her attunement with the air spirit, Sylph, to prevent the sound from traveling.

My father lurked on the edge of the circle. He gave me a small nod as his eyes flicked from Mav back to me. Which might be the warmest greeting I've gotten from him in years. It's okay, I probably don't need therapy.

"Matthew, what the hell was that?" Dawn demanded as soon as I stepped through the noise-cancelling bubble. I felt my ears pop slightly at the change in air pressure.

"What the hell was what?" I asked, caught flat-footed as the dozen or so Fae turned to look at me.

"The Hunter said he would stand for our readmittance into the

Constellation Congregation, and when we walked in, he was *silent*," she snarled.

"Whoa, whoa, whoa," I said, holding up my hands. Maybe I should have kept the other badge on if I was just going to be playing defense for the Hunt the whole time. This whole multiple-jobs thing was starting to make my head spin. "The entire room was waiting for him to explode like a powder keg, and he was cool as a cucumber. Besides, you and I both know that was just an appetizer event. There's plenty more race to be run, and Orion will do as he promised."

"The agenda did feel a little targeted, didn't it," Dawn murmured, cocking her head. "That is an astute political observation. I wonder why none of my other advisors thought to bring it up." She gave a scathing glare to the courtiers across from her.

I had never seen her act quite like this. Dawn is a performer; she wears whatever mask will serve her best in a situation. But this was something else. This was nervous Dawn, I realized. If she were a tiger, she would be pacing the length of her cage, roaring her frustration.

She wanted back into the Constellation Congregation badly. Which wasn't a particularly deep or shocking revelation; everyone knew that. But there was more to it. She was chasing her mother's dream, but in her own manner. Having ghosts watch over your shoulder while you try to live up to their expectations is a heavy burden. I know a thing or two about that.

Still, I was confused what she was so worked up about. It was out of character. Did she know something I did not?

"Why did the Hunter's silence trouble you so?" I asked softly.

"Who says it did?" she shot back, arching an eyebrow.

"The cowering aides are a pretty good clue," I replied dryly.

Dawn glanced back at them as if seeing them for the first time. "Shoo," she commanded. They scurried out of the privacy bubble, only too happy to be free from Dawn's gaze. Seven of us stayed behind: my father, Robin, me, and the other three seasons of Gloriana's progeny.

"If you keep noticing things like this, I may have to make you an ambassador, Matthew," Dawn threatened. She drummed her fingers on the table for a moment, staring at me with her golden Faerie eyes, as if struggling to make a decision. Finally her gaze fell to my Dandelion Court badge, and an amused smile broke across her face. She reached out with a finger and tapped it once. I guess I had made the right call about that.

"Do you know why the war between Hunter and Faerie started?" she asked.

"Uh, I think someone told me once the Hunter was like a mortal protector and took issue with how the Fae were treating humans or something," I answered, doing my best to sound neutral. I was wearing the Dandelion badge after all.

"An excuse," Dawn replied, waving my answer away. I arched an eyebrow in surprise. Not that there was more to the story, I knew that. But I was shocked she seemed willing to tell it. Fae hoard secrets more aggressively than they do gold.

"Your Majesty," Robin interrupted, a pained look on his face.

"Do you not trust him, Robin?" Dawn asked dangerously, her eyes half lidded. "Did I not hear you advocate on Matthew's behalf to my mother without ceasing?"

Robin was silent, head bowed.

"Then he has earned the truth." Dawn turned back to me, a strange look on her face. "It began over Ascalon, the very lance the Hunter now holds."

I blinked in surprise. I remembered the look on Orion's face when he took it in his hands. How they had trembled slightly. I had just thought he was excited. What kind of warrior wouldn't be excited to get his hands on a dragon-killing weapon?

"The Hunter made a deal with a Faerie for Ascalon, to aid him in his war against Draco. But when the time came for him to receive his weapon, it was never delivered, and the Hunt did not have it at their final stand against Draco and the Dons."

"How?" I asked, dread settling on my shoulders like a wet blanket. "How did they break the deal?"

"It's simple," Dawn said, eyeing her fingernails. "The Faerie who made the bargain was dead. Torn to tiny little shreds."

"If you're going to tell him the truth, at least tell him the whole thing," Robin said, his face hard.

"The Faerie who made the deal with the Hunter was named Oberon," Dawn relented. "He was King of All Fae until my mother killed him and took the crown for herself. She didn't feel the need to honor what she saw as a personal agreement and decided that the Fae should keep the weapon."

It took an extreme amount of willpower to close my hanging jaw. I could almost picture a grief-ridden Hunter slaking his rage on the Fae who had betrayed him and left him unable to protect his Hunt. I remembered his fury when the Faerie assassins attacked us in Goldhall. How could that not be triggering for someone who had been through what he had? Suddenly his hatred and lack of trust for Gloriana made sense.

"That's why she swore to my deal on the Dandelion Throne," I breathed. "She knew Orion would never have let her out of the same loophole again."

"Quite astute of her," Dawn agreed, giving me a smile that was all teeth.

"You were always going to give him Ascalon, weren't you?"

"I thought he might appreciate it more if he took it from me," Dawn admitted, a hint of amusement glinting in her eyes. "I meant what I said, Matthew. I am not my mother. I have no desire to be one of the Hunter's enemies." I wondered if she thought colluding with

Samael wouldn't put her near the top of that list. I decided to keep my mouth shut.

"Then you will have to keep showing him that," I said slowly, trying to figure out where to put all these brand-new puzzle pieces on my mental table. "Orion's mind changes slowly, like a glacier."

"Very well, I will trust your judgment. Don't let me down." She didn't need to add *or else*; I heard it in the silence just fine.

I tried not to let that terrify me. I had complete faith in Orion to keep his word. While he might not be bound to keep it the same way that a Fae was, I got the feeling that to break it would be painful for him in a way it wouldn't be for a mortal like me. Even so, managing the behavior of immortals was a lot of pressure for a twenty-five-year-old with a fake college degree.

"He'll do it," is what I said instead. It was fewer words.

I noticed Tania hovering behind her sister's shoulder, a golden collar that matched Mav's around her throat. The last time I had seen her, Dawn had been dragging her unconscious body around by the ankle. I was still surprised she was alive. "I see you took my advice." I nodded toward the two rebellious sisters without looking at them.

"I listened to the advice of *several* of my advisors, Matthew," she said coolly. "Not just you."

"What's with the prisoner aesthetic?" I asked, ignoring her jibe.

"I have bound them to me," the Queen said in awful tones. "Those are not collars, but knives. They have both sworn an oath of obedience to me, but each of them has also sworn an oath of mortality to their collar. All I have to do is this"—she snapped the fingers of her right hand—"and the collar will do the rest."

So that's why Mav didn't try to murder me. It wasn't better judgment but a supernatural shock collar stopping her in her tracks. I didn't have much sympathy in the tank for either of the Faerie Princesses. Both had tried to kill me in one way or another, and I didn't appreciate that. But even for my worst enemies, the collar sounded terrible. A cold shiver ran down my spine as I met the dead eyes of Tania, sitting behind her sister. She had wanted to be free but now was more a prisoner than ever.

Was their word so literal for the Fae if they promised to die, they would? I filed that one away for later. You know, just in case I ever wanted to kill a Faerie for some reason.

"As long as you think they're under control," I said, giving Dawn a small smile. "I'm just glad they're here."

BY THE TIME I managed to extricate myself from Dawn's clutches, Carina had vanished. The glass she had been drinking from was still on the table, wet with condensation. Frustrated, I switched my badge back to THE HUNT and set out to find my missing Argonaut.

I had been able to steal some food off Ash's plate while stuck in the business meeting that would never end. That might be the best perk of being betrothed so far.

Before I could even consider getting some food of my own, I was cut off once again.

I don't know who enjoys socializing like this, but they should be shot. How are you supposed to actually do anything when you're constantly being interrupted? I was so frustrated I could scream. But since it was Polaris himself who'd intercepted me this time, I decided it was wiser to rage only in my mind.

"So, you are the mortal whose existence threatens to rip the world apart," the North Star said without preamble.

"You, uh, know about that?" I asked in surprise.

"You are a danger to my people. It is my duty as a leader to watch out for threats like you." The ancient Nephilim spoke with the tone of a scientist eyeing a mildly interesting specimen in a microscope.

"I'm not trying to be a danger to anyone. I'm just trying to, you know," I whispered dramatically, "not get darned to Heck when I die."

"If you were not protected, I would cut your throat myself this very moment," Polaris replied, tilting his head to study me. His dark eyes reflected none of his alleged humanity.

I felt my stomach do a double backspring and totally flop the landing. I had no doubt he meant it. He had the face of a man who could slaughter an entire village and cook breakfast in the ruins.

"Speaking of which, thanks again for the bread. It was delicious," I replied. I wanted to make it extra clear that I was an official Guest— just in case.

"The day that Orion disgraced himself enough to allow mortals and runts to join the Hunt was the day of his undoing," Polaris said with a shake of his head. "You are a disease spreading through the Congregation, and I shall see that you are amputated before you rot the entire body."

I opened my mouth to make a dumb joke about how he must have studied medicine back when they were still using leeches, but as if summoned by the look on my face, Orion appeared with Alex in tow. He placed a heavy hand on my shoulder and looked from Polaris to me.

"Time to go," he said.

We stole a move from Doyle's people and pulled an Irish goodbye, leaving without saying a word to anyone. Which, given the mood I was in, was probably better for our political futures. Once we got outside the windowless Hall B, I was surprised to see how long we had been in there. The sun was already beginning to set, casting long shadows over Downtown LA. Time flies when you're fighting for your soul, I guess.

We were quiet as we made our way out of the convention center and through the crowds of mortals blissfully unaware of the supernatural event they were funding. I still couldn't quite wrap my brain around that either. The more I learn about Constellations, Conventions, and everything in between, it often feels like the history of humankind is that we are suckers, and everyone is laughing at us.

The grounds of the center were swarmed with vendors selling street dogs, people in cosplay taking photographs, and a small group of religious protesters with large signs.

"Depart from this den of iniquity!" a man called on a bullhorn as we walked past. "Satan and his devils seek to make you like them!"

Heh, if only he knew.

Dark shadows fell across the streets as the tall buildings began to block out the setting sun. We made our way back to the parking lot. I zipped up my jacket against the slight chill. LA has pretty dreamy weather, but the desert tends to get cool fast once dusk settles in.

"That Polaris guy doesn't seem to be a big fan of... any of us," I said cheerfully as we walked.

Orion grunted noncommittally.

"So, what next?" I asked after a moment's pause. "We have two more days of this."

"Tomorrow is the Fae membership vote, and then the censure of the Hunter," Alex told me, holding up a small pamphlet with a schedule on it.

"Sunday is the Dragon Don's request?" I guessed. Alex nodded in confirmation.

"The first thing we are going to do is get the lance checked," Orion announced firmly. "To make sure it is what it's supposed to be."

"Do you think the Fae would give you a fake?" Alex asked in surprise.

"Dawn told me the story," I said quietly.

Orion's shoulders tensed ever so slightly, like the faint quiver of a mountain before an avalanche. Alex shot me a confused look. *Later*, I mouthed to him. I tried to not feel a small amount of satisfaction for finally knowing a piece of lore that he didn't.

"Oberon was my friend," Orion replied in the ghost of a whisper. "The Knights of the Hunt were my friends. I may have gotten them all killed, but Gloriana's treachery made their deaths certain."

Alex shot me a terrified look, his eyes as round as saucers. I gestured with my hands for him to stop thinking so loudly. Orion's hearing is so good that sometimes I think he can hear the muscles in our foreheads when we raise our eyebrows.

"Do you still know that priest?" Orion asked after a tense moment.

"Father Pike? Yeah, I talk to him from time to time. Why?"

"Ask him if he's able to look at something for you tonight. Tell him it's urgent, but don't put what it is in writing." I nodded and pulled out my phone to text my priest. Well, he wasn't *my* priest. He was my friend who was a priest. A year and a half ago, I had wandered into his parish on a desperate whim and told him the whole story. We're talking everything from Dan the Demon to Lilith the VP of Hell. Father Pike had listened, and even better—he had believed me.

Ever since, he had been researching whether there existed some sort of reverse exorcism he could use to pull my soul back in. We kept in touch, but there hadn't been much progress on that front.

I sent him the message and slipped my phone back into my pocket. "Okay, assuming he says yes, we take it to him and make sure it's real. Then what? We're juggling a lot of balls here. We're supposed to help the Fae get back into the Congregation, stop the dragons from getting Draco released, and then not get the Hunt shut down."

"Don't forget not dying to the aforementioned dragons," Alex pointed out.

"Or getting killed by the freaking North Star. What a stupid star to be. It's not even a Constellation. Isn't he technically just a part of the Little Dipper? Couldn't even make it to the Big Dipper, honestly kind of lame."

"He is the star of Destiny," Orion said grimly. "He points in the direction we are to go."

"Speaking of North Stars, what was the deal with the South Star being absent? What do they do?"

"The South Star is supposed to be the balance to the North. As Destiny looks forward to our future, the South Star is supposed to frame it with wisdom from the past. I do not know why she is not here, but it is a troubling sign."

"I don't suppose she was one of your bigger allies traditionally by any chance?" I asked, confident I already knew the answer.

"You might say that," Orion replied absently. "She is my aunt."

"Awesome," Alex groaned.

"This whole Congregation is a setup, isn't it."

"Seems like it." Orion didn't pause his determined walk toward the car.

"I should have given all this up and gone to med school in the nineties," Alex muttered to no one in particular.

We were a block away from the parking garage when my phone vibrated. I pulled it out of my pocket and saw it was from Gerald. "The good father says we can bring it by Saint Sebastian's tonight if it's urgent."

"It is," Orion grunted.

"Yeah, yeah, I already told him," I muttered back.

"Guess we're going to Friday-night Mass," Alex said with a false cheer.

"Alex?" a woman's voice called from my right. "Alex, is that you? Alex, please! I need help!" Her voice cracked with a sob. I realized it was Nika a second after Alex exploded into motion, cutting across me to race toward the alley.

With a horrible feeling brewing in my gut, I turned to chase after my friend. I heard Orion let out a curse behind us as he spun to see his two squires sprinting into the dark. He had no one to blame but himself—this is what he had taught us to do.

I followed Alex into the trash-filled alley as Nika's tortured voice cried out for him again. My training took over, and I reached behind my back to draw one of the pistols that rested there. I kept my gun pointed at the ground, finger off the trigger as I raced behind Alex.

"Alex, *please*," Nika begged, her muffled voice coming from the shadows.

I drew up short as I saw a hog-tied figure lying on the ground. Slowly, I raised my pistol and settled into a shooting stance. Something was wrong. A similar idea must have sunk into Alex's panic-ridden brain, because he skidded to a stop just outside of the darkest part of the shadows where she lay. Belatedly, he drew one of his shoulder-holstered pistols.

A cloaked figure stepped out of the unnatural darkness around Nika. A low chuckle came from the depths of its hood as it watched us set ourselves for a fight. "Poor scared children, did you lose some-one?" a woman's voice said. A trickle of fear ran down my spine as I wondered who would dare lead the Hunt into a trap.

Brilliant light burst out behind me as Orion drew his sword. The blade's flames seemed to dance, banishing the shadows, lighting up the alley as if it were noon. On the other hand, luring the Hunter into a closed space with his magic sword wasn't the best trap I had ever heard of.

The figure drew back its hood, revealing a brown-haired female Nephilim with black eyes and pointed ears. "Right on cue," she breathed in a sultry tone. She raised her hands from beneath the cloak she was wearing, revealing a curved short bow, nocked with a wickedly barbed arrow. She wore leather armor like she had just walked off a movie set. I recognized her from the roll call. This was Sagittarius the Archer.

"What have you done to her?" Alex demanded, raising his gun.

"What have we done to her?" she mimicked. "Terrible, terrible things. If only you weren't a powerless runt."

Alex was shaking, rage and horror fighting for control of his motor functions. Unsure what to do, I inched forward, trying to be closer to him when this inevitably turned violent.

"Who sent you, Sagittarius?" Orion asked, his voice low and dangerous. The Nephilim gave him an impish smile, her eyes dancing with the reflected light of his blazing blade.

"Why would someone need to send me? You're a traitor and a fool. I've been waiting for the chance to see you die for centuries."

I snorted in disgust. There are few stupider things I can think of than deliberately picking a fight with the Hunter.

Sagittarius's eyebrow twitched as she glanced in my direction, her expression thick with condescension. "Quiet, little mortal. Your betters are talking."

"Besides," a low, guttural voice called from behind us as two more Nephilim stepped out of a dark doorway. "It's high time that someone more worthy became the Hunter." I glanced over my shoulder to see Bellerophon and another Nephilim cutting off our path back to the street, naked black swords in hand.

Okay, maybe it was a better trap than I had originally thought. I licked my lips, glancing between the two prongs of attack we were facing. As the guy in the middle, I had to figure out which of my friends would need more help.

While technically Orion was facing down two opponents, I was pretty sure Bellerophon wasn't on the same level as the Hunter. He didn't have his own Constellation. Plus, I didn't think it would be a good idea to show the Archer my back. Taking an arrow to the spine would be a super-lame way to punch my one-way ticket to the Downstairs.

"You cannot be the Hunter if you are dead," Orion said with a sad shake of his head. "You have come to die."

"You can't do anything to us anyway," I sneered between the smug-looking archer and the two swordsmen behind us. "We are Guests. You cannot harm us."

"Oh no, I hope we don't get reported by all these witnesses." Sagittarius chuckled sarcastically, glancing around the abandoned alleyway.

That, I had to admit, was a good point.

It was also apparently the modern-day equivalent of "draw" for the gunslingers of old. In one fluid motion, Sagittarius pulled back her bow and sent an arrow flying at me with blinding speed.

Only my year and a half of training with the Hunter saved me. My legs went limp as I dropped to the pavement like a bag of cement, letting the arrow whistle over my head.

Alex launched himself forward at the Archer, his pistol barking. With the fluid grace of a master of martial arts, Sagittarius slipped backward from his rush, dodging the first shots from his gun.

Doggedly, Alex pursued her, trying to keep her moving so she couldn't nock another arrow. The Constellation let her cloak slip off, revealing a hip-mounted quiver bristling with arrows like an inverted porcupine. She grabbed another shaft, but Alex managed to catch it with his left hand and wrench it out of hers. I leapt back to my feet and ran to Alex's aid. I didn't dare risk taking a shot with him that close to her.

Sagittarius's black eyes narrowed in annoyance, and she spun, blurring with speed as her leg came up in a roundhouse kick. Her boot slammed into the side of Alex's head and lifted him off the ground. He flew several feet before crashing back down to the asphalt. He rolled onto his back, blinking rapidly as he tried to shake off the hit. The Archer turned her attention from the grounded Alex and fixed her stare on me. With a sinister smile, she drew another arrow from her quiver in a slow, deliberate movement.

So I shot her.

My first bullet hit her high in the right shoulder. Her body rocked backward from the force of the round punching into her, but she stayed on her feet. I thought I heard a faint sizzle as the cold-iron seared into her.

"You'll pay for that," she snarled, setting arrow to string, even though there was a hole in her arm. Cold iron burns supernatural beings—the way silver is supposed to do to werewolves—although it doesn't pack enough punch to kill an Immortal. Still, most Nephilim were the lowercase, budget version. Her human DNA made her susceptible to old Death, and I was more than happy to make an introduction.

So I shot her again.

I blinked in surprise as she took the bullet in the gut with only a grunt, as if it had been a mild punch. Nephilim might be more mortal than most supernatural beings, but that doesn't mean they don't take some extra killing.

Sagittarius snapped her bow back in a draw and sent another arrow hurtling toward me. I leapt to the side, and this time I *did* feel it as the barbed tip sliced a cut on the edge of my wrist as it whizzed past.

With an enraged shout, the Nephilim leapt at me, slinging her bow over her shoulder in a fluid motion. Tossing my gun to the side, I dropped into a fighting stance and ordered Willow to burst into flames. I might not have as much firepower in the mortal realm as I did in the Faerie Lands, but I was confident I had enough to serve up one Kentucky Fried Constellation.

She charged about three more steps before Alex, now back on his feet, grabbed her as she ran past. Sagittarius let out a gasp of surprise as his hands dug into her with crushing, vise-like strength, stopping her in her tracks.

"How?" Sagittarius hissed as she wriggled in his grip.

I stared in horror and fascination at the black mask that glowered at me over her shoulder. It was a strange-looking thing, like the kind they used to use in Shakespearean plays. The style probably has many names, although I remember my drama teacher calling it a mummer's mask.

More importantly, this was a demonic mask, from Samael herself. It made the wearer stronger and faster.

My friend didn't seem interested in answering any of her questions. Silently, he lifted her off the ground and threw her against the wall like a Frisbee. The Constellation slammed into the bricks, and several of them shattered from the force of her impact.

Alex stared at me for a long moment, ignoring the Nephilim he had just sent flying. His chest was heaving, and his entire body shook with rage. Slightly terrified of my souped-up friend, I raised both of my hands in a placating gesture.

"You got her, dude. Still on your side," I said.

With a slight huff that reminded me of far too much of the minotaur for my liking, Alex turned toward the downed Sagittarius, who had finally taken a blow she couldn't just shrug off. Silly me, using bullets instead of an entire building.

With the threat from one side taken care of for the moment, I spun to check on Orion. The Hunter was locked in a duel with the two Nephilim, but his stone-like face was unbothered, despite being outnumbered. I have watched Orion duel some of the greatest living swordsmen. I have watched him cross blades with a fallen angel. They don't give Constellations to just anyone, and I could tell immediately that there was a reason neither of his two attackers had one.

Bellerophon's scars looked sinister, twisted by the snarl on his face as he slashed his blade toward the Hunter's head. Orion leaned backward, letting it slice past before grunting and snapping fully upright in time to catch the next attack when the second Nephilim struck from the other side.

With a neat disengage, Orion turned a quarter step, forcing the two attackers to rotate to maintain their even positioning on either side of him. It was an old master's trick. It took his opponents four steps to move along the outside of a circle, but Orion only a fraction of one to turn. By making them take extra steps he would eventually tire them out. Granted, when we're talking about Nephilim the process could take hours... maybe even days.

I saw no reason to be a good sport, so I raised my gun and sighted in on Bellerophon's unprotected back. Before I could squeeze the trigger, I was tackled by a freight train. I slammed into the pavement with a grunt, all the air in my lungs shooting out in a strangled *whuff.*

I managed to get on my back as I grappled with my opponent. It felt like I was wrestling with the iron tentacles of a monster squid. Slowly, he wrenched one of his arms free, and his hand clamped around my neck with machine-like force. As I gasped for air in the alley, the sparse lighting from the building next to us reflected dimly off the matte black of Alex's mask.

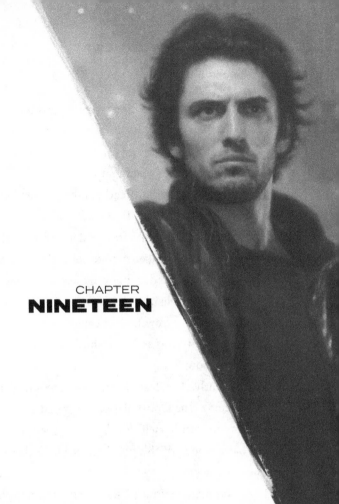

CHAPTER
NINETEEN

I **HAD ONLY A** second to register Alex's masked face before
his hands clamped down on my neck, cutting off my oxygen
as effectively as an air lock. I slammed my fists into his elbows
as Orion had taught me, trying to relieve the pressure on my neck.
I might as well have punched a pair of steel rods. There was no give
in his muscles.

I struggled with my friend, unable to breathe. There was a burning in my lungs that was hotter than any flame Willow could conjure.
Taking that flame as a personal insult, both of my hands surged with
more of the fire spirit's power.

Even with black fuzzing the edges of my vision, I hesitated. I could
see my flames reflecting in the dull black of Alex's mask. I didn't want to

burn my best friend. I didn't want to hurt him. But I *needed* to breathe!

"Behind you!" Nika screamed in warning from the side of the alley. The iron grasp on my throat vanished in an instant as Alex spun to face the threat sneaking up on us.

I took a gasping breath, and the world stopped fading on me. Scrabbling to my feet, I inhaled as much as my hurting lungs could handle, trying to reinflate the dang things. They were the sweetest breaths I had ever taken despite being ripe with the scent of rotting LA garbage. I staggered as I got my feet under me, feeling light-headed.

Alex's right hand was in front of his face, fist wrapped around the still-quivering arrow he had caught with his bare hand. A haggard-looking Sagittarius stared in shock from where she was hunched over with her bow.

Silently, Alex leapt at the Archer, right fist drawn back for a vicious hook. The Constellation staggered back a few steps, raising her bow to protect herself. Alex's fist smashed through it like it was made of balsa wood. With lightning speed, he slammed his left hand into her stomach.

Gasping, Sagittarius staggered, dropping the ruined remnants of her weapon. Alex didn't hesitate, fists flashing as he vented his rage on her. Weakly, she crouched into a sweeping kick trying to knock him over. Her foot bounced off Alex's leg like she had tried to trip a tree.

I watched the beating with a mixture of satisfaction and horror. I had no sympathy for the Archer who had kidnapped one of Orion's students. That's like playing with enriched uranium and being surprised to get burned. But on the other hand, I didn't recognize the rage in Alex. It was like his humanity was gone, devoured by the darkness of the mask.

Sagittarius might have been caught off guard, but she was still a Constellation. Her left hand flashed, and a wicked little curved knife blurred from somewhere as she slashed at Alex. My friend danced back, kicking at her hand trying to knock the weapon away.

But the knife was just a trick. The Archer's right hand dove into her quiver and snagged an arrow. In one fluid motion, she leapt forward, the shaft extended like a miniature spear, aimed directly at Alex's heart. Her attack was so smooth and direct that I think even the Hunter would have struggled to counter it.

Alex should have died. I practice against him every day, and I know there is no way he should have been able to stop her thrust. But his whole body rippled with speed, and he leapt off his one remaining foot, spinning backward like a soccer player performing a bicycle kick. His foot connected with Sagittarius's wrist, and she screamed as a loud snap echoed through the alley.

The arrow clattered to the asphalt from her nerveless fingers.

Alex's back slammed into the ground next to it a moment later. In one fluid movement, he leapt to his feet and tackled the Constellation. Sagittarius's head slammed into the alley wall as they slid to the ground, her body going limp.

This seemed like the moment when I needed to start worrying about my own safety. Whatever influence the mask was having on Alex, it definitely seemed to struggle with distinguishing friend from foe. Once Sagittarius was down for the count, I might be next on the hit list. I needed to get it off him before I had some broken bones of my own. I even thought I knew how.

It was a really stupid plan—but it was a plan.

Whatever demon magic was pumping up my friend's physical powers must have been boosting his hearing too. I took my first step, and his head whipped around. Before I could even take a breath, he charged.

I let out a panicked yell and rushed to meet him. We hurtled toward each other like an unstoppable force and a fragile guy who didn't want to get hit.

As we got in range, I leapt into the air, using Willow to create a small explosion that launched me higher in the air than my mortal legs could ever hope to do. Not to be outdone, Alex and his demon passenger launched themselves to meet me.

That was step one. In the air he would lose his maneuverability, but thanks to my Willow, I kept some of mine. All I had to do was move a little to my left and—

Wham! Every bone in my body shook as Alex slammed into me with the force of a thousand normal Alexes. My forward momentum vanished immediately, and I felt my back clench in expectation of a gruesome landing on the pavement below.

In panicked reflex, I managed to swing my right hand behind me and trigger a blast. The collision spun us like a top, rotating me to the top of our pile as we crashed to earth.

In my defense, he's a Nephilim—he can survive the landing better than me.

Besides, I'm not the one who put on the demon mask and went insane.

Alex-sized cushion or no, the landing was far from delicate. If we had been an airplane, no passengers would have been tempted to clap. If we had landed any harder, I'm not sure I would ever have been able to clap again.

As I lay there trying to restart my brain, I felt Alex shift below me, hoping to claw his way free of our tangled pile. In desperation, I grabbed for his mask. One of his hands clamped down on my wrist with terrible strength. Fear surged in my chest as I struggled to move it.

I said this was a stupid plan, and I meant it.

I managed to snake my other hand to the mask without getting caught, and I pulled for my life. With a *pop*, it came free, and I hurled it across the alley like a live grenade.

"Blurgbhlhlhl," Alex gasped, as if he had just woken up from an underwater nightmare. His blue eyes had begun to bleed into the dark-eyed stare of a demon. Deep black veins stood out on his face, twisting snakes of corruption.

"You're welcome," I grunted, rolling off him and lying on my back, gasping for breath. Faintly in the night sky, even through Downtown LA's light pollution, I could make out Orion's belt—three stars in a straight line—twinkling down at me.

I found that irritating for some reason.

"Couldn't. Control. It." Alex panted from where he lay on the pavement next to me. "It wanted to break everything."

My vision of the few stars actually visible in the LA sky was eclipsed as someone leaned over us, a nocked arrow pointing directly at my eye. "Honestly, I can relate," Sagittarius seethed through what sounded like a mouthful of cotton balls. Her face looked like it had just been smashed a brick wall, which made sense. Blood streamed down her cheeks, but the Nephilim was still standing.

"You've got to be kidding me—" I started to shout, when the Archer abruptly vanished with a squeak. I looked over in time to see Orion slam his fellow Constellation against the wall, fingers buried deep in her long brown hair.

I dragged myself to my feet and held a hand down to Alex, pulling him up after me. Glancing down the alley, I saw no sign of Bellerophon and the other Nephilim who had tried to duel the Hunter. I guess seeing Sagittarius get manhandled by Alex was enough to send them running for the hills.

Orion's sword was back in its sheath over his shoulder. With a smooth motion, he drew the black Desert Eagle that had once been Zagan's from behind his belt and jammed it into Sagittarius's eye.

"What have you done to my student?" he demanded. His voice shook with a consuming hunger for violence, like an open grave ready to consume.

While she was not technically a member of the Hunt, the Law of Predators would dictate that she was a part of the Hunter's greater... territory, maybe, or ecosystem? I don't know—the analogy breaks down a little, but the point is she wasn't some random person to the Hunter. It was an extra level of insult between beings who are already easily insulted about that kind of thing.

"Poor Hunter," Sagittarius cackled, a bubble of blood popping in her lips as she spoke. "Still can't protect his herd."

Orion cocked back the hammer of his .50-caliber pistol with a deafening click, underlining a threat he didn't even need to make. Alex and I both took a big step back. If he pulled the trigger, there would be a splash zone that I had no interest in being in. Way less fun than SeaWorld.

"You wouldn't dare," she cackled. "A Constellation killing another Constellation is forbidden. You of all people should know tha—"

Without the slightest hesitation, Orion dropped the pistol from her eye to her thigh and pulled the trigger. The roar of the miniature cannon going off in the close quarters of the alley was deafening. Her screams grew louder.

I made a conscious decision not to look.

"What did you do?" Orion screamed, raising the gun back to her head. Sagittarius's face was painted with a mixture of pain and horror as she stared down that unblinking eye of the Desert Eagle. She must've really thought the Hunter cared about what was "forbidden" on a hunt.

Play stupid games, win stupid prizes.

"We didn't touch her. We didn't! She's fine!" Sagittarius screeched, recoiling into the wall, desperately trying to get away from the bore of the gun.

"I'm okay," Nika groaned in confirmation.

"Untie her," Orion growled at Alex, who sprinted toward the still form of Nika.

The alley was completely silent except for the sound of Sagittarius's leather armor scraping against the wall as she struggled in the Hunter's grip. Two pairs of black eyes stared into each other, waiting to see which one would give. I don't know what the Archer saw in the dark depths of Orion's gaze, but a terrified whimper came out of her mouth.

Freed of her bonds, Nika stalked over to glare down at the broken Constellation. The younger Nephilim had a wicked bruise on her face but otherwise seemed fine. Alex hovered over her shoulder like a helicopter boyfriend.

"See, she's fine." The pleading tone in Sagittarius's voice was totally alien.

Orion cocked the hammer back once more. I braced myself to see something that no amount of therapy would ever be able to scrub out of my brain. Sagittarius let out a wet sob.

"Are you okay?" he asked, turning to his student.

"I'll live," she replied darkly.

"I told you we didn't hurt her," Sagittarius panted to no one in particular. She sounded like she was hyperventilating.

"Where did she get the second bow from?" Alex asked me. I shrugged.

Orion shot her in the other leg.

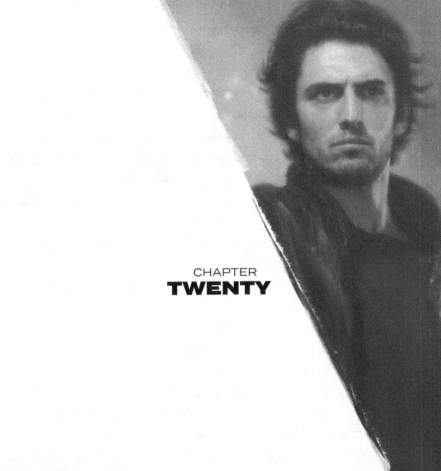

WE LEFT SAGITTARIUS where she lay, broken and bleeding. Mercy is not one of Orion's personality traits. The Archer had attacked the Hunt and was paying the price. As far as he was concerned, that was what the scales of justice demanded.

I felt a little cruel, but Nephilim are not mortals. A human would need metal rods and years of physical therapy to even dream of walking again after having both legs blasted like that. If they didn't bleed out on the sidewalk in fifteen minutes first.

The Archer would live to arch—and walk—another day.

Sirens sounded behind us as we trotted out of the alley and made our way back to the parking garage. I was only too happy to hustle. The last thing I wanted was to get caught at the scene of another gunfight this week. Detectives Jones and Rodgers would be all over me.

"What next?" Nika asked breathlessly, looking at Orion.

"You are going home," the Hunter replied, his eyes glittering darkly.

"Home? Why? A Constellation just kidnapped me!"

"Exactly," Orion snapped. "This is not a place for you. You are not ready."

"But they are?" She gestured at Alex and me with a wild flail. "I'm a better fighter than either of them."

"And yet it was you who was tied up on the ground," Orion remarked softly.

Nika fixed both of us with a glare. I gave her a small shrug. I knew better than to try to convince the boss when he was like this. It's more efficient to argue with a cinder block. I don't know why Nika was so eager to get into the thick of this. I didn't want to be here; I had to. Furious, she stormed away from the scene of the crime to call a car. Alex watched her go with a broken expression on his face.

The van was right where we left it, with all its doors and windows intact. A minor miracle for Downtown Los Angeles. A small part of me had half expected us to come back to find the windows smashed and Ascalon missing, only to turn up in some pawnshop a few blocks down the road.

But Saint George's lance was still in the back, so the three of us piled in. Orion insisted we leave his bike there overnight. That seemed like another bold decision to me, but he wasn't willing to be separated from the lance for even another second.

Carrying our holy cargo, we joined the slow-moving river of traffic exiting Downtown on a Friday night. GPS estimated it would take us over an hour to get back to Northridge, which was fine with me. I needed at least that long to mentally prepare myself before I stepped into a church. I sent Father Pike another text letting him know we were en route, then leaned back, letting the leather seat coddle my bruised body. Alex's van was far from luxury, but it sure beat the asphalt I had just been dribbled around on like a basketball.

I could already feel a dull ache setting into my bones as the adrenaline began to wear off. I promised myself I would put a large glass of water and an entire bottle of ibuprofen on my bedside table before I went to sleep tonight. I had a feeling I was going to need it.

We spent the first fifteen minutes riding in a silence that might have been described as *stony*, though I think I prefer the term *awkward*. The tension was reasonable: One of us had beaten the crap out of another. Sure, there were some extreme circumstances, but that didn't make it just go away.

"So that was fun," I said, when I couldn't stand the silence anymore. When things get too quiet, I sometimes imagine I can hear the brain rot in my head eating me from the inside out. At least if I'm talking, it covers up the sound of the chewing.

"Every time," Alex groaned.

"You would benefit from a new catchphrase," Orion agreed.

No one appreciates my art. "That's a lot of judgment from a guy who just went nuts on demon magic and tried to choke out his so-called best friend." I shot Alex a glare. He hunched his shoulders behind the wheel as if I had hit him.

"Yeah, sorry about that," he muttered.

"What did it feel like?" I asked.

"Like I was riding a rhinoceros. It's big and strong and could destroy anything I pointed it at, but at some point it realized I didn't have the mass to make it obey. The longer I was riding it, the less it listened to me."

I shuddered a little at the thought of a demonic rhino stomping me to death with its tree-trunk-sized hooves. That was definitely not on the list of ways that I hoped the lights would finally go out for good.

"Well, I don't know about anyone else, but I vote we maybe don't use the mask with uncontrollable battle rage again." I looked around the van, hoping for unanimous buy-in, but all I got was tense silence.

Surprised, I turned back to Alex, who was staring straight ahead, his hands holding the steering wheel in a death grip. "Alex?" I prompted. "Please tell me you're getting rid of the mask."

"What am I supposed to do?" he snapped, not looking at me. "I don't have a magic sword or a fancy fire spirit. When the chips are down and you guys are counting on me, I'm practically worthless."

"You're not worthless," I said softly, hearing the echoes from our conversation the other day. Alex didn't respond. I tried to put myself in his shoes. While I didn't think I had leveled up to a point where I had left him behind, I had to admit Willow did give me an edge.

Whether it's true or not, feeling left behind is a cancer that can eat someone from the inside out. Which meant that this wasn't my choice to make; it was something Alex had to decide for himself.

"Okay, well if you're gonna keep it, can we at least wait until a safe time for you to practice with it?" I asked. "Because we can't do that again. Maybe start meditating or something to get your brain strong enough to handle the power?"

"Yeah, I won't use it until we can do some testing with it," he promised. I nodded. That was good enough for me.

Orion was silent. But his judgment of Alex using the demonic mask was loud enough for both of us to feel. He's not a man of many words, the Hunter, but that doesn't mean he doesn't communicate. I could feel a chill in the car that even switching Alex's heaters on couldn't banish.

"I gotta say, Nephilim politics are much more exciting than I thought," I offered, turning to glance over my shoulder at the brooding Orion. "I don't think human congressmen get in gunfights in back alleys nearly as often."

"Yeah, what the hell was that about?" Alex asked. "Someone trying to prove themselves?"

"There are many who wish to be the Hunter," Orion replied coolly. "But there can only be one."

"So Bellerophon is some sort of couch quarterback," I said, remembering how snotty he had been when he had seen Alex and me. "He thinks he could do it better. I don't know who the other guy was—"

"Perseus," Orion offered mildly.

"Sure, that was Perseus. Why not? He killed Medusa, right?"

"That's the one," Alex agreed.

"He also wants to be the Hunter?"

"He has long maintained killing one of the Gorgons should have earned him a Constellation, but there's never been much support," Orion replied.

"Okay, so the two of them I kind of get. They both think if you were dead there would be a slot for a new Constellation, and it might be their turn?"

"Something like that," Orion agreed.

"But what about Sagittarius? She already is a Constellation. Why would she want you dead?"

"You may not have noticed," Alex interjected in an amused tone, "but our boss is a little different from most of the other Constellations."

"Different how?"

"Usually once you become a Constellation you sort of retire. Kick back and rest on your laurels. What else is there for you to accomplish?"

Orion snorted in disgust.

"Did you know there are references to Orion and his Constellation in *The Odyssey*? By the time Homer was telling one of the earliest stories of recorded history, Orion was already legend. Since then, he's slain several Immortals, including a dragon. They don't let you have more than one Constellation, but someone is dangerously close to eclipsing the rest of them."

"What did you have to kill to become the Hunter in the first place?" I asked, turning to look over my shoulder at Orion. "Was it a *T. rex*? You have to tell me if you killed a *T. rex*."

"One," Orion replied grimly.

"One of what?"

"One of everything."

Oh. Well, that was certainly a lot to process. It was also, I noted, not a denial that he'd killed a *T. rex*. As far as I was concerned it counted as an admission.

My obsession with dinosaurs aside, Alex's explanation made a lot of sense, but I found myself disappointed there was such a small reason for such a large amount of jealousy and hatred. But then again, isn't that often the case? "What was the bit about killing her being against the rules?"

"Constellations are forbidden from killing each other," Orion replied. "It's supposed to help keep the peace."

"Seems like it works well," I sneered. "I'm guessing that rule doesn't apply to anyone who isn't a Constellation?"

"If another Nephilim can take down the Hunter, then maybe they deserve to be the Hunter," Orion agreed with a grunt.

"So, the two lackeys were there to kill Orion while Sagittarius took care of Alex and me?" I frowned as I said it. Something felt wrong, like I was forgetting an important piece of the puzzle. If I had learned one lesson in my year and a half of surviving the plots and plans of Immortals, it was that there was never just one thing going on. "Is it possible we're giving too much credit to the whole jealousy thing?"

"What do you mean? They literally said they were there to kill Orion," Alex protested.

"True," I agreed. "I'm not saying that's not part of it. But it's a little convenient to me that fifteen minutes before all this happened,

Polaris told me he'd slit my throat himself if I weren't a Guest."

There was a tense moment of silence as the two Nephilim processed this news.

"You might have a point," Orion mused grimly. He didn't sound too surprised.

"But we *are* Guests," Alex raged. "Surely Polaris wouldn't violate the sanctity of an event he's hosting."

"You heard Sagittarius," I said, shaking my head. "There were no witnesses, and I bet there wouldn't be a lot of pressure from the top to investigate our untimely demises."

"You think he wants you dead that badly?"

"That's the impression I got from our brief conversation. He seemed to know all about me and my missing soul and said something about me being the mortal who could 'destroy everything.' Next thing you know, we get jumped by a bunch of lunatic Nephilim, including a Constellation."

"That's a lot to give you credit for," Alex offered. "I don't know if you could destroy *everything*. A lot of stuff, sure. But not all of it— wouldn't want you to start thinking you're too important."

"Thanks… I think?"

"You're welcome."

"You still tried to choke me to death less than thirty minutes ago."

"Ugh, are we still talking about that? Learn to let things go, man."

"I'm just glad you let go of my throat so I can breathe."

THE GPS ESTIMATE turned out to be a little ambitious, we arrived at the church ten minutes later than I had told Father Pike we would. But by LA standards, anything under fifteen minutes late is on time, so we were fine.

St. Sebastian's doesn't necessarily look like what immediately comes to mind when I hear the term *Catholic church*. Usually, I think of steeples and bell towers. Instead, the church was a squat one-story building with a domed, white roof that had probably started peeling before I was born. It reminded me of my neighborhood: a little banged-up around the edges and in need of some paint, but not going anywhere. It had the sturdiness of a tree stump. Anything trying to uproot it and pull it out would have its work cut out for it.

The parking lot was almost empty; despite Alex's prediction, we had apparently missed Friday Mass. That was okay with me. I would have felt a little out of place. Then again, I was the only member of the group without demon blood in their veins walking into a church. I wondered if there were any potential issues to that.

Neither of them seemed concerned, so I decided not to think about it. I had more than enough stress for a young man, thank you. Together, the two of them carried Ascalon, still in its black duffel bag.

"I don't like churches," Alex confided in me as we walked toward the building.

"Bad childhood experiences?" I asked.

"No, I just don't like spending time in ruins, no matter how many people are inside."

I led the way, opening the hefty front door of the church to let Alex and Orion tenderly guide the lance through the opening without hitting anything. No one burst into flames, which I took as a good sign. Ahead of us, the solid doors that led to the sanctuary were closed, but a hallway on either side led to the rest of the administrative rooms. We trooped our way through the narthex, which is a fancy word that means something like "lobby," and headed toward Father Pike's office.

A disapproving sniff greeted us as we crossed the empty room. I turned to see my old friend Father Bryant eyeing the three of us distastefully from the far hallway. The first time I had come to St. Sebastian's, I had told him the story of my stolen soul, and he had condemned me as someone who deserved to go straight to the Pit of Hell. It irked him to no end that Father Pike and I hung out. "This is a church," he sneered, "not a circus, despite what you seem to believe, Matthew Carver."

"That's for me actually, Father Bryant," Gerald's voice interjected smoothly, cutting off my plans to ask him why, if that were true, they let a clown like him work here, which I am mature enough to admit might have been for the best.

Father Bryant let out another sniff but didn't protest any further, turning on his heel and marching down the hallway he had been lurking in. I've never been very clear on who is the boss between the two fathers. It would be convenient if they had ranks like Sergeant Father or something for us laypeople. Granted, I'm still not clear on some of my military ranks either. If a colonel is so high up there, why does the most famous one only serve fried chicken?

"This way, please." Gerald gestured down the opposite hallway. Wordlessly, the two Nephilim caddies followed his instructions, each holding one handle of the long duffel and carefully swinging it wide to avoid obstacles as they entered the hall.

Father Pike held out his hand for me to shake and gave me a broad grin. "It is good to see you, Matthew," he said, his bright-white teeth shining in contrast with his dark skin. Gerald is a native of Uganda who came to the States to tend to a people he felt needed him. As such, his English is tinted with a hint of a British accent, and he loves tea. He was dressed in a traditional black suit, with the white collar of his office peeking out at the top. The lights above reflected brightly on his waxed bald head.

"Father Pike, it's been a while," I replied, giving him a firm handshake. As itchy as religion and folks like Father Bryant make me, I always felt a little lighter every time I saw my friend. He's good people.

Father Pike led us down the long hall to where his office door waited, open and inviting. It took a little bit of pivoting, but we managed to get Ascalon through the door without scratching the walls or bumping into anything. If this whole Hunt thing didn't work out, we might have a career as movers to fall back on. Alex and Orion are both extra strong, and I'm a great supervisor.

The priest's office was unchanged from the last time I had been here. The wall-to-wall bookshelves on either side of the room were overflowing with too many books to ever properly fit. More piles of knowledge were stacked around the room in some sort of filing system that made sense to no one but Gerald.

His desk was also coated in a thick layer of papers and open books. He scooped up some of them and gestured for Alex and Orion to lower the lance onto the desk, heedless of the leftover papers. For a moment, he stared down at the black duffel, then held his hand out to the Nephilim.

"I'm Father Gerald Pike," he introduced himself, shaking hands with them. I could see his eyes wandering over my two friends' inhuman features as he greeted them. Gerald was in the know to some extent. He believed there were demons and monsters, but he'd had much less exposure than I had, lucky him.

"Two Nephilim in my office," he murmured to himself. "What a day."

"Oh, we're just getting started," I told him with a grin. "You're not going to believe this."

"What have you brought me?" The priest looked down at the bag on his desk, then picked up a pair of horn-rimmed glasses and slipped them on. A faint shadow of excitement hovered just out of reach on the corner of his face. He's a good man, but he's also a huge nerd.

"We were hoping you could tell us," Orion answered, opening the long zipper and tugging the bag down to reveal the weapon.

This was my first real look at the lance of Saint George, and I leaned forward to drink it all in. I already knew Ascalon was long—I'd guess that it was over eight feet from end to end. The butt was fitted with a bronze grip and a small round piece that looked like a cross guard. Four square red crosses were stamped around the edge of the circle. The wood was dark oak, beautifully polished; it glowed under the lights of Father Pike's office. The lance ended in a six-inch tip sheathed in leather. It looked more like a work of art than a weapon.

Once again, the feeling of immense dread descended upon us. It was as if the baleful eye of a sleeping giant had cracked open, and it was taking in its surroundings. I stayed very still, like I would with a feral dog, as the presence stared at me. When its gaze moved on, I let out a relieved breath.

Gerald also froze when it turned to him. My tension grew as the fury seemed to pause, focusing on the father for longer than it had stared at any of us. Then suddenly, there came a relaxing of the pressure in the room, as if the presence had let out a long sigh, and the eye closed.

Father Pike was silent for a long moment. Reverently, he reached out with a shaking hand, but he stopped himself an inch short of touching Ascalon. I noticed the weapon didn't growl at him the way it had when Orion tried that. Pulling his hand back, he tilted his head forward to stare at us over the rims of his glasses.

"Is this what I think it is?" he demanded, a troubled look in his brown eyes.

"The one who gave it to me claimed it was Ascalon, the weapon Saint George used to slay a dragon," Orion replied calmly. "But we were hoping you could confirm it."

Father Pike sat down hard in his chair, his hands coming up to move his glasses to the top of his head and wipe his face. He paused to stare at the lance again, slipping his glasses back down onto his eyes. "That's certainly Saint George's mark," he mused, studying it closely. "Where on earth did you get this?"

Orion glanced at me, his black gaze questioning. I shrugged and nodded for him to continue. Father Pike could handle the truth.

"From the Faerie Queen."

Gerald let out a gasp that sounded both horrified and excited, his gaze never ceasing to roam over the lance, as if he were trying to drink it up with his eyes. "It's beautiful," he murmured. I could only agree.

Despite being close to a thousand years old, Ascalon looked as if it had just been crafted last week. "It certainly looks like it is a weapon worthy of Saint George the Dragon Slayer," he added, standing up and looking at us. "But I'm not sure how exactly how I can verify it as a relic. I could have it sent off to the bishop of our diocese, but I suspect that isn't quite what you were hoping for."

"You can't just... tell?" Alex asked, a note of disappointment in his voice.

"Were you hoping I would get a tingle in my collar and sense its holiness?" Gerald replied in a wry tone. "I'm a priest, not a wizard, Nephilim."

"So you can't confirm it's legitimate?" Orion asked, frustrated.

"I can tell you what you already know," Gerald said, pacing around the lance, eyeing it appraisingly. "The tales of Saint George and the dragon were recorded in the eleventh century, but it is often believed that he actually lived as early as the fifth century. I've seen ancient wood from a similar time—it didn't look like that."

"You think it's fake?" Alex pressed, a frown darkening his face as well as Orion's.

"I didn't say that," Father Pike asserted, holding up a finger to stall the questions. "I said I've never seen ancient wood in this good a condition. Which leads me to suspect it is either fake—or exactly what you think it is. If it is truly well over a thousand years old, then I do not know how else to account for its condition."

"Surely the whole malevolent force thing counts for something," I insisted. That seemed like the more obvious piece of the puzzle to me.

"There are plenty of forces in the world that are malevolent, Matt," Gerald replied softly, his eyes distant. Slowly, he reached his hand out toward Ascalon's hilt. I tensed, waiting for the lance to snap at him, but the presence did not stir as the father laid his hand gently on the weapon. The four of us were silent, staring at the alleged relic sitting on the table in front of us, unsure what to do next. While it was impressive looking, I understood his hesitance to declare it anything other than a well-made lance in the style of Saint George.

After a long moment, Father Pike reached toward the sheathed blade at the front of the lance. "May I?" he asked, directing a glance at Orion. The Hunter shrugged, arms still crossed.

With a loud *snap*, he undid the clasp, and the blade slid free. The four of us stared in wonder as the steel was immediately enveloped by a familiar flame. The weapon's presence burst into focus, filling the room like a thick fog as if we finally had Ascalon's full attention. The cheery bright fire sent light dancing around the room. Gerald hastened to slide some of his scattered papers away from the blaze, but he needn't have worried—the papers were never in any danger of combusting.

It wasn't that kind of fire.

Father Pike took a step back, crossing himself. With wide eyes he glanced up at the three of us. "Well, I think I can more confidently comment on its veracity as a relic," he breathed in awe.

Orion's face split into the leering grin of Death as he stared down at Ascalon. I shuddered to think what was coursing through his mind. Reverently, the Hunter reached out to touch the lance, but again the weapon almost seemed to hiss in warning. The flame on its burning tip crackled as it grew in size. It seemed only Father Pike had its trust.

"What do you plan on doing with it?" Gerald asked, his voice barely above a whisper.

"Now that you know it's real, are you going to suggest we give it to a museum or the church?" Alex replied, drawing up stiffly.

"I'm going to kill a dragon," Orion answered over his squire.

Father Pike was silent for a long moment, his eyes unfocused as he stared into the dancing flames on the head of the lance. Whatever he saw in the fire made him smile. He looked up, boldly holding Alex's and then Orion's gaze.

"I suspect if it's showing up after all these years, Saint George would think that it's exactly where it should be," he said warmly. Orion grunted noncommittally. It might have been my imagination, but I thought Ascalon's fires settled slightly, like a smug cat.

"Let me bless it. Just in case." An amused grin twisted his face as he glanced at the three non-Catholics standing before him. "You did bring it to a priest," he chuckled. Orion shrugged and took a step back, motioning for him to proceed.

Father Pike pulled a flask from his desk and poured some water into his palm before using it to inscribe something on Ascalon's shaft. I knew from personal experience that the good father always has holy water lying around, just in case. As he drew, he closed his eyes and murmured something in Latin, which I still don't speak. After he was done, he opened his eyes and looked at Orion for a long moment.

"I do not know you, Nephilim," he said somberly. "But I do know this is an instrument that has been made for terrible and mighty deeds. Use it in the defense of the weak, and it will not fail you. But if you use this weapon to oppress those you should defend, then know that this blessing is a curse. He who lives by the lance will die by it."

Orion stared at the priest for a moment before a small smile cracked the corner of his lips. "Have no fear, Father," he said. "I'm familiar with the responsibility." Gerald bowed his head slightly in acceptance. The tension in the room winked out, gone in a heartbeat.

Slowly, Orion reached for the hilt of the lance. This time Ascalon did not object. The four of us exchanged glances. I guess it was on board now. Maybe it just needed its permission slip signed or something.

"I'm glad to see you've been staying out of trouble since the last time we spoke," the priest remarked to me as the Hunter began to put the weapon away.

I realized I hadn't given the father some of the key updates on my life. "That reminds me," I said, unable to help myself, "I sort of got betrothed."

He must have been able to tell something from my voice, because Father Pike's gaze snapped up from the lance, and he fixed me with a withering stare that only a holy man could muster. "Go on," he urged.

"She's really nice," I replied, feeling an embarrassed flush creep up my neck. "She's, uh, a Faerie princess."

Father Pike's eyes narrowed like a seasoned investigator's, clearly sensing there was more to the story. His steely gaze reminded me of Detective Jones. I guess they were both used to hearing confessions. "Why do I get the sense I'm not going to like whatever it is you haven't told me yet?" he asked.

"She's, uh, also the Devil's daughter," I muttered under my breath.

Father Pike sat down, pulled out a different flask from his desk, and without hesitation took a long draw from it.

TWENTY-TWO

THE HUNT DRAGGED themselves out the front door of my fortress house the next morning. Orion brought up the rear, cradling Ascalon like a long-lost child. The Hunter had slept, or done whatever the demigod equivalent is, on my couch. I wouldn't be surprised to discover he spent the night cuddling the legendary weapon now that it no longer seemed to hate him.

I let out a groan as I dropped into the passenger seat of Alex's van. My body had finished cataloging the road rash on my knees and back from yesterday's alley showdown and was more than happy to register their pain as a dull throb, like the bass of a neighbor's music at 3 a.m.

My first action of the morning had been to pop more than the doctor-recommended amount of ibuprofen into my mouth. To be fair, it was also my last action before going to sleep, but I was still unbelievably sore. I counted myself lucky that I had joined the Hunt in the era of leather seats and shocks instead of having to stand in the back of a chariot. The ride to the con could have been much less comfortable.

I cast a disgruntled eye at Alex, who looked no worse for wear despite having been beaten up about the same amount as I had yesterday when Polaris's cronies ambushed us. Stupid supernatural healing genes. Not for the first time I wondered if I could take a blood transfusion or something and get a little of extra resiliency for myself.

"Big day," I commented to the car as we fought our way through traffic like salmon swimming upstream.

Orion grunted, which in Hunter speech usually translates to "Yes, obviously" or "No, shut up." I didn't let Orion's reticence slow me down. The votes today would have major repercussions for my chances of getting my soul back—which is a little self-centered, I know.

If the council voted to admit the Dandelion Court back into the fellowship, then, as a dual citizen, I would be eligible to complete an Impossible Task and make Dan's contract null and void. Orion still had complicated feelings on the matter, and now that I knew the depths of Gloriana's betrayal, I understood them a little better.

But Gloriana was dead. Long live Dawn, the new Queen of All Fae.

As far as I could tell, there were only upsides for me if the Dandelion Court got their status back, and the only possible downsides died with Gloriana. But as I glanced in my rearview mirror at the brooding Hunter, I could only hope he agreed. Because if the vote did not go Dawn's way, I was going to get kicked to the curb to fight off Hell on my own.

"What are we going to do about the Draco vote?" Alex asked, reminding me that not everything is about me. "There's no way it passes, is there?"

"I don't know," Orion replied, his gaze focused out the window. He seemed unusually broody and pensive, which is a bit like saying Seattle was rainier than normal. "Centuries ago, I would have said there was no chance it passed. But after yesterday, I fear there is more afoot than I know."

"Yeah, getting jumped in an alley by another Constellation doesn't make me feel great," I remarked, "but that might be the bruises talking."

"Still bitter," Alex muttered. I chose to take the high road for once and ignored him.

"If Polaris has decided he would rather see the Hunt go extinct than keep that monster in chains, it is very likely many members of the Congregation will follow his lead," Orion stated far too calmly.

"How bad is that exactly?" I asked. "I know you said he was as close to a god as a dragon gets, but I don't know what that means."

"Remember how dragons are cursed, and they can't adopt their true forms?" Alex said, glancing over at me with a serious look on his face. "Draco can get closer than all the rest."

"Oh. That sounds pretty bad."

"He is the eldest dragon, the first of their kind. One of the last true monsters," Orion added from the back.

"Okay, so hypothetically..." I paused, trying to figure out power scales in my head. This was always so much easier in video games, where everyone had a mathematical number attached to all their stats. "...who would win in a fight, Zagan or Draco?"

Orion was silent for a moment as he thought about it, which was already scary enough for me. I had been hoping the answer was *Zagan*, with no hesitation. I already had enough terrifying creatures to fight, thank you very much.

"Depends," he finally answered.

"Depends on what?"

"Whichever one of them lets loose first, I think," the Hunter replied grimly.

Filled with troubling thoughts of a monstrous lizard man, we eventually made our way to the same parking garage and left Alex's van a few spots over from where Orion's bike waited. I grabbed another pistol from the back to replace the one I had lost in the fight yesterday and pulled my Hunt badge over my head.

The lines of mortal nerds were even longer today, snaking out and around the convention center like an endless quagmire. Angelenos huddled in their coats, bundled up against the crisp sixty-degree weather. I didn't blame them—spending your whole life in the Summer Lands of California will absolutely ruin your body's ability to process the cold.

Once more our industry badges let us breeze through "security" unquestioned, and within moments we were inside the convention center. This might have been my first convention, but I could get used to skipping lines. Standing in that mess of shivering humanity didn't seem like how I ever wanted to spend a Saturday.

"Wow, I made good time," Alex complimented himself, looking at his watch. "The Congregation doesn't convene for about an hour. Can we go buy some nerd stuff?"

Orion relented with a grunt and followed Alex and me as we headed to the main floor in Hall A. I was blown away by the scale of the operation that was waiting for us. Booths were set up in the style of a sprawling flea market, marked off in rows and lanes, as thousands of convention guests wandered around, admiring art, games, and more.

Eager as a kid in a toy shop, Alex led us down an aisle, stopping to admire giant drawings of famous characters and worlds, which is entirely on brand for a two-hundred-year-old superhuman whose walls are plastered with fantasy posters. I had to admit it was pretty cool. Orion trailed behind us, radiating tension. Even mortals didn't seem eager to stand too close to the brooding Hunter, which made shopping in the crowd easier.

Alex was animatedly bargaining with an artist over a framed poster of some old book cover when I spied a familiar face farther down the aisle. My heart lurched in my chest as I recognized Violet and Connor dressed in subdued cosplay working their way toward us.

Instinctively, I ducked to the other side of Orion, trying to use the sturdy Nephilim like the trunk of an oak tree. All I had to do was scootch my way around him as they passed by, and I would be in the clear. I didn't need this complication, not right now.

"Matt! Alex!" Connor shouted in cheerful greeting. With a defeated sigh, I leaned around my Nephilim shield and did my best to fake surprised delight at seeing my friends.

"What are you guys doing here?" I demanded in playful tones. Behind me, I felt Orion withdraw, his looming presence pulling back like the sun passing behind heavy clouds. Fearless warrior that he is, he doesn't like mortals much. I wonder if he feels about us how I feel about cockroaches.

"Violet won tickets in a contest and insisted we come and check it out," my college friend explained with a grin. "What are the odds?" I felt a chill run down my spine as I considered that. What were the odds indeed. Probably better than they should be, when Dan's deal is involved. "I had no idea you were into this nerd stuff."

Somehow when he said it, it wasn't as complimentary as Alex. I didn't blame him; this wasn't really poor Connor's kind of thing. My lean friend looked out of place in his brown tunic and elf ears. He works in finance; it takes your soul in a different way.

"Of course he is!" Violet insisted brightly, stepping forward to give me a fierce hug. A chill settled over me as I returned her embrace, which was a little too tight, a little too comfortable. Since Dan messed with her mind, something has been off with our interactions. I know whatever he did to her made her think she loved me, but whenever I looked in her eyes, they were clouded in a way I could never unsee. One more person counting on me to tear this contract to shreds.

"Are you calling me a nerd?" I asked, my mouth moving automatically.

"Of course." She punched me lightly on the shoulder. "In the best kind of way." I thought that was a little rich coming from a woman wearing fake pointed elf ears, and a daisy chain crown in her blond hair. Her green eyes sparkled brightly as she smiled at me.

"I'll have you know I'm only here because I'm working," I protested.

"We just got here, is there anything cool to see?" Connor inquired, his eyes drifting to the posters Alex was haggling over. "Wait a second, is that a *Lord of the Rings* and Chargers mash-up?" He wandered off toward the booth, his eyes narrowed in fascinated horror.

Goose bumps flared on my arms as Connor left. That had started happening more and more, as if Dan's impetus made him easily distractible when he was around Violet and me. He always seemed to find a reason to leave us alone.

"How have you been? You got a job! Tell me everything," Violet ordered, slipping her arm through mine in a parody of the way Ash often walked with me. She had never done that before, but it felt very deliberate. For a moment, a small beacon of loneliness burned in my chest. Before I had been sucked into the supernatural world, Violet and Connor were my best friends; their companionship had kept me sane after my family was killed. I missed having them as the comfortable foundation of my found family. But the dark secrets that spanned between us were chasms too wide to cross.

"Yeah, I got a job," I replied, using my arm to brush my hair back, forcing her to let go. Now all I had to do was figure out how to explain being a member of the Hunt to her. "One of Alex's friends runs a gym that does fantasy combat training."

"Like magic and spells?"

"No, but close. Swords, spears, that kind of stuff."

"So you're, what, helping teach people how to be extra cool at the Renaissance fair?"

"Sometimes, yeah. His more advanced students are like stunt doubles and stuff."

"Oh, that's cool. Are you going to be in a movie?"

"One step at a time," I said with a smirk. "I still have a lot to learn from him."

"Well, you look great." She squeezed my biceps with her hand. "The workout regime is clearly agreeing with you." My stomach did a weird flip-flop of pleasure and terror. I couldn't do this, not today. In less than an hour, the Congregation was going to vote on whether the Dandelion Court was allowed back into the fellowship. My soul quite literally was hanging in the balance.

"I'm so glad you guys are here," I told her, freeing my arm for the second time. "My break is almost over, and I gotta get back to the booth before my boss murders me. Maybe we can meet up when my shift is over?"

We couldn't. But in LA it's polite to pretend you might socialize with someone at a future moment even if you have no intention of doing so. Don't ask me why, it's all part of the ritual.

"That would be so fun," Violet gushed, giving me another bright smile. "When are you done?"

"I'm not really sure, it's kind of one of those depends-on-how-it-goes…" I lost my train of thought as a dragon walked behind her. Doyle stalked through the main aisle, his little round sunglasses covering his weird pupils.

Suddenly, I remembered Samael had promised to deliver the weapon to Doyle today. It was too early for the Congregation to start, and I doubted the dragon was a plushy collector. So why was he here, prowling through the nerd collectibles?

That seemed like something both my bosses would want to know.

"Crap, that's my manager. I'm late." I patted her on the shoulder and sprinted past her, following the Dragon Don. "I'll text you guys!" I lied over my shoulder. I spotted Orion a row over and jerked my head at the back of the dragon. He gave me a somber nod and tilted his head to the other side. I tossed him a lazy salute, and we split up, leaving Alex to his poster shopping.

I slid out into the main hall and did my best to follow the lizard without him noticing. Thanks to the fantastical expectations of the convention, no one gave Doyle's scaly face more than a second glance as he moved through the crowd. His bright-red hair sure did stand out, so following him was easy.

I took point, making sure to stay close, while Orion trailed off to my left, flitting like a specter the next row down, nearby but never getting in the dragon's line of sight. It was a lot easier for me to blend in than the six-foot-six Nephilim with a sword strapped to his back.

Doyle marched straight down the center of the convention floor, never even casting a curious glance at any of the booths he passed, which only heightened my suspicions. He definitely wasn't here to sightsee; this dragon was on a mission. He walked to the end of the hall and pushed through a pair of metal doors that swung open into a hallway on the back side of the building. The Dragon Don vanished behind the doors as they swung closed behind them.

Heart pounding, I waited a handful of seconds before I strolled up to the doors, doing my best to look like I was supposed to be there. I glanced over my shoulder and made eye contact with Orion, still a few rows over. With a shrug, I gently pressed on the bar and eased the door open, trying not to make enough noise to wake the dead.

I peeked through, just in time to see Doyle walk into another entryway across the narrow service hallway. I slipped through the door and caught it as it swung back behind me, stopping it from slamming shut. I made my way down the hall, treading softly as Orion had taught me. As I drew close to the open entrance, I again stuck my head out to see if the coast was clear.

The hallway opened into another cavernous convention hall, similar in size to the one that held the booths, but unlike its neighbor, this one was empty. Most of the lights were off, except for a few in the middle.

Standing in the pool of light in the center of the windowless room, Doyle waited with his arms crossed. His forked tongue flicked out in irritation as he looked around the dark. I slid into the back of the hall, crouching in the inky shadows to avoid notice.

I didn't have to wait long.

Doors on the far side of the convention hall opened, letting morning light pour in as three people entered. I shut my eyes against the burst of brightness until I heard them slam shut, plunging us back into the dark.

Blinking against the spots dancing behind my eyelids, I crouch-walked my way along the wall, inching closer to the group in the center. Three humans strode into the puddle of light to meet the Don. The Chinese woman in the center wore a charcoal pantsuit, and her black hair was wrapped up in a tight bun. She looked familiar, but I couldn't place her. One of the men with her carried a black leather briefcase in his hands.

"Dragon," she said by way of greeting.

"Is that it?" Doyle asked.

The woman nodded sharply. "As promised."

"Give it to me." Doyle extended a clawed hand, stepping forward to collect the case from the woman's assistant. She snapped her fingers, freezing the lizard in place.

"Do not waste this on one of your weak kin," she said in steely tones. "Only the strongest among you can hope to master it and not be consumed."

"Spare me your lecture, you *disease*," Doyle snapped, although I noticed he didn't take another step toward the small woman. She gave him a sour look but seemed to relent. She nodded to her bodyguard, who held out the case.

"You understand what is required of you?" the woman asked the Don as he accepted the package. "He shows tremendous trust in you."

"I do. I shall not fail," Doyle promised, surprising me by inclining his head slightly. I didn't know the Irish Dragon Don well, but I didn't think he'd be willing to bow to most mortals.

"See that you do not. My master has promised me a new pair of dragon-leather boots if you do." She turned away, her job done. "Red is not my color, but I might make an exception if you waste my creation."

TWENTY-THREE

HID IN THE shadows as the two groups dispersed. The humans exited out the back while Doyle hurried off with whatever weapon he had just been given. I racked my brain, trying to figure out what kind of weapon a dragon might want. Maybe it would let their fire burn hotter? But dragonfire was already plenty hot. Maybe it was some sort of armor. I suppressed a shudder at the thought of being chased by a scaled monster encased in steel. I didn't need a dragon knight on my list of problems.

I forced myself to be patient and stayed hidden in the shadows. I trusted Orion not to get caught, but for all I knew Doyle had paused in the hall to check out his new toy. The last thing I needed to do was run into him because I was impatient. Eventually my paranoia was satisfied. The coast had to be clear by now. With my heart beating loudly in my ears, I slowly rose to my feet and tiptoed out of the abandoned room.

A man was waiting for me in the hallway.

I froze in guilty shock. The stranger wasn't a dragon; in fact, I was pretty sure he was just a guy. He was very short, with dark hair and a perfectly trimmed goatee. He wore a black suit and a pair of black square sunglasses indoors. My heart continued its plummet as he held up a badge that read FBI in big letters, because I didn't even have to read it to know he was a Fed; his entire persona just screamed it.

"Mr. Carver, can I have a word?"

"Ah, sure," I replied hesitantly, glancing around as if I wasn't in an off-limits hallway, and this was a big impediment to my very busy day. The fact that he knew who I was only made my apprehension worse. "I have a few minutes. What can I do for you, Agent...?"

"Richter," he said, folding his badge and slipping it back into his jacket pocket. "I'm with the Supernatural Crimes Division of the FBI. Do you know what I mean by that?"

My eyes narrowed as I realized the implication of his question. While I had been worried about the cops getting involved in the past, that had mostly been because they had no idea what was going on. An informed law enforcement department was a whole new can of worms.

My understanding was that individuals knew about the supernatural world but not governments. Jones and Rodgers had certainly seemed oblivious in all our interactions. But if there was an entire division of the FBI devoted to it—then my life might get much more complicated.

"I think I have a guess," I replied.

"Great," he continued without a shred of emotion on his face. "Would you mind answering a few questions?"

"Do I have a choice?"

"Several nights ago, you were at the scene of a shoot-out between elements of a supernatural mafia and other unknown perpetrators." I blinked in surprise as he ignored my response.

"While being questioned by LAPD detectives Jones and Rodgers, a Class A Supernatural Type often referred to as a Faerie interrupted your statement and performed some sort of unknown psychic attack to erode the detectives' free will and take you from the scene of the crime, which is at the very least an obstruction of justice."

Not exactly how I would have explained it, but close enough.

"Analysis of the recordings indicates this is a previously unknown Faerie capability, indicating this is a high-level operator within their organization."

"Sorry," I said, cutting him off. "I'm not exactly hearing a question." I could feel my blood pressure rising. How closely was I being watched?

"Last night," he continued, showing no emotion at being interrupted, "you engaged in a firefight with unknown supernatural persons in an alley not far from here. You fled the scene of the crime before law enforcement could arrive."

"Hold on, excuse me—shouldn't that be like allegedly or something?" I demanded, feeling a flush growing at the base of my neck. How did he know?

Agent Richter gave me a flat look, reaching into his jacket pocket and pulling out my missing pistol that had been bagged and tagged by some evidence team. "Does this look familiar?" he asked.

So that's where that went. Oops.

"I made it one count of obstructing justice, two counts of exposing mortals to the supernatural, one count of using a supernatural creature to beguile mortal man, and at least three more counts for reckless endangerment," Richter continued, in the same even tone as if he were telling me the weather. "I could probably lump in assault of an officer with a supernatural power and a few other things if I really wanted to. Detectives Jones and Rodgers have some very interesting theories about a lab that burned down last year. I should mention that thanks to your interference, I've been forced to recruit them to the FBI."

"Still not hearing a question," I replied, trying to sound braver than I felt. The thought of Rodgers and Jones having the power of the Feds behind them was terrifying. The last thing I needed was to spend my remaining years in a prison cell. That would be a death sentence.

"Just now you almost ruined a major operation monitoring a deal between two supernatural organizations." I didn't have to fake how wide my eyes went as I stared at the agent. The FBI had been watching the exchange between Doyle and Samael's people? Maybe I should have kept my nose out of it. This must be how curiosity always got the cats.

"Wait, you guys are watching Doyle?" I asked, sounding as shocked as I felt. "I didn't know about that, I wasn't trying to step on any toes—"

"Are you aware that a large contingent of supernatural leaders are meeting here in LA?"

"…yes," I replied after a moment of thought, once more having to resist the urge to glance at the convention walls around us. If he already knew, I couldn't get in trouble for confirming it, right? I assumed I wasn't supposed to go around telling everyone about it, but if they wanted to hide it, maybe they shouldn't have sold tickets.

"Do you know what they are gathered for, what they are planning?"

"Uh, not really?" I replied. I didn't know what I was supposed to do here. Did he not know he was standing in the very center of the storm he was describing and then asking me about it? "My understanding is it is sort of a routine meeting, nothing too dramatic." Richter's face didn't change as he processed my response, his dark eyes watching me with the cold interest of a bird of prey.

"Several leaders of supernatural mafia organizations are on American soil for the first time in decades," the agent scoffed. "Nothing routine about it."

"I don't know much about them." I held up my hands. "I'm new to all this, and that's a whole different ball game." The more he talked, the more confident I started feeling. This guy didn't know everything, only enough to be dangerous.

"Do you know where this large meeting will be held?" Richter pulled out a notepad and jotted down some notes.

"That's a bit above my pay grade," I replied with a shrug. "You gotta be somebody to get an invite to something like that, I think." Richter nodded and wrote some more.

"Mr. Carver, I think you're a good, mortal man caught up in something you don't understand." The arrogance was practically blinding. "I think we can help each other."

"Oh?" *This should be good.*

"My department is willing to overlook some of your, let's call them felonies, in exchange for good work in helping me keep an eye on the mafia while they are here."

"Are you trying to make me some sort of confidential informant?" I asked, feeling a little stunned.

"If you'd prefer, I could start processing all the paperwork I have about you on my desk." Richter's flat voice told me I really didn't want him to do that. "Maybe write up both of your super friends while I'm at it. The Class B one with the sword and the Class D you live with were both in the alley altercation with you."

I resisted the urge to blink in surprise. As a human, I had briefly felt a hint of relief that my government knew about the supernatural world. That's one of the things a government is supposed to be *for*, the care and protection of its people, right? Serve and protect and all that jazz.

The fact the FBI had a Supernatural Crimes Division that was breathing down my neck was annoying, but I had, for a short moment, felt a little safer on my mortal friends' behalf. I'd even entertained the idea that maybe the United States of America could negotiate with Hell to get my soul back.

But the more Agent Richter talked, the more that good feeling went away.

If for some reason they thought Robin was a higher tier of power than Orion, then we weren't any safer with their help. Whoever was running the shop over there clearly thought they knew more than they did. But whatever they did or did not know, I didn't see a way for me to get out of this without playing ball with them—at least a little bit. I was sure there was some little tidbit I could feed them that would keep Richter off my back.

"I don't want any trouble," I said, raising my hands in a placating gesture. "I'm happy to do what I can to help. This *mafia* are no friends of mine, and if you looked through the reports, then you know I was attacked at Balsamic."

"Good." Richter nodded as if I was being very reasonable and playing nice.

Only a lifetime of training to be a smart-ass kept me from rolling my eyes. "What do you need from me?" I asked.

"I will expect reports."

"Naturally." I nodded.

"I want to know what they are up to, what they are planning, and where they are meeting."

"On it," I said.

"Here's my card. Call me as soon as you hear anything." I glanced down at the small piece of FBI-branded paper with his name and number. Apparently, our Agent Richter was a Steven. He kind of looked like a Steven.

"Oh, Matt?" Richter called over his shoulder as he walked away. "Do a good job. I'd hate to have to bring you in."

"You got it, boss," I replied, tossing him a mock salute.

Feeling unbelievably lucky to have survived two different close calls, I dashed back out into the main floor as soon as the agent was gone. It only took me a matter of moments to spot Orion towering over the convention-goers. The big Nephilim was wound tight; his black eyes looked relieved to see me in once piece. Alex had bought the poster and somehow managed to shake Violet and Connor. He carried his purchase neatly wrapped in a long cardboard tube like a baton.

Together we made our way out of mortal Hall A and toward Hall B while I caught them up to speed with what I had seen and my encounter with Agent Richter.

"A dragon knight, huh? Sounds dumb," Alex offered after I finished. The small frown on his face told me he felt left behind once again.

"Whatever wickedness the serpents are up to, we will handle it the same way," Orion promised grimly.

"Wild they have spooky FBI agents again, though," Alex remarked. "I didn't think they were still doing that, not since the Pinkertons. Remember the Pinkertons, Orion?"

The Hunter grunted in a tone that could only be described as sour.

I could feel my tension building like a low cello note as we got closer to the hall. It was almost time for the Dandelion Court vote. I could practically feel a giant scale hovering above me waiting to pass judgment on my soul.

To my surprise, Bellerophon stood guard at the door again today. He looked no worse for wear, but his dark eyes glittered madly as he watched us approach. Orion ignored the lesser Nephilim's pointed looks. The eagle does not notice the chirping of sparrows—unless he is hungry.

Never one to miss a chance to be petty, I gave him a friendly eyebrow wiggle as we slid past.

The interior of Hall B was much as we left it yesterday, the stadium bowl already full of Nephilim and thrumming with an eager energy.

My gaze strayed to the side, where I spotted Ash and the rest of the Dandelion Court lurking in the cocktail area. My betrothed gave me an urgent wave, beckoning me over.

With a nod to Alex and Orion, I split off and jogged past the empty buffet line. Hopefully that would be full once the vote was completed. I'd want to either celebrate or eat away my sorrows. I slowed down to a more appropriate pace as I stepped up next to the Autumn Lady. She was dressed in a white and gold outfit that looked like it had been modeled after a Roman legionnaire but smiled in welcome as she reached a hand toward my wrist.

"How are things?" I asked, glancing past her to where Dawn simmered, dressed in a similarly martial fashion.

"Tense," she murmured, following my gaze. "Is everything on your end—you smell like perfume."

"As ready we can—sorry, what?" I stumbled over my words as I processed Ash's change of topic. I turned to meet her green gaze but found myself staring into two golden pools instead. She did not repeat herself, and I felt the back of my neck grow warm as an embarrassed heat filled me. I don't even know why; I hadn't done anything wrong.

"We ran into some mortal friends of mine, must be from one of them," I rushed to explain. "I didn't even notice."

"Matthew!" Dawn snapped from inside the Fae huddle, her harsh tone slicing through this delicate moment like a chef's knife. "Is the Hunter going to do as he promised?"

With superhuman effort, I managed to tear my gaze away from Ash's unhappy stare and turned to the Queen. "He's a man of his word, Dawn."

"Yes, but he can lie," Dawn hissed as she stalked toward me. Her ornate armor rustled as she moved. Her golden crown shone in her bound hair; she looked like a warrior queen ready for combat.

It's probably hard for a Faerie bound by the rigid rules of her kind to have faith in a being that isn't restricted in the same way she is. But this was Orion we were talking about. If I couldn't trust him, who could I trust?

"We're good," I promised, meeting her golden gaze with my calmest stare. I did my best to ignore Ash radiating a cold so deep she could have been the Lady of Winter next to me.

"See to it that we are," she snarled, her eyes boring into mine, "or you will have to find yourself a new sponsor for your Impossible Task." I had never seen the Queen this raw before, which told me how much this vote was eating at her.

"Yes, you've been very clear," I told her dryly.

"Yet you are still here." Dawn's eyes flashed. "Shouldn't you be wrangling the Hunter?"

I tossed Ash an apologetic look, and her icy one in return told me our conversation was far from finished. I fled Dawn's stress bubble and trotted back up the bowl to join the rest of the Hunt in the same seats we used yesterday. The bitter-faced stranger was in the chair next to me again. His oddly colored eyes glinted like prisms in the lights as he glanced my way. I gave him a friendly little smile and sat, gazing at the arena before us.

"Of course they kept the rejects next to each other," the man grumbled to me, shifting in his seat.

"Sorry?" I replied, turning to look at him. I never was a popular kid in school, but the term "reject" still stung a little. I was a Squire of the Hunt. I had earned my place in this room.

"The mortal and the mutt," he laughed, gesturing between us. "Half these pointy pricks would love to see us six feet under, not sitting in their meetings dirtying up their air with our *impure* bloodlines."

Nephilim tend to take a lot of social standing from their genetic makeup. The ratios of human and demon DNA in their bloodlines literally dictate how strong they are. I understood why it was a thing, but it definitely made me feel itchy whenever it came up.

Orion had been harsh toward Alex when they first met because of the difference in their blends but had slowly changed his opinion of us both. Given my new neighbor's attitude, I wondered if being willing to change like that was unusual for the elder Nephilim. I knew it was for elder humans. I can only imagine how set someone might become in their ways after a millennium.

"I'm new," I replied with a shrug. "I know I'm a mortal, but I don't know what Polaris meant when he called you... *that*."

"It means what it sounds like," the man replied, shifting agitatedly in his seat again. "The Nephilim are descendants of demons and men. To be a member of the Congregation, you must be a Nephilim."

"But dragons..." I said, not meaning to interrupt.

"But dragons indeed." He gave me an approving nod. "You must be a Nephilim or a suitably *worthy* exception."

"Oh, it's one of *those* clubs."

"Nephilim like to act as though they are all there is," he hissed. "They tolerate the Fae because they're cousins, and they kept their own line *true* after they forked from the Nephilim tree."

"But you're not a Fae or Nephilim?" I asked, gently, hoping that would not be an offensive question. He'd brought it up; I was just trying to understand what we were talking about.

"I am everything." He laughed bitterly. "Not all of our ancestors followed the rules."

"You're a supernatural melting pot," I breathed, surprised I hadn't thought about that before. Most of my exposure had only been to demons and Nephilim, but I knew there was more.

"I had a great-grandfather who was a Nephilim." He raised his chin proudly. "I can trace at least two different werewolf lines, and a dozen other lineages have been forgotten among my ancestry."

Even though he was a little unpleasant, I couldn't help but feel bad for the guy. I couldn't imagine how hard it would be to be supernatural but... different. Well, maybe I could. Now that I thought about it, it sounded very similar to being a mortal but in the supernatural world. I didn't have anyone else like me around who could understand.

Some days were lonelier than others.

"Last time when you, uh, tried to speak, you said something about a group of the Forgotten?" I asked, understanding beginning to form now that I had a better frame of reference for what had happened during the last session.

"It's the name we've given ourselves," he replied, strange eyes fixed on the empty podium below. "A place for the forgotten by-blows of monsters and men. We've been begging to be admitted to the Congregation for a century, but you saw how that usually goes."

"Not great," I agreed, giving him a sad look.

"That is why I am here." He leaned past me eagerly trying to catch Orion's eyes. "If more Nephilim were like you, Hunter, we might stand a chance of getting into the Congregation. Would you stand for us?"

Orion was silent for a long moment, his black eyes staring at the man. I wondered if he was wrestling with old judgments or merely struggling like Atlas under the weight of his burdens. The guy had a lot on his plate.

"I fear you would not want my help, Gregor," he said at last, turning to look at the entrance. I followed his gaze and stared in shock as Sagittarius walked in, her legs working far better than they should have, although she moved with the hint of a limp.

I felt the urge to take another ibuprofen.

It just wasn't fair.

"But you're the Hunter," Gregor protested, incredulity running across his narrow face. "No one here would dare stand against you."

"We'll see about that," Orion replied dryly.

Gregor's pleas were interrupted by the note of the first bell sounding. Immediately the room went silent, all the conversations around us dropping dead like a man on the gallows.

The second bell rang, its clear notes sounding the clarion call of the Congregation. I felt adrenaline course through my veins, the scrapes and bruises suddenly fading from my consciousness as my body switched over to battle mode.

This was it.

The third bell sounded and let loose the dogs of war—or in this case, the Nephilim of politics, which might be worse.

Polaris and the Coronas processed in as they had the day before. Once again Borealis called the roll, with every Constellation present except the South Star, Octantis. As the "Absent" call faded from the room and Ariadne furled her scroll, Polaris once more stepped up to the podium.

"You know what we are meeting today to discuss," he said without preamble, black eyes sweeping the room as he stared at different Constellations before settling his gaze on Orion. "Let us begin. The Ruling Council sees fit to bring before the Congregation a motion. We propose the readmission of the Dandelion Court to our august membership."

As he spoke the doors opened, and Dawn led her sisters to the podium. All four wore matching white legionnaire armor and had their hair in tight ponytails. They looked like soldiers instead of courtiers. Mav and Tania still wore their golden collars, which gleamed in reflection of the powerful lights above. My eyes sought out Ash, but her attention was focused on her sisters. She hovered at the back of their diamond, watching over everything.

"Dawn, Queen of All Fae, will present her case, and then we shall discuss." Polaris stepped back from the podium and gestured for her to take his place.

Dawn strode to the front of the room, her eyes fully golden. She looked every inch a Queen. As much as I hated Gloriana, I knew she would be proud of her daughter.

"Centuries ago, the Dandelion Court was voted out of this Congregation," Dawn began, her voice bold and strong. "I believe the results of that vote were correct and just."

Surprised murmurs broke out in the crowd.

"My mother led her people in the way she sought fit," Dawn pressed. "When she came to power, she broke faiths that should not have been broken. We Fae have paid for those broken promises in oceans of blood." The Queen of All Fae inclined her head in Orion's direction.

Another round of muttering rippled throughout the room.

I watched Orion out of the corner of my eye, but the Hunter was stone-faced, patient. A faint tickle of dread ran down my spine. Maybe Dawn was right to be worried about the Hunter's ability to lie. Was I wrong to trust him?

"I say again that we Fae have been punished for our crimes. My own mother has reaped the final reward of being estranged from the fellowship of this Congregation. Her body now lies encased in the marble mausoleum of my ancestors."

I blinked once in surprise at her words. Gloriana's fall had been due to her daughter being desperate to be free and the whispers of demons. I wasn't sure how they were related...I knew Ash and Tania had never been allowed to leave the palace of Goldhall because of their mother's paranoia. Had that been enough to drive Tania to kill her own mother? I suppose you could make that argument.

"My mother is dead. I am Queen now. Already I have begun to right her wrongs." That sentence seemed like one for the Hunter more than the Constellations gathered here. "My people have suffered enough for oaths they did not break and at the hands of enemies they did not choose to make. It is time for us to be allowed to rejoin our cousins and sit once more in fellowship with this body."

With another slight incline of her head, Dawn, Queen of All Fae, stepped back and gestured for Polaris to resume his perch. I did my best not to let out a little cheer. That was a pretty good speech.

The ancient Nephilim leaned on the podium and looked around the room, one white eyebrow arched. Tension vibrated in my chest like a thousand thrumming butterflies. Many of the Constellations were leaning forward in their seats, waiting to speak.

"Well," the North Star said dryly, "what do we think?"

At least twenty Nephilim leapt to their feet, waving their hands, screaming their lungs out, demanding to be heard.

"Order!" Polaris snarled, looking around the room. "Grus, I saw you up first."

The rest of the yelling Nephilim dropped into their seats, leaving a tall, thin man with birdlike legs standing alone. I found it more than a little ironic that one of the longest-lasting government bodies in the world operated on a who-stood-up-first model like we used to use in preschool.

"What right have you to claim membership in this Congregation?" he demanded, pointing down at Dawn. "Your mother was Faerie through and through, but you're not."

Shouts of approval echoed around the room. I don't know how the acoustics in a three-quarter-bowl stadium work, but it sure sounded like there had been less volume in the cheers for Dawn than the ones for this Grus guy.

Dawn stepped forward, golden eyes dancing with fire. "I'm more than enough Faerie to throw you through whichever wall you prefer, Crane."

Roars of approval echoed from other sides of the bowl.

"Gemini, you wished to say something?" Polaris shifted his head. A pair of identical women rose to their feet. They spoke in tandem, alternating which of them said the word.

"We—wish—to—know—what—the—Hunter—thinks," they intoned.

No one cheered. The collective weight of eighty-six other Constellations' attentions descended upon us in a crushing wave.

Slowly, the Hunter rose to his feet as Gemini sat. Orion's face was cold. An eternity passed as the two enemies stared at each other. I felt my nerves begin to build.

Something felt wrong. Why had he not voiced his approval? What was he waiting for? This had all been agreed, and the Faerie had already made good on their bargain this time. He had Ascalon. All he had to do was give his support, and we had a chance—I would have a chance.

But I knew that look on his face, it was one of awful, unrelenting judgment. It was the last thing many monsters had seen over the millennia. There was no more give in him than a mountain.

"Please," I begged in a panicked whisper.

Down below, Dawn tilted her head to the side, a wicked understanding glittering in her eyes.

"I vote no!" roared the Hunter.

I felt my stomach crumple in on itself in despair as the room exploded, Gregor cheering loudly. At the head of the chaos, Polaris gave Orion a small, annoyed smile before turning his attention to the tumult around us.

"Order!" screamed the North Star once again, his commands going unheeded as the Constellations continued shouting at one another. I stared straight ahead, looking at nothing, unable to comprehend this door being slammed shut in my face. My chance to get my soul back and protect my sister was gone. Dashed to the floor by the Hunter's rage.

"Order!" Polaris demanded. Again the sea of noise ignored him.

"I said order!" The elder Nephilim's voice echoed around the room, this time exerting Presence with a capital *P*. My mouth dried up in fear. I could not have stood up if my life depended on it. The shadows in the room danced around Polaris as he extended both hands in dark command.

There was Order. The angry shouts of the Congregation were strangled out by the North Star's will until only silence remained. For a long moment, Polaris kept his hands extended, glaring. Satisfied that he had regained control, he lowered his hands, and the Presence withdrew, like a light being hidden under a bushel. Whatever that means.

No one dared to speak. My stomach felt queasy. I wasn't entirely sure what the North Star had just done to the room. It reminded me of Ascalon's furious aura, but stronger by an order of magnitude. I now knew he hadn't earned his position based just on his good looks.

"The Hunter has cast his vote," the North Star said coolly, as if he hadn't just screamed at all of us. "We will now proceed with the rest of the Congregation's votes, in an *orderly* fashion." A flash of anger glinted in his eyes as he paused to look around the room again. No one made so much as a peep.

Polaris gave a satisfied nod and stepped back to allow Ariadne to take his place. She unfurled her scroll once more and read out the first name with a clarion voice: "Andromeda."

Dawn stared up at us, her face composed. But I knew her well enough to see the rage hiding in the way she slowly rubbed her fingers together. Her blazing golden eyes weren't fixed on the Hunter; they locked on me. Ash too shot me a worried glance, and I tried to give them a smile but couldn't quite muster one from the ruins of my hope.

I was going to Hell.

A tall, dark woman with a crown, sitting at the right hand of Cassiopeia, rose from the sea of the Constellations and spoke: "I vote yea."

"She voted *against* the Hunter?" Gregor gasped quietly next to me.

Even though I knew there were many more Constellations to go, I felt a small flame of hope rekindle in that moment.

"Antlia," called the Corona Borealis.

"Yea," a voice replied from the bowl.

The muted whispers grew, like the building tension of an orchestra's wood section. So it continued down the list. One by one, the Constellations were called and voted to admit the Dandelion Court back into the Congregation.

I was over the moon. There was to be no dashing of my hopes on the ground. The Hunter's face was impassive, carved from something harder than granite, as his peers voted against him.

I didn't understand that something was wrong until they called on a familiar face. Cassiopeia rose from her seat beside Andromeda—her daughter, I realized—and stared at Orion for a long moment, a thoughtful expression on her face.

I consigned myself to the fact that she would vote no. She was the Hunter's friend and ally. Without her aid, Lilith would have killed me. She would vote with Orion, but I promised myself I wouldn't hold it against her. She had no way to know that I needed—

"Yea," Cassiopeia said and sat back down.

Something wasn't right.

Gregor, who had become increasingly agitated at each Constellation vote, finally boiled over. "How dare they, Hunter," he hissed over me at Orion, who had not moved a muscle since the vote had started. "How dare they disrespect the one who saved them—"

Orion cut him off with a raised fist, not even bothering to turn away from where he stared at Dawn.

Certain I was missing something, I sat back in my chair to think. A year spent with Ash and Robin had helped me expand my understanding of politics, but by no means was I a master at it. Still, something tickled my consciousness like a faint breeze. Cassie had clearly figured it out. Now I needed to.

I followed Orion's gaze down to the center, to see what he was looking at. Dawn was practically glowing, her earlier rage banished like the morning fog by the sun. Her delighted face tracked each Constellation as they rose, beaming at them as they cast their vote in her favor. Orion wasn't staring at the Queen of All Fae, I realized. He was watching Polaris standing at the edge of the dais. The North Star's eyes were narrowed as he glowered up at the Constellations. As if he felt the weight of my scrutiny, his glance swept back up and paused on me before flicking over to Orion, measuring the Hunter's reaction. It took much of my self-control not to shiver while he was looking at me.

The yeas continued unanimously until we got to Sagittarius. The Archer rose to her feet slower than most of her peers, her face mottled with rage. "No," she screeched. "No, no, no."

It was seeing the Archer panic that made me realize the clever Hunter had set a trap of his own. Or more accurately, there had been a trap, and Orion had avoided it. Once, few would dare to stand against the Hunter's will, especially when it came to the Fae.

But if Orion was right, this entire Congregation had been a setup to bring him down. If Polaris was half the politician I suspected he was, than he had puppets in the crowd under orders to vote *against* whatever the Hunter voted for. By voting no, Orion had actually made it possible for the Fae to get in. If he was right, it was a brilliant read of the situation.

But that sentiment did not bode well for the rest of the Congregation, I realized with a sinking feeling. How many of these votes were Constellations who'd figured out Orion's game, and how many were Nephilim brazenly defying the Hunter?

I guess we'd find out.

The vote continued. I ran out of fingers and lost count, but even I could tell it was a landslide victory. The Dandelion Court was going to be a member of the Constellation Congregation once more.

I had done what Dawn had asked of me. I could complete an Impossible Task.

I could get my soul back.

Below me, Dawn's smile lit up the room like her namesake. Even icy Mav looked pleased. After the last member—Vulpecula—finally answered "yea," the vote ended. A few more Constellations had voted nay, but I wasn't sure if that was because they were smart enough to realize what the Hunter was doing and wanted to oppose him, or if they wanted to support him and were too stupid to see what he was up to. I did notice that all the reptilian votes were against us: Hydrus, his wife Hydra, and Serpens all voted no. So did Scorpius, who I think technically counts as an insect. But their votes were too little too late.

"With a vote of sixty-five to twenty, and two abstentions, the yeas have it," Corona Australis intoned in a booming voice.

"Let the will of the Congregants be done," Polaris replied. "The Dandelion Court is to be reinstated as a full member of the Congregation on the advent of the new year." As he spoke, he raised a small wooden mallet and struck the podium with a sharp crack. Dawn's eyes flared slightly at the stipulation. All around the bowl, the room broke into awkward, offbeat applause. I saw more than a few Constellations exchange confused glances, unsure if they were happy or sad about the outcome.

"The what now?" I whispered to Alex. "Why not immediately?"

"Could be like health insurance," my friend said, shrugging. "You have to join during the enrollment period. There's always some sort of stupid bureaucracy in these things."

"Or?" I pressed.

"Or someone doesn't want them to have the protections that come with being a card-carrying member this weekend," he finished, his own theory matching mine.

"Exposed and unable to vote," I agreed grimly.

"With the first item on the agenda resolved, we are adjourned until the afternoon session," Polaris announced, returning to the podium. "We will resume promptly at three p.m. to pass judgment on the complaints against the Hunter."

Somewhere, the bell rang again, signifying the end of the meeting. Immediately, Constellations began to get to their feet and the volume of conversation rose. I glanced at Orion, who had still not moved from his seat. A wry smile twisted his mouth, like someone who had just seen an ex-girlfriend with her new lover.

"That was quick thinking," I whispered to him. Even with everyone talking around me, I was trying to be careful. There were about a hundred people in this room who could hear a butterfly's wingbeat. Orion gave a small shrug but didn't reply.

"What's got you bummed out?" Alex asked, looking at Orion in surprise. "We won, didn't we?"

"You didn't expect that many to vote against you, did you?" I realized with a flash of insight.

"That was... worse than I feared," Orion agreed grimly.

"Some of them figured it out," I protested. "I'm almost certain Cassiopeia knew."

"The Canis brothers may also have figured it out," Orion offered with another small shrug. "They have always been loyal friends."

"But the rest of the votes against you..." I didn't finish my sentence. Realistically, while this vote had been important for me personally, it was the least important on the grand scale—for the world. Orion might have managed to trick a few people into voting how he wanted on this first one, but the truth was it was only possible to trick them because his view had changed.

When Orion himself was called before the Congregation, if the room was stacked against him, there would be no fooling the crowd on which way to vote.

"Hunter!" Dawn's voice interrupted our little pity party with ease. "What in all the depths of the Hungry Abyss was that?"

Dawn and her sisters made their way up to us, energy radiating off her like a storm. She cut her way through the exiting crowd with ease. Even Constellations didn't want to get in her way when she was fired up.

"Dawn, it's not what you think—" I rushed, leaping to my feet to put myself between the two of them before she could start a fight. Orion was in a sour enough mood that he might take her up on it. I just needed to make her understand that when he'd voted no, it had actually been in her best interest.

"It was brilliant!" she crowed, ignoring me. "I didn't know you had that kind of guile in you."

"Oh, never mind, it is what you thought it was," I said lamely, getting out of the Immortal's way.

"Inspired," the Queen of All Fae continued, her giant grin still shining bright. "It took me a second to see it, but the moment I did, I knew we had won." She paused, tucking a strand of blond hair behind her ear, composing herself. "Thank you." She inclined her head in respect. "I will not forget this thing that you have done for me and for my people."

"You're welcome."

There was a moment of companionable silence, as if a hundred-year-old wound had finally gotten its first stitches, which isn't how wounds work, but I digress.

"Even with your ploy, I didn't expect that many to vote against you," Dawn murmured in more serious tones after the healing moment had passed.

"Once, they would not have dared," Orion grumbled softly to no one in particular. "But it seems that since the Fall of the Hunt, they have forgotten who I am."

"Well, we've got about an hour," I said, checking the clock on my phone. "Think we can remind them a little?"

THE COMBINED DANDELION-and-Hunt swept out of the bowl into the reception area with an entourage that would be impressive for any celebrity. Dawn only made it a dozen feet before she was swarmed by Constellations congratulating her. Suddenly there were plenty of Nephilim who wanted to be on her good side.

The rest of us left her behind, driven by the almost audible ticking of Time's clock. The final grains of sand were trickling out of the hourglass until the next vote began. As I followed Orion into the throng, a warm hand wrapped around my left arm in a familiar way. I turned to smile at my betrothed, Ash, still wearing her legionnaire outfit.

"Congratulations," I said, giving her a warm smile. "How does it feel?" I could only hope that such a huge victory would put whatever little speed bump we had hit before the session in the rearview mirror.

Ash was silent for a moment as she gazed around the room. Thanks to her father, she shared as much kinship with the beings here as she did with the Fae. But there was no warmth in her green eyes as she evaluated her cousins. "Empty," she answered after a few moments. "Endless bureaucracy that amasses power for its own gain."

"Around here, we just call it politics," I told her.

"I don't know, Squire Carver," an elegant voice interjected. "Some of us call it keeping everyone else alive." The North Star appeared at our elbows, holding a glass of red wine and a faintly bemused smile, like a grandfather who has just watched his descendant pull a cookie out of the cookie jar without realizing she's been caught. "Congratulations to the Dandelion Court," he continued, giving a small bow to Ash that was somehow polite and mocking at the same time.

"Thank you, Polaris," Ash replied formally. "It is wonderful to be restored to fellowship with our peers."

"I'm sure." His dark eyes sparkled as he took a sip of his wine. "It was well done by the Hunter, to change his vote," he offered without any pretense. "I must confess I thought that he wouldn't notice how the winds have shifted over the centuries."

I blinked in surprise as this blatant admission that he'd manipulated the vote against Orion. While no one can resist a good monologue, even the dastardliest of villains rarely spills the beans after the opening round. Especially if they lost it. I guess the North Star was certain the next vote would go as planned.

"I think you're proving the lady's point," I replied. "You're rigging the game against a member of the Congregation to consolidate power. Sounds like politics to me."

"You think this is about power for power's sake?" Polaris's white eyebrows scrunched down as he scowled at me. "I was just beginning to think you might be a bit brighter than you look."

"I get that a lot."

"This is about survival." The North Star waved my banter aside as if it were a gnat, not worthy of his time or attention. "The world has changed in the last five hundred years, whether the Hunter wants to admit it or not. Power has been amassed, lines have been drawn, deals have been made. It is much the same in the mortal world. When your ancestors learned to tear apart the fabric of the world, everything changed."

"You guys have nukes?" I asked, terrified at the thought of Hell with access to an arsenal capable of wiping out the entire world.

"Why would we need those?" Polaris sounded annoyed. "The Hunter still thinks he is a Viking warrior, raiding and plundering as he sees fit. Or maybe a Knight of the Round Table, dispensing what he believes is justice. But the world has moved on." His eyes glinted with flinty knowledge. "He is a spoiled child in a new era of civilization, and he is going to get us all killed. Starting with you and your fellow squire if history repeats itself at all."

As Orion's friend and student, I wanted to dismiss Polaris's degradation of him out of hand. He was certainly not spoiled or a child no matter what some ancient Nephilim said. No one has any business being that dangerous and still considered a kid.

But part of me, deep down in the part of my mind where I'm actually honest with myself, had to admit he had a point. Orion could be rash. His solution to a wrong was to kill it until it was right. There was a certain... barbarity to how he saw the world, and who could blame him? He was the Hunter. He had been hunting for thousands of years.

It was clear that in Polaris's view, that made my mentor dangerous—a problem to be solved. But there was more to Orion. He was also someone who stood up for the little people, like me, for example. He wasn't afraid to draw a line in the sand and defend it against evil with his life. I'm pretty sure he's saved the planet at least once.

I felt a growing sense of distaste for anyone who sees it as necessary to cut those people out of the world "for the good of everyone." That sounds exactly like an ideology Zagan would agree with.

"You're wrong about him," I said, meeting Polaris's eyes with my best determined stare.

"Oh well, thank goodness for your insight," the North Star replied dryly. "I've only known him for a thousand years, so I'm glad your year of friendship can shine some light on the Hunter for me."

"Year and a half actually," I replied, raising my chin.

"Every little bit helps," he agreed sagely. "Well done on the first round. I wish you luck on the next." With a cheery little salute of his wineglass, the eldest Nephilim turned away, gliding through the assembled Constellations like a maestro walking through his orchestra.

"That could have gone better," I muttered to Ash. A mild sense of despair began to form in the back of my mind. I have faced some terrifying monsters, but none of them had ever seemed so methodical and composed as Polaris. Even Zagan had let me get under his skin, but the North Star had a path he was leading the Constellation Congregation down, and I didn't see any way to stop him.

"Well... yes," she agreed after a moment of thought.

"Gee, thanks," I huffed, giving her a mock glare.

"What?" she protested, holding a hand to her chest. "Darling, you know I am a Faerie. I cannot lie."

"Yeah, but usually that works out better for me," I grumbled. Still, on the inside I was trying to hide a smile of relief. It seemed like I wasn't in trouble anymore.

"Usually." I could hear the smug grin in her voice without even looking at her.

"Hey, I just wanted to apologize," I said, changing topics. We both stopped, and she turned to look at me, a curious expression on her face. "I know this Congregation thing has got us both spinning in different orbits, and that means our schedules aren't really lining up…"

She gave me a long look, one that seemed to ask, *Do you really want to do this now?* Which made me panic, but it felt important to say. I'm not great at expressing my emotions out loud. It's too personal and weird. It makes my brain feel naked, and I don't like it.

"I just mean we haven't been able to spend as much time together as usual, and I'm sorry. When this is all over, we can do something special to make up for it."

"You're being ridiculous," Ash laughed, cocking her head at me. "This is our job. A job that neither of us can afford to fail at. Of course we're going focus on the convention. Besides, when this is over, we will have the rest of our lives—" Her eyes widened as she abruptly cut herself off. For a moment, I think she'd forgotten my clock was counting down while hers was frozen.

"Spending time together with someone special," she whispered almost reverently. "I understand now." I guess my lesson from our date had finally gotten through. All she had to do was face my mortality.

"I hate to ruin the moment," I murmured, clocking a familiar face over her shoulder. "But the lizard is on the move." Ash's eyes narrowed, and she turned to watch as Doyle made his entrance. The Don was alone, none of his dragoons trailing behind him.

It was clear that he was still on the hunt, because his spectacled gaze fell on a pair of Constellations in the corner of the room, and he slithered over to them without a moment's hesitation. One of the reptilian Constellations, Hydra, I think, tried to get his attention but was rebuffed with a firm wave.

The two Nephilim watched the dragon's approach with apprehension. I was pretty sure the man on the left's name was Bootes, because I thought it was funny. I couldn't remember the woman's name. Both of them had voted against the Hunter in the last session.

"Fancy a little wander?" I asked my betrothed, offering her my arm. Her eyes sparked with a hint of excitement before she slipped her arm through mine.

"It's such an interesting room, we really should explore a little."

We began meandering directly toward the corner where Doyle had the two Constellations backed up against a wall. Bootes's face was tight as he listened to whatever the dragon was saying.

"—your flocks will burn," Doyle hissed in threatening promise as their voices abruptly leapt into focus. We were too far away for my mortal ears to pick up their conversation. But as the hairs on my arm stirred ever so slightly in a light breeze, I glanced across the room to see Dawn watching me with a bemused stare. She tossed me a wink when our eyes met. Once again, having a Lady of Wind on my side proved to be very useful.

"Please," Bootes begged. "I want no part of this. I'm no warrior, just a herdsman who cares for his people."

"Then care for them, or one of my kin will bring fire and blood to your villages."

My hands closed into fists, as rage began to burn inside of me at Doyle's threats. It was one thing to challenge the Hunter. Predators have to fight to reach the top of the food chain, I get it. But threatening to murder entire villages just to get your way? That was beyond the pale.

Before I knew what I was doing, I pulled myself free from Ash's arm and stormed over to the Dragon Don. I had no real plan, I didn't even have a way to kill the Don, but I did have one perk. He couldn't touch me without getting in a lot of trouble. The kind of trouble that might jeopardize his vote.

"Is threatening a member of the Constellation Congregation really following the rules of being a Guest?" I asked the dragon's back as I closed in on him. Doyle hunched in surprise before turning to face me.

For a moment he simply stared, his tiny round sunglasses hiding reptile eyes. A forked tongue flicked out of his mouth once, tasting the air. Slowly a crocodile smile spread across his scaly face as he decided he liked whatever he saw.

"Now that you mention it," he hissed, "I seem to have forgotten to break my bread." He took a lazy step in my direction, and a weight of panic settled over me. I took a small step backward, my mind racing to find a way out of this. I felt like a Chihuahua that had caught a Rottweiler.

This was a bad time for me to remember that he hadn't been present when Polaris had invoked the rite of a Guest for all the attendees. If he also had skipped the stale bread, I don't think he was a Guest, which meant I wasn't protected from him. Then as I followed that train of thought, I felt a toothy grin spread across my face. That particular decision was a two-way street.

"Hey Orion," I called, not bothering to turn around. I knew he would hear me just fine. "Did you know our friend Doyle here isn't a Guest?"

The room went very, very quiet.

A hundred pairs of immortal eyes slid slowly between the advancing dragon to the Hunter lurking behind me. The perfect silence shattered beautifully at the sound of a sharp sword clearing a scabbard.

Doyle stopped, cold as his blood.

Slowly his sunglasses turned from me toward the buffet line deeper in the room. I could practically hear the calculations running through his head. Would Orion really attack him in this room? The answer to that one was yes. Was Doyle confident that he could fight off Orion? If not, how bad would it look to cower before the Hunter?

I heard a pair of booted feet moving across the carpet behind me as Orion strode toward the dragon. I chuckled as I watched the Don hesitate. No matter what happened in the next few moments, the damage was done. Everyone knew that for all his bluster, Doyle still feared the Hunter.

With a muttered Irish oath, the dragon dashed to the side in a shocking burst of speed. He sprinted across the happy-hour space to the buffet tables. Without pausing, he snatched a roll from one of the silver platters and stuffed it into his mouth before storming out of the room without looking behind him.

The Hunter let him go with a hint of wry amusement on his face. He gave me a slight nod as he slid his burning blade home in its sheath over his shoulder once more. That might have done just enough.

The black eyes of the Constellations around the room watched us with renewed interest. Orion ignored them, striding toward the corner of the room, toward Bootes and his companion.

Cassiopeia and her daughter Andromeda followed suit, as did other Nephilim I didn't know. I joined the circle in time to hear Bootes explain what I had overhead. "He threatened to murder my people if I dared to support you."

"You know I would not let that happen," Orion seethed.

"They got to me right before the session started," said one of the Constellations I did not know, a tall, gruff-looking man with muttonchops.

"It was the same with us," Andromeda agreed. "They waited until there was no time for us to warn you."

"He is a Guest now," Orion reassured them "He cannot threaten anyone in these halls without breaking the law."

"Orion, they claim they found a way to break the curse," Cassie pressed.

The Hunter's head snapped around. "Are you sure?" he demanded. I resisted the urge to groan. I had only found out about the curse a few days ago, and they had already found a way to break it?

"They told me the same thing," the gruff Constellation replied. I wondered if he was Canis Major. If so, that would make the smaller, similar-looking man next to him his brother, Canis Minor.

"They didn't exactly *demonstrate* it," Cassiopeia snarled, "but that is not an idle threat."

Suddenly the North Star's concern about Orion getting everyone killed with nukes made a lot more sense. "Polaris knows," I hissed. "He implied it to me earlier."

"What do you mean?" Orion asked, looking at me.

"He said the world had changed, and if he didn't do something, you were going to get the whole Congregation killed."

"If what the dragons claim is true… and the Dragon Dons do not get Draco back," Cassiopeia began.

"Then they have a way to go nuclear on the whole Congregation," I finished for her. I hoped all the Nephilim were up on their modern weaponry. My grandparents struggled with email, and they were in their seventies. I would understand if something similar happened to beings over a thousand years old. From the grim looks on their faces, I knew they had tracked my meaning. I guess that particular world event was a hard one to miss, no matter how old you were.

"Samael told him it worked," I gasped in horror. I thought I knew what the briefcase was for now.

"That what worked?" Cassiopeia asked.

"Something the Devil made for Doyle—something that had been tested on dragons. She said it worked. I thought it was a weapon or something." I had literally been there when Doyle had been promised the equivalent of the presidential football: the briefcase with the nuclear codes. I just hadn't realized what I was hearing. No wonder Samael had said it was too late to stop them. Who could stand against an unchained dragon?

"There's only one!" I blurted out, remembering more of the conversation between the demon and the Don. "Samael told him he would only get one because they didn't trust him."

The circle of Constellations didn't find that as heartening as I'd hoped. I guess even one fully fledged dragon was enough to cast fear into anyone's heart.

"You know me, Hunter," Canis Major said regretfully, "I love a good fight, and you have always been a good friend to me. But if the dragons' curse is truly broken—I am not you. I am no dragon slayer."

"None of us are," Cassie said sharply. "I suspect that is rather the point."

In my head, the trajectory began to make sense. The dragons had found a way to lift their curse, giving them a superweapon, for lack of a better term. They wanted their god back, and they saw Orion as the backbone of their opposition.

So they went to Polaris, threatened the entire night sky's worth of Constellations, and demanded that Draco be restored to them. To make that happen, Polaris had to defang the Hunter. So, when the Constellation Congregation had been called, it had been built from the ground up to poke and prod Orion, to erode his support base and leave him alone—unable to act.

"They finally found something scarier than you, Hunter," the man at Cassiopeia's side said. He had answered to the name Cepheus during the vote.

"It was never about being scared," Cassiopeia admonished him, placing a hand on his shoulder. "But only a fool stands in the way of a raging dragon."

"I have been called worse," Orion murmured. His rage had vanished, replaced by a quiet resilience that I had seen in him once before. A rare, genuine smile lit up his face as he looked around the circle of Constellations, perhaps the only peers of his that he considered friends. "I am not your lord; you owe me no fealty," he said spreading his hands in a peaceful gesture. "Do as you must—as will I."

A chill ran down my spine as I imagined what the Hunter might consider necessary. Cassiopeia frowned at him, genuine concern etching her beautiful features. "I have known you too long to have any hope that what you think you must do will end peacefully," she said sadly.

"The lines for this battle were drawn long ago," Orion murmured, his expression distant. "If it is finally time for the bill to come due, then I shall see to it that they pay what they owe in full."

THE INTERMISSION WAS all too brief. An hour feels like an eternity when it's the last one of the work shift or the lecture of a particularly dry professor. But the truth is that sixty minutes is only thirty-six hundred seconds, and they go by quickly.

With a heavy sense of dread, we marched back into the stadium bowl and took our seats. Gregor was already perched in his. He gave me a tight smile that had too many sharp teeth to feel comforting. I'm not sure he was trying to be comforting anyway. He's kind of weird.

"Maybe you'll know what it's like to be on the outside soon," he said in a polite tone, even if the substance was rude. I gave him a thumbs-up and dropped heavily into the chair next to him.

Alex sat next to me with a grim look that said, *Here we go again.* I held up a fist. He rapped his knuckles against mine and leaned back in his chair, his hands gripping both of his armrests tightly.

By contrast, Orion, the one with the most to lose, seemed as cool as a cucumber. I have seen more concern on a smooth rock that is about to be skipped across the surface of a lake. He was silent as he watched the Nephilim passing us on the way to their seats.

Most of them avoided looking at him.

Sagittarius stared boldly, unafraid to meet his eyes. It takes a special sort of coward to lash out at others on the way down.

The room was thick with a nervous energy, as if a cold front was sweeping in. There was no murmur of conversation, only a hungry silence, waiting to be filled. The bell to invoke the session rang, but it felt unnecessary. Everyone was already balancing on the knife's edge.

"The next matter before the Congregation is the question of censure of the Hunter," Polaris said simply. He leaned forward on the podium in a casual manner, his dark eyes scanning the room. "Complaint has been brought before the Constellation Congregation against him."

The North Star paused again, as if waiting for some sort of outburst, but the only response was the absolute stillness of prey avoiding the notice of predators.

"It is a request for censure with three accusations: namely, that the Hunter did not have the authority to reinstate the Hunt after its dissolution, that he has sullied the establishment of the Hunt with runts and mortals, and finally, that he has used this unauthorized Hunt in reckless endeavors that have antagonized other members and our forefathers, to the detriment of us all."

I frowned in confusion. I had thought this was about the dragon stuff. But these accusations were about different things. In fact, it really seemed like they were all things that had to do with... me.

I know, I know, everything isn't about me.

But just this once, maybe it was—a little. Orion *had* restarted the Hunt after learning about my soul being stolen. He had done so to protect Alex and me and to take us under his wing. I hadn't realized it at the time—I was too new to the supernatural world. But now that I had looked behind the curtain for more than five minutes, I could recognize the move for what it was.

As far as filling the Hunt with runts and mortals went—guilty as charged, I supposed. But it was the third charge that really sealed the deal for me. I didn't want to assume too much, but given that the Nephilim are the descendants of mortals and demons, I was willing to bet they considered the denizens of Hell their forefathers.

I'd only killed the Devil's girlfriend, Lilith, made a personal enemy of his CFO, and gotten betrothed to his estranged daughter. I don't know what Hell had to be upset about.

All these pieces fit together like a puzzle, and I suddenly understand why dragons and demons would be only too happy to work together. Both sides stood to gain things they desperately wanted: The dragons would get their leader back and get revenge on Orion, and Hell would strip one more layer of protection away from me.

If Orion lost the Hunt, it was going to be because of me. For some reason that was a sacrifice I could not bear. My friends had risked life and limb for me without complaint. But to see the Hunter without the Hunt... my mind couldn't begin to process it.

Polaris folded his hands and looked around the hushed room before settling his eyes on Orion. The ancient Nephilim's gaze was as steady as a surgeon's as he measured the Hunter's reactions After a moment, he inclined his head. "Would you care to respond, Orion?" he asked mildly.

The Hunter rose, his expression neutral. The room seemed to rear back in anticipation, as if a hundred pairs of lungs all inhaled at the same time. Orion glanced down at Alex and me for a long moment, the ghost of a smile playing at the corner of his lips.

With a roll of his head, he squared his shoulders and stared down at the North Star. "Not really," he said with a shrug. "There doesn't seem to be much point when the dragons have already intimidated all of the Congregants in this room into compliance."

A tiny murmur rose around the room, like a distant wave.

"So you admit to re-forming the Hunt even though you had not been given the authority?" Polaris pressed, ignoring the barb.

"I am the Hunter. What more authority do I need?"

"You were given special approval to form the band during the last troubles," Polaris replied, a note of anger creeping into his voice. "After the Hunt's demise—"

"At the claws of Draco," Orion interjected with a voice full of steel.

"—the Hunt was officially decommissioned at the last Congregation, and as such you had no right—"

"I AM THE HUNTER," Orion shouted, his voice echoing off the walls with the harshness of a landslide. I saw half a dozen Constellations flinch. "Look up at the sky tonight and find my belt. I earned the title. The Hunt is not yours to give or to take away. It is *mine*. What right did you have to tell Jason that he could not re-form the Argonauts or to deny Achilles his Myrmidons?"

Polaris stared at Orion for a moment, a stoic frown carved on his face. The murmurs began to grow.

"Do you deny that in this new Hunt you have filled its ranks with lesser beings—mortals and impure Nephilim?"

"I have filled its ranks with Hunters I have judged to be worthy of its name," Orion said, dismissive.

"Do you deny that you have antagonized other members of this august body as well as strained our relationship with our forefathers?"

Orion was silent for a moment, gathering his thoughts. I thought I knew why: Of the three crimes, this was the one with the most weight behind it. The Hunt *had* pissed off the forefathers, but that was mostly on my behalf. Orion was not a Faerie, but I knew he had his honor and his pride. He would not lie, but he also wouldn't snitch.

I never made the conscious decision to stand up. But the moment after I realized Orion was trapped between truth and politics, I was on my feet. "Technically, I killed Lilith before I was a member of the Hunt," I projected into the room. As I processed the decision my brain had just made for me, I did my best not to let my knees knock together in terror as the North Star's furious eyes turned to me.

"Oh no," I heard Alex mutter under his breath, rising to stand with us. I ignored his complaints. I may not have thought this through, but it was the path I was walking now.

"Silence, Squire," Polaris snapped. "Your betters are speaking." His disgust was so strong it almost knocked me back into my seat. It rivaled anything the cheerleader version of Dawn had ever aimed in my direction.

But even as my legs buckled, something cold and iron filled my spine with a stubborn resolve. I glanced over at Orion, who was watching me with curiosity. Not sensing any reproach from him, I decided I would not be sat down. I would not be silenced.

Not today. Not when my friend's legacy was on the line.

"Better you might be," I allowed, "but I am still a badge-carrying Guest of this Congregation." Polaris's eye twitched slightly at the word "Guest." I gave him a smile full of teeth. "As such, I give my eyewitness account and swear on my badge that I killed Lilith before I was a member of the Hunt."

"Very well," the North Star replied, nonplussed. "If we are opening the floor up to witnesses, does anyone else have any statements to make?"

As if on cue, Sagittarius screeched, "I do!" and leapt to her feet. Which, given the tremendous damage that had been done to her legs less than twenty-four hours ago, should not have been possible. "The Hunter and his pack of mongrels tortured me outside this very hall for fun. They destroyed my legs and ignored my pleas for mercy."

"Is this true?" Polaris demanded from Orion in a performance that should have been nominated for an Oscar. As if he didn't already know. He probably ordered it himself.

"If I had wanted to torture you, Archer, you'd still be trying to grow new legs," Orion replied, looking over at Sagittarius. "I'll be happy to demonstrate the difference next time." The Constellation's face paled slightly at the Hunter's threat.

"Is this all you have, Polaris?" Orion continued, leaning forward to stare down at him. "Petty complaints and half-truths to try to take away what is *mine*? You claim I have endangered the relationship with our forefathers. Who will prove such a thing?"

"I will." A voice like an ill wind swept in from the entrance. A single figure strode down the red carpet, dressed head-to-toe in black.

Samael.

The Poisoner.

The Seducer.

The Dark Whisper of the Devil himself marched to the podium with every eye glued to her. The pale demon didn't seem to notice the weight of the attention on her. Her black eyes were fixed on me, like a falcon preparing to dive on its prey. Primal fear leapt in my chest.

"You honor us with your presence, Elder," Polaris intoned, bowing at the waist toward the demoness. Orion snarled in disgust. I felt my own lip curl at the sight of the ancient Nephilim sucking up to the Devil's aide.

"I do," she agreed, still not looking away from her target. "I have been sent by the Dark Star to bear witness to the loyalty of his children in exile."

A hungry murmur swept through the room. I thought a saw an

expression of yearning on the faces of a lot of Constellations. I had never considered Orion's hatred of demons might be rooted in some unresolved daddy issues, but as I watched a room full of demigods twitch at a hint of being included in the roster of the Devil's family, it made sense. Nephilim straddled the line between two worlds, which I knew from personal experience made it hard to feel like you belonged anywhere.

"Lucifer has sent me with a message for the Constellation Congregation, North Star," she continued, striding up to stand next to him. The North Star stepped away from the podium without complaint.

"And what does the Dark Star ask of his descendants?" Polaris asked, in a tone that told me he already knew the answer. I wondered who had written this script. It needed some work.

"He told me to tell you that he is considering a change to the Edict of Banishment," Samael replied, the capitals obvious in her tone. Another shocked murmur swept through the room.

"No way," Gregor gasped in disbelief.

"What's that?" I muttered out the side of my mouth to Alex.

"Nephilim that are *too mortal* aren't allowed to associate with Hell," he whispered back. "Not pure enough."

Huh, I guess that idea came straight from the top—or bottom.

"But he is troubled," Samael continued, ignoring the reaction to her words. "He is eager to be reunited with his estranged family, but when he sends his servants to prepare the way, what do we find? That the Constellation Congregation is festered with those who would plot against him."

There were no murmurs now, only a petrified silence.

"Among your number are those who plot the downfall of the Lord of Hell. Not only were several Constellations here involved in the brutal murder of his paramour, Lilith, but the Hunter and his little pups continue to spread dangerous lies about the provenance of Hell's claim to a mortal soul."

Samael's face was as smooth as ice as she stared at me, each word another nail in the coffin of the Hunt. I knew what she was going to say before she finished her threat. The carrot was already dangled: a chance for the unwanted and forgotten to belong. If she gave them a little push, they were hers.

"My master is eager to be reunited with his children, but he worries that while you harbor such dangerous and insidious people and ideas, we could never be whole."

"Who says we want to be whole?" a voice on the other side of the room demanded. Cassiopeia rose to her feet to challenge the demoness. "Hell did not want us when we were children; now that we are adults it suddenly finds us valuable? Why should we serve a master when we have become our own?"

A soft mutter of approval rose, raising my hopes with it. It seemed that not everyone had lost their mind. Belonging is nice, but some things aren't worth it.

"Yes, you've done very well for yourself," Samael replied dryly, pointedly looking around. "Renting Hall B of the Los Angeles Convention Center is much better than anything we could offer."

I can't believe I ate tacos with her at a pool party once. Never again, I promised myself. No matter how good the tacos were, I was a man of principle.

"Better a convention hall than a chain around our neck," Cassiopeia spat. Another mutter of approval met her words, louder this time.

"A strong accusation from someone who is complicit in the murder of Lilith," Samael replied, unruffled. "I wonder if you might have a more selfish reason for your opposition."

"Is it true?" Sagittarius struggled back to her feet, calling down to the demoness. "We would be welcomed home?"

"Eventually, I suppose," Samael answered. "There would no doubt be some work to be done before the happy homecoming could occur. But that's what therapy is for, isn't it? Decide as you will about the Hunter. I shall carry the news of this Congregation's decision to my master."

Another murmur surged as the Nephilim voiced their interest. Gregor grumbled in disgust at my left elbow. I had to assume this was more than a little triggering for the misfit.

"Shall we call a vote then?" Polaris asked, stepping up next to Samael. "Those in favor of censuring the Hunter and removing the Hunt from the Congregation?"

Horrified, I looked at my friends. "What do we do?" Between the Dragon Don's threats and Hell's promises, I didn't think there was any way that this vote went our way. Around us, silence fell.

"Andromeda!" the Corona Borealis called, unfurling her scroll.

"We suffer what we must," Orion replied, his voice cracking with emotion.

Andromeda rose to her feet slowly, a frown pulling at her face. Her gaze flicked from the podium to Orion and back to the podium again. For a second, I thought she might be the match that started something, but she was not Atlas and could not bear up under the weight.

Her shoulders slumped, and her voice was dejected as she spoke her vote while slinking back down into her seat. "Yea."

So the vote continued, decided before it even began. It made me wonder how often it went down this way in the mortal Senate or House. Something told me I wouldn't like the answer.

Cassiopeia voted yea; so did her husband Cepheus.

The Canis brothers, Major and Minor, voted yea.

Aside from Orion, only three other Nephilim voted no.

"Not again," Carina spat. "You did it once to Jason, and we stood by. Not again. I vote no."

Puppis and Vela, the other two former Argonauts, also voted no, united in common disgust, despite none of them being seated together.

"The yeas take it, eighty-three votes to four," Corona Australis reported to the North Star. A leaden weight had settled in my gut, as if I had eaten a dozen rocks. At some point, the votes started to feel like kicks while we were down. We had already lost, what was the point? I glanced at Orion, but he was staring through the podium, eyes unfocused.

"So let the will of the Congregants be done," Polaris intoned, raising his little wooden mallet and striking the podium sharply. "The Hunter is hereby revoked of his right to lead the Hunt. Effective immediately the Hunt is disbanded." The elder Nephilim gazed up at us with black, merciless eyes.

"As such," he continued, with the severity of a judge reading off a death sentence, "the badges of any members of the Hunt are hereby also revoked. They are no longer welcome Guests."

Murmurs of surprise swept across the bowl. Alex and I were very careful not to twitch as a room full of predators looked at us with new eyes. My brain whirled, tracing the path of the web that had been spun around us. By dissolving the Hunt, the Congregation had effectively removed Orion's legal right to be our protector.

When we were part of the Hunt, if someone messed with us and Orion stabbed them, it had been his *right* to do so. But now, on paper at least, that was no longer the case. They had also stripped us of our protection as Guests while we stood in a room of enemies— but they hadn't taken away *his*. If someone attacked us here, there was nothing he could do to stop it without triggering some serious repercussions.

"Polaris, I must object," Cassiopeia shouted, leaping to her feet. That's a thing I loved about the Constellation of Beauty: She was always there to keep me from an untimely death. "This is highly irregular—"

"You are not recognized," Polaris snapped, interrupting her. A savage grin twisted his face as he pointed up at Alex and me. This had been his plan the whole time, the monster. "I am the host of this event, and I do not extend Guest privileges to them in their new roles." Sagittarius was practically drooling in her seat.

"Jokes on them," I muttered, fishing my hand into my pocket for my Dandelion Court badge.

"Don't," Orion grunted, hand shooting out to grab my arm in an iron grip.

"Why? I'm a dual citizen; they can't kick me out," I whispered back.

"You are correct. But if you play that card, Alex will be alone in the gauntlet they have set up for you," he replied softly. Orion finally turned to face me, a somber light glinting in his black eyes. "You will need each other for the challenge to come."

The Hunter reached under his jacket and pulled free the black Desert Eagle pistol he had used to lame Sagittarius. Wordlessly he held it out to me in his open palm. "You may need this," he said gravely.

A shiver ran down my spine, but I nodded and released my grip on my backup badge to take the hand cannon from him. He was right, I couldn't leave Alex stranded. I shoved the gun into my waistband next to my other holstered ones.

I pulled the lanyard with my Hunt badge over my head and tossed it out into the bowl with as much disgust as I could muster. Alex's joined mine in its plunge a few seconds later.

Polaris watched our badges flutter to the ground like a pair of dying butterflies with a sardonic smile on his face. He turned his bemused, victorious gaze back on us and called for the guards. "Security, please escort these wayward pups out of the hall. They are no longer welcome."

I saw our old friend Bellerophon and a handful of Nephilim enter from the doors at a trot. "Guess that's our cue," I said, turning to Alex. He held out a fist, and I rapped his knuckles for good luck.

"Give them Hell, boss," I told Orion.

"I shall give them something far worse," the Hunter promised.

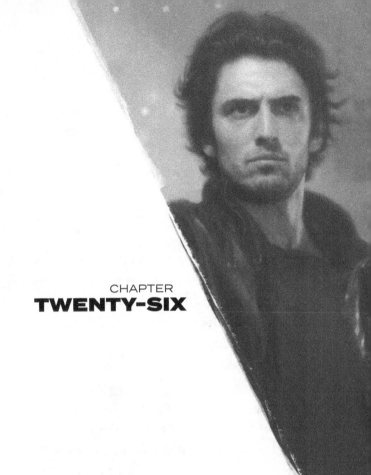

JUST REMEMBERED, I think we're supposed to be somewhere else," I remarked to Alex, eyeing Bellerophon and his squad of Nephilim coming to collect us. The bowl was loud as the Congregants began to debate Polaris's judgment.

"That's right, we do have an appointment doing... anything other than this," my friend replied coolly.

"Shall we?" I asked, jerking my head toward the back of the bowl's stadium seating.

"Right behind you," he answered grimly.

I slid past Alex and the Hunter, pausing only to clap my former boss on the shoulder as I stepped into the aisle. "See you on the flip side," I called to him as I left.

"Hey, can you bring my cardboard tube out with you?" Alex asked, pausing on the stairs. "It's a limited-edition poster..."

The Hunter didn't reply.

I glanced down at the side where Dawn and the Dandelion Court were seated. The Queen of All Fae gave me an irritated look as if reminding me of my spare badge, but I shrugged and pointed at Alex. Dawn rolled her eyes.

Behind her, Ash shot me a concerned look. Seeing my reply to Dawn, she reached for her own badge, as if to take it off her head. I waved my hand to stop her before she could go too far. The last thing we needed was to make this a bigger incident than Orion was no doubt going to turn it into. My betrothed frowned but relented with a small slump of her shoulders.

"I hate to interrupt, but we are sort in the middle of a chase scene," Alex grumbled from behind me. Not wanting to waste any more time, I shot Ash a wink and turned to sprint up the stairs. I could feel the structure rumble as Alex pounded along at my heels. Surprised shouts followed our progress as we dashed past seated Constellations. My eyes fell on Carina as I ran. The stoic Nephilim watched us for a moment before giving me a slight nod. Surprised and a little confused, I returned the gesture. I wasn't entirely sure what we were communicating, but I'd take a friend wherever I could get one right now.

Alex and I reached the top of the bowl stadium and without pausing vaulted the back rail. Instead of leaping off the structure, I flipped my grip and dropped down the side, lowering myself onto the exposed wood crisscrossing its way down the back of the structure in the shape of an *X*.

Letting gravity help our descent, Alex and I dropped from crossbeam to crossbeam like a pair of monkeys on the jungle gym. We were only thirty feet in the air, so it was a matter of seconds before we were close enough to drop to the floor safely. I landed in a crouch, brushing some sawdust off my hands as Alex landed next to me.

"Okay, now what," I asked him, looking around the empty hall. Outside of the little cocktail area at the front of the room, there was nowhere to hide or go. No matter what direction we went, we'd be impossible to miss.

"I say we get somewhere public as fast as possible," Alex grunted. "Make them make a scene if they want to do anything to us."

"I love scenes," I agreed.

Someone shouted above us as Bellerophon and his gang made it to the top of the stadium and looked down. I decided to exercise the better part of valor and broke into a sprint, with Alex right behind me as we dashed around the side of the bowl and raced for the entry doors at breakneck speeds.

I heard a loud *thump* as someone landed hard on the ground behind us. Stupid Nephilim and their stupid strong knees. One of them must have taken the thirty-foot drop in one go to catch up to us.

I didn't bother turning around, just let the mental image of a bloodthirsty Bellerophon chasing us for revenge give me wings. I might have come close to breaking a land speed record as I shot across the open room and through the empty cocktail area to slam into the metal swinging doors of Hall B. The doors burst open with a crack like a gunshot, and Alex and I whizzed out like bullets.

Barreling at high speed, we almost ran smack into a lounge of dragoons waiting for us on the other side of the door. I skidded to such an abrupt halt that I was surprised I didn't tear the carpet. Two of the dragons looked like the poisonous green ones that had ambushed us at Balsamic. but I couldn't be sure. I have trouble telling alligators apart. I'd never gotten their names, so I decided to call them Green One and Green Two from now on.

The third was a similarly horrible mash-up of man and reptile, but its scales were a dark brown and green from the palate of jungle camouflage. I named that one Cammy. All of them wore fancy suits, and none of them seemed the slightest bit surprised to see us.

The door clicked behind us, and I turned to look over my shoulder in time to see scarred Bellerophon giving me an evil grin as he pulled the door shut. "Have fun," he called in a lilting voice. He locked the door loudly.

Orion had been right: They had set up a gauntlet for us. A low grade of anger had been burning in my gut all day, like a pilot light. At the sight of the dragons waiting for us, flames of rage leapt to life. These miserable reptiles thought they could hunt the Hunt? Well, I guess technically we weren't the Hunt anymore, but in my heart I was. That had to count for something.

"Not gonna lie," I panted to Alex as we stared at the three lizards, "this is the worst checkout process I've ever experienced."

"I will definitely be leaving a review," my friend agreed, his gaze firmly fixed on our new opponents.

"We have been sssent to collect a debt," Cammy hissed. "You will come with us." Its forked tongue tortured the *s* sounds in its words, dragging them out until they sizzled like bacon on a hot griddle.

"I'm sorry, I know this is so rude," I replied, holding up my hands. "But I just can't understand a word you're saying. Is there anyone with you who speaks English?"

"Do you have a pen and paper?" Alex suggested. "Maybe if you wrote it down, we'd be able to communicate a little better."

"You just need a good elocution coach. Have you tried any tongue twisters? Here, say this one with me—she shells seashells down by the she shore. Wait, no, that's wrong. Hang on—sorry. She sells seashells down by the shell. Wow, this is harder than I thought."

"The last word is supposed to be *seashore*, I'm pretty sure," Alex offered.

"Enough!" the dragon roared, rage bubbling. "Grab them," it

shouted to its companions. The green dragoons stepped toward us, raising their horrible claw-hand appendages.

"You know, I understood that one perfectly fine," Alex told me.

"Yup, I think that's enough free teaching for one day," I said.

The dragoons blocked the way in front of us but hadn't bothered with the hallways that cut to the sides. By unspoken agreement, we dashed to the left as the reptiles came for us. I put my head down and accelerated as much as I could, clawing at the air with my hands, trying to get every ounce of speed I could out of my body.

Alex surged a little ahead of me, his nephilic gifts allowing him to cruise right past me. I was reminded of the age-old question, "How fast do you need to run to escape a dragon?" The answer was, "Faster than the other guy."

No thank you.

I lowered my head and leaned into my sprint with my entire weight, letting the momentum pick me up like a runaway boulder on a landslide. I could hear the reptile's clawed feet thumping on the carpet as they lumbered behind us. I risked a glance over my shoulder and let out a terrified squeak as I saw the monsters gaining on us, hurtling at a terrifying speed.

We ran out of hallway before the chase really got going. Alex pumped the brakes as we raced toward a wall of closed metal doors. Thick chains interlocked them, holding them fast.

"Right or left?" my friend shouted, glancing at the only two doors we had available to us.

"Right!" I called. Left felt like it would take us back toward the Congregation in the bowl, which was one of the only other places on God's Green Earth that I wouldn't rather be right now.

Alex rushed to the door and shoved it open. I followed him in, and slammed it shut. The dragoons were getting close; I could feel the floor shaking under their combined weight. Glancing around for something to barricade the door with, I pointed at a heavy looking table along the wall.

Alex and I sprinted to the it and dragged it to block the door. Just as we got it in place, the door slammed into it. The table shifted a few inches but held.

"We will crack open your bones and drink your marrow, human!" one of the dragons hissed through the crack, shoving at the door again. The table wiggled but did its job.

"Bite me," I panted, turning to look at the room we had sealed ourselves in.

"I think he was saying that was the plan," Alex remarked, joining me.

"Not my best work," I agreed.

Together we started down the hallway, trying doors as we went. Behind us, our barricade rattled as the reptiles smashed into it over and over. Worried we had trapped ourselves, I broke into a jog, and Alex kept pace with me easily. We seemed to be in some sort of staff hallway; the locked doors were all marked things like CLEANING SUPPLIES or AV.

"There's got to be another way out," Alex muttered after the fourth locked door.

"Oh, there is," I told him confidently. "I'm just hoping it isn't inside a dragoon's belly."

"They wouldn't eat us," Alex protested. "Well, they wouldn't eat us *here*," he amended after a moment.

"That's the spirit," I told him, finally finding an unlocked door. I led Alex into the dark room, both of us stopping dead in our tracks as we realized it was a giant industrial kitchen. That felt a little too on the nose. "Then again, it's never the wrong time for a snack," I commented.

Behind us, something crashed as the table blocking the door finally gave in. We looked at each other and sprinted farther into the kitchen. This must be where all the catering for major events was done. Gleaming stainless-steel workstations lined the room in rows, enough for thirty people to cook at once.

I raced down to the end of the room, dropping into a crouch to hide below a chopping station's counter. Alex copied my move a row over. Hunkered down in the dark, I tried to find my center, slowing my heavy breathing. I work out, but being chased by dragoons will take anyone's breath away, trust me.

Belatedly, I reached under my jacket to draw one of the pistols that was holstered on my belt. I wondered if it packed enough firepower to punch through their scaly flesh. It felt a little like I was getting ready to go after an elephant with a BB gun. I just found comfort in the familiar weight of a weapon in my hand. Despite my doubts about the smaller caliber firearm's effectiveness, I left Orion's Desert Eagle in my waistband. I didn't have any extra magazines for it and didn't want to waste it.

Distantly, I heard crashes as the dragoons threw themselves at the locked doors we had tried. Mentally, I kicked myself for hiding in the first unlocked room—it was too obvious. With a loud bang, the kitchen door burst open, light spilling in from the service hallway. I risked a peek, leaning out to see a single dragoon illuminated as the door swung shut behind it.

Slowly, the monster made its way through the room. I could hear it hiss as it stuck out its forked tongue to taste the air like a snake. Gently, ever so gently, I shifted my body, turning to crawl over to another aisle, keeping low below the countertops.

The reptile continued to stalk, a deep growl rumbling from its throat. I held my breath as I heard it pass by me on the other side of the chopping station. The dry rustle of its scales triggered in me a primal fear of snakes. My heart was in my throat, doing its best to run away on its own since my body clearly wasn't getting it done.

Now I knew how those kids in *Jurassic Park* must have felt, hiding from velociraptors.

As the dragoon made its way down the aisle, I resumed my crawl, hoping to make it to the end of the row before the monster turned around. It was a maddening type of stress; I had to move slow enough to be noiseless, but fast enough to get away in the small window of time I had.

I gritted my teeth and prayed that Alex was doing the same thing on his side. The dragoon had walked between us, so we each had a fifty–fifty chance it would choose our aisle next.

"It stinks of fear in here," the dragoon hissed softly. "Where are you, little mice?"

I slid another few feet. Considering what snakes do to mice for fun, I wasn't even a little tempted to make a sarcastic remark. No, just this once, I was more focused on living than having the last word.

I was about two-thirds of the way up my aisle when everything went wrong. The dragoon let out a pleased hiss, and one of the workstations toppled over with a crash. Worried that Alex had been squashed underneath a stainless-steel avalanche, I leapt to my feet, settling into a shooter's stance.

Alex was on his feet, backpedaling from Green One, or maybe Green Two, which was chasing him down his aisle. A fallen counter lay between them like a makeshift barrier. Unable to get a clear shot, I jogged down my aisle, trying to flank the dragoon. My friend opened fire with his own pistol, the shots lighting the darkness with bright flashes as he tried to slow the monster's advance.

Alex's bullets slammed into the creature's chest, tearing up its suit, but it stayed on its feet and kept lurching forward. Drawing a bead with my own pistol, I opened fire, hammering it from the side.

Caught off guard, it teetered for a second, its balance knocked askew by the force of my bullets. Trapped between two angles of attack, the dragon staggered and fell. Both of our pistols continued to roar in the echoey kitchen as we emptied our weapons into the downed creature.

There was an abrupt silence as we both ran out of ammo. With practiced movements, I slipped one of my spare magazines out of my back pocket and reloaded my gun. My ears were ringing.

"Did we get it?" I shouted to Alex.

I knew the dragoon wasn't dead, but I hoped the repeated blows had at least stunned it a bit. It let out a low growl and rolled, trying to find its feet.

"Negative," Alex sighed, racking the slide of his pistol with an ominous click.

"Screw this," I snarled, vaulting over the two cutting stations that separated our aisles. The dragoon had gotten its arms underneath it and shook its head like a dog as it pushed off the ground. Tossing my worthless 9mm pistol on the counter, I pulled the Desert Eagle from my waistband and pointed it down at the creature at my feet.

"Let's see if your scales like this any more than a Constellation did," I hissed and squeezed the trigger.

I had fired the Desert Eagle once before, but I'd forgotten how much kick a .50-caliber round had compared with my usual pistol. I was used to riding rocking horses, but this gun kicked in my hands with all the fury of an untamed bronco.

As bad as I had it, Green Two had it much worse.

The round slammed into its back with all the force of a collapsing building, knocking it onto the floor. Unlike our other bullets, this one penetrated its scaly skin, punching a vicious hole.

Hands shaking, I started to lower my pistol, but as I did, the monster stirred, arms impossibly moving to push off the ground once more. I stared in horror, unable to believe that it could keep going despite the mangled mess that it was, I put two more rounds in the back of its head. The dragoon flopped to the ground and stopped trying to get up. I had never been so grateful it was dark. I didn't need to see the aftermath in full high definition. My nightmares are already vivid enough.

I had just enough time to worry that we were forgetting about something when the kitchen door burst open and Green One stormed in. Operating on panicked instinct, I spun, raised my gun, and fired a shot.

The artillery shell that the Desert Eagle uses as a bullet hit the dragoon high in the chest, picking it up and throwing it against the far wall. I felt the slide of my pistol pop open, ejecting the slim hope I'd just begun to feel.

I was out of big-boy bullets.

Stuffing the empty Desert Eagle back into my waistline, I scooped my regular pistol up off the counter and turned to Alex. "We should run now," I said as emphatically as I could.

"Right behind you," he agreed.

The nice thing about industrial kitchens is that they're designed for lots of people to come and go at the same time. There was another door on our side of the room that exited to a service hallway, far away from where the second dragon was struggling back to its clawed feet.

We burst out into the hallway and right into Cammy coming to investigate all the noise. This dragoon didn't hesitate. The moment it saw us, it put its head down and charged at us like it was a minotaur rather than a reptile. Alex and I raised our guns and opened fire on the scaly freight train.

It staggered under the force of our bullets, but as it built up steam it seemed to notice them less and less. Both of our pistols clicked on empty, and together we lowered them, watching the monster bear down on us. It raised its head and opened its horrific snout, revealing a sinister red glow.

A jet of unbelievably hot fire erupted from its mouth. I raised my hands, kindling Willow and commanding the spirit to extinguish the flames rushing toward us. The dragonfire vanished, and a slight breeze wafted over us like a warm summer night instead of Pompeii Part Two. The dragoon slid to a stop, shock apparent on its human-reptile face. I guess it had never seen a Lord of Flame do his thing before.

"You're not the only one who can do fire tricks, worm," I taunted, giving it my toothiest grin and settling into a fighting stance, hands still burning. If I could neutralize its fire long enough, maybe we could knock it down like we had the others.

"Sorry in advance," Alex said grimly. Confused, I turned in time to see him slip the black mummer's mask out of his jacket.

"I thought we agreed on no masks!" I shouted at him as he started to place it on his face.

"Do you have any better ideas?" he snapped, pausing for a second.

I let out a groan of annoyance. No, I didn't. We were trapped; I was out of big-boy bullets and running low on magic propane. We both knew it was only a matter of time before one of the lizards got us.

"If I survive three of these dragoons only to be strangled to death by you, I going to be so pissed," I complained. He took that as an agreement and finished setting the mask on his face, striding to intercept Cammy.

Supercharged by the dark powers of the mask, Alex closed with the dragoon. Dismissively, it raised its clawed hands as the Nephilim stepped in range. Alex pulled his right hand back and clocked the monster in the face with the pistol he was still holding. The dragoon staggered back a few steps, hissing in surprised anger.

Cammy raised a disbelieving claw tenderly to its face, its cat-eye pupil widening as it stared at Alex. My partner didn't give it any time to recover. He pressed his attack, feinting with his left hand before lashing out with the pistol again.

Alex danced around Cammy's clumsy swipes, fists raining down a punishment on the flabbergasted monster. Every time there was an opening, his pistol struck in another brutal blow. A thrill of hope ran through me as the scaled creature began to retreat under the ferocity of his attack.

As I watched Alex beat the ever-loving crap out of one of the most feared monsters in the known universe, I began to worry about my own chances of survival. If he could knock out a dragoon, what chance did I stand against him one on one? He dashed forward, ducking under the dragon's clumsy right hook, and wrapped his arms around the monster, wrenching it to the side.

Cammy fell to the ground, and Alex rode it down, pinning it under his knees before he went to work, fists pounding the dragon hard enough that he looked like he was trying to turn it into schnitzel. Cautiously, I began to sneak up behind Alex, trying to time my attack so that I wasn't saving the dragon, only myself. I just needed to get the mask off before it was my turn to get battle-raged on...

Alex's demon-fueled attack was focused entirely on the downed lizard, and I managed to get within a pace or two of him without him noticing. Heart hammering in my chest, I reached out to grab the mask, hands hovering behind his head.

Was it too soon?

The dragon looked pretty done, but I have no idea what their recovery time is. Like I said, from all the hype, I'm pretty sure they take a lot of killing. I didn't think the one I had double-tapped was really dead. It was unlikely that twenty blows to the snout was enough to put this monster down for good, hellish strength or no.

But that was probably good enough for us to make a break for it.

My hand snapped forward to snag the mask, but Alex must have heard me somehow. His head shifted to the side so that my hand barely grazed the edge of his mask. He spun, leaping to his feet and stalking toward me.

"Hey, buddy, I'm really gonna need you to snap out of this," I hummed, retreating. I glanced at my still-burning hands. "I don't want to hurt you."

But whatever the mask was doing to Alex's brain, he didn't seem at all concerned by my warning. I cursed and dropped back, casting a wary eye on the downed dragoon. The lizard was twitching but didn't seem ready to get back on its feet. I wasn't sure if that was a good thing or a bad one for my chances.

With a sigh, I slid my hand to my back holster to grab my second pistol. As my hand went for the gun, it brushed my thigh and reminded me that I am an idiot.

A giant, unbelievably stupid, idiot.

I jammed my hand into my pocket and pulled out the Key of Portunus. That sure would have come in handy a couple of minutes ago when we were trying to find an unlocked door to escape through. A portal to a dimension the dragoons couldn't follow us into would have worked perfectly.

But that moment had passed. I didn't see the key being helpful in getting Alex's mask off or in stopping me from getting my skull caved in. For a second, I considered opening a door to the Between and throwing myself in, but I couldn't abandon Alex.

Even if I had wanted to, my friend had no intention of being left behind. He rushed forward in a full-body tackle, hurtling toward me like a spear. His arms wrapped around me, and we crashed to the ground with bone-jarring impact. The key bounced out of my hand. Visions of the beating the camouflage dragoon had just gone through danced in my head. My scaleless body wasn't nearly robust enough to handle a fraction of that abuse.

As Orion taught me, I raised my flaming forearms in front of my face to block the hammer blows that Alex would rain down on me. But before the first strike could land, a feral growl sounded behind us. Both of us turned to regard the angry reptile on all fours, its animal pupils burning with hatred. It seemed Cammy had managed to recover its wits.

I don't know exactly how the programming inside the demon mask works, but even it seemed to recognize the important of dealing with the bigger predator. Alex got off me and turned to face this new threat. But Cammy didn't give him any time; it leapt forward, making a terrifying impression of an alligator.

The two of them fell to the ground, rolling in a vicious wrestling match, each trying to pin the other. I scrambled to my feet, eager to get out of the way. I didn't have enough claws or superpowers for that battle. Cammy seemed ready for Alex's strength this time and was playing for keeps. The dragoon fought its way on top of Alex and slashed at him with its vicious claw-hands. Talons screeched against the black mask.

With a jolt of fear, I realized the lizard wasn't trying to kill Alex—well, not with that move. It was trying to take off the mask. It had figured out the source of his strength. As much as I didn't want to get stuck alone with Alex while he was all raged up, I was counting on him to take out Cammy first.

"Get off him!" I snapped, thrusting my right hand forward and triggering one of Willow's concussive blasts. The shock wave wasn't enough to hurt the dragoon, but it sent the beast flying a handful of feet, freeing Alex.

Quick as a nightmare, Cammy was back on two feet, and this time it decided I was the easier target. Hissing in fury, the dragoon rushed toward me, jaws open wide. I let out a terrified screech and turned to run, and as I took my first steps, I spotted the glinting key lying on the carpet ahead of me.

Better late than never, I suppose.

I bent low as I dashed past the key, scooping it up in my hand.

Behind me, I could hear the huffs of the dragoon as it chased me, and I thought I heard the swift footfalls of Alex as he chased the beast. What a bad day to be at the bottom of the food chain. I stopped at the first door down the hall and shoved the Key of Portunus in the lock. Fortunately, some magic makes the key always fit, because my hands were shaking too hard to be accurate.

I twisted the handle and shoved the door open to the Between. I had just a second to see the eternal office hallway before I spun to face the charging dragoon. Its reptilian eyes gleamed in hungry delight as it closed the final distance between us. Summoning the last dregs of Willow's power, I raised my left hand and swatted it at the beast as it closed in, dancing out of range as I triggered another concussive blast.

I thought I heard a surprised shriek as Cammy was bowled over, rolling right through the open door like a perfect soccer goal. With my right hand, I slammed the door shut and wrenched out the key, trapping the dragoon in the space between worlds.

Leaving me alone with a very dangerous Alex, hurtling toward me like a bullet train.

Before he could crash into me with enough force to shatter me, the kitchen door behind him exploded open. Alex's head snapped around, and he slowed as the dragon I had winged earlier lunged through, scaled snout pulled back in a snarl. It let out a roar of anger at the sight us, and without hesitation reared back its neck before lunging forward to spit out a tsunami of fire.

I have no idea what might influence how much flame a dragon can produce. It could be an age thing, a result of training, or have to do with how much spicy food the beast had for its last meal. All I know is the maelstrom of fire that poured out of this second dragon's mouth was an order of magnitude larger than the one I had extinguished with Willow earlier.

The world seemed to slow. The flames spewed out of the dragon in a fiery geyser that filled the hallway. As the inferno swept toward us, I called on the minuscule juice Willow still had, trying to command the oncoming fire.

It seemed like the closer the fire got to us, the slower reality itself moved. I raised both my hands at a glacial pace and shouted a command, each syllable lasting an eternity. "Exxx-ting-uishhhh," I cried. Even as I did, I knew my will would not be enough. I was a single tree standing against an avalanche.

Inch by painstaking inch, the flood of flame swallowed us. Its heat was indescribable—so hot that it burned cold. I had just enough time to see my hands begin to blur and vanish as they were devoured. Everything went bright as my world was consumed—

—I stumbled into Alex as my left foot didn't land properly. He gave me a confused look as he caught his own stride and we fell back into our frantic sprint.

We were running.

Why were we running? Had we always been running? I didn't think I had been running...

I glanced over my shoulder at the two green dragons that were chasing us. Green One and Green Two hadn't been ready for us to make a break for it, but they were gaining fast.

By unspoken agreement, Alex and I had cut to our right, along the closed doors of Hall B, toward the connecting hallway that took us back to Hall A and the main convention floor. I felt a pang of concern about that as I ran. We were leading the monsters toward the crowds of mortals, which was not the best plan to limit civilian casualties.

For a second everything around me flickered, and I was in two places at once. One felt like the middle of a raging inferno, with heat consuming me on all sides; the other was a pretty room-temperature convention center. Then I was only in one place, but still sprinting. I shook my head to clear it of the visions that were distracting me.

If we had been smart, we would have gone to the left and so we could run *away* from the innocents, but it was too late now. The die was cast, and there was no going back. Our retreat was blocked by a literal offensive line of lizards.

"Why didn't we go left?" Alex shouted. "This is a terrible idea!"

"I was following you!" I yelled back. He had been the one to go right first, hadn't he?

"Me? I was following you!"

The runway for our argument ran out abruptly as we burst through a pair of metal doors and into the open atrium in front of Hall A. Brightly dressed nerds gave us confused looks at our loud entrance, but no one said anything. Groups of people gathered around cosplayers dressed as their favorite characters, or minor celebrities taking pictures with fans.

Terrified at what would happen when the reptilian freight train that was hot on our heels burst into the room, I started screaming as I ran. "Dragons! Everyone run!"

Unlike medieval Europe, where that might have caused more of a panic, no one screamed or fled—a few people laughed. Most people just gave me a weird look, like I was embarrassing myself.

We should have gone to the left.

Behind us, the metal doors smashed open, and the two dragoons shot out into the open area. Attendees began to cheer as they saw the monsters chasing us.

"That's such a sick cosplay!" I heard one dude shout.

"You guys look so good!" a girl dressed as some anime character called.

Gritting my teeth in frustration, I gave up on trying to warn anyone. The Constellation Convention truly was a brilliant concept. Humans were so conditioned to believe the supernatural world wasn't real that there was no undoing it. I was about to be torn to shreds in front of a host of mortals whose only reaction would be to cheer on our awesome performance.

Still, there was a silver lining: Instead of cowering away, my fellow humans pressed forward to get a better look at the "insane dragon costumes," making it impossible for the dragoons to keep track of us. They were too busy getting caught in selfie attempts to hunt two nice young men.

No one thought our costumes were cool, so Alex and I skittered among the gathering crowd like a pair of cockroaches, ducking through gaps and circling the room, working our way out of the epicenter in a counterclockwise fashion.

"There you are!" a bright voice called as we cut our way through the crowd. "Is your shift over already?" Alex and I froze mid-dash, turning in shared horror to see Violet jogging toward us with a giant grin on her face. She was still dressed as an elf but now had several bags full of purchases. Connor was nowhere to be seen.

"We were just about to go see what's in the other hall," she told us. "Apparently it's a special section or something."

"Oh—it's really not worth seeing," I assured her, staring over her shoulder at the two green dragons being forced into selfies. They seemed to have lost us in the press of the crowd, but I didn't feel safe sticking around.

"Yeah, it's super lame," Alex agreed, a note of impatience in his voice.

"What is it?" Violet asked.

"Shadow puppetry," I lied.

"Really bad shadow puppetry." Alex shot me a glance that told me I was an idiot. I know, I don't know where that answer came from, I just panicked.

"Oh," she said, sounding disappointed.

One of the green dragoons turned, its reptilian eyes locking on

Alex and me across the room. Its forked tongue tasted the air, and it bent its snout into an evil smile as it saw us talking to Violet.

Dammit.

"We gotta go," Alex told me.

"I know," I sighed, already regretting this. "But they saw us."

"Who saw you?" Violet turned to look over her shoulder in the direction we were gazing.

"Violet, I need you to trust me."

"Of course." She turned to stare at me with her bright-green eyes. "Always." Although the spell she'd once held over my heart had long since faded, I would be lying if I said I didn't still feel a twinge of nostalgia as I met her gaze. But this wasn't about anything other than saving her life.

"Where's Connor?"

"He went to the bathroom." That was fine; the dragons would never notice him. But they had seen Violet with us, which meant we couldn't leave her here alone. She'd be snapped up before she knew what happened.

"Okay come on, we gotta run now."

"What do you mean? He'll be right back."

"Matt," Alex warned as one of the dragoons began shoving its way through the sea of admirers. Time to run again.

"Trust me!" I snapped, reaching out to grab her wrist with my right hand. She let out a shriek of surprise but didn't resist as Alex and I resumed our dash for the exit.

The dragoon in pursuit let out a furious roar as we burst out the front of the building. I could dimly hear the crowd cheering in appreciation before the doors slammed shut, cutting the sound short.

Violet didn't ask any questions as we raced the three blocks to the parking garage and leapt into the van. Alex locked the doors as if that would do anything to stop a lounge of angry dragons from breaking in. Still, I couldn't deny it felt nice. I put on my seat belt too.

Just in case.

For a long moment, we sat there, staring at nothing, trying to catch our breaths. After a few moments, Alex raised his fist, and I rapped my knuckles against his without looking. It was not the most daring or epic escape in the history of Alex and Matt, former Squires of the Hunt.

But it was *an* escape.

CHAPTER
TWENTY-SEVEN

A T A LOSS for what to do next, we decided to take Violet to safety. She texted Connor, asking him to pick her up at my place, and we set off. Violet tried to engage me in bright, bubbly conversation a few times, but eventually even she got the hint that I wanted some time to myself. Alex and I were both lost in our own thoughts, processing what it meant to no longer be a part of the Hunt.

In some ways, it felt like I had lost my soul for real. I know this had all started because of the whole soul fraud thing, but I still couldn't tell you what my soul actually was. I didn't feel its absence the way I would a missing limb. I felt no different. Maybe that was because I hadn't lost the dang thing yet, just had its return-to-sender address changed.

Losing the Hunt hurt so deeply because it felt like losing part of my identity, a segment of who I was. That might seem stupid, given I had only been in the Hunt for a year and a half, but that didn't make it any less true.

It was the death of a part of me. I had been Matthew Carver, Squire of the Hunt; now he was dead, and I was someone new. Who that was, only time would tell.

Alex pulled into the driveway, and we piled out of the van. I unlocked the front door and led the group inside. Alex slid past me, heading toward the kitchen. I hoped he was going to break out the whiskey—I could use like twelve drinks.

Violet hesitated at the doorstep, staring at me like I was a stranger.

"Please, come in, Violet," I urged. "I'll explain everything."

She gave me a slight frown but acquiesced, stepping into my house.

"So, this is your new place," she murmured mostly to herself as I led her to the living room. As predicted, Alex joined us with a bottle of whiskey and three glasses. "How do you two afford it?" she asked, a disbelieving eyebrow arched.

"We got a good deal," Alex offered.

"Not that good," I muttered under my breath, thinking about what the five million Zagan gave me had cost.

"Are you finally ready to tell me what is actually going on?" Violet demanded, settling into one side of the large couch, a spark of true anger in her eyes. "You've been lying for a year and a half now."

"Okay," I said with a sigh. "I'll tell you everything." I wouldn't, of course. For one, I suspected whatever claws Dan's deal had put in her would prevent her from understanding. But certainly, she didn't deserve to get drawn into this. This was my problem, not hers. It was okay, I'd had this lie ready to go for months.

Alex started pouring drinks, bless him.

"It has to do with Meg," I told her. Better to start with a shred of truth. My sister *was* involved.

"Do you know where she is?" Violet leaned forward.

"Not quite, but we think we've identified one of the gangs involved."

"Have you told the police about this?"

"They've given up."

"So you're, what, doing it yourself?" A note of horror entered her voice, and she glanced between the two of us, connecting enough dots that I didn't even need to tell her the rest of the story. "Are you trying to get yourselves killed?"

Alex took a sip of his whiskey and nudged the other glasses to the center of the coffee table. I leaned forward and snagged mine, but Violet was too focused on the conversation to be distracted.

I didn't really know how to answer that one. I was a dead man walking, and technically I was trying to undo that. "We have help; we're not completely stupid."

"The same PI you've been talking about for forever?" I nodded. "So you're working the convention to tail this gang, is that why you were running?"

"That's a pretty good summary." I winced.

"And they saw me?" A note of panic entered her voice. Totally reasonable and fair, but I didn't think she had much to worry about. We had gotten her away from the dragoons, and she was just one mortal in a sea of many. It would be almost impossible for them to figure out who she was.

"I think you're fine," I promised. "We got out cleanly but didn't want to risk you being seen."

Violet was silent digesting this information. After a few moments, she leaned forward and collected her whiskey glass. I offered a cheers and a small smile as an apology.

The three of us clinked our glasses and drank, and I felt my shoulders relax as a bit of the tension I had been carrying bled out. Today had not been a success by any stretch of the imagination, but it certainly could have gone way worse. I could have died! That would have been bad.

Alex distracted Violet with stories of our adventures with Orion, heavily edited to fit the gang narrative, but they did the trick. I shot him a grateful glance as I sipped my whiskey. Yup, it had been messy for a few minutes, but we had pulled it off.

The doorbell rang.

So much for the peace and quiet. My heart sped up as I walked toward the front. I paused to snatch a gun from the front closet—just in case. I looked out the peephole and felt a whole new kind of panic when I saw who was waiting for me. Ash and Robin were still wearing their convention outfits and matching grim expressions.

I pulled my phone out of my pocket—it was dead. Uh-oh. I tucked my pistol in my belt and opened the door, prepared to take some well-deserved punishment.

"Hello," I said with an embarrassed grimace.

"Oh good, you're alive." Ash's icy tones almost made it sound like I would have been in less trouble if I were dead. Robin shot me a glare from behind her. I wasn't sure if he was upset because he had been worried or because he'd had to suffer Ash's bad mood on my behalf.

"I'm alive," I repeated slowly, trying to think of what I should say, how I could apologize for not letting her know. If Ash had been sent through the gauntlet and I had to wait, I would have been pissed if she didn't call me too. I got it—I did. I was just too caught up in trying to manage the mortal we had to save to think about it.

"I was worried. I thought you might have—" A shadow passed across her face, and she fell silent. She didn't have to say anything else. The cold edge of her disappointment sliced at me like a sharp knife.

"That's fair," I admitted, bowing my head in shame. "I was a little overwhelmed. I'm sorry." Ash remained silent, perhaps evaluating my apology. "Please, come in," I offered, standing aside to usher the two Fae in.

It didn't occur to me until I led them back into the living room that I was going to have a hard time explaining Violet's presence. She was still rocking her elf ears, which I suddenly worried was offensive. Ash didn't look surprised to see her. My betrothed's face had settled into a frozen mask that would have impressed Mav.

"Violet, this is Robin and Ash," I said by way of introduction, a very bad feeling creeping up my spine. Ash had reacted strangely to a whiff of Violet's perfume earlier. Finding her here after I forgot to call probably wasn't going to earn me any points.

"More co-conspirators?" Violet asked coolly, watching the two Fae warily. "Love the costumes."

"We told her about the *gang*." I stressed the word to respond to Robin and Ash's confused looks.

"We ran into Violet while we were making our getaway and thought it wisest not to leave her behind," Alex offered, standing up to get more glasses. It seemed he had learned some manners while being my manservant in the Faerie Lands. Maybe I was imagining things, but I thought some of the hard edges went out of Ash's shoulders at our explanation. Not completely. Her face was still tight and her body stiff, but I thought she understood.

"So what's the plan, you guys are going to bring down this gang all by yourselves?" Violet sounded skeptical, which was more than reasonable if I was still the Matthew Carver she knew.

"We're going to find Meg," I answered to spare my friends who couldn't lie.

"Oh, Matt, she would never forgive you if you got yourself killed trying to save her." Her words stung in a way that she couldn't know. I knew exactly what that felt like, I'd had to live it when Megan died.

I closed my eyes against a sudden wave of grief and took a long breath.

"We're doing our best," Robin promised, placing a friendly hand on my shoulder before accepting one of the glasses from Alex.

We sat in a tense limbo for a while, drinking our whiskey and forcing small talk to keep the room from falling silent. It turns out that mortals and Immortals have little in common, even with Alex and I there to act as a bridge.

Ash was silent the whole time, watching Violet sip her drink.

It took what felt like an eternity for Connor to pick Violet up. "Don't worry," Violet said, announcing his arrival, "I won't let him come in. I'm guessing you have actual things you want to talk about after we're gone." A note of bitterness filled her voice as she rose.

"I'll walk you out," I replied, not sure what else to say. It was better for them both if he stayed outside, but for some reason it hurt a little too. It felt like I was a kid again, telling my friends I was about to move to a new school. This goodbye felt heavier, even if it wasn't forever. It wasn't her fault that there was a chasm between us. It wasn't really my fault either. But the yawning expanse felt impassable.

"Hey, I don't think you guys should go to the convention tomorrow. I'm not sure it will be safe," I told her as we walked. She nodded but didn't respond.

I led Violet to the door and opened it for her. Connor waved from the driveway; I could just make out his silhouette over the headlights of his car. She paused, and mentally I braced myself for one of her aggressive flirtations. But she only gave me a sad smile and a pat on the arm.

"Take care of yourself," she begged, walking out my front door.

"Yeah," I croaked over the odd lump in my throat, surprised by her kindness.

"Oh," she called as she walked toward the car. "You should keep working out, you look good." She tossed me a wink before getting into the car.

Ah, there it was. I gave her a flat smile and waved at the car as they drove off.

Squaring my shoulders, I braced myself for the next round as I returned to my frigid living room. Alex handed me a refilled glass, a look of commiseration on his face. I accepted it with a nod of thanks and sat down next to the ice sculpture that was pretending to be my betrothed.

"Who was she?" Ash asked in a too-calm voice. My stomach did a little flip. I had never heard her sound like that, not even when she had been standing over the bodies of dead assassins who had tried to kill her.

"An old mortal friend," Robin offered, trying to defuse the situation. Ash shot him a glare and turned to stare at me.

So I told her the story. All of it. How I used to live with Connor, and how the two of them had been included in Dan's meddling. How I had once felt something for Violet, but that had been lost to the veneer of whatever manipulated her now.

"She was actually more normal than usual," Alex remarked, draining the last whiskey from his glass. He wore a glum expression as he stared at the bottle, trying to decide on a third pour. I knew the demise of the Hunt was eating at him.

"For the most part," I muttered, thinking about her final comment from the driveway.

Abruptly, Ash leaned forward and poured herself more whiskey and refilled Alex's glass as well. My friend blinked in surprise at the gesture. Ash wasn't that spoiled by royalty standards, but it's not every day a princess gets you a drink.

"Orion thinks you're dead," she said after she took a sip. "We came here to find you before he does something rash." Alex and I exchanged ashamed glances. Wrapped up in our own emotions, we had forgotten our master.

"There's a party tonight. Your presence is required to keep Orion from going too far."

"Sorry, did you say party?" Alex asked incredulously.

"Yes, Dawn has decided the Dandelion Court should throw a celebration to thank the Congregation for voting them back in."

"Tonight?" I gasped. "When did this get planned?"

"Matthew, please. We're Fae, last-minute parties and clothing are sort of our thing." Ash sounded a little indignant that I would even question how they had conjured a party out of nowhere.

"Please tell me it's not Downtown."

"It's Downtown."

"The traffic is going to be a nightmare," I groaned. "Can't we just call him and tell him we're fine?" Even as I asked the question, I knew that wouldn't be enough. Orion wouldn't be mourning just our hypothetical deaths but also the demise of the Hunt itself. We should be there.

"Matt, you need to come." Ash's voice was emphatic. "Dawn wants you there. Plus, I'm not sure how... rational Orion is at the moment."

"I don't blame him; it has been a day."

"True, but I don't think the alcohol is helping," she said with a nervous tone.

"Orion's drinking?" I asked incredulously. I had seen the Hunter have a drink or two before, but never anything I would classify as "drinking." Alex shot me his own doubtful look from across the couch. I couldn't begin to imagine what he would be like tipsy, let alone drunk.

"Dawn is worried he might try to strangle Polaris with his bare hands," Ash insisted.

"Would that be such a bad thing?"

"Yes, it would, and you know it would. There's still the dragon vote tomorrow. If Orion lashes out, we lose any chance at winning it." She was right. As frustrated as I was, Orion murdering the North

Star would only end poorly. It might be satisfying, but it would come crashing down on us like a game of Jenga when a foundational piece is pulled out.

"I guess we're going to a party," I muttered into my glass as I polished off my drink. Alex groaned but followed suit.

Ash made me change my outfit three times before she was satisfied that I was presentable. On the plus side, that gave my phone plenty of time to charge. My betrothed seemed to enjoy playing a classic Faerie role, and the mood between us warmed up as she sent me back to try something else on over and over.

Robin drove us in one of the ridiculous golden SUVs that Dawn favored. I barely had time to buckle my seat belt before he gunned it, and we peeled out of my street and back toward Downtown.

I've only ever had the misfortune of riding with a Faerie driver a few times, but any gray hairs growing on my scalp are a direct result of those experiences. I don't know if it's a symptom of being Immortals, or because there are no cars in the Faerie Lands, but to call them reckless would be like calling a *T. rex* a lizard. It's technically correct but so small in the scale of what it is trying to encompass that it isn't even close.

The SUV's engine roared as Robin inserted it in gaps in the flow of traffic that should never have been big enough but somehow always seemed to work out. I don't think we spent even twenty seconds in a single lane as we carved a path back to Downtown LA.

"Are all Faerie from New York?" I muttered to myself as we cut off another car trying to merge, our chauffeur leaning on the horn as he barreled by. "This feels like I'm in NYC traffic."

"Oh no," Alex said, "New York drivers are even worse."

For once, Robin didn't join in on our banter. That scared me even more than the dragons had. When Gloriana had been stabbed in front of the entire Fae kingdom, my lawyer had gone back to cracking jokes in a heartbeat.

It seemed that to him, this was much more dire.

"How bad is it?" I asked him from the back.

"Many things teeter on the edge of a knife," Robin said, not turning from staring out the windshield. I'd never seen him so focused on a single task before. "The Hunter is furious in a way I have never seen. Even when Gloriana refused to give him Ascalon all those centuries ago, I do not think he was quite as angry."

I tried to picture Orion getting furious, but it was hard. He was so stoic; I was used to thinking of him having the emotional range of a mountain. The only images that came to mind now were of a volcano erupting, molten fury pouring down on the world below.

"To make matters worse, there are others who share his rage."

"Yeah, we're pretty pissed off," I agreed.

"Not you," Robin said, his voice dry with derision. "Nephilim who have suffered similar fates, who share his proclivity for violence."

"The Argonauts," I breathed, remembering they were the only Nephilim to stand with Orion. If he was hanging out with that crew, it was another good reason for me to get over there. Surely one of them could tell me how I could get myself assigned an Impossible Task.

"The very same," Robin agreed. "Do you know what was done to them?"

"I know some of them became Constellations for their participation in an Impossible Task," I said, remembering Nika's story. "I assumed they couldn't stand one another and had a falling-out after that, like the Beatles or something."

"No, Carina said the Congregation did this to them too," Alex pointed out.

"Polaris and the Crowns feared Jason's popularity and his power," Robin told me. "After he completed an Impossible Task, they were afraid they were losing control of the Congregation. So they forced the Argonauts to disband."

"I bet that went over well," I remarked bitterly.

"Jason and his companions refused."

"Well, they seem pretty disbanded now," I pointed out.

"Yes, they do."

Oh.

"Where is Jason?" Alex asked. "I've never heard much about him."

"They made him the example, and when they were done with him, they tore the Argonauts apart. Did you know that the Constellation Argo was once the largest in the night sky? When they killed Jason and disbanded his followers, they tore it to pieces and gave the scraps to the survivors as a threat, not an honor."

The jaws of the trap felt like they'd finally closed around us, and I could see the teeth for what they were. All of this had been about neutralizing Orion, but it wasn't just about taking away his power or forcing him to get back into line.

It was about getting rid of him.

Every single step of this Constellation Congregation was choreographed with the intention of riling him up so he would cross the line and defy them. Then once they had the excuse, they were set to release the perfect weapon to bring him down. They were hunting the Hunter.

A low growl rumbled in my throat. I might not legally be a member of the Hunt, but what does a lion care about rules and regulations? It can't read them. It only cares about its territory and its pride. Beside me, I felt a similar rage roil off Alex.

"Come on," Robin groaned, "be *smarter* than the Argonauts, please. They were many, and still they were broken. You are but three."

I was silent for a moment, thinking about what Robin was trying to say. This trap had been laid with care and precision; I could practically feel the webs closing in from all sides. I wondered if that was Samael's doing, or if Polaris had cooked it up himself. The only way out of this mess that I could see was for Orion to become something he was not.

If he sat there and took the injustices being heaped upon him by Polaris and the Constellation Congregation, then there was nothing they could go after him for. No, I realized with a trickle of dread, it wouldn't even be that easy. By disbanding the Hunt, they had exposed Alex and me as targets. Orion would have to stand idly by and watch while his enemies hunted us. He had no political right to protect us anymore.

Yeah, I didn't think there was any chance he'd let that happen.

"He's right," I said. "We're going to have to be much smarter than the Argonauts if we're going to win this."

"I don't know if you've been watching the same life I have," Alex replied, "but historically that's the part we're the worst at."

"I must agree," Ash sniffed from the front seat.

"Well, put your thinking cap on," I snapped at him. "If we don't come up with a way out of this, you and I are going to be dragon food by the end of the weekend."

DAWN'S PARTY WAS clearly planned with a desire to one-up Lazarus and anyone else who had even thought about throwing an event during the convention. The Dandelion Court had taken over an old theater-turned-music-venue in the heart of Downtown. The DJ was playing so loudly that I could feel the bass thrumming in my chest the moment we got out of the SUV.

The vertical sign out front read THE BOLTON in giant old-timey letters, complete with fluorescent bulbs glowing brightly into the night. The old-school billboard read DANDELION RAVE. It was a strange blend of the old entertainment world and the new, but as a LA native, it wasn't anything I hadn't seen before.

A line of people were waiting at the doorway, conferring with the staff who were diligently checking the guest list. I'm sure they were being *very* thorough. I know from personal experience that Dawn doesn't like having her parties crashed by uninvited guests.

Robin led Ash and us past the waiting guests to the front, holding up his hand to expose a glittering gold band around his wrist. As we walked past, several of the people nudged one another, no doubt irritated that we got to cut the line. The burly security guard nodded as he saw the bracelet and unhooked the red velvet rope blocking the entrance without any hesitation.

Robin paused at the check-in stand as we waltzed in, deftly nabbing two more of the golden wristbands and tossing them to us with a careless air. Alex and I looked at each other and shrugged. I guess we were VIPs again. The band was overengineered for a disposable bracelet. You had to fold it over itself and then fit a button through a hole—it's not important, all I'm saying is it wasn't embarrassing that Ash had to help me with mine. It could have happened to anyone who isn't an origami master.

The inside of the party was packed with supernatural beings. If Lazarus had hosted a quaint little happy hour, then Dawn was throwing the weekend's rager. The giant open lobby was scattered with circular bars; closed doors led to what I presumed was the original theater. Judging by the wall of sound emanating from that direction, it was the current lair of the DJ.

Dancers hung from the ceiling on golden silks following elegant choreographies that didn't match the beat or vibe of the blaring electronic music in the slightest. These are the growing pains of a city obsessed with what it was and what it was becoming: Nothing quite lines up.

The main floor was crowded by a sea of partiers trying to take advantage of the free drinks, except for one spot. The bar in the center only had four figures seated at it, with their backs to the door. Even from across the room, I could feel the dangerous air radiating from them. It was so strong that people were willing to wait an extra five minutes to get their beverage rather than risk bothering the predators. Orion and the three former Argonauts were surrounded by a graveyard of empty glasses so large my liver hurt just looking at them.

"Good luck," Ash murmured to me, giving my arm a gentle squeeze as she and Robin stepped to the side. It seemed even they weren't interested in bothering the Hunter when he was riled up. From my right, Alex mumbled something I couldn't make out over the cacophony of music and people.

"What?" I shouted, leaning toward him.

"This is worse than I thought," he yelled back, into my ear.

I had never seen Orion have more than a few drinks, and I've always assumed that if being a Nephilim means you barely need sleep it probably also works wonders for your alcohol tolerance. But I don't care how much demon blood you've got running through your veins, Poseidon himself would have drowned under the flood of booze that had filled those glasses.

With a growing sense of trepidation, I followed Alex through the swirling party and into the empty bubble surrounding the four Constellations. I felt a heavy amount of scrutiny from around the room as people watched us enter the no-man's-land. I understood their interest: Who would dare bother this group of beings? But while the residents of the table were intimidating, I wasn't worried. I knew which side my bread was buttered on.

Even with having drunk more alcohol than an entire Viking clan's mead hall, the warriors were still sharp. The moment we crossed into their space, they all turned to evaluate us with abyss-filled eyes. I have no idea how they knew we were coming; it was too loud for even someone with their super ears to have heard us.

Orion's face betrayed an unusual amount of emotion as he gazed at us with unabashed relief. Seeing his expression, I wondered if glasses were piled around him not to mourn the dissolution of the Hunt, as I had suspected, but in memoriam of Alex and me. Which if he had just *answered his phone* could have been fixed. Then again, I had forgotten to call Ash, so who am I to throw stones in a glass house?

"We lived, by the way," Alex said as we approached. Shame flickered across the Hunter's face.

"Hail to the survivors!" cried one of the Argonauts—Puppis, I thought it was. He was short and wiry for a Nephilim, but his eyes were as black and ears as pointy as the rest of his kindred. "Another round to celebrate the ones who lived!"

The rest of Jason's old crew cheered and turned back to the bar, pounding it with their fists, making the empty glasses on the surface rattle like a sea of wind chimes. Only Orion didn't turn. He stared at the two of us like a man dying of thirst seeing an oasis on the horizon.

"You survived," he said. I could barely make out his words over the thumping of the music. "How?"

For a moment, I was a little offended. What did he mean, how did we survive? All we had to do was turn right down the hall and run out of the building. That's all it had been, right... or had it been left? For some reason, the events of our escape felt cloudy in my mind, it was like trying to remember a dream. I could picture it, but I couldn't think of a single word to describe the experience. Maybe I was feeling that whiskey more than I thought.

"What can I say, we paid attention," I told him after I gave up on trying to figure out how to explain.

A weight seemed to lift from Orion's shoulders. With a giant grin he leapt off his stool and grabbed both of us in a bear hug. I let out a grunt as the large Nephilim crushed us against his washboard abs. I don't know what it says about a guy that his embrace makes you feel like you're between a rock and a hard place, but that's how Orion's are.

"Easy big guy," Alex panted from his prison next to me. "You might finish what the dragons started." I patted his back weakly, hoping it would trigger his steel-trap-like arms to release us. After another moment, our teacher let us go, taking a step back to snag a pair of shot glasses off the counter and handing them to us.

"We must drink!" he shouted in joy, more happiness shining on his face than I had ever seen before. "To celebrate the return of my squires!" I caught myself raising a hand to shush him before he said that part any louder. It was great that the big guy was happy we were alive; I was happy too. But we weren't *technically* his squires anymore, at least as far as the government was concerned.

Carina handed him a glass, and the Hunter raised his drink in a solemn salute. Wordlessly, Alex, the Argonauts, and I followed suit. Orion was still for a moment, his lips pursed in a thoughtful frown. Slowly, he looked around the room, making eye contact with each of us. At last, he seemed to find the thread he was looking for. Squaring his shoulders, he looked over our heads at his glass.

"To those who have gone before: the Myrmidons, the Argonauts, and the Hunt."

The surviving Argonauts grunted their agreement all around us. I felt my stomach clench as he pondered his next words. I didn't think that I was going to like where this was going.

"May what we do next honor their sacrifice." This time the Argonauts roared their angry approval as the Constellations cheered with us, and everyone took their shot. I knew from the first whiff that it was going to burn on its way down. I have some bad associations with tequila. The first time I ever drank it was the time Dan showed up to steal my soul. The taste is linked in my brain with demons. Baggage aside, I managed to choke the shot down and eagerly bit into the lime wedge hanging on the rim of my glass, letting its citrus flavors cancel out the burn.

"You did well today," Orion said with a bright smile, clapping both of us on the shoulder with his giant hands. The force of his approval was almost enough to make me stagger, but I managed to bear up. "I am proud to have the two of you known as members of the Hunt."

I won't lie, a genuine warmth began to burn in my chest at his words, but the heat faded soon enough as I realized he was doubling down on the Hunt terminology. I wasn't surprised, not really. Orion has a jaw cut from granite and is more stubborn than any mineral Mother Earth can produce. It didn't matter what happened to the Jason and the Argonauts, he would walk his own path.

"About that," I shout-whispered, leaning in closer to our mentor. "You gotta play it cool about the whole squire bit for a while."

"I will not be told by Polaris, or anyone else, what the Hunt can or cannot be," Orion said, brows furrowing like dark storm clouds. "I am the Hunter, they are not."

"We know, we know," Alex agreed, joining me in making shushing gestures with his hands. "But that doesn't mean you should be so *loud* about it."

"I'm not afraid."

"I never said you were, but this isn't a game."

"I know it's not a game," Orion snapped, some heat flickering in his black eyes. "Do not forget that I have been here for *millennia*, Matthew Carver. The gravity of what has occurred has not escaped my notice. You are a clever squire, but you have not learned all my tricks yet."

Slightly embarrassed, I lowered my head in shame. "I didn't mean to—"

"The Hunt is *mine*. You are my squires. I knew this day would come the moment I heard your tale. I chose this path then, and I choose it now."

Surprised, I blinked at the large Nephilim. Cassiopeia had hinted as much, the night I met her in the back of the Olympus Bar and Grille. She had asked Orion if he was willing to go to war over what had been done to me, and he told her that he already had.

Chills ran down my spine as I realized the Hunter wasn't lying. He had been hunting this prey the whole time. I had begun to think myself smarter than the Hunter, that I was sharp enough to see traps he could not. Perhaps it was merely that the tiger does not concern himself with the web of a spider, for he knows it cannot hold him.

"You knew?"

"I suspected." Orion sat down heavily on the barstool behind him, a world-weariness tugging at his shoulders like a yoke made of granite. "I saw what happened to Achilles and to Jason when they outlived their purpose to Polaris and the Crowns. I knew I would be stepping onto that same path."

"And you did it anyway?"

"I did it anyway," he agreed. "You are owed justice, and Alex is owed respect that is not given to him by our people. Those were causes worth going to war over."

I didn't really know what to say. All my panicked arguments about how this was all a trap to kill Orion seemed useless now. He knew that better than I did. That had been the point before the Constellation Convention had even been called. Everyone else knew that's what this was about. Alex and I were the ones late to the party.

"You could have just told us that from the beginning," Alex complained, a similar look of frustration on his face.

"It's rude to brag about how noble you are," the Hunter said with a tiny, amused smile as he accepted another drink from one of the Argonauts. I barely managed to stop myself from rolling my eyes. I guess he deserved one lame joke for his friendship.

But only one.

"Isn't that right, Squires?"

"Yes, sir," we responded in unison.

"This is very touching and all," I said, trying not to sound too unappreciative, "but do you have a plan for this war? Or are we figuring that part out as we go?"

Orion was silent for a moment, swirling his whiskey in a cheap glass before quaffing it in a single gulp. "Tonight, we drink," he said, sounding more Viking than he ever had. "Tomorrow, we fight."

"Isn't there a way that this ends without turning into a giant fight?"

"No."

Puppis and the rest of the Argonauts let out another cheer as the short Nephilim slid in, holding another round of shots on a tray. My stomach roiled in protest, so I waved him off. I was pretty sure my organs would stage a mutiny if I tried to go shot-for-shot with a bunch of demigods.

Not feeling particularly encouraged about our potential plan, I slid past them to the bar to get myself a normal cocktail. I've found that holding a beverage helps prevent people from trying to force more drinks on you. Having an empty hand at an event like this is a beacon to the party bullies. They'll make sure you get a drink if it is the last thing they do.

I made my way to stand next to Carina as she waited for the bartender. The brunette Argonaut was almost as tall as I am, with broad shoulders and a square jaw. I was pretty confident she could crush me even without her superhuman strength.

I gave her a friendly nod as we waited and got a stern one in return. I stared at my hands, desperately trying to figure out how to break the ice. I could feel my heart speeding up. I'd rather be chased by those dragoons again than figure out how to make small talk. All I had to do was strike up a conversation with a lady at a bar. Sure, in this case I had no romantic agenda, but historically I have struggled in moments like this. The irony that my future might depend on such a basic human interaction was not lost on me. It shouldn't be hard—*just find some common ground.*

"What are you drinking?" I asked, knowing it was a lame question before it was even out of my mouth.

"Bourbon."

"Oh, nice."

We stood in silence as the music of the party raged around us. I felt like an ice climber sliding down a mountain, my fingers scrabbling for purchase on a cold, smooth surface.

"Can I admit something?" I asked, not bothering to wait for her answer. "I don't really know what the difference is between bourbon and whiskey."

"I like bourbon more."

"Oh, well maybe I should give bourbon a try. I'm not sure if I actually enjoy whiskey, or if I just like that it's not tequila. I had a bad tequila experience, and now I try to avoid the stuff."

The bartender approached us, empty glass in hand. He looked at me, and I decided to try to keep things going by bluffing my way through the order.

"Two bourbons, please," I told him.

"Neat!" he said, which was a weird thing to say. I guess it was neat that we were both ordering bourbon. I would've figured it wasn't that unusual at a *bar*, but hey, what do I know. The bartender stared at me for a few more seconds, which made me begin to suspect I was missing something. Was that a question? Now that I thought about it, it sounded like a question.

"Neat," Carina confirmed from next to me. The bartender gave me a weird look but nodded.

"I thought he was saying our order was cool," I confided to the stoic Constellation as he went to work, pouring two fingers of the brown liquid into a pair of glasses.

"Neat means it is served on its own," she explained.

"Ohhhh," I said. "That's… neat, I guess?"

Carina looked at me, exasperated. All I could do was give her a mildly ashamed shrug. It was right there; I couldn't help myself. An irritated chuckle escaped her lips as she accepted her glass from the bartender.

"That was terrible."

"If you think that was bad, you should hear the rest of my jokes."

"I think I'll pass." The Argonaut gave me a salute with her drink and started to turn back to her companions. Desperate, I threw any attempt to be charming and normal to the wind and called after her.

"I need your help."

The Constellation paused, turning back to me with a strange look on her face. Slowly, she placed her drink on the bar and folded her hands next to it. "Why would you need my help when you have the Hunter in your corner?"

"Because you know something even he does not."

"And what is that?"

"How to be given an Impossible Task." Whatever Carina had been expecting me to ask for, it was clearly not that. Shock rippled across her face in a wave before she schooled it back to smoothness.

"Do you have a death wish, manling?" she asked.

"No," I said with a shrug, "it's more of a death date really."

"Ah, you mean your deal with Hell has a time limit on it."

"Sorry, is it that bad?" I glanced down at one of my armpits and gave it a sniff. I had put on extra deodorant, but it doesn't seem to help with whatever it was that supernatural beings could smell on me.

"Are you unhappy with how long your contract lets you live? If you wish to end your life early, there are easier ways."

"What do you know about my deal?" I asked. I hadn't been quiet about what Dan had done to me. Polaris had also referenced it in his list of Orion's crimes, but that didn't mean every Constellation had heard the truth.

"Why, did you ask for something special?" Carina asked, arching a brown eyebrow. I guess the word really hadn't gotten around. Maybe I should hire a PR person or something.

"I didn't ask for anything at all. I never signed anything either."

"Then why do you reek of sulfur and demons?"

"Because a demon forged my signature and stole my soul," I replied fiercely.

Carina's eyes went wide, and she took a sip of her whiskey before dropping the cup to the counter and tapping it for the bartender to refill. I followed her lead, doing my best to exhale the gasoline-like fumes of the bourbon so I wouldn't choke on them. I didn't tell her, but it tasted no different than whiskey to me.

The bartender obliged us with another neat round. Carina didn't say anything while he poured. Her black eyes bored into mine, as if she were trying to drill into my mind and see if I was telling the truth.

"Who knows about this?" she demanded, apparently deciding I was.

"Orion, the Fae, a few others." I deliberately kept my answer vague. I appreciated that the Argonaut had voted with Orion today, but that didn't mean I trusted her completely.

"Did Lilith know?"

I gave her a small nod as I took a sip of my new drink. She cursed something under her breath that I couldn't quite make out over the music. I'd never considered what the death of Lilith must look like to someone who didn't know she had been involved in taking my soul. Maybe some thought Orion had finally snapped and gone after prey above his station in the food chain. That might explain why so many were willing to turn on him. If he was killing the Devil's girlfriend, why not them next?

"What does an Impossible Task have to do with this?"

Now it was my turn to stare into her black eyes and take her measure. How much did I trust this Nephilim? I had heard of Jason and his Argonauts before, but I had never heard a peep about Carina or Atalanta before this weekend.

She seemed decent, but then sometimes the worst of us do. My hesitation was that I didn't know how much Hell knew. Zagan had clearly read Dan's custom contract well enough to know that he had to give me five million dollars every year. But had he caught the part about the Impossible Task?

Even if he had, he didn't know for sure that Robin had seen it, which meant that there was less of a chance for him to be ready to run interference. Did I trust Carina? Not really. But there weren't many people alive who had completed an Impossible Task, so who else was I going to ask?

"It's a way out," I told her.

"A way out of what... your contract?" A surprised look fluttered across her face. "I've never heard of anything like that being a part of an infernal deal."

"It appears the fraudster gave me something of a custom deal," I said with a wry smile.

"Well, I wish I had better news for you, friend, but that's not much of an out." Carina shook her head, leaning back on her barstool. "The only people I know of who could give you an Impossible Task are long dead."

"What do you mean, they're dead?" I asked, feeling a little indignant. I had earned the right to get a task. Someone should have mentioned if they weren't giving them out anymore. "Who is dead?"

"To get yourself an Impossible Task, you need to find a Sorcerer King."

"A what now?"

"A king who is a sorcerer."

"Oh, okay, thank you, saying it backward makes it make so much more sense."

"A king who is more than just a king. Someone like Solomon. Our task came from one called Pelias. A queen would work just as well. If you manage to dig up Cleopatra, maybe she'd be willing to sort you out."

A leaden sense of despair settled around my heart with a strong grip. We didn't really do kings or queens the same way anymore. Even if we did, I had no idea how you were supposed to know if they were a sorcerer or not. Was that more like a wizard or a magician? Would a royal who knew how to do card tricks qualify?

"So there aren't any living ones?" I asked.

"It's been centuries since the last one I knew of died, and they don't really make royalty like they used to. I'm sorry." Her expression softened, and she held up her glass to me in a silent salute. "You may not believe me, but you should be grateful."

"You're right," I said, echoing her cheers. "I don't."

"The only thing worse than dying in the pursuit of an Impossible Task is completing one."

I stopped drinking after our conversation. Part of that was because I was on DC—Designated Constellation—duty. But a bigger part of it was because of what I had learned from Carina. In my head, I could picture Zagan's cruel laughter as I discovered the loophole wasn't really a loophole. I wondered if some poor sucker had actually negotiated that into their contract only to learn the same thing I just had.

Robin had been wrong: There was no easy way out. Hell had me wrapped in their coils, and they were not going to let me go. I had 103 months to live. With a doom cloud like that looming over me, maybe I should have been the one drinking. Deep down I had always suspected this wasn't going to be a way out for me. I had been losing the game from the first move; the only thing I could do was try to lose slowly.

But I wasn't the only one who had lost something today. Orion's grief was fresh and raw. So I let him drink to mourn the second passing of the Hunt, and I retreated to the corner of the bar to mourn my own future death in private. It seemed only fitting—after all, you die alone. Everyone would get to go to my funeral, but I wouldn't be invited. I wondered if this was how terminally ill patients felt, able to see the end with a clear vision that their peers could never understand.

The oppressive music isolated me as I sat in my sorrows, cutting me off from hearing anyone's conversation. The low light made it feel like everyone was far away. I was only a few feet from the group, but it might as well have been miles.

A most unwelcome visitor stormed into my bubble of seclusion, sucking out the tranquility and ruining my attempt at rationally accepting my future death. My father wore his gray peacoat buttoned all the way up to his neck. His golden eyes burned with distaste as he scanned the room of partiers.

"Tomorrow," he said by way of greeting and explanation.

"Tomorrow?" I repeated, not sure what we were talking about.

"Tomorrow, we strike."

Oh, that. In all the drama that had happened today, I had completely forgotten about my father's machinations for revenge. One more plate to keep spinning, I guess.

"Are you sure it's the best time?" I asked. "Did you see what happened today? Do you know what's probably going to happen tomorrow? We sort of have a crisis on our hands right now."

"It's been arranged," he informed me coolly, not an ounce of hesitation visible in his firm face.

"But the Hunt—" I protested.

"Being free of the Hunter's clutches is a good thing," my father interrupted. "In time you will learn how lucky you are not to be tied to that madman. Now you can focus on things that are actually important."

A low burn of anger prickled across my scalp at my father's casual dismissal of my friend. Orion had risked his life for mine more times than I could count—more times than Damien ever had.

I opened my mouth to let him have it, but some instinct warned me it would only be wasted breath. My father wasn't interested in my opinion. My mouth snapped shut so hard my teeth clicked against each other. My progenitor gave me a knowing glance but didn't comment.

"When everything comes to a head tomorrow, the Powers That Be will be distracted," he continued as if nothing had happened. "That's when we will exact revenge for your mother and sisters."

"How will we do that exactly?" I asked, feeling my heart pound as my father casually planned the assassination of a Faerie princess. "That sounds less like a plan and more like the idea of one. Mav is an Immortal; how exactly are we going to snip her life thread?"

"I've procured an immortal-killing weapon," Damien mused, raising one of his flameless hands to inspect it lazily. "But we still start with fire." A chill settled over me as I pictured how much we would have to burn the Lady of Winter in order to extinguish her life. "It seems only fitting. She drowned my family, so we shall burn her."

"Our family."

"What?" he asked, sounding annoyed that I was interrupting his monologue.

"She drowned *our* family."

"Yes..." he agreed after a moment, as if he was agreeing to something so simple, he couldn't believe we were discussing it. With an irritated sigh, I let it go. I don't know what else I expected.

"How will I know when it's time?"

"You'll know." Damien hesitated before turning to face me, a serious look on his face. "You have been a disappointment on many levels. Do your best not to add another reason to the list tomorrow."

Stunned, I stared at my father, with no idea how to respond to that. I couldn't believe he'd actually said it out loud. It wasn't like I didn't know, but to hear it clear as a bell was not something I'd been ready for.

A weird cocktail of shame and despair began to curdle in my guts, like milk and beer being mixed. My father was not someone I looked up to or wanted to emulate, but the disdain of a parent is a blade that cuts through any armor.

"You know I didn't sign the deal, right?" I stuttered after a few seconds of poignant silence. My father watched me with the eyes of a master chef, waiting to see if his soufflé would settle. "They really stole my soul. It wasn't me. I didn't do it!"

"And yet," he said in cool tones, "here we are."

Here we were indeed. I may not have signed the deal, but my mother was dead, one of my sisters was dead, and the other was currently in a limbo-like state, being tortured by the denizens of Hell.

Here we freaking were.

"I hate to interrupt what I'm sure is a touching father–son conversation," Dawn said as she appeared at my right hand, "but I'm afraid I need to borrow the former squire, Damien."

"He's all yours," he grunted, turning on his heel and striding back into the party as if he was late for an appointment. I couldn't help but feel like he meant that on more than one level.

I eyed the bar with a hint of despair, as Dawn slipped her left arm through my right. After that conversation, I could really use a drink. But I doubted this was a social call.

"It seems, Matthew, that things have changed between you and me," the Queen said after a moment as we wandered through the party. A cold wave of fear rushed through me as I realized she was talking about our deal.

"I did what you asked," I replied defensively. "I helped manage the Hunter and get the Dandelion Court back into the Constellation Congregation."

"Yes." She laughed warmly. "You have done very well. I told you to prove yourself, and you have done so."

"But?" I prompted, narrowing my eyes at her.

"But how do I know I can trust you?"

"How do I know I can trust *you*?" I shot back.

"Oh, darling, you shouldn't trust me." Dawn laughed again. A shiver ran down my spine. I knew she truly meant that.

"You seem to enjoy Samael's company a little too much for me to do so," I snapped. I didn't mean to let that slip, but I couldn't take wondering anymore. If we were going to be allies, I needed to know.

"So you saw that, hmm? I never took you for a Peeping Tom. No one ever overhears anything pleasant while eavesdropping." A bright smile shone on her face as she regarded me.

"That does not inspire a lot of confidence in our relationship."

Dawn was silent for a moment, a rare pensive look on her face. She stopped walking and turned to stare directly into my eyes. "The Poisoner killed my mother," she said very softly. I had to lean forward to hear all her words. "You of all people should know what that feels like, Matthew Carver."

Goose bumps ran up my arms as she leaned closer to whisper directly into my ear. "The best way to catch a spider is with many flies, and that takes a lot of honey."

"You're going to kill her," I breathed, a hint of awe in my voice. I couldn't even conceive of killing an Immortal like Samael. Killing a fallen angel? Was that even possible?

"We shall see," she mused, a hint of something pleased lurking in her voice as we resumed walking. "But enough of that fantasy. It seems you now only serve one master. Let us discuss your status tomorrow," Dawn continued before I could interrupt, trilling her *r*'s.

"Tomorrow?" I choked. How had she overhead what Damien had said? I know I had been going along with his plan, but that didn't mean I was going to actually help him *kill* Mav. Not that I didn't like the idea—she *had* murdered my family and tried to kill me. I just wasn't sure I was the cold-blooded type of killer. I have ended lives before, but not premeditated. That felt more twisted somehow.

"Yes tomorrow, at the convention." Dawn clicked her tongue in annoyance. "I assume you will be attending as a member of my court?"

Now that Alex was outside and safe, I didn't see any reason I couldn't use my other badge to get into tomorrow's vote. Otherwise, we both would just be stuck outside, waiting for the bad news.

"Yeah, I'd like to," I told her. "I think it would be good for me to be in the room."

"Very well," Dawn said with an accepting nod. "If you are going to be representing the Dandelion Court, can I count on you to be on your best behavior?"

I thought about my answer for a moment. I had a very bad feeling that tomorrow would be more of the same scheming and backstabbing. Misbehaving as a member of the Hunt had been one thing, but tomorrow I would be a member of the Fae nobility. Dawn had just managed to get her people a seat back at the table, I could understand why she wouldn't want me to upset the apple cart yet.

"If I'm being honest, Dawn, probably not," I admitted with a helpless shrug.

"Excellent." The Queen gave my arm an affectionate pat and released me, swirling off into her own party like a piece of confetti dancing on the wind. My emotions did the same sort of flight pattern inside my brain, corkscrewing all over the place.

Glancing back at my friends, I thought it might finally be time to go. The Argonauts stood in a little group swaying, and I couldn't tell if it was in time to the music or because of the ocean of alcohol they'd consumed. Orion and Alex remained at the bar, both lost in their thoughts. As I walked back to join them, a familiar figure cut across the room, walking past the bar without any hesitation.

Nika wore a bright-red cocktail dress, and her blond hair flowed down to her shoulders, freshly blown out. She was dressed to kill in more ways than one. I couldn't believe Dawn had let her in.

"Nika!" Alex called as she entered his vision. He popped out of his chair and held a hand up, trying to catch her attention. "Nika!" You didn't need pointy ears and Nephilim blood to hear his shout over the loud music. The svelte warrior did not pause as she strode through the doors and into the concert hall. Alex's shoulders slumped as he dropped back onto his stool.

I've both lived in LA long enough to know what happens when your social currency runs out. We may have escaped with our lives, but it seemed not everything had survived.

THE FINAL DAY of the convention dawned dark and foreboding. LA is often thought of as the land of eternal sunshine, where no one has ever seen the rain. That's mostly true—we're smack dab in the middle of a temperate desert, so we rarely see any kind of weather at all. But there's one thing that often gets overlooked: When we get weather, we get *weather*. The iron-gray clouds that gathered in the sky promised buckets of water would be dumped down upon our dry city very soon. I was glad I wasn't driving today, because LA people have no idea how to drive in the rain.

My phone rang as I was getting dressed. My eyes narrowed at the unknown number, but I answered on instinct. "Matt's phone, how can I take your order?"

"Are you trying to screw with me, Carver?" a familiar governmental voice demanded in clipped tones.

"Ah, Agent Richter, no, sir," I replied. In all the excitement I had almost forgotten about the supernatural FBI breathing down my neck to make me a snitch. Maybe I should start writing some of this down.

"Well, you've certainly not given me a damn thing I can use!" Steven hissed. "It's like you think I won't lock you up."

"No, no, I take you very seriously," I assured him as earnestly as I could. "I just have been working my way in deeper trying to figure out what's going on with the big meet."

"So it's happening?" A hungry note entered his voice.

"Yes, sir, one hundred percent," I told him, feeling almost bad for the poor guy. He was just a little out of his depth. "I'm confident something huge is going down today, and I think I have a way to get inside."

Agent Richter was silent for a moment as he considered my news. "Okay, you better find something good. I swear, you screw me and—"

"Yes, heard loud and clear," I promised, cutting off his rant. "I've got a good feeling about today, sir. I'll get you something you can use."

"I hope so, for your sake."

We filed into Alex's minivan and headed Downtown for the final session. Orion sat in the backseat, a pair of sunglasses over his eyes as he nursed whatever the immortal version of a hangover was. The fact that he had drunk almost an entire distillery's worth of whiskey last night and was only minorly uncomfortable now was clearly a superpower all on its own.

"I hate this," Alex remarked as we made our way closer to the center.

"Which part?" I asked dryly. "There's so much to love."

"The part where I have to sit outside and wait while you two go in to actually do something."

"Hey, man, you're not being fair to yourself. You're doing something."

"I am? What am I doing?"

"You're keeping the car warm for later."

Alex rolled his eyes but didn't rise to my barb. The final meeting of the Constellation Convention was to address the most dangerous topic of them all, and we were all on edge.

I'm not ashamed to say that I was afraid of Draco being released. While I think we have been exceptional squires, I am willing to admit the previous roster was a bit more *deadly*. I didn't have high hopes that a second showdown with the dragon god would go better with us as the backup, even if Orion did have Ascalon now.

My mood was as bleak as the weather as we pulled back into the garage, parking next to Orion's bike.

Alex turned off the van but didn't take his hands off the steering wheel. I saw his knuckles whiten has he gripped it in frustration. I gave him a reassuring pat on the shoulder as I opened my door and slid out. Six months ago, when I had blown the dandelion candle to escape being squished by Zagan, I had abandoned my friends in the middle of a battle with a fallen angel. The stress and guilt I felt while on the sidelines had been more painful than the crushing force he had applied to my rib cage.

I grabbed a pistol from the armory in the back of the van and slipped it under my belt, taking a small amount of comfort in the duffel-bagged form of Ascalon waiting for its moment. At least we were loaded for dragon today.

"Call me if anything goes down," Alex grumbled dejectedly from the front seat. "I'll be there in a jiffy."

"You got it," I promised him, tossing my friend a wave as I followed the Hunter out of the parking garage. I hunched my shoulders against the crisp October wind as we made our way down the street.

Orion and I breezed through security with the same casual indifference. Except this time, I was rocking my Dandelion Court badge instead of my Hunt one.

Bellerophon was on guard at the entrance to Hall B again. His black eyes sparkled with malevolence as he spotted me approaching with Orion. The scarred Nephilim stepped toward me, hand on the hilt of his sword. Two other guards I didn't recognize followed in his footsteps, like a wolf pack on the hunt.

"Brave of you to show your face here without being a Guest," Bellerophon called as he trotted toward me. He eyed the Hunter with a devious smirk as he challenged me. Orion ignored him, not even pausing his stride as the warrior closed in on his former squire. That might have hurt my feelings if I didn't understand the game we were playing.

In the eyes of the Constellation Convention, Orion had no claim to protect me anymore. The law had taken Alex and me away from him. If he rose to the bait and picked a fight with Bellerophon, he would be in the wrong. It was a trap, just not a particularly clever one.

Fortunately, I didn't need Orion to step in and protect me. I had a different shield to hide behind. I gave Bellerophon my best condescending Robin smile and held up my lanyard for him to see.

"There must be some sort of confusion," I said brightly. "Are members of the Dandelion Court no longer welcome Guests at the convention? Does the Queen know? I will be sure to inform her immediately."

Bellerophon stopped dead in his tracks, as did his shadows. A flicker of fear crossed his face before it vanished behind an angry mask. The idiot had almost caused an international incident by enjoying being a thug too much.

"Of course not," he muttered through gritted teeth. "I merely misspoke, please forgive my ignorance. I did not mean to imply anything other than the utmost respect for the Dandelion Court."

Say what you will about these immortals, but they sure do know how to apologize. Some of our politicians could learn a few things from old Belphy.

"I appreciate your words," I told him, smug smile still fixed firmly on my face. "I will make sure that they are carried straight to the Queen's ears." Unable to protest, Bellerophon stepped to the side and gave me a stiff nod, as if we'd just had a friendly exchange. I wondered if this was what Dawn was talking about when she asked if I would be misbehaving today.

Probably.

Orion had already vanished through the doors into the hall. None of the other guards dared check me, so I strode alone into the reception area as a representative of the Dandelion Court. Even though it was early, many of the Constellations were already milling about. I felt an immediate weight of attention as beings marked my entrance. A lot of them looked surprised to see me in one piece.

I followed Orion's cue from the hallway and ignored him back, making a beeline for Dawn and her posse who were huddled around a pair of standing tables. Let the people wonder what was going on—it was good for them.

"I suppose you think you are very clever," an acerbic voice observed from next to me.

I turned to face Polaris and resisted the urge to tell the ancient Nephilim the answer was yes. The North Star was sipping wine from a fancy silver goblet even though it wasn't yet noon. He eyed me with an overt scowl.

"I'm not sure I follow," I said slowly, as if I were trying to piece together something very complex. "What do you mean?"

"Do not play games with me, boy," the elder hissed. "A different badge might protect you as a courtesy to your betters, but that does not make you welcome here."

"It's okay," I confided to him. "I don't really want to be here either."

"If you truly understood what was at stake, you would not be."

"Ah yes, watching you aiding and abetting the dragons to black-mail your little congress into releasing some sort of draconic god from prison was tempting to miss, but I decided to come check it out anyway. I was already in the neighborhood, and you guys have great catering."

A cruel sneer grew on Polaris's face. I might have imagined it, but I thought the wine in his glass was shaking. I snagged a little crudité off a passing plate while the ancient Nephilim seethed and took a loud, crunchy bite.

"What? It's not like it was subtle," I said around a stalk of celery. Too bad it wasn't a carrot. I felt a little like Bugs Bunny talking down to Elmer Fudd. "I'm honestly a little embarrassed for you. Our congress at least pretends they're doing their best—well, sometimes, I guess."

"If you had an inkling of what an unchained dragon is capable of—" Polaris snarled, but I cut him off.

"Yeah, yeah, fire and destruction. Very bad, I'm sure. Have you heard of the Cold War? I've gotten this whole spiel before, *Ronald*."

Polaris's eyes narrowed in anger, and he took a step closer to me. I took another bite of celery. He couldn't touch me. If he broke the faith as a host right here, right now, I was confident that the room would tear itself apart, and Orion would be in the thick of it. Part of me wanted him to start something, just to see what the Hunter would do to the North Star.

"You and that runt should have died yesterday. Time will run out on you eventually."

"Matthew, there you are, darling." Ash's warm hand hooked through my arm as my betrothed slid in beside me. I turned to give her a smile and received a bright one in return. Her red hair was coiled into a tight braid that rested over one shoulder. She wore a black dress that ended just before her knees with what appeared to be thigh-high biker boots.

"Polaris, how are you this fine day? It is good to see you."

"It is lovely to see you as well, Lady Ash," the North Star replied smoothly, changing from a furious conspirator to a charming old man in the blink of an eye.

"Do you mind if I steal him away from you?" Ash patted my arm affectionately, but I got the sense I was being extracted.

"Of course." Polaris raised his morning wineglass in a small salute. "To young love."

Which, first of all, whoa, whoa. Ash was my betrothed. She was great. Smart, funny, beautiful, you name it. But throwing around the L word seemed aggressive. Just because we were getting married didn't mean he had the right to bring up love! I know he's a villain, but the audacity still shocked me.

"You're welcome," Ash murmured in my ear as she steered me toward Dawn and the rest of the Dandelion Court.

"Saving my bacon as always," I chuckled, patting her hand.

"What else are betrotheds for?"

"You look nice," I said without even thinking about it. I like her, don't get me wrong. I like her a lot. But who's to say when like ends and love begins? Not me, I'm no philosopher. I don't even have a real college degree.

The Dandelion Court was out in full muster today. Tania and Mav wore similar outfits to Ash, plus the golden collars that ensured their obedience. My father lurked next to Dawn, his aristocratic face narrowing in focus as he spoke with the Queen.

Robin was bedecked in his classic white and gold suit; he twinkled his eyes at me with an amused hello as I joined. I gave him a nod and warm grin in return. It was objectively funny that I had been kicked out yesterday, and they had to let me back in because I had a different badge. It only happened because of terrible circumstances, but it was still funny.

"Matthew, are you behaving?" Dawn drawled, her eyes a solid gold as she watched me approach.

"Not particularly, Your Majesty," I replied. For some reason, here in this formal moment, I got the vibe that addressing her by her name instead of her title would have been a betrayal of trust. Just because I had known her before she was Queen didn't mean that I didn't have to respect her office.

"Good." Dawn looked around the room with an unashamed stare, measuring the Constellations that had already arrived. "Keep it up. We don't have much time left."

I took that as permission, and with Ash on my arm went off to cause more chaos. If the whole room was already so intimidated that they had voted against the Hunter, I didn't know what she was hoping I could do. But then again, as I had told Polaris, it's not like the situation was *subtle*. I might as well swing for the fences.

I led Ash to where Cassiopeia and her family were standing. The Constellation of Beauty gave me a polite nod as I approached, and I returned it with a genuine smile. Cassie had saved my life when Lilith ambushed me, so no matter what happened, I'd always be grateful to her for that.

"Your Majesties," I said, bowing slightly at the neck to Cassiopeia and to Cepheus her husband, both royals in their own right. "Have you been introduced to my betrothed, Lady Ash of the Dandelion Court?"

I knew the answer was no, Ash had never been allowed to leave the doomsday bunker that was Goldhall until her mother had died, but it seemed rude to assume. Cassiopeia greeted Ash warmly before turning to me, expression growing harder.

"If you are here on the Hunter's behalf, know your breath will be wasted."

She's a real straight shooter, that Cassiopeia.

"Orion did not send me," I reassured her. "He couldn't even if he wanted to. I don't know if you missed it, but I'm no longer his squire." The stunning Ethiopian queen scoffed dismissively. That's fair; if I were in her shoes, I probably wouldn't have bought it either.

"If I come on behalf of anyone, I would say it is on behalf of everyone."

"Having now been excommunicated from the Hunt, you've taken up the mantle of everyone? How noble," Cepheus mused into his cup. I guess immortals really don't have the same rules about drinking before noon that those of us susceptible to liver failure do.

"Someone had to, since the rest of you are letting the Dragon Dons walk all over them," I replied, holding the Nephilim king's eye. He looked away, lips twisted in irritation. Point for Matt. A petty point, but a point all the same. I take them where I can get them.

"It is very easy to criticize when you have never seen a rampaging dragon," Cassiopeia scolded me sharply. "You do not know what you are asking for."

"Everyone keeps telling me that," I replied with a small shrug. "I'm sure they're terrifying. But if a regular one running around doing its dragony thing is so bad, what do you think happens if Draco is released? I can only assume his final form is even more dramatic. Otherwise what's the point of this whole game?"

Cassiopeia was silent for a moment, a troubled frown on her face.

"The way I see it, they're using the threat of their current stick to get a bigger stick, and that one has nails and spikes sticking out of it. If they really can do what they say, how does letting them become even more powerful make standing up to them in the future any more possible?" The two Nephilim shifted uncomfortably, unwilling to meet my eyes. I guess it's easy to get lost in fear when the gun barrel is right in your face.

"You ask us to take an incredible risk," Cepheus managed after a few moments of intense silence.

Somewhere behind us a bell sounded, calling the Constellations to their seats.

"I'm not sure I'm asking," I told him.

Since the Dandelion Court had not been a formal member of the Congregation when it had convened, we had been given some leftover seats in the first row of the bowl, along the edge. I followed the delegation and slid into a seat between Dawn and Ash, which felt weird. Six months ago, I could not have imagined this ever happening.

They were by no means good seats, but they were perfect for heckling the speakers. Dawn had told me to misbehave, and I had every intention of taking advantage of that carte blanche.

The session began with the now familiar ceremony. Polaris and the two Auroras strode down the hall and ascended to the dais after the third chime sounded. Borealis began to call roll from her giant scroll. Everything went exactly as it had the last two days—until she read the final name.

"Octantis, the South Star."

"Present!" a strong female voice boomed from the entry behind us.

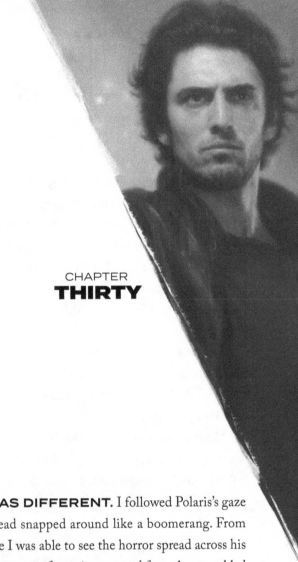

THIS WAS DIFFERENT. I followed Polaris's gaze as his head snapped around like a boomerang. From my angle I was able to see the horror spread across his ancient features. A low murmur of surprise emerged from the assembled host as they saw the missing Constellation enter.

Like Polaris, Octantis was aged. She wore a long purple gown that trailed behind her, pooling on the ground. The blindfold made of cloth torn from her dress and wrapped around her eyes was even more striking. Despite her eyes being covered, she looked around the room as if she could see. She reminded me of something, but I couldn't quite place my finger on what it was.

"Did you think I would sit idly by and let you bring about ruin?"

she murmured as she passed Polaris. A faint spark of hope flickered in my chest at her words. Anyone who was not on the North Star's team was a welcome addition to the party, no matter how late they decided to show up.

He didn't bother to answer, instead turning to grip the podium as he prepared to address the Congregation. However much he didn't want Octantis there, it seemed there was nothing for him to do about it.

"On this final day of the Constellation Convention, we have one major motion to discuss," Polaris said briskly to the room. "The Dragon Dons wish to petition the Congregation for the release of their master, the Constellation Draco. The Poles and the Crowns have agreed to allow them to present their case—"

Octantis let out a disgusted snort. I was starting to like the South Star more and more. If only she had been here yesterday, maybe I'd still be in the Hunt. Polaris gave her a withering glare but pressed on with his opening remarks.

"Much has changed since the time that Draco was given his sentence. To that end, we have agreed to let the Dons speak." Behind Polaris, Don Doyle appeared, decked out in his Italian suit. Octantis's blindfolded gaze followed the dragon's movement with unerring accuracy, like a hawk watching a mouse.

I got the feeling she saw more than I did, not less.

Doyle stepped up to the podium, accepting the place Polaris offered him. The red-headed dragon smiled, revealing the wicked-sharp teeth hidden behind his human-looking lips. If it was supposed to be friendly, the gesture failed. It was only threatening.

"Almost five hundred years ago, you lot voted to lock up Draco on account of his beef with the Hunter," he said without preamble. I guess there's no need for flowery speeches when you've already personally threatened all the voters.

"On that black day, you didn't punish the Hunter for his transgressions, but you chose to throw our master into the darkness. I'm here today to request that you set him free and put the Hunter in his place. Draco's done his time, he has, but where's the punishment for the dragon slayer? What justice has he faced for his actions?"

Whatever else the Dragon Don might have planned for his speech was lost in the horrified gasps echoing around the elevated bowl of the Congregation. I thought I saw a faint echo of the room's shock on Polaris's face, as if he hadn't been expecting this either.

This was so much worse than just getting their big bad boss back. I craned my neck to the left to look up at the Hunter, who was perched in his center seats, staring down at the dragon. The Hunter's face was impassive, chiseled like a mountain. Doyle's demands might as well have been the wind rushing past for all they seemed to bother him.

I tried to catch Cassiopeia's eye across the bowl, but the queen wasn't looking my way. This is what happens when you tell predators you are weak. If a mouse wouldn't be satisfied with just a cookie, why did anyone think the dragons would stop with getting Draco released?

This was the dragon's insurance policy on the plan, I realized. They had been baiting the Hunter, to try to kill him. But if he didn't fall for it, locking him away in a prison cell for centuries would be close enough.

"All right, all right, order!" Polaris demanded, stepping back up to the podium, shooing the dragon out of it. "We will now discuss the Dragon Don's... request."

"This is an outrage!" barked Canis Majoris, the big Nephilim I had met with Orion, leaping to his feet. His smaller son also stood and voiced his own displeasure at the dragon's request.

A dark murmur rippled through the room. It rang of resentment and brewing anger. It seemed the masses were perfectly fine watching Orion be stripped of his rights, but now that they realized he might not be around to watch over them, it was going too far. I suddenly thought I understood a little of Orion's disgust for his relatives. Is there anything more pitiful than watching someone with power cower behind others?

"North Star, I would speak!" a woman shouted over the barking canines.

"The Congregation recognizes the Archer Constellation, Sagittarius," Polaris shouted instantly, almost as if he had been waiting for it. "Silence!" he bellowed, glaring at the two dog Constellations until they begrudgingly sat down.

"Don Doyle speaks true," Sagittarius said as soon as the room was quiet once more. "Draco has more than paid the price for his crimes—"

Octantis let out a peal of mocking laughter that silenced the Archer as effectively as a guillotine. In front of me, I saw Polaris's hands tighten as he gripped the podium in fury.

"You have something to add, South Star?" he asked, turning to face the blindfolded woman.

"The Archer seems to think that she is able to see when a debt has been paid, to have the wisdom to proclaim when Justice has been satisfied. Bold of her to claim to know what is in my domain." Her tone was so sharp, I half expected Sagittarius to start bleeding.

The room was unbearably silent. Octantis's threat could not have been more apparent if she had crossed the room and backhanded Sagittarius in the face. Suddenly, I remembered what she reminded me of. Give her a pair of scales and a sword, and she would be the spitting image of Lady Justice.

"I cede to your wisdom, South Star," the Archer said after too long a pause. Sagittarius dropped into her chair, a flush of embarrassment on her face.

"Well, I like her," Dawn mused to no one in particular. I had to agree.

"So the Dons claim their master has paid for his crimes, do they?"

Octantis asked, strolling up to take control of the podium from Polaris. The North Star relented with a grimace, but he seemed unable to deny her.

"That we do," Doyle said from behind her, an uncomfortable look on his face. It seemed the return of the Justice Constellation was making everyone uneasy.

"Fascinating—have I died and gone to a different plane where the serpents have become known for their love and appreciation of the law?"

No one was brave enough to answer her.

"I thought not," she chuckled to herself. "But perhaps there is something I do not know. Maybe I have forgotten the details of Draco's crimes. Shall we check the scales and see if Justice has been satisfied?"

Again, there was only silence.

"For the murder of the five immortals of the Hunt, Draco was sentenced to two thousand years in Tartarus. It has been"—her lips turned down in a dour frown—"five hundred and seventy-eight years."

Every single person standing on the dais with Octantis was gritting their teeth so hard that I thought I could hear a grinding sound. It took a superhuman effort to keep from laughing. She and Orion were definitely related.

"Justice does not seem to be satisfied," she intoned. "One wonders what reason *other* than justice might be allowing this farce to progress even this far."

A legion of horrified gasps leaked out from the assembled Constellations. Even Dawn let out a small grunt of surprise. The South Star did not beat around the bush, not even a little.

"You dare accuse this council of corruption?" Polaris thundered after he recovered from shock.

"'Corruption' seems too weak a word for this evil you have allowed into our halls, *North Star*." She somehow managed to make his name a curse word, full of venom and spite.

"You would do well to be careful, old crone," Doyle spat, taking a step toward Octantis, scaled claws flexing.

A single chair creaked under the strain of the Hunter rising to his feet. The ruby set in the pommel of his sword glinted fiercely where it peeked above his shoulder.

Doyle froze in his tracks, his catlike pupils tracking Orion's movement the same way a diver watches the sharks swimming around him. For a moment the two enemies stared at each other, practically quivering.

"It seems, honored Polaris," drawled the South Star, "that the Hunter wishes to speak."

The North Star glanced between the two beings, a scowl on his face. "The Congregation recognizes the Hunter Constellation, Orion," he said begrudgingly.

The hushed attention of all the Constellations in the night sky flitted to where Orion stood immobile and unyielding. His black eyes locked on the dragon down below him like a falcon about to stoop on a mouse. For a second, I thought he might decide to let politics be damned, draw his sword, and leap on Doyle. With a Herculean effort, Orion tore his gaze away from Doyle and looked around at the starry sea of his peers.

"The Dons have all warned you what will happen if they don't get their way. They have threatened you with ancient terrors of fire and blood, the likes of which have not been seen in millennia."

Octantis let out an angry hiss at Orion's words but didn't interrupt him.

"But serpents have ever been liars. They tell you they have broken the curse, but that is not the whole truth. They have merely bent it, not broken it. It may be true that the dragons have found a way to return to their final form, but it is *not* true that all of them can. They can only give this power to one dragon. Why do you think they have not demonstrated it before now? They seek to release their elder and use him as a weapon."

Disconcerted murmurs spread throughout the room. It seemed Cassiopeia and her husband weren't the only Constellations living under the fear of an entire wing of fully freed dragons descending upon them.

Doyle's face burned with rage, which only served to make his orange scales and red hair even fierier. He looked like a draconic tea-kettle that was seconds away from whistling. I smirked, hoping the dragon would glance my way, just so I could add some insult to injury.

A sixth sense prickled up and down my neck, telling me I was being watched. I turned to my right and found Dawn staring at me, a blond brow arched over one of her golden eyes. I got the feeling that I was too well behaved for the Queen's tastes. I'm not usually good at following orders, but this was a command I could get behind.

I rose to my feet, hands clasped behind my back, doing my best to school my face into a warm, pleasant smile that I directed at the North Star. Polaris ignored me, his glare focused on the Hunter looming above him. I shuffled slightly, trying to make enough motion to catch his eye. I figured I should follow the rules until the moment was right. I didn't want him to shut me down until it was too late.

After a few seconds of tense silence, I raised my fist to my mouth and gave a polite cough. Polaris's head whipped around, and his black eyes narrowed as he saw me standing next to the Queen of All Fae.

"The Dandelion Court is not yet an actualized member of this Congregation," he snarled in my direction. "The Congregation does not recognize Matthew Carver."

"Let him speak." Octantis's voice cracked like a whip over Polaris. He didn't flinch, the old Nephilim was too tough for that, but it was obvious he wasn't willing to get in her face. Maybe Orion's reaction to the last person who had threatened the South Star made him nervous.

"Fine, say your piece, mortal." Polaris threw his hands up in the air in disgust as if we were the ones ruining the sanctity of this hallowed organization.

"I vouch for Orion's testimony. It will only work for one dragon, not all of them."

"Of course the little squire echoes his master's words," Sagittarius sneered from above me.

"I beg your pardon?" I turned to stare up at the Archer, who was about half a dozen rows above me. "I am *not* the Hunter's squire. Were you not paying attention yesterday? If you need someone to explain what happened to you, that's okay, no one will think less of you." A few dark chuckles echoed around the room as Sagittarius leapt to her feet, her face purpling with rage. I plowed on, not giving her a chance to speak.

"I give this witness as a member of the Dandelion Court." I held up my lanyard for her to see. "Everyone knows the Fae cannot lie. I would never jeopardize the reputation of my Queen by telling a lie in her name. Is that what you are accusing me of?"

Dawn slowly rose to stand next to me, a delighted, predatory smile on her face as she stared up at the Archer. She looked like a kid who'd always wanted to punch the school bully and had finally found an excuse. Sagittarius's face, on the other hand, had gone very, very still.

"Oh, come on, Sag," the Queen of All Fae encouraged. "Call us liars."

Sagittarius sat down very slowly.

Dawn gave me a satisfied smile before settling back into her chair, ceding the room back to me. It was not lost on me what had just happened. The value of my testimony had been questioned in front of the entire Constellation Congregation, and the Queen of All Fae had just made it clear that I spoke with her approval. To dismiss me was to dismiss her, and that was a much more dangerous thing to do.

It reminded me of the time Gloriana made Dawn her executor in hunting down the assassins who had tried to kill the gang and me in Goldhall. She had told everyone that Dawn spoke with her voice. For at least the next few minutes, I was doing the same. It was kind of fun being on Dawn's good side.

"Constellations of the Night Sky," I began, turning to take in the whole room. My heart was in my throat, and I did everything I could to keep it from choking me. "I come to tell you that you have been lied to."

Dark murmurs spread through the room.

"I witnessed Doyle being given a device that would allow a dragon to resume its original form," I said, spreading my hands wide to gesture to the stadium around me. "He was told there was only enough for a single dragon and that the transformation could only be successfully performed by one of sufficient strength, or it could fail."

Doyle's reptile eyes stared at me with the murderous promise of an alligator. I ignored the fear in my chest and made myself smile at him.

"Who told him this, boy, who instructed him in the use of this weapon?" Octantis asked, setting me up for the perfect spike delivery. Something told me the old Nephilim already knew the answer.

"Samael gave him his orders and commanded him to follow her master's bidding," I said as loudly and confidently as I could. "She came here and offered reunion, while at the same time giving the dragons the very stick that they threaten us with." Horrified murmurs swept through the room. I bared my teeth in a satisfied grin. They should have known better than to trust the Devil's Dark Whisper.

"You lie!" Doyle hissed, taking a step toward me. His path was blocked by the avatar of Justice, her blindfolded gaze staring into his eyes without wavering. Doyle blinked first, which was a little unfair since he was the only one in the staring contest who had... eyes.

Anger began to boil around the bowl as more and more Constellations who had been terrified became angry enough to forget their fear. The Canis family were back on their feet, and more Constellations I didn't know joined them.

The acoustics of the stadium collected all the outage into a dull roar and channeled it into the center of the ring. I thought I saw Doyle stagger slightly under the weight of the noise. Octantis wore a tight smile that filled me with more hope than anything else. If Lady Justice thought there was a way out, then all was not lost.

I glanced over at Dawn, who gave me a satisfied smile of her own and a slight nod of praise. I had misbehaved to my Queen's satisfaction. I sat down and nudged Ash with my left elbow.

"How'd I do?" I asked.

"Oh, were you doing something? I must have missed it."

I shot my betrothed a mock glare, and she winked back at me, which sent weird little shivers down the back of my neck. *Focus, Matt, now is not the time.*

"If makes you feel any better, I'm sure you did great, darling."

"It does make me feel a little better, now that you mention it."

"WE WILL HAVE ORDER!" Polaris roared, banging on his podium until the raging of the Congregation was eventually still, like a calm sea after a storm passes. Begrudgingly the Constellations returned to their seats, even the Canises.

But not the Hunter.

Polaris stood at the head of room for a long moment, his irritation seething off him in waves so thick they almost produced a mirage. This entire convention had been orchestrated and choreographed down to the moment, but the final number was not playing at the tempo he had been conducting to. I wondered if he had known the dragons could only back up their threats with one dragon, yet still allowed himself to be blackmailed, or if he just loved power so much that it never occurred to him to do anything different.

"This has been a disgraceful showing—" the North Star began.

"Call the vote!" someone roared from up toward the top of the bowl.

"Call the vote!" another voice cried on the other side of the room.

"Call the vote!" I chanted along with much of the crowd as more Constellations took up the cry. The arena seethed with an immortal anger. In the center of the stadium, Orion still stood in a sea of shaking fists, glowering down at the dais like a gargoyle of judgment.

"We will not call the vote until reason has been restored—" Polaris began again.

"Ariadne, begin the vote!" Octantis interrupted. The roar of the night sky's approval was so fierce that it shook the stadium, which made me wonder what would happen if a real earthquake hit. I'm not sure Constellation construction was up to OSHA standards.

The Aurora Borealis shot Polaris an apologetic look but obeyed the South Star, unfurling her giant scroll. My heart leapt in my chest as I looked around the room, trying to count how many votes we had freed from the dragon's intimidation. Many of the Nephilim were chanting, but plenty others were silent, black eyes unreadable as they evaluated their options.

"Before any of you vote," Doyle shouted as Ariadne opened her mouth to begin, "just remember that even if we only have one full dragon, those flames will be hot enough to burn the lot of you!" There was a moment of stunned silence, but the current of anger was out of control. The room booed the Don's threat until the dragon took a step back, an angry snarl on his twisted face.

"The question of the release of the dragon Draco and the pun-ishment of the Hunter has been brought before the Congregation," called the Aurora Borealis. She glanced down at her scroll and read the first name: "Andromeda."

Cassiopeia's daughter rose slowly out of her seat as an eerie hush settled over the room, the way the jungle goes silent when a tiger moves through it. I perched on the edge of my seat, trying to inject my own stubbornness into the princess with my eyes. But Andromeda needed no help. She raised her chin in defiance and tossed her long braids over one shoulder as she looked Doyle square in the face.

"Nay!" she cried out boldly. Half the room erupted in cheers; the other was silent. I saw Polaris's face tighten in a grimace as the first vote was cast against them.

"Antlia," Ariadne called.

"Yea," a voice answered from somewhere behind me, deflating some of the mood. I guess even the threat of one dragon is enough to scare some people. Polaris's face relaxed a little. We had come so far! All we needed was a little more belief.

Apus voted no, but Aquarius voted yes. Ara abstained to boos from all around. Aries voted yes also. I guess the astrology gang likes to roll together. The Constellation I had caught Doyle threatening, Bootes, voted no, which was cool. If we won, he was definitely invited to the afterparty.

The Canis guys voted no, but the Canes Venatici voted yes. Don't ask me the difference—I don't know. Cassiopeia and her husband Cepheus both voted no in solidarity with their daughter. I struggled to keep count of the votes and eventually lost track. I only have so many fingers. But even I could tell it was close.

Horologium, a Nephilim I had never noticed before, was one who surprised me. He rose to his feet and ran a hand over his chin, looking between Orion and Doyle as if weighing up two fighters. He wore a long tan robe that was open at the front over a white shirt and black jeans. His brown beard and hair were neatly trimmed. I had no idea what a Horologium was supposed to be, but he looked far more comfortable in the mortal world than most of his peers.

"No," he mused after a moment of thought. Excited murmurs

spread throughout the room as he settled in his seat. It seemed that a lot of the stars were very interested in his vote.

Hydra and Hydrus, unsurprisingly I suppose, voted in favor of the dragon's request. We continued with the back-and-forth until at last the foxy Vulpecula voted no, and it was done, all the ballots cast. The room sat in silence as Ariadne tallied her records. My heart was slamming into my rib cage as I waited. It was going to be very, very close.

"With a vote of forty-four to forty-three and one abstention. The nays have it!" the Aurora Borealis pronounced.

The room erupted in a deafening cacophony as everyone leapt to their feet. We cheered and hugged one another. The losers cried in terror of the threats that had been made. Something warm pressed against my cheek as Ash gave me an enthusiastic kiss. I squeezed her as tightly as I could, a thrill running down my spine, for more reasons than one.

The dragon's god could keep rotting in the dark.

As we parted from our embrace, I looked to the dais and the North Star. Polaris's face had taken on a delightfully ashen hue. Doyle, on the other hand, had turned purple with indignation. The Dragon Don leapt off the dais into the center of the room and pointed a scaly claw at Orion.

"You'll burn for this, Hunter!" he screeched, forked tongue slipping as he raged. The dragon reached down to his torso with both arms, grabbing at the base of his shirt like he was about to rip it off. Orion's hand shot to the hilt of his sword.

"Cease this idiocy at once." Octantis's voice sliced through the noise like a blade, killing all the commotion in a single blow. Even furious Doyle froze in his steps under the blindfolded glare of the South Star.

"You. Are. Still. A. Guest," she hissed at the dragon, each word packed with the force of a meteor slamming into the ground. The Don twitched as if each one affected him physically. After a moment he recovered and stood up straight, popping his suit jacket once to reseat it.

"For now," he agreed ominously, turning on his heel to storm out of the stadium.

"How much longer does the convention run?" I asked Dawn, who was watching the dragon somberly.

"The floor officially closes at eight p.m., but being a Guest is more complicated than that. Properly it ends on the beginning of a new day," she told me with a knowing look. I glanced at my watch; it was already a little after two. We had just under ten hours to prepare for a dragon.

WELL DONE," POLARIS sneered into the silence of Doyle's departure. "When the dragonfire comes to devour you all, remember that I tried to protect you."

"Silence, you corrupt fool," Octantis cried, rounding on her counterpart. "That was the bright future you've been planning for us? You'd trade our freedom for a collar made of scales."

"What do you know of the future?" Polaris demanded, not backing down. "You're so fixated on the past, you can't see that we're in danger of losing everything!"

"If we forget where we come from, then we are already lost," Octantis replied in an even tone. "It is not in the stars to hold our destiny, but ourselves." For some reason, that reminded me of the room's reaction to Samael dangling the hope of being reunited with their ancestors. They should know better, but when you're lost and hurting, hope is as addicting as any narcotic.

Polaris snarled in disgust and spun, pointing a long finger up at Orion, who had released his grip on his sword. "Don't forget, *Hunter*," he hissed. "The dragons are still members of this Congregation and Guests. There will be no leniency for the side that breaks the peace."

Orion didn't reply, his black gaze fixed on the North Star, rich in judgment. The elder Nephilim blinked first, turning away in disgust. With a snarl, he grabbed his little gavel and slammed it into the podium with a dull thud.

"The final session of the Constellation Convention is adjourned." Without a glance over his shoulder, Polaris followed in the dragon's footsteps and stormed out of the bowl.

"Now what, Hunter?" called Cassiopeia from her side of the bowl. Silence fell as the Constellations around the room looked to Orion for guidance.

My friend still stood in the spot where he'd challenged Doyle. There was a rigid tension in his stance, like a knife resting in its sheath. He turned to face the Constellation of Beauty, his face hard.

"Now we find out if the demon told the dragon the truth," he said simply.

"And if she did?" another voice called from above.

"Then I will slay another dragon."

No one was brave enough to question the Hunter. Dawn struck up a round of applause the room joined in with halfheartedly. I got the sense more than a few Nephilim were having a case of voter's remorse. Orion needed to work on his pep talks.

On that awkward note, the room began to disperse, people trailing back out to the cocktail area to gossip and stress about the impending dragon attack. As far as I knew, the gist of the plan was to let Orion stick the lizard with Ascalon and call it a day.

"Come, ducklings," Dawn said, rising to her feet and glancing at her entourage. "We must prepare a war council." The rest of the Dandelion Court followed the Queen to reclaim some of the tables in the foyer. I eyed the closed clamshells of the buffet as we passed. I wasn't sure if war councils were a snackable event or not.

"You're hungry, aren't you?" Ash murmured to me.

"I didn't eat breakfast," I protested, turning away from the food to look at her. As I did, I made eye contact with my father over her shoulder. He arched a single, imperious eyebrow and gave me a slow nod.

My gut dropped. In the heat of the draconic moment, I had forgotten about his assassination plans. Mav walked at Dawn's right hand, hovering like a bird of prey. The golden collar around her throat glinted in the reflection of the industrial lights above us.

Did Damien really intend to do this now? It was kind of a bad time. Who was I kidding? My father never let anything get in his way; a dragon would be no different. Part of me—the bitter son and brother part—agreed with his sentiment. Mav had killed my mother. She had drowned my sisters. Seeing her burn would be more cathartic than any amount of therapy.

But there was a dragon coming, and it didn't just want to burn me, it wanted to burn my friends and most of the people I had met this weekend. Some of them I could live without; I wouldn't pour out my drink to extinguish Polaris if I saw him on fire. But some of them I cared about very much. Maybe revenge could wait a little longer. I had to survive to enjoy it.

Mav was a monster, but she was also the Lady of Winter and followed the Path of Water. I hadn't been lying to Dawn when I suggested her sister's powers might be more useful against dragonfire than my own flames had been. Killing Mav this very moment felt a little like taking your own queen off the board before the first pawns had even been moved.

I tried to catch my father's eyes and shake my head, but he ignored me. Whatever he had planned was already in motion.

"Now then," Dawn said, taking a seat at the raised table as we huddled around her. "Obviously things are going to get interesting in a few hours. You're my advisors, what do you advise?"

"We should leave," Tania offered instantly. "There is still time to depart before the Guest protection fades. We can be safely in Goldhall in an hour."

"We are bound to stand with the Hunt when they strike at the dragons," Robin objected mildly.

"An excellent point, dear Robin," the Queen noted, her golden eyes moving around the circle of advisors. "Anyone else have anything to add?"

"We are bound." Ash shrugged as she agreed with Robin. "Hard to argue with that."

"It would be," Dawn agreed, nodding somberly, her gaze settling on me like an anchor. "If the Hunt still existed." I felt my eyes go wide. Frantically, I tried to remember the terms of her deal with Orion. What had she agreed to? Horrified, I realized she was right. She had pledged her support to the Hunt against the dragons, but the Constellation Congregation had dissolved the Hunt. There was only the Hunter now.

"Is that really what you want?" I asked, trying to keep the panic out of my voice. "All this work to make peace with Orion, thrown out over a technicality?" Suddenly I wondered if she had been planning this when she had talked to me about trust last night. If I stayed with the Hunter without her blessing, it would probably give her an excuse to get rid of me.

"Darling, we are Fae. Technicalities are what our empire is made of."

"And how's that working out?" I shot back, thinking of their marble fortress floating in the abyss. Dawn blinked once in surprise, which might as well have been a spit-take from her when she was wearing the face of the Queen.

"Of course the mortal wants us to die for the Hunter," Mav hissed venomously, her own golden eyes sparkling with hatred in my direction. "Let us leave and be done with this."

Maybe my father was right: Now was the time to kill her.

"Until the dragons come looking for the gold they love so much," Ash murmured somberly. That took some of the wind out the assembled Fae's sails. Even Mav looked a little unsure about how to counter her argument.

I definitely picked the right sister.

"Thank you for your wise council," Dawn said, waving us away like a cloud of gnats. "I shall consider your words. In the meantime, go, mingle, find out what our peers are planning."

I wasted no time scampering out of the Fae team huddle to follow the Queen's orders. The first conversation I was going to open was with the buffet line. There was a fight coming, and I was going to need all the energy I could get my hands on.

On my way to the food, I was distracted by something far more interesting. It's really hard to distract me from a solid buffet, but if there's one thing that will do it, it's a juicy piece of drama between Orion and his ancestor.

The Hunter strode up to the South Star, who stood alone in the middle of the room. The lesser Constellations seemed even more hesitant to enter her aura than they were to orbit Orion. The woman raised her blindfolded gaze to meet the Hunter's stare as he stopped in front of her.

"Hello, nephew," she said, tilting her head in a slight greeting—which didn't necessarily confirm they were related. Nephilim have a weird habit of blending generational respect and friendship with terms we mortals use for blood relatives. Before Alex and Orion had become close, Orion had referred to my friend as his nephew, but it had everything to do with the diminutive amount of demon blood that ran in Alex's veins compared with the Hunter and nothing to do with genealogy. It was kind of like how we used Mister or Miss.

"Aunt," Orion replied grimly.

The two demigods stared at each other for a long moment. There was a stiffness in both of their spines that made me think they actually could be kin. Only family could have reunions this specific flavor of awkwardness.

"You're late," the Hunter grumbled after a few minutes.

"Justice is never late," Octantis replied cryptically.

"And yet you were not here when an injustice was done to me and mine."

"Poor Hunter, he suffers for an opportunity to right an ancient wrong." Sarcasm dripped from the elder Nephilim's tone. Orion stared at her, his black eyes questioning.

"You of all my students should have learned justice is never late, but that does not mean it comes when you want it to. It is a not a dog."

Still Orion was silent, his gaze demanding an answer to a question I didn't know.

The South Star sighed in surrender, her blank gaze sliding away from him in some sort of admission. "I was called upon to pass judgment on a god for breaking the faith of a host." She clicked her tongue in irritation. "I too find the timing suspicious."

"And what sentence did you order?"

"A millennium in the cells of Tartarus."

A shiver passed down my spine as I thought about being imprisoned for a millennium. I don't think I would make it a year, never mind the 999 more.

As if he felt me listening, Orion turned his head and narrowed his eyes at me hovering a dozen steps away. Suddenly this conversation felt way over my pay grade. I gave him a friendly nod and resumed my original trajectory toward the buffet.

Now it was time to eat—oh crap. I had forgotten about Alex, sitting badge-less somewhere outside, waiting to find out if the elder dragon was being released from his prison. Diverting myself from the food yet again, I headed toward the exit of Hall B to place my call in private. It wasn't the moment to be overheard gloating about how we had stuck it to the dragons and Polaris.

I slipped out the doors and took a left, down a short hall that ended in a series of locked doors, chained shut. For some reason, I felt a sense of déjà vu, but I couldn't say why. Confident I was out of earshot from any supernatural beings with batlike hearing, I pulled out my phone and dialed Alex.

"I swear if you're not dead, I'm gonna kill you myself," my friend said as he answered. I winced in sympathy. If it had been me stuck waiting in the car, I could only imagine the hyperdrive my imagination would kick into.

"Definitely still alive, and you might want to hold off of on the murder until you hear my news."

"How bad is it?" he asked.

"So, you remember how the dragons had threatened everyone with a super dragon attack if the Congregation didn't vote to release Draco?"

"Yes, I've been paying attention," he snapped.

"The countdown for super dragon attack has officially started."

There was a pause as he processed this. "Wait," he gasped after a moment. "The Congregation didn't vote to release Draco?"

"By one freaking vote," I cackled, pumping a fist in excitement. "The South Star showed up and turned the whole thing upside down." I gave him a summary of everything that went down, up until Doyle and Polaris both stormed out. I didn't tell him about the loophole the Fae were considering. That felt like crossing my wires in a way I wasn't comfortable with. While in my heart I was loyal to the Hunt, I had some legal responsibilities to the Dandelion Court. Just in case I ran across one of those elusive Sorcerer Kings, I needed to keep my membership in the Constellation Congregation active. We'd burn that bridge when we came to it.

"Holy crap, you actually did it," Alex breathed in shock when I was done.

"It was a team effort," I protested. "I just grumbled in a few Constellations' ears. Octantis did most of the heavy lifting."

"So, a dragon attack is scheduled for midnight?"

"That's the theory."

"Let me guess. I should stay in the car until then?"

"Well, the convention apparently closes at eight, but I don't know what that means for us."

"Do I at least have time to grab a burger?"

My stomach gurgled in sympathy. "I would guess. If it makes you feel any better, I can't even get near the catering right now."

"That actually does make me feel a little better," he confided.

"Listen, get your burger, and wait for the call, okay?" I told him, jealous of his freedom to get food.

"Copy, extra cheese."

I hung up on him. I knew he was feeling left out, but I was hungry enough that I would have given him my badge in a heartbeat if it meant I could hunt down some food. I turned to head back into Hall B, but paused, struck by another thought.

I had promised Agent Richter something juicy to keep him off my back. A rampaging dragon in the middle of LA felt like exactly what the doctor ordered. I pulled my phone out and called his number. He answered on the second ring.

"Richter."

"This is Matt Carver—"

"Got something worth my time, Matt?"

"Yes, sir, I think I do."

"Well, I'm all ears, lay it on me."

"I have reason to believe the Dragon Dons have figured out a way to undo the curse that prevents them from achieving their full dragon form, and they plan to unleash this power here in Downtown sometime around midnight."

There was a moment of shocked silence on the other line. I understood—this was no small tip. If the agent and his team hadn't caught wind of the dragon's threats yet, this would be a huge surprise.

"I'm sorry, did you say dragons?" Richter said after he recovered.

"Yes sir, the Dragon Dons."

"You're telling me a dragon is going to attack Los Angeles, tonight at midnight?" An incredulous tone that I did not like had crept into his voice.

"Correct."

Richter let out a disappointed sigh. "Matt, I had hoped we were going to be able to work together. I really did. How stupid do you think I am?"

"Uh, what? Why wouldn't we be able to work together?" I asked.

"Dragons? Really? I can understand you might think I'm an idiot, but everyone knows there's no such thing as dragons, Matt. Don't call me again unless you're going to take this seriously." Richter hung up on me with an aggressive click.

Stunned, I stood there for a couple seconds with my disconnected phone still against my ear. What did he mean, there was no such thing as dragons? Did the... did the mortal supernatural FBI not know about dragons?

They were going to be in for a rude awakening in a few hours.

WE WERE WRONG.

The dragons didn't wait until midnight to attack. They barely waited thirty minutes. I set a loaded plate down on one of the standing tables, ready to devour my final harvest of the buffet tables, when my phone rang. With a sigh, I pulled it out of my pocket and answered it.

"I thought you said the dragons were coming tonight?" Alex demanded.

"That's when the Guest protection is over. Why?" I asked, spearing some prime rib with my fork.

"Because I see about a dozen of the lizards walking down the street right now, armed to the teeth."

I paused mid-bite, surprised. "Are you sure?"

"They're kinda hard to miss, dude."

"Right, I get that. But it's too early, what do they think they're doing?"

"Matt." Alex's voice took on a horrified tone. "I think they're going to—"

There was a long, awful silence. My mind came up with a thousand things the dragons might be doing, each worse than the last.

"They're going to what?" I shouted, forgetting where I was for a moment. Immortal faces turned to regard me as my cry echoed around the room. I ignored them. Somehow, I already knew the answer before he told me.

"They're attacking mortals." Alex's voice was tight with hatred.

My fork dropped out of my fingers as I pictured what Alex was saying. Of course they were. Mortals on the street were not Guests of the Constellation Convention. They were under no protection; they had no safety. Under the supernatural laws dragons were free to do to them whatever they wanted.

This was bait.

Slowly, I turned to look for Orion. The Hunter was already heading toward me with a determined stride. The ruby hilt of his sword glinted angrily in time with his steps.

Wordlessly, I handed him the phone.

I already knew how this was going to go.

Over Orion's shoulder, Dawn caught my eye, her own narrowing as she took in my expression and the stiff form of the Hunter. I shook my head in despair. There was no way the Fae were going to back him in this.

"I'm coming," Orion told Alex, hanging up my phone and handing it back to me. Without another word he surged toward the exit of Hall B, not bothering to check who was following him.

I took a step in his direction, but instinct stopped me from taking another. I turned to find the Queen of All Fae standing right behind me, something primal in her eyes. She had never reminded me more of her mother than in that moment.

Suddenly nervous, I licked my lips as I stared into Dawn's demanding gaze. I no longer served two masters, as far as the law was concerned. Following Orion would have been a gesture of contempt for Dawn's wishes. I was the Faerie Queen's now, totally and completely. Well, at least until Hell came to claim what was theirs. But for now, I was *hers*, and if there's one lesson supernatural beings don't learn in kindergarten it is how to share.

"Well?" she murmured in dangerous tones.

"The dragons are attacking mortals outside the convention center," I told her.

"Fools!" Dawn snarled. "Are they so desperate to die they cannot wait a few hours?" Surprised by her anger, I kept my mouth shut. I had been afraid as soon as I told her, she would order us all to head for the marble halls of the Faerie Lands.

But as I looked into her golden eyes, I realized she was torn. Technically, according to the terms of the deal she'd made with Orion, she was free to turn her back on the Hunter. She got everything she wanted and had kept her word. By Fae accounting, it might have been one of the greatest bargains ever struck.

Gloriana would have walked away with a smirk on her face.

But as much as she resembled the deceased Queen sometimes, Dawn was not her mother. She was just as cold and calculating, but lurking somewhere beneath that arrogant exterior was the tiny sliver of a heart. The problem was, it wasn't enough for her to *want* to help. The trap Doyle had set for Orion would catch her just as effectively.

Polaris had declared there would be no leniency for anyone who violated the safety of being Guest. The Dandelion Court had just gotten their membership back. It would be a shame to lose it a day later.

"Well, we are here," Dawn said with a small sigh. "We might as well go and see what all the fuss is about."

That sure sounded like permission to me. Not waiting for her to change her mind, I turned and bolted toward the door, my feet pounding on the carpeted floor even faster than they had when the dragons chased me through the halls. I pulled my phone out of my pocket and called Alex as I ran.

"Talk to me, Goose," I shouted as he answered.

"It's not good, man, not good at all." My friend's stress reached straight through the phone. I could hear things clinking together in the background as he rooted through the van.

"Is he out there?"

"Oh yeah." Alex sounded both impressed and horrified at what he was watching.

"Has he broken the Guest rules yet?"

"Nope, but he's got the sword out."

"I'm almost there!"

"Hurry."

I hung up on him and doubled down on my sprint, slamming through the crash doors and into pandemonium. The main lobby was full of terrified people huddled in masses. The metal detectors were knocked sideways, smashed by the stampede of folks who had forced their way in to escape the nightmare outside. I shoved my way through the crowd, fighting against the current like a salmon swimming upstream.

"Move!" I shouted. I bounced off people and squeezed into spaces that should not have fit me. I did not apologize; I did not slow down. I had to get outside before it was too late.

The crowd screamed as they were parted in front of me as if they had been split by a pair of giant hands. Dawn's air spirit, Sylph, casually shoved the mass of people back, clearing a space for us.

"Make way," the Queen snarled, leading her people through the gap like a cavalry charge. A little stunned, I allowed myself to be swept into her wave and carried out the door.

Outside was a madhouse of a different caliber. Screams of fear echoed off the tall buildings. Terrified people cowered behind benches, trees, and food trucks. Others streamed around the edges of the building, getting away from the showdown that was occurring right in the middle of the street. In the open spaces lay still bodies that couldn't run anymore. Something dark and hot twisted in my guts.

A full wing of dragoons holding assault rifles flocked around Don Doyle in a semicircle. The redheaded leader of the dragons clutched a familiar black briefcase in one of his hands and was staring at Orion ravenously. The Hunter stood between the serpents and the mortals, his sword blazing in his hand.

Alone.

I took a step into the street, ready to stand with my friend. An invisible leash of air swirled around my torso like a lasso and tightened, stopping me in my tracks. I shot Dawn a furious glare, but she ignored me, her golden eyes locked on the two predators ahead of us.

"Excellent!" Doyle cried, spotting the Fae contingent. "Now we have witnesses to the Hunter's treachery. This Constellation has threatened me, a Guest of the Congregation, with violence. I call upon you to remember this should it result in bloodshed."

I gritted my teeth in frustration, straining against the invisible bonds of Sylph's will. The logical part of me knew Dawn was holding me back because getting attacked was exactly what Doyle was aiming for. He was trying to start a fight by coercing someone else to take the first swing. But those bodies on the ground made me eager to oblige him. As angry as I was at her for holding me back, I understood why. I was a member of her court. If I broke the Guest rules, it would be on her, not Orion.

"Get out of my way, Hunter," Doyle snarled. Orion's only reply was to raise his blade and settle into a fighting stance, knees bent, both hands wrapped around the hilt of his fiery sword.

The Dragon Don broke eye contact with Orion, his gaze sweeping the street before landing on a family cowering behind a planter beside an overturned stroller.

With a cruel snap of his taloned fingers, he pointed at them. One of his dragoons immediately turned, raising its rifle to aim at the innocent mortals. The bottom of my stomach fell out as if I had just leapt out of a plane.

This was it!

Somewhere next to me, Dawn let out an annoyed sigh. Sylph's air bonds went slack a heartbeat before Orion's blazing sword buried itself in the dragoon's chest with a vicious *thunk*. Unable to reach the monster in time, the Hunter had simply thrown his weapon end-over-end like a tomahawk. With a dry hiss, the beast fell to its knees. The sound of its rifle falling from its nerveless claws and clattering to the paved ground was as loud as a gunshot in the sudden stillness.

Doyle's reptilian eyes flicked from the fiery sword embedded in the chest of one of his minions to the now weaponless Nephilim standing before him. A sinister smile spread across his face.

"Help," he drawled in an amused tone. "The Hunter is trying to kill me."

Orion, in turn, put his head down and charged the dragon and his lizard army. The dragoons raised their rifles and opened fire. Either talons make for terrible trigger fingers, or he's just that agile, but as the Hunter cut sharply to the right, nothing hit him. Or more likely, I realized as I felt a whisper of wind rush past me, the air itself refused to carry the bullets to him.

Surprised, I glanced at Dawn. She had not moved, but a small, self-satisfied smile tugging on one corner of her lips confirmed my suspicion. But why would she help Orion, why risk being dragged into his—

My question died as Dawn crashed to the ground. Horror bloomed in my brain as three spots of blood began to grow on her white dress. The Queen was down. They had shot the Queen. I rushed to her side, dropping to my knees, hands extended to help stanch the blood pouring out of her. Her golden eyes bored into mine, seething with anger at my response.

Then I remembered Dawn was an Immortal—an Immortal who could control the winds. A green dragoon standing on the closest edge of the semicircle stared at us with its reptilian mouth hanging open in shock. I'm no lizard expert, but I was pretty sure it was one of goons that had attacked us at Balsamic, where this exact thing had happened before.

Understanding clicked. The dragons hadn't *shot* Dawn. Well, not on purpose anyway. But a few of the bullets meant for Orion had magically found their way instead into the Queen of All Fae—a Guest of the Congregation.

While it might not hold up in a court of law, technically the Dandelion Court had been attacked by the Dragon Dons while under the mandated Guest peace. For a Faerie, that inch was good enough to run with for miles.

But something was different than the last time she took a bullet. I saw Dawn's face shift from arrogant pride to pain, and I thought I caught a whiff of something burning. I glanced down at her wounds again and saw a faint line of smoke emerging from her chest. The dragoons had brought cold iron this time. Robin dropped to his knees at my side, his golden eyes taking in the damage in a glance.

"Falling Stars," he swore as he realized what the bullets were made of. "Go. I got her."

"They shot the Queen," I bellowed, leaping to my feet. I screamed as loud as I could to make sure everyone watching heard the pretense. "The dragons shot the Queen of All Fae!" All around me, the Fae shouted in perfect outrage. It could not have been better orchestrated if I had been a conductor and they, my musicians.

At my cry, Doyle's head whipped around, his catlike eyes narrowing as he saw Dawn on the ground. With a subconscious nudge, I summoned Willow's flames on my hands. Leading the rest of the Fae contingent, I stepped into the street, entering no-man's-land.

Immediately the closest dragoon raised its rifle toward me. Knowing fire was not the most effective element against a dragon, I threw my right hand forward, shaping Willow into a fiery whip with my will. The spirit sizzled as it cut through the air, coiling around the barrel of the assault rifle. With a flex of my wrist, I pumped heat through the whip, turning Willow's bright red into a searing white.

The whip sheared the front barrel off with a *pop*, and it clattered to the ground. Quick as a thought, I released the flames, allowing them to return to their normal form, burning around my hand like a boxing glove. The dragoon growled in anger and tossed its ruined weapon to the side. Its teeth and claws were more than enough to handle a little mortal, fire or no fire.

But the Dandelion Court isn't only a court of fire.

Somewhere far above Los Angeles, a gray cloud carried molecules of water too light to escape the updraft of its winds. Eventually, some of those droplets merged, becoming heavier and heavier, until finally they were too substantial for the cloud to hoard them any longer.

Succumbing to gravity's siren call, they plummeted toward the ground. Most precipitation that falls in this manner splats harmlessly against the earth as life-giving moisture, not icy daggers. Then again, most rain doesn't have the Lady of Winter commanding it to forge itself into weapons as it free-falls.

A swarm of tiny droplets of razor-sharp ice slammed into the advancing dragoon like a hundred rounds of buckshot. The reptile collapsed bonelessly, its scaly flesh torn to shreds as if it had just gone through the wash with a spool of barbed wire. The beast didn't even twitch. One moment it was alive and ready to eat me, the next it was chopped liver—and everything else.

With a crack of thunder, the rest of the clouds burst, and a heavy rain began to pour on our battle. Mav, the Lady of Winter, stepped up next to me, her golden collar glowing softly. She gave me a disdainful sneer, then leapt past me, charging the next dragon in line. Her hands were coated in gloves of thick ice that ended in sharp talons, mimicking the reptiles' own claws.

I knew if that collar hadn't been wrapped around her neck, she would have been more than happy to go after me instead. *It's been arranged,* my father told me. I'm not sure what he had planned, but an all-out brawl between the dragons and Fae was a wonderful opportunity for a little assassination on the side.

A thrill ran through me as I saw the rest of Dawn's coterie racing toward the dragoons. Ash shot forward, hovering above the ground, her hands lit with the same Willow's fire as mine. Next to her, the golden-collared Tania raised a hand as she called on her spirit, Gome. A chunk of asphalt tore itself from the street and speared an unsuspecting lizard in the gut.

Feeling safer among my charging allies, I turned my attention to Orion. The Hunter was still trying to recover his blade, which was sticking out of the chest of the dead dragon like a more gruesome version of Arthur's sword in the stone. Doyle and his lounge pushed him, knowing that keeping him away from the magical blade was their best chance at survival.

Mav leapt on a dragoon, her icy claws tearing into the creature's flesh. Cognizant of my dwindling fire reserves, I held both of my hands behind me angled toward the ground and triggered a short explosion of fire.

With a jerk, I shot forward in a leap that human muscles could never have produced. We needed Orion to get his sword quickly, before the dragoons overwhelmed us with their superior numbers. Maybe my flames could help buy my friend time.

As I soared like an ICBMatt missile, I aimed my feet at the back of one of the dragoons that was focused on Orion. The stupid dinosaur didn't know what hit it. My combat boots slammed into its torso, bowling it head-over-tail. I crashed down onto the pavement with much less force, thanks to my scaly airbag. I rolled twice and leapt back to my feet, turning to face the monster I had just picked a fight with.

The lizard in question had the same horrific snout as the rest of its kin, but its scales were a dull copper color. Catlike pupils glinted dangerously as it pulled back its neck and opened its maw wide.

Familiar with this trick, I raised both my hands, calling upon Willow to meet the dragonfire as it poured from the creature's mouth. I knew my fire spirit probably didn't have enough gas in the tank left to extinguish the flames, so I decided to try something new.

With Willow acting as a rudder, I split the wave of fire that shot at me, allowing it to pass by me on either side harmlessly. Stunned, the dragoon sat there for a few seconds, jaw hanging open in shock.

Deflecting dragonfire was all fine and dandy, but it didn't really tackle my bigger problem. How the heck was I supposed to kill a creature that was immune to fire? The dragoon's mouth clicked shut with an audible snap, and I could tell its reptilian brain had already come up with a new plan. It wasn't a particularly creative one.

The monster squared its shoulders and rushed me. Uninterested in a wrestling match, I held my left hand out to the side and triggered another concussive blast, which pushed me out of the way of the dragoon's charge.

As it careened past, I summoned my fiery whip again and sent it streaking at the dragoon's stomping feet with a flick of my wrist and a thought. I'm not sure whether I have some unusual talent with whips or if Willow understood what I wanted, but the whip lassoed tightly around its right ankle. I challenge any cowpoke to do it better.

Gritting my teeth, I set my feet and pulled with all my might. The sheer mass of the dragoon yanked me forward a few steps before I caught my balance. But my weight was enough to throw its gait off kilter, tripping it as effectively as if I had tied its nonexistent shoelaces together. The copper dragoon slammed face-first into the pavement with enough force that I felt a faint vibration under my feet.

The lizard levered itself off the pavement, staying on all fours like its cousins from the animal kingdom as it turned to face me. Hatred seethed in those inhuman eyes as its forked tongue flicked out. I licked my lips and set myself in a fighting stance. I wasn't sure what to try next. I had used all my tricks just to give the dragon a bit of road rash.

I wiped my forehead to clear the now sopping-wet hair out of my vision and heard some of the raindrops sizzle as they fell into Willow's nimbus and the fire consumed them. My eyes narrowed as some half-forgotten physics lessons started to give me an idea.

Dragons seemed to be immune to fire, or at least the strongest one I could whip up. But I had seen with my own eyes that they did not have the same tolerance for ice. Did that extend to any other elements? I could only control fire, but that didn't mean I didn't have options.

Readying my flames, I threw my right hand out, shooting a blast of fire at the dragon's head. But this time I didn't pour all my power into trying to burn through the monster's scaly hide. Unimpressed by this mild blaze, it didn't even look away, taking my firebolt straight to its ugly face.

The lizard had forgotten it was raining. The water pooling on its snout and nestling in its scales sizzled as the heat turned it from a liquid into steam. The super-heated gas seared into the dragon's exposed eyes, and it let out a shocked scream of pain.

Mrs. Bowman, my ninth-grade physics teacher, would be so proud of me. Well, she would probably be a little horrified. But I think once she understood the broader concepts of the struggle I was in and accepted that dragons were real and *evil*, she would be proud.

Grinning, I sent another wave of fire at the dragon. This time it backed up, eyes screwed closed as it tried to escape the hissing steam. My mind raced, trying to figure out my next move. I didn't think the rain was enough water to actually boil the dragoon alive. I might have figured out a weakness of the lizards, but it wasn't enough to kill them. I needed another solution before I dried the dragon off and went back to square one.

Instead, one of my allies came up with a better plan. Something slammed the dragon into the ground with the force of a sledgehammer. A massive chunk of flesh was missing from its neck. A few heartbeats later, it convulsed again as another shot hit it. Stunned, I turned to look up the street. The parking garage Alex was waiting in was only half a block away. It paid to carry a sniper rifle in your van, I guess. I tossed him a salute before turning back to my downed opponent.

I don't know if a .300-caliber sniper round packs enough blunt-force trauma to kill a dragoon, but the copper-scaled beast stayed down, its dark blood mingling with the rain on the asphalt. That was fine with me. There were plenty more dragons to go around.

I turned toward Orion and saw my distraction had helped. As I watched, he leapt around one of the reptiles trying to tackle him and grasped the hilt of his sword. With a vicious wrench, he pulled it out of the dead dragoon's chest. Snarling, he raised his flaming blade and dove into the middle of the remaining lizards, scattering them like a fox in the henhouse.

The monsters that had been murdering humans only a few minutes ago were now fleeing the wrath of Orion. Justice is never perfect, but I can't deny the satisfactions it offers.

My smugness faded a little when I realized Doyle wasn't running. The Dragon Don stood on the other side of his panicking pack, his reptilian eyes watching Orion without blinking. The Hunter noticed too, letting the rest of the dragons flee as he stared at their boss.

"Well, dragon slayer, it seems it is time for you to prove your name," Doyle called. "I am not a hatchling you can defeat so easily." Orion didn't reply, simply raised his blade and took a step toward the dragon. Doyle accepted the invitation and strode to meet the Hunter.

With blinding speed, the Don slashed at Orion, his human hand shifting into the clawed talon I had seen him threaten Dawn with days ago. The Hunter dodged the attack, stabbing forward with his burning blade. Doyle spun, a tail growing out of his backside, which he used to swat Orion with a meaty *thwack*!

The big Nephilim staggered back a step, and my heart leapt in my throat as Doyle pressed the attack, both hands now savage claws. A few of his talons tore deep rents in the Hunter's leather jacket, but Orion stayed on his feet, retreating under the assault.

I don't know what was different about the Don that let him shift his body so effortlessly, but it was clear he was much more powerful than his dragoons. For a moment I worried my friend had finally met his match.

But the Hunter hadn't earned his Constellation with his charming personality. He dodged a swiping claw and slashed his blade at Doyle's hand. The dragon let out a hiss of rage, shaking his claw like it had been stung.

This time it was Orion's turn to go on the attack, blade flashing. Doyle fell back as he took a dozen little cuts fending off the burning sword. My heart surged.

But serpents are tricky, cunning creatures.

With another blurry spin, Doyle sent his heavy tail out like a whip, creating a little space between himself and the Hunter. He leapt backward, widening the gap to at least a dozen feet.

"You're very good, Hunter," Doyle hissed with a triumphant smile. "But I don't think you're good enough."

Where was the briefcase? The Dragon Don wasn't carrying it anymore. This had to be the moment Samael had given it to him for. What had he done with it? I spun, looking everywhere, and after a moment spotted the open case lying on the ground next to the body of a dead dragoon.

It was empty.

With a slash, Doyle's left claw ripped his expensive shirt open, exposing a scarred chest dotted with more of his orange and red scales. He raised his right hand, revealing a syringe gun with a large tube screwed in, full of a black liquid that seemed to eat the light around it. The Dragon Don didn't hesitate, plunging the needle into his chest and squeezing the trigger. The serum instantly began flowing into his veins.

The effect was immediate and horrifying. Doyle screamed, his shoulders hunching, as if he had developed a pair of humps. But he didn't let go of the trigger, and the dark liquid continued to flow into him, the syringe already half empty. Without thinking, I threw out my right hand, using Willow to hurl a fireball toward the gun. My aim was true, and the fiery projectile slammed into the dragon's hand holding the device.

Whatever was in that tube was apparently combustible. An explosion erupted from the front of Doyle's chest, sending him flying backward. I raised my arms to shield my face from the force of the blast.

When I lowered them, the Dragon Don was lying on his back, his right hand a mangled ruin. For a beautiful moment, as I stared at his still form, I thought I had killed him and saved the day. *Matthew Carver, Dragon Slayer*, has a nice ring to it.

But this isn't one of those stories.

With a horrific series of cracks, his entire body seized, folding in on itself. The scales on his torso began to swell, and new ones popped out of his flesh like a rash. Doyle's hands changed into paws, all ten fingers elongating into claws. His face warped as his mouth transformed into a long, tooth-filled snout. Still screaming in pain, the Don managed to struggle to his feet as his body changed.

Then he began to grow.

Doyle had never been a small guy—dragon—thing. But as the serum flooded his body, his mass enlarged. In moments, he was ten feet long; after a few more, he was as big as a house.

I could only stare in horror as Doyle metamorphosed into a real dragon. I didn't think I wanted to be here anymore. Could I get off this ride? I took a few steps to stand by Orion, who was also transfixed by the spectacle. This was the supernatural nuclear option, and here I was at ground zero.

A pair of giant leathery wings burst from his orange shoulders and stretched at least thirty feet across the street. My heart skipped a beat as I found myself in their fell shadow.

We were so going to die.

With a final crack, Doyle rolled his neck and fixed us with a triumphant glare. He opened his giant mouth and let loose a roar against the rainy sky that was so loud I felt it in my bones. Car alarms all over the street went off, only adding to the terror of the scene.

"Well, I think the mortals are going to have a hard time explaining this one away," I muttered. No sooner were the words out of my mouth than I felt the unveiling of a PRESENCE.

It was like when Polaris dropped his mental hammer on the Congregation—times a million. I saw a shadow forming in the air like a shimmering wall that spanned multiple city blocks. It felt like some POWER had placed its giant hands around us, cutting us off from the rest of the world.

"Uh... what is that?" I squeaked, despair hanging over my heart.

"It is the blessing of someone mightier than Doyle," Orion replied grimly, his eyes taking in the shadow circling us. "A problem for the future, if we survive."

"Is it *him*?" I asked, remembering whose orders Samael had been operating under when she commanded Doyle to kill Orion.

"I don't know." The Hunter shot one more look at the awakened dragon and turned to sprint back toward the me and the convention. I'm all for being brave, but if Orion was running for his life, I was only too happy to follow his lead. The Hunter fell in stride with me as we raced out of the street toward the little garden in front of the convention center. Everyone else had already been smart enough to get out of the street; I didn't see a single being other than us.

Doyle let out another victorious roar behind us as we fled.

Abruptly, Orion stopped and grabbed my shoulder. "I cannot order you to do this," he began.

"Shut up," I snapped. "What do you need done?"

The Hunter gave me a long, measured look. Wordlessly, he held out his hand, offering me the hilt of his blazing sword. Full of trepidation, I reached out. The last time I'd tried to hold this blade, it had burned an imprint into my palm, a scar I still bore. Today the sword accepted my grip without complaint.

"Buy me time," he said softly.

Abruptly I understood. The sword was powerful, but it simply wasn't big enough to stab a creature the size of several elephants. Doyle would need something bigger.

Like a lance, for example.

Our only hope was for Orion to use Ascalon to kill Doyle. But the lance wasn't here. It was a couple of blocks away, locked in the back of a minivan. Someone had to keep the dragon's attention until Orion could retrieve it.

"Oh," I said, stupidly. This is what I got for offering to help. "Yeah, sure thing."

"Stay alive," Orion ordered, clasping me on the shoulder. Then he was gone, sprinting into the rain like the world depended on it. Behind me, the giant dragon let out another roar.

THIRTY-THREE

DOYLE KEPT ROARING, and I did my best to not pee my pants. Fortunately, it was raining, so no one would ever know if I failed or not. Holding the Hunter's blade, I turned to face the monster. I'm no dragonologist, but now that I was farther away, I could see there was something wrong with his transformation—an unevenness that looked unhealthy. His entire body, while terrifying, was warped and malformed.

One wing was bigger than the other, a leg longer than its brothers. Even the right fang sticking out of his red maw was shorter than the left. Muscles bulged in parts of his chest but were missing on the other side. He looked like the dragon equivalent of someone who had only exercised their left arm and right leg. His right foreleg was mangled from the explosion, just bigger and more disturbing now.

Seeing his deformities gave me a little more confidence. Matt versus a totally healthy dragon seemed hopeless. But facing off against a twisted, cursed dragon? That was much more manageable.

Probably.

"Hey, big guy!" I yelled, not sure how else to get Doyle's attention. The dragon's long neck whipped around to stare at me, standing in the rain, holding the burning sword of the Hunter. "Can you keep it down a little? There's a noise ordinance, and I wouldn't want to have to call the cops."

He narrowed his eyes in irritation and opened his massive jaw in what I could only assume was the precursor to him vomiting an ocean of fire on me. But before he could spew his flames, a thousand icy missiles slammed into him from above. Doyle let out a roar of surprise but didn't go down under the barrage. He took a giant hopping shuffle step toward me, like an eagle bouncing around its nest.

"If you do not wish to die, manling, you should run," Mav hissed, appearing at my side, her black hair slick with rain. She cut to our left, running away from the convention center across the empty street. Not wanting to be left alone with the big scary dragon, I followed her, fast.

There was a heavy thump behind us, and I glanced over my shoulder to see Doyle spreading his uneven wings. He ran after us in lumbering, uneven steps, pinions flapping as he gained momentum. It was like being hunted by a pterodactyl. Or maybe one of the other winged dinosaurs. Pterodactyls might have been vegetarian, I can never remember.

Ignoring the crosswalk lights, the Lady of Winter and I sprinted through the intersection and down the street, turning the corner on the dragon behind us.

"Go, go, go!" I shouted at the Faerie princess ahead of me, pouring all the speed my body possessed into my run. Mav shot me an annoyed look but picked up the pace. Downtown Los Angeles rattled as Doyle roared his way into the air, herking and jerking on uneven wings.

As stunted and flawed as Doyle's transformation was, it was still awe-inspiring to see him soar above us. Too bad he wasn't on a movie screen for an action hero to deal with.

With a few more flaps, Doyle was gone over the buildings, heading farther Downtown. I let my sprint slow into a jog, watching until I lost track of him behind a skyscraper.

Ahead of me, Mav slowed to a stop, and I joined her, careful to stay out of reach of her icy gauntlets. Orion's blade still burned in my right hand, its flames and heat different from Willow's.

"Well, I guess he didn't want to play with us after all," I said to the Lady of Winter between gasps. "Where do you think he went?"

"He isn't gone," Mav had just enough time to hiss before Doyle emerged at the head at the street, flying back toward us. He hadn't been flying away after all, just getting ahead. The red dragon's jaw was open wide, revealing his forked tongue and uneven teeth.

His need for draconic braces faded from my mind when I spotted the massive fireball forming at the back of his throat. With a terrifying whoosh, the lurching dragon spewed fire down the street in a molten tidal wave. Horrified, I watched as the flames swept over abandoned cars on their way toward us.

With grim determination, I set my feet, calling upon whatever strength Willow had left. I doubted my new trick of diverting dragonfire would work with Doyle's flames. Something told me they were of a higher—and therefore hotter—caliber.

"Get close!" I shouted at Mav, not sure why I did. What did I care if Mav survived the inferno? As far as I was concerned, a fiery lake was exactly the fate she deserved.

As the fire drew close, a wall of heat slammed into me, hotter than my grandmother's leather car seats after they had been out in the summer sun. I knew it was worthless, but I called upon Willow to create a bubble of air around us and let the flames pass by.

The fire swept over us, and somehow my dome held. I gasped in shock as I felt the power leaving my body to combat Doyle's flames. It reminded me of the first time I had used Willow and burnt down Lazarus's lab. Pushing the fire spirit past its limit had consumed my own energy and caused me to black out. On the bright side, if I fainted now, I probably wouldn't feel anything when the fire claimed me.

Slowly, my bubble began to shrink as Willow's energy waned. I dropped to my knees, and Mav crouched next to me, the fire raging all around us. It was getting hard to breathe; the flames had devoured most of our oxygen. I slumped my shoulders, pressing against Mav as we played the world's most dangerous version of limbo.

My vision was going black around the edges. I couldn't hold this much longer. At least if this was the end, I would get some small taste of vengeance in my final moments. I wasn't avenging my family per se, but knowing their killer was dying with me was a small comfort. Not the kind of comfort that made the fires around me feel less hot, but it was something.

Willow's flames on my left hand flickered and went out. I gritted my teeth and dug deep for one final push against the fire. I took as deep a breath as I could in our limited oxygen and consigned myself to the Pit. I imagined it wouldn't actually be that different from where I was right now. I'd close my eyes in one fire and wake up in a different one. Willow clung to my right hand, flickering on and off like a lightbulb on its last legs. The edge of the bubble was practically touching us now.

"*I'm sorry, my friend,*" I sent mentally at the little spirit. I knew they couldn't speak to me in this realm, but I felt like I should apologize for one more of their coals going out.

Suddenly the sphere began to grow. The temperature dropped a dozen degrees, and I could breathe again. I had done it! I had found some final reserve of strength to—I glanced at my right hand in time to see Willow's fire wink out. I hadn't done anything; my tank was empty.

But the bubble did not shrink.

A figure moved within the inferno, stepping through the barrier to join us. Ash, Lady of Autumn, walked amongst the flames, and they did not burn her. Her hands were covered in fire as her Willow protected us with a strength I could only dream of.

The roaring wave of Doyle's flames around us abruptly receded, like someone had just turned off the hose. With a gesture, Ash dismissed her Willow's defensive dome, and the three of us stared out on a wasteland of destruction. Dragonfire had devastated everything it touched. There were no hard edges left on the cars or buildings that had been caught in his flames—they had all melted off.

The asphalt of the road had turned to putty and was sticky underfoot. Steam sizzled off everything as the rain fell on the superheated street. The whole block was burned and blackened, like it had been in a toaster oven for too long. Only the small area that had been within our bubble was untouched, an oasis in an apocalypse. This is what an unchained dragon was capable of.

"Darling, you know I would never let you go on adventure without me," Ash said with a beaming smile. "If I hadn't needed to tend to my sister's wounds, I would have been here faster."

"Is Dawn okay?" I didn't think cold iron was strong enough to kill a true Immortal like Dawn, but that didn't mean it was good for her either.

"Robin and I removed the bullets. She is weak but will recover swiftly."

"Well, I hope she hurries," I grumbled, making my way to my feet. "Having someone who could knock Doyle out of the air would be real handy."

The dragon let out a furious roar as he saw us alive and unburned.

Lowering himself into a hunting pose, he leapt toward us, an ungainly move that still was terrifyingly fast for how clumsy it looked. My Willow was completely out of juice, and I didn't really want to put Ash's reserves to the test of another firestorm. Looking around for a way out, I saw an alley intersecting the street.

A chance to escape.

"This way," I shouted, cutting to the left toward the mouth of the open alley. The giant dragon was faster than we were in a straightaway sprint. But he was big and unwieldy. I had been able to use that against Apis the minotaur once upon a time. Maybe it would work on an even bigger baddie. I led the two Fae princesses into the small alley at a breakneck pace. If we could make it to a cross street, Doyle would have to take to the air again to chase us, and this time we would hide. It was a good plan—a great one even. But there was one fatal flaw to it.

The alley was a dead end.

Instead of cutting all the way through the block, it ran straight into the back of a large commercial building that spanned the entire length the street. Panicked, I raced up to the massive doors that granted access to its trash dumpsters and tried to wrench them open.

They were locked. We were trapped.

Except a door is never truly locked for me. With a giant grin, I dug my hand into my pocket and pulled out the Key of Portunus. I wonder if even Gloriana knew how powerful a tool she had given me. I jammed the key into the handle, and the lock morphed to accept the ancient thing. Resisting the urge to chuckle to myself, I unlocked the door and pulled it open for us. *Let's see Doyle follow us to the Between.*

But the eternal hallway wasn't waiting for me on the other side. Instead of humming fluorescent lights, the doorframe was filled with the same inky darkness that filled the sky. I didn't need to be a genius to know I shouldn't touch whatever it was. The mysterious POWER that was locking down this area really didn't want us to leave. I shuddered to think of what—or who—could block access to other worlds just with their will.

With a curse, I slammed the door shut and pulled the key out. Here in the mortal world, it was locked again, as if I had never opened it. Desperate, I stabbed the tip of Orion's sword into the door near the dead bolt. The burning blade cut through the metal like it was butter. Mav slammed into the doors with her shoulder, rattling them, but they did not budge. Behind us, I could hear the dull thuds of the dragon's footsteps. My hands were shaking with fear, but I kept cutting.

"How much power do you have left?" I shouted at Ash as I sliced at the door.

"Not enough," she said grimly, casting about the alley for another avenue of escape. "Especially in close quarters like this where he will be able to focus his heat."

I had led us into a funnel for the dragon's fire. With a dull *clunk*, the deadbolt finally snapped free of the door. I shoved on it, but it still wouldn't open. Realizing there were locks at the top and bottom too, I reached up and sheared through the upper one with a single stroke. As I leaned down to get the second, everything went still.

Beside me, Ash and Mav froze in silent horror. There were no more thuds. I knew without turning that time had run out. The Dragon Don, in all his unchained glory, was at the mouth of the alley.

Slowly, almost against my will, I turned to face the beast that had us cornered. I had a moment to process his open maw and the flame at the back of his throat. Ash raised her hands, Willow's light burning bright. Her icy sister did the same, setting themselves for one last desperate stand.

The wall of fire filled the narrow alley completely, rushing toward us in a flaming avalanche. I stood between the two princesses, holding Orion's blade. Maybe if it survived the fire, my friend could use it to avenge us.

Heat slammed into us like a runaway eighteen-wheeler, and I staggered back a step. I had hoped to meet my death on my feet, but I was a leaf in the wind of the titanic force crushing down on us. I closed my eyes against all the horror sweeping down on me.

And then the world went silent.

I couldn't hear the *whoosh* of the rushing flames or the steady beat of the falling rain. Now that I thought about it, the heat was gone too. Confused, I opened my eyes and looked around. Everything was frozen—not in ice, this wasn't some trick of Mav's. But nothing moved. The Fae princesses on either side of me were locked in place. Even the flames rushing forward had paused, each individual tongue completely still. The only thing other than me that seemed unaffected was the undulating shadowy curtain in the distance, which still rippled, moved by some unseen wind. Whatever PRESENCE was there still felt very freaking present too.

With a flicker of movement, a man appeared before me. He wore a brown robe that was open at the front over a white shirt and black jeans. He had a neatly trimmed brown beard, and in his right hand he carried a long black staff. His black eyes bore into me with the unfathomable weight of the abyss.

With a start, I realized I recognized this Nephilim. He had voted against the dragon's request in the Congregation today. He had a weird name, Horologius or something.

"We have got to stop meeting like this," he chuckled, leaning on his staff with an amused smirk.

"I'm pretty forgetful, but I can't say I recall being stuck in drag-onfire and getting resc—" The words died in my mouth as something blazed in his dark eyes, and I *remembered*.

I remembered everything.

We didn't go right. We went left. The dragoons chased us through the kitchens, and we died. In a blaze of fire and fury we died. Or we should have. But instead, we went right. We escaped.

My head began to throb with a sharp pain as two timelines, two realities, tried to form and exist inside my head. I was dead. I was alive. I felt myself splintering as two Matts tried to exist inside my body at the same time.

Horologius tsked in irritation and waved his hand dismissively. The pressure in my head abated immediately, and only one of me was there. I was still aware of the other timeline, the other me, but it lurked in the back of my mind, where I could acknowledge it out of the corner of my eye without looking at it directly.

"Try not to think about it too deeply," the Constellation advised sagely.

"What did you do to me?" I managed to gasp out through clenched teeth. If all of the king's horses and all of his men had managed to put Humpty Dumpty back together, I think the egg-man would have needed a moment to collect himself too.

"So far I've saved you twice. You're welcome."

"Who even are you? Horo—something, right?"

"Horologium."

"Yeah, I'm not going to remember that."

The Nephilim laughed warmly, standing up straight and beginning to walk toward me. "Then perhaps just remember it means 'clock' and that will be close enough."

Time. This was the Constellation of Time. My eyes stared at the frozen wave of fire hovering a dozen feet away. Horologium had simply paused time to speak with me. That's it, nothing crazy.

"You can control time," I said, stupidly.

"I cannot control it," he replied, coming to stand a few steps in front of me. "No more than you can control fire. But I can guide it a little."

"I don't suppose you could rewind me all the way back to when

Dan the Demon stole my soul and let me skip this whole thing," I asked.

"If my desire was to destroy the very fabric of the universe, that would be an excellent way to do it," Horologium chuckled softly. "Time left unchecked will devour as happily as the flame."

"Why save me then?" I demanded. "Leave me alive to suffer more?"

"The appointed hour of your death has not yet come," he told me. A chill ran down my spine as I remembered Samael had told Doyle that very same thing.

"Are you working with the demons?" I demanded, brandishing Orion's blade and taking a step toward him. I'm not sure what I was hoping to accomplish. How do you stab a guy who can control—excuse me, *guide*—time? Although if time was already frozen, could he freeze it again? Or would he have to unfreeze it in order to refreeze it, and would I have enough ti—Well, the point is, who knows, but I had an immortal-killing sword and a bad attitude, and if I was going to go down, I was going to go down swinging.

"I may have demon blood in my veins, but I do not answer to the Dark Star," Horologium told me with a broad smile. "You are the bringer of change. A new flame that flares in the dark. I would not see you go out before you can do your work."

I didn't find that as comforting as I think he thought I would.

"Time runs out on us," he said, raising his staff a few inches off the ground. "We have tarried in the Stillness too long. We will speak again, in the flowing world."

"I'm thrilled you don't want me to die today," I said before he could unpause everything or whatever it was he was about to do. "I love it, I'm on board. But how exactly are you going to help with that? The fires are *very* close."

"I can give you another chance," he told me seriously. "But I cannot keep saving you. Already I have pushed my power too far in too short a time. When you go back, choose wisely. There won't be any more redoes for a while."

"What should I do? How do I stop a full-blown freaking dragon?"

Horologium was silent for a moment. He glanced up at the black barrier with a thoughtful air before responding. "My advice? Stop going left."

"I can't believe Time can't just wave his hand and fix this," I grumbled.

"I'm not Time," Horologium told me, an amused smile spreading across his face.

"You're not?"

"Time is my father." With a firm *crack*, he slammed the butt of his staff into the ground.

I was in the middle of the burned street, its heat still oppressively strong. Doyle's charge carried him toward us like a limping rhino. Two alleyways beckoned to us, promising escape from the rampaging dragon. I staggered a step to the right, as my fractured identities battled for control of my being. All I wanted to do was go left. I needed to go left. I *was* Left Matt. But I wanted to be Right Matt. Right Matt lived at least thirty seconds longer than Left Matt.

I remembered how it felt when Horologium purged my mind and tried to copy that sensation. With a savage twist, I shoved the interloper into a shadowy box and stacked it in the back closet of my mind, next to the other abandoned fork of myself that died in a service hall. Somehow, I doubt that's something therapy can fix.

"Mav, can you ice up our getaway?" I shouted, turning to run right. "Get the front of this alley too." If this was truly my last chance, I wasn't going to waste it.

The Lady of Winter stared at me for a moment, her golden eyes burning with stubbornness.

"Do you want to die, *Viking*?" I demanded.

"*Obey*," Ash commanded, her voice dark with power. Was it my imagination or did the golden collar around Mav's neck glint slightly? The dark-haired princess glared at us for another heartbeat before shivering and turning to follow my command.

Ice erupted on the pavement, steaming as it melted in the face of the incredible heat Doyle's fire had left behind. Mav had to keep coating the asphalt, cooling the ground so the ice could last more than a few seconds.

Doyle drew closer. He was less than a half a block away now.

"Time to go!" I shouted, cutting to the right and leading the two Fae into the alley. "Make sure the entrance is fully covered," I called to Mav. She rolled her eyes but complied, coating the ground again and again.

Looking ahead, I breathed a sigh of relief: This alley went all the way through to the next street. Maybe Horologium was onto something. Putting my head down, I sprinted as fast as I could, leading the two Immortals down the narrow straightaway. Having an exit was great, but we still had to get out before Doyle turned this into a blast oven.

The heavy thuds of the charging dragon drew closer. I risked a glance over my shoulder as I ran and was rewarded with the sight of a giant, red-scaled beast sliding past the entrance to our alley and roaring in frustration as he hit Mav's ice.

It would only delay him a few seconds, but that was more than enough time for us to make our escape. Panting, I rushed out of the alley and turned away from the convention center. The last thing I wanted to do was lead the rampaging dragon back to the huddled masses.

I almost slammed smack dab into one of the dragoons that had fled from Orion when he got his sword back. This muddy-green-scaled beast had been hiding until its master came back to save it from me and my friends.

The dragoon hissed as we pounded out of the alley, knocking over the mailbox it was hiding behind, which I'm pretty sure is a felony. Acting on instinct, I raised my hand holding Orion's blade and commanded Willow to sear the lizard—then remembered that I'd already burned through Willow's magical battery.

I was so surprised when the flame on my right hand actually did burst into being that I almost dropped the magic sword. Willow's flame spiraled along the length of the blade, pulling some of the magic sword's flame with it. The two distinct fires melded into a swirl, never quite touching, then shot forward like a spear, slamming into the dragoon and punching through its chest with the ease of a brick through a window. The lizard let out a surprised gurgle and fell sideways, its slitted pupils wide.

"*Wow, special fire,*" Willow commented gleefully into my head, making me almost drop the sword again. Willow had never been able to speak to me in the mortal realm like they did in the Faerie Lands. "*Are you sure it's okay we borrowed some of it? I don't know if we're really allowed...*"

"How are you talking to me right now?" I asked the fire spirit. "Have you been holding out on me?"

"*I told you, I'm magic fire, I need magic to burn. That sword is some deep magic.*" Somehow, I didn't find that surprising. Packing the power to kill an Immortal wasn't exactly anything to sneeze at.

"Can you borrow some more of it to recharge yourself?" I suggested.

"*...I'd rather not.*" If I didn't know any better, I'd say Willow sounded uncomfortable. "*This is an elder flame. I wouldn't want to overstep.*" A chill ran through me at the spirit's hesitation. Not for the first time, I wondered what exactly the sword Orion carried was.

"How do you feel about dragonfire?" I asked on a hunch.

"*Delicious!*"

"Boy, do I have good news for you," I muttered.

"*Time to go, I don't want to presume,*" Willow sent, and the fire on my hand immediately winked out, leaving me more confused than when we started. Then again, that's how most of my conversations with Willow go.

"Come on, we gotta get off the street," I said, turning away from the dead dragoon. The sisters followed me without complaint. I scanned the sky, getting raindrops in my eyes as we ran. I could feel someone watching us. I assumed Doyle was above us, circling like a bird of prey.

Part of the way down the street I found an abandoned food truck, its door hanging open. I guess whoever had been manning it had run when the fighting started. I would too.

I motioned to the princesses, and we slid into the back, pulling the door shut behind us. Doyle would never think to check a food truck, would he? Unless he was hungry, because these taco fixings smelled heavenly.

"Now what?" hissed Mav as we crouched, waiting for any sound of the hunting Don.

"We wait," I whispered back, leaning my head against the cool metal wall. The steady drum of rain on the roof was calming. My heart rate finally began to go down. We were safe, for a moment at least.

The three of us sat in silence, recovering a little from what we'd just gone through. I wondered if either of them remembered the timeline fork. Was it a fork if it went back, or was it more of a splinter? I don't know, I've never actually read any Hawking.

I almost screeched in surprise when a shock rattled through the entire truck as something heavy landed near us. The three of us exchanged concerned glances. I felt smaller rumbles as the dragon paced down the street. I could hear the thud of his tread growing louder over the rain as he drew near.

I was too scared to breathe. My heart was pounding so hard in my chest I was worried that he would hear it. I could hear him clearly, just on the other side of the wall of the truck, sniffing deeply.

My cell phone rang.

I'm not a monster. My phone stays on silent. There was no obnoxious ringtone that blared out our location. But it sure did vibrate in my jeans pocket, rattling against the metal wall of the food truck that I leaned against.

Startled, I pulled it out, desperate to stop the buzzing. There was a horrific crash as a heavy claw slammed down on the top of the truck and began shaking it so hard, I thought it might shatter. Mav kicked the back door open, and the three of us raced out like it was a fire drill. The screen on my phone said the call was from Alex, so I answered it.

"The cavalry is on its way!" Alex shouted into my ear over the roar of an engine. "Where are you?"

I glanced over my shoulder to see Doyle resting on his back legs, one of his forearms grasping the taco truck. His lizard eyes were fixed on me and the Hunter's sword, burning with hate. The dragon opened his mouth and let out a roar of triumph at having found us.

"Follow the sounds of the angry dragon," I squeaked, hanging up on him to run.

QUICK AS A cobra, Doyle spun after us, his long neck drawn back for a strike. Ash and Mav scattered. I didn't bother to run. There was nowhere to go; the dragon was looking only at me.

I heard a sound like the hiss of an open gas line as fire formed in the mouth of the Dragon Don. I stood, facing my death on my feet. I knew I only had one chance to survive, even if I had to do the thing I hate the most.

I listened to my father.

As the torrent washed down on me, I took a deep breath, much the way I did when I recharged Willow in the Faerie Land. The flame swept over me, and I welcomed it. Instead of pushing it *out* with Willow's strength, I pulled it in.

My lungs burned. Each breath felt like I had volcanoes in my bronchioles, erupting in fire and ash. I was boiling, but I did not burn. The heat inside my body grew to match the heat coming from the outside, easing some of the discomfort, but not all.

Doyle's assault continued. My entire world was made of shades of red and orange. Still I pulled the flame into me. The pressure mounted as my body struggled to contain all the power I was absorbing. Worried I was about to pop, I used Willow to burn some of the excess flame out my right hand, like a kettle's spout.

Just when I thought I could not hold another ounce of magic, Doyle's attack stopped. His torrent of flame faded to reveal me standing in the center of the charred patch of earth, hands burning with bright flame, Orion's blade still firmly in my grasp. Dragons have big dumb lizard faces that aren't good at conveying human emotions, but I took the Don's mouth hanging open at the sight of me unharmed as a measure of his shock.

Fire burned within me, rage at this dragon that had come to my city, hurt my friends, and murdered my people. Abruptly, I realized I was glaring at the dragon at eye level, instead of looking up at him. Startled, I looked down at the ground, only to discover I hovered a dozen feet above it.

That was new.

Even more surprising, I noticed my hands weren't the only part of me on fire. My entire body was wreathed in the thick, angry inferno of Willow. Steam hissed as the rain fell on me. Beyond my feet I saw Ash staring up at me with a face of awe.

"*Heh, heh, heh,*" Willow cackled, their voice crackling with unusual intensity.

The power of a dragon sang in my bones as I stared down at the predator. Doyle's wide eyes betrayed a hint of fear. I guess he wasn't used to someone stealing his fire. Maybe I was the second coming of Prometheus. But he never used the gods' flame to burn them. With a savage snarl, I drew back my fist, still wrapped around the hilt of Orion's sword, and thrust it forward with all the force I could muster.

A brilliant beam of fire shot out of my fist, bypassing the blade entirely. The column slammed into Doyle's jaw and lifted him off his feet, tossing him down the street like a to-go cup caught in a tornado. He rolled end-over-end before sliding to a stop thirty yards away.

Doyle's reptilian eyes were no longer shocked; they glared at me with a cold malice. The overwhelming pressure stored within me had lessened, but I still had gas in the tank.

Giving him no time to recover, I threw both fists in front of me and shot a second beam, this one thicker than the first. It slammed into Doyle, driving him backward.

I held the attack as long as I could, channeling all the stolen fire I had at my disposal. I fed every ounce of anger and rage to the drag-onfire in my body and sent it to burn its master. I didn't even notice I had begun to sink until my foot touched down on the asphalt. With a sputter, my beam flickered and died. I glanced down and saw I was no longer wreathed in flames.

I was just Matthew Carver, former Squire of the Hunt.

My chest heaved as I tried to catch my breath. It felt like I had just run three marathons at the same time. Doyle was still on his feet, but there was a scorch mark on his red and orange scales, a spot of black and char on the front of his chest and on his face. I felt some savage satisfaction at seeing the ruin I had dealt to him.

I would have felt even more satisfaction if he had died, but beggars can't be choosers.

Doyle let loose a furious bellow and hunched, ready to pounce. I guess he figured my ability to absorb his fire wouldn't be that useful if he bit me in half. I couldn't fault his logic.

A different kind of roar interrupted the dragon's leap. A black motorcycle driven by the Hunter hurtled out of the intersection behind me. In his right hand he held Ascalon, the lance of Saint George, free from its sheath, its blazing tip pointing to the dark sky like a knight of old, just with significantly more horsepower.

The weapon pulsed, sending out its rage like a wave. I felt it wash over me, but I was not its target and it slammed into Doyle with tremendous force. The dragon seemed to stagger back a step from the relic's mental assault. I might have imagined it, but I thought the shadowy veil surrounding us rippled with its aftershocks.

My heart soared at the sight of my friends coming to save my bacon yet again. *Cavalry indeed*, I thought. Alex clung to Orion's back for dear life as they screeched to a halt beside me. My friend's eyes widened at the sight of the sword in my hand.

"Off," Orion called, his black eyes locked on the dragon. The younger Nephilim scurried to comply, jumping next to me, an assault rifle clutched in his white-knuckled hands.

"Glad you're not dead," Alex said, still staring at my unburned hand holding our former master's blade.

Orion didn't give us time to settle our nerves with banter. "CROM CRUACH!" he roared, glaring dark daggers at the dragon down the street. "Come and meet your end."

Doyle, or whatever his real name was, seemed only too happy to face the Hunter. His giant eyes were fixed on the fiery lance of Saint George with a furious hate. The dragon let loose a deafening roar and leapt forward, its lopsided stride eating up the distance between them. Orion gunned the throttle of his motorcycle. The rear tire spun, drifting the bike sideways as he held the front brake for a few seconds. Then with a savage twist, the bike shot forward, sending the Hunter out like a dragon-killing bullet.

The earth shook as the monster raced to meet the knight. The blazing tip of the saint's lance lowered, extending in front of Orion like the finger of judgment, pointing at Doyle. At the last second, Orion swung his bike to the right, avoiding a swipe from the beast's claw. As he cut to the side, he lashed out with the lance, its fiery blade slicing through the dragon's shoulder, causing Doyle to cry out in anger. Alex and I roared our approval. After running from the monster for so long, seeing him bleed filled me with fierce joy.

Then the Hunter was past his prey. He shot down the street, lance up in the air. His tires screeched and water sprayed as he executed a hairpin turn, flipping back toward his target. There was no joy in the face of the Hunter, only the marble mask of an executioner. This was vengeance centuries in the making. Doyle twisted around to meet the Hunter. Orion gunned his engine, and the two charged again, drawn together by their hate.

But dragons are slithery, sneaky creatures, and Doyle was one of the most ancient and wicked of their fell breed. As Orion raced at him, the dragon twisted, spinning his bulk to whip his long tail around in a familiar move. I could only watch in horror as the tail swept across the street, batting the Hunter and his bike like a baseball, sending them flying.

Orion flew free of his motorcycle, rolling across the pavement for a dozen yards. My body winced in sympathy for the road rash he would suffer. Ascalon landed near him, slipping out of his grasp as he hit the ground.

A trickle of fear ran down my spine, even colder than the rain that had found its way below my shirt. For all the Hunter's prowess, Doyle was relatively unhurt; he was bleeding from the wound on his shoulder, but it looked superficial. It's very hard to stab something the size of a house to death, especially when its skin is made of armor.

Orion pulled himself to his feet, shaking himself like a wet dog. Water sprayed out of his drenched black hair, and his eyes blazed with fury. Slowly, he bent down and picked up Ascalon, holding the lance in his hands as if it were a spear. Doyle let out a growl as he began to stalk toward the dismounted knight. To no one's surprise, the Hunter strode to meet the dragon head-on. I could almost see the souls of the dead members of the Hunt riding on his shoulders, watching him avenge them.

Doyle struck first, his head shooting out like a snake, trying to catch one of Orion's arms. The Nephilim danced to the side, jabbing with the lance. The dragon hissed and dodged backward, narrowly avoiding having his head sliced by the burning blade.

Carefully, they circled each other in a deadly dance. Doyle hissed and turned, whipping his tail at Orion with blinding speed. But the Hunter had already learned that trick. He leapt over the dragon's attack, rushing toward him as the tail continued past him. Quick as lightning, the Hunter stabbed Ascalon forward, its blazing tip streaking toward Doyle's chest like a missile.

The Don let out a roar of anger and pain as the weapon bit into his bright-orange scales. I raised a clenched fist in victory, but my shout of joy died on my lips as I saw the weapon stop short. Orion jerked to a halt; his momentum stopped as Ascalon failed to punch through the armored hide.

I guess that's what the horse is supposed to be for.

Without his bike, Orion didn't have enough force to shatter Doyle's thick scales. The Hunter wrenched the lance free and leapt back, dodging the dragon's swipe as he struggled to reset the fight. I turned, looking to see if there was any chance his bike was still in riding condition.

I'm no mechanic, but I'm pretty sure you need both of the wheels to be on the motorcycle for it to work. We weren't getting any more horsepower out of it until it spent a long time in a repair bay. Cursing, I tried to think of another way we could jam Ascalon's pointy tip through Doyle's cold heart.

Then I saw it, the crack in his armor.

"Orion! The charred scales!" I shouted, pointing at the portion of Doyle's chest that had weathered Willow's attack with his stolen fire. The Hunter gave me a slight tilt of his head to acknowledge he heard me, his eyes never leaving his target.

Furiously, Doyle swiped his front claw at Orion, who merely stabbed it, causing the dragon to shriek in pain. The earth around us shook as the injured monster stamped its rage into the asphalt. Tired of being on the back foot, the Hunter advanced, jabbing with the lance, trying to find the timing to strike.

Doyle gave ground, backing up until his scaly hindquarters were pressed up against a tall apartment building. Fully cornered, he let some animalistic instinct take over and lunged forward, mouth wide, seeking to devour Orion. In one fluid motion, the Hunter sidestepped the attack and stabbed viciously at the Don.

The tip of the lance bit deeply into the blackened and burned flesh I had hammered with stolen dragonfire. The brittle scale shattered under the force of the blow. Ascalon dove hungrily into Doyle's chest, the burning blade sinking its entire length into the beast. It was so firmly buried that it was ripped out of Orion's hands as the strength went out of Doyle's legs, and the dragon collapsed to the ground. Alex and I raced toward our friend, unable to believe what we had just witnessed.

Everything except the still-falling rain was silent.

Orion stood over the downed Don, his face as unreadable as the dark clouds above us. The monster shifted weakly, trying to gather the last of its strength to stand up to the Hunter.

My former master stepped past the beast's jaws and wrenched Ascalon free. Doyle let out a pitiful cry as Orion slammed the lance down into the dragon's chest a second time, spearing for his black heart. The tension flowed out, and with a great sigh he was still. Doyle, the unchained Dragon Don, was dead.

The black shadow that had cut us off from the rest of the world abruptly vanished like someone had turned on the lights as the PRESENCE hovering above all of us like a giant eye winked out.

"Dragon slayer," Alex murmured in awe.

"Dragon slayer," I echoed in the same tone.

Orion ignored us, staring down at the Doyle' carcass, his face a mask of rage. I could only begin to imagine the emotions he was wrestling with, the traumatic memories this brought back. I hoped he could lay some of those souls he carried on his shoulder to rest now.

Something in the hunch of his shoulders told me that the answer was no.

I felt a light brush at my hand as Ash stepped close to me. She stared at the Hunter with the same reverent awe that I felt reflecting in her eyes. The three of us waited in silence for the Hunter to speak. This silence was his to break.

After an eternity, Orion turned, Ascalon grasped firmly in his right hand. His iron face relaxed slightly as he saw us waiting with bated breath. Slowly, he raised the holy lance into the sky and gave it a vicious shake, freeing us from our silence.

Alex, Ash, and I roared our approval at the Hunter's triumph.

"*Sic semper tyrannis!*" Alex cried.

I shot him a weird look. "I'm not quite sure how 'thus always to tyrants' is applicable here," I told him.

"His face kinda looks like a *T. rex*," Alex explained with a shrug. "I figure that's close enough."

"And you say my Latin jokes are bad."

"They're *terrible*," Ash moaned from beside me. I gave her a friendly shove with my shoulder, and she jostled me back as we turned away from the dead lizard.

"Well, that wasn't so bad," I commented, glancing around the destroyed street full of overturned cars and smashed light poles. "We only destroyed maybe two blocks. What was everyone so worried about?"

"We have broken much more than that," Orion promised darkly. The Hunter was looking past us, toward the convention center. I followed his gaze to find a dozen Constellations making their way toward us, with the North and South Stars in the lead. Octantis's expression was blank, but Polaris was practically beaming. That couldn't be good.

"Hey, wait a minute," I said, looking around our merry little band. "Where did Mav go?" Ash glanced behind us, a concerned expression growing on her own face.

I had a very bad feeling I knew the answer to that question. Suddenly nervous, I turned to go hunt for the Lady of Winter, before pausing mid-step to look at Orion for guidance. Technically we were not part of the Hunt anymore, but I didn't want to abandon my friend if he needed me.

"Go," he said with a firm nod. "I will be all right."

I shot a worried glance at the approaching Nephilim, but nodded and dashed off to the side, magic sword still in hand. It hadn't started to burn me yet, which I took as permission to keep hanging on to it.

Heart pounding in my chest, I sprinted across the street in the direction Mav had gone when we split up after Doyle had tried to burn me into a cinder. The rain made looking for footprints or markings impossible—everything was wet.

As I worked my way down the street, I tried to think like Damien. Where would I have taken the Lady of Winter? It wouldn't be far. He would want to capitalize on the distraction Doyle was providing to exact his revenge and be gone before anyone noticed.

Footsteps sounded behind me, startling me into action. I whirled, blazing sword held in a low guard, only to find myself staring into the amused eyes of my betrothed. Feeling more than a little stupid, I lowered my sword and relaxed.

"Did you think I would let you go looking for my sister without me?" she asked, arching a quizzical red eyebrow. I had no good answer, so I shrugged and turned back to my hunt. Inside, my stomach boiled with stress. I strongly suspected we were about to discover a dead or dying Mav, and I wasn't sure how Ash would react.

On the one hand, the two sisters weren't what I would describe as close. Mav had personally tried to have her sister assassinated more times than I could count. On the other, no sibling appreciates it when an outsider gets in the middle of their rivalry.

I almost missed the breadcrumbs Mav had left for us. Six tiny ice marbles were tucked by the gate of a towering apartment building construction site. They had been there for a while, melting away bit by bit. My heart sank; they were all the confirmation I needed that the Lady of Winter had been taken. Wordlessly, I pointed them out to Ash. Her lips pressed into a flat line as she processed their meaning. I reached out and tested the big lock holding the chain-link fence closed. It was open. Together we slipped through the gate of the abandoned yard.

The construction site was part of a multiyear project to build even more apartments Downtown, where no one wants to live. The metal bones of the structure stretched into the sky forty or more stories, promising to become something mighty when it grew up. Scattered around the yard were the tools of industry: trucks, machines, mobile homes set up as offices.

We crept across the gravel, ignoring the signs ordering us to wear a hard hat and steel-toed boots. I doubted the Queen of All Fae recognized the authority of OSHA over her subjects anyway. Ash caught my attention by lightly tapping my elbow and pointed toward one of the trailers, where a few ice balls lurked among the gravel in front of its stairs. Instinctively, we both kept silent, unsure what listening ears might hear us if we spoke.

Step by agonizing step, we made our way across the treacherous footing. Each footfall had to be as precise as an ice climber's. All it would take was one careless move to trigger a miniature rockslide and alert whoever had taken Mav—almost certainly my father—to our presence. Thankful for the drumming of the rain to mask our movements, we closed in on our target.

I paused before stepping on the metal stairs that led up to the office door. A hunch told me they were cheap things that would creak when I stepped on them. Holding up my hand to Ash, I took a pair of steps to place my ear against the lower part of the trailer. But the drumming of rain on the metal wall made it impossible for me to hear anything.

With a frustrated sigh, I turned back to Ash and shrugged. But the Lady of Autumn hadn't waited for me. She was halfway up the stairs, a dark look on her face. She reached for the door and wrenched it open, her Willow wreathing her hand in fire.

Gulping at what we might find, I dashed up the stairs after her, careful not to trip and stab myself with the magic blade. I'm pretty sure the rules about running with scissors also apply to swords.

The office was a simple affair, a long single room with a pair of desks and a few metal chairs scattered between them. Mav sat in the middle of the room, bound with cold-iron shackles on her hands and feet. A muzzle covered her jaw, leaving only her furious golden eyes peeking above.

Behind her stood my father. Damien wore his traditional gray peacoat and was as dry as a bone despite having dragged the Lady of Winter through the rain not too long ago. A thick pair of rubber gloves rested on the desk in front of him. His golden eyes flicked between us with an amused light.

"Ah, Matthew," he said after a moment. "I see you've brought a date."

CHAPTER
THIRTY-FIVE

ASH'S GAZE SNAPPED to me, her face calm and calculating. I didn't meet her eyes but stared at my father. I had helped make this happen, but now that the moment was here, I had mixed feelings about it.

I wanted revenge, vengeance, justice, whatever it was called, for my mother and sisters. But for some reason, I couldn't get the bitter hollowness of Orion's body language after he slew Doyle out of my head. The Don was only one of the dragons responsible for the death of the old Hunt; Draco still lived. Mav was the last piece of the Carver family revenge mosaic. Maybe once you complete it vengeance is more satisfying than I've seen.

"The three living nobles of Fire in one room," my father mused, an arrogant smirk growing on his face. "Each of us with a grievance against the Lady of Winter."

I was lost. I didn't know what I wanted to do. I didn't know what was right, but my conscience whispered in the back of my mind that this wasn't it.

"It is fitting," my father continued, stepping around the desk to approach us, flaming hands held wide in greeting. "She sought the extinction of our power, of our line. It is only just that we three bring about her end."

Suddenly I realized what was setting off all my alarm bells. My father seemed *happy*. There hadn't been a single biting comment, not one rude remark. I couldn't remember the last time that had happened.

"Well?" he asked, a cruel, aristocratic smile spreading across his face. "Who would like the honor of the first cut?"

"You would risk the wrath of my sister?" Ash asked coolly, her face unreadable.

"I have sworn to serve your sister and protect Dawn," Damien shrugged, pulling a sheathed knife from inside his jacket. "Mav has proven herself a threat to the Dandelion Court a hundred times over. This is within the bounds of that promise."

I glanced at the Lady of Winter, shackled in her chair. Her golden eyes gaze met mine, intense and unyielding. There was no fear or begging in her gaze, just the unblinking stare of a predator waiting to see what its target would do.

Mav had protected me today. She'd tried to kill me in the past, but today she had saved my life, and I had saved hers. Killing her after surviving a dragon's rage together felt weird. But this wasn't killing her, was it? Not really. This was *murder*. Justifiable murder perhaps, in an eye-for-an-eye kind of way. But that tends to leave the whole world blind.

For some reason that made me think of Octantis and her blindfold.

Ash strode forward to stand in front of her sister, her face pitiless as she held the Lady of Winter's gaze. I could only guess at the thoughts swirling behind her eyes. "Very well," she breathed after a few moments. Mav twitched in surprise.

"'Very well'?" I repeated, a little stunned. Ash might be the only person in the world with more grievance against Mav than my father and I, but I had not expected her to be on board with this. Dawn had once mocked me for treating her and her sisters like humans. Maybe I made that mistake again.

"So glad to have your permission," my father sneered, stepping closer to Mav. "But I was not asking for it."

"And yet you are a lord of *my* house," Ash said, the steel in her voice stopping my father in his tracks. "You are the prodigal Lord of Fire, who has returned to the court and laid low my greatest enemy." Damien was still, a cold expression sweeping across his face. I wondered if Ash was thinking about Dawn threatening to marry her to him if she had not earned her keep.

"This is not your vengeance, my lady," he snapped. "I made this happen, not you."

"It is mine if I say it is. Unless you are prepared to betray your house?" Ash did not raise her voice to match his tone. She reminded me of her mother, cold and composed. With steel in her spine, she held his gaze until he nodded, snarling. Ash stared at him for a few seconds longer, just to make sure he got the point.

I resisted the urge to cheer. Seeing Damien back down was an item near the top of my bucket list, way above meeting a dragon. I hadn't expected to live to see either. What a day.

"Well then, my lady," he grumbled. "What would you have us do?" He eyed the burning blade in my hands. "We seem to have the means to end an Immortal right in front of us."

Ash turned an appraising eye on the fiery sword, and me holding it. A chill ran down my spine at her too-calm expression, which would have been more at home on Dawn's face.

I looked down at the sword. I still didn't really trust that it wasn't going to start burning me any second. I felt like a toddler who had been allowed to touch a hot stove once for his own good. I knew there was danger, but I didn't understand it.

My eyes flicked from the sword to Mav, unsure if I had the grit to do what my father was proposing. I was a killer, but I wasn't sure I was ready to become a murderer. No sooner had that thought crossed my mind than the hilt in my hand flashed a warning pulse of danger-ous warmth. Startled, it took every ounce of self-control not to drop the sword.

"Ah, I think the sword says no," I announced, breathing a small sigh of relief as its handle immediately cooled off.

"What do you mean it says no?" my father demanded, staring at me like I had just uttered something unbelievably stupid.

I don't know what the sword is. Orion never talks about it, and my searches on the internet have been unhelpful. But I have ears. I pay attention some of the time. I have a guess or two about what sort of power fuels it. It says a lot that Willow is afraid to borrow any of its fire. If I'm right, I'm pretty sure that source takes a dim view of murder.

"You know what I mean," I replied, jutting my chin out defiantly. Damien's eyebrow twitched, but he didn't push it.

"Fortunately, I came prepared." He pulled the sheath off the dag-ger he was holding. I took a step back as I recognized the black knife Tania had used to murder Gloriana. Mav's eyes widened in horror. It pulsed with a wicked darkness in my father's hand.

"Where did you get that?" Ash's voice was frigid with anger.

"Everyone forgot about it that night, but I didn't."

Of course he hadn't. My father had returned to the court to thwart Gloriana in her plans to unlock the Path of Fire and get revenge for the death of our family. Seeing her die in front of him was an early Christmas present. Toss in an Immortal-killing weapon that would work on Mav? There was no way he would be distracted from getting his hands on it.

"Unlike your weapon, Matthew, this one has no qualms about a little vengeance," my father gloated.

Ash and I stared in uncomfortable silence at the demon-fueled weapon he held casually in his hand. I felt an oily stain on my mind. Not to draw too rigid line in the sand, but if the demon knife *wanted* to kill Mav and my blade didn't, that sure made me think. I don't like demons or Hell. I'm willing to admit a prejudice there. It's the same one I have against dragons and alligators now.

Damien took another step toward Mav, raising the dagger. All I had to do was stand to the side, silent, and I would have my revenge. But as I gazed down at the bound form of the Lady of Winter, it felt like a hollow victory.

The empty pang of family taken before their time would not be filled. There would just be another emptiness next to the first, the hole where my morality used to be. If I was lucky, this new void would be big enough to swallow the first, but somehow I doubted it.

The knife in his hand glinted darkly in the fluorescent lights, reminding me of something Dawn once told me: That Hell and its demons didn't want the Fae to return to their former glory. They profited from having their competitors weak and powerless. It was in their best interest that the Path of Fire did not return to the Dandelion Court.

I wondered how they would feel about Mav, the icy executioner, being removed from the board. I didn't have to think very hard. I knew they'd love it. Dawn had told my father she needed her sister in order to solidify her rule. Mav was a mad dog, but junkyards use them for a reason—it keeps the jackals out.

My father stepped into striking range, his golden eyes burning with a pleased fire. Something about this felt wrong. Not just on a moral level, but on a choreography one. This isn't how I had expected this to happen. *It's been arranged*, he'd told me.

"Wait," I shouted, holding out my left hand. Ash and Damien looked at me with oddly similar questioning looks. "Something's wrong about this," I insisted, taking a step toward Mav. "You want to use a *demon knife* to kill the Lady of Winter?"

"She's an Immortal, boy. How else did you think we were going to kill her?" my father shouted at me. He seemed almost frantic. I guess he had been dreaming of this moment for a long time.

"We're not going to kill her." I tried to make my voice as imposing as I could. Standing up to my father felt a little like trying to intimidate a boulder. He loomed over me as an unmovable object, and I was a very stoppable force.

"We aren't?" he snarled. "Did you not hear the lady of our house give her blessing?"

"Why?" Ash asked, turning to look at me, tiny, concerned cracks appearing in her frozen face of judgment. It almost broke my heart.

"Because"—I pointed at the inky-black dagger in my father's hand with the blazing sword Orion had loaned me—"that's exactly what the demon who gave Tania that knife wanted to happen."

"Idiot, it was to kill Gloriana."

"Killing Gloriana does the same thing killing Mav does," I insisted, refusing to rise to my father's bait.

"And what is that?"

"It weakens the Dandelion Court," Ash breathed in understanding.

"It does Mav's work for them," I snarled, glaring at the Lady of Winter. Just because I was speaking for her life didn't mean she was forgiven for killing my family or for trying to kill me.

"You cannot stop me from claiming what is mine," Damien hissed, drawing the knife back. Without thinking, I extended the fiery sword in my hand and took a step to shrink the distance between us. My heart raced in my chest as my blade hovered a few inches away from my father.

"You would strike down the last member of your family to spare the one who killed the rest?" he asked, his golden eyes hard.

"Killing either of you does the demons' work for them. I'd rather you both live."

We stared into each other's eyes for an eternity, channeling the same genetic stubbornness. It must come from his side of the family tree.

The sound of a slow clap behind me broke our staring contest. I whirled to find myself face-to-face with Dawn. The air around the Queen of All Fae shimmered as some sort of illusion faded away, revealing her lounging in an office chair like a bored employee.

Her white blouse was stained red on her chest and stomach where the cold-iron bullets had pierced her, and she was a little paler than usual, but otherwise she seemed fine. She wore a sardonic smile that didn't quite reach her eyes.

Unsure how to react to her sudden appearance, I lowered my sword. I felt a little like a kid who had been caught with his hand in the murder drawer, which is similar to the candy drawer, only worse. The more I learned about the power of Sylph, the air spirit, the more I began to secretly suspect that they were the most powerful of all the Paths by far. I was just careful to think that in the back of my mind, where Willow couldn't hear it.

"Oh hey, Your Majesty," I said lamely. "I didn't see you there."

"I bet." If Dawn appreciated me using her formal title, she didn't acknowledge it. Leveraging herself up from the chair, she rose to her feet, looking at the four us with judgmental eyes. She was enjoying our confusion, I realized. Dawn loved nothing more than seeing everyone off balance.

"I told you," she mused, glancing at my father.

Damien didn't respond but slid the black dagger back into its sheath. His golden eyes were still trying to bore holes into my skull. I don't think he appreciated me pointing a sword at him. I kind of enjoyed it.

"What do you mean you told him?" Ash demanded, turning to face her sister. "Was this one of your games?"

"Of course it was, dear." Dawn sighed, gesturing at my father to free Mav from her chains. He pulled a key from his pocket and tossed it on the floor in front of her feet with a disappointed frown.

"This whole thing was a test to see if I would go along with murdering your sister?" I asked, trying to catch up. "What was the point?"

"Both of you fled the cuckoo's nest after my ascension. You are members of my court, but I did not know if I could trust you."

"What about him?" I cried, pointing an accusing finger at my father. "This whole thing was his idea."

"Your father's loyalty is secured much better than with a vague promise of fealty," Dawn laughed. "Did you think that when I became Queen, I forgot all the lessons I had learned from my mother?"

"But he said he wanted to kill her..." I trailed off, trying to wrap my head around the mind games Dawn had subjected us to. My father was a Faerie; he could not lie. He wanted to kill Mav.

"He does. There was every chance Mav might die in this little test. I've promised him her head in seven hundred years. This just would have been sooner."

Something told me my father was more than a little disappointed I had proved Dawn right. The more I thought about his words, the more I was certain that he had wanted me to kill Mav. It hadn't been a test for him, but an opportunity.

"What of me, sister?" Ash asked, crossing her arms to stare at the Queen. "If I had taken my revenge on the one who murdered my court? What would you have done?"

"I would have understood," Dawn replied, without a smile on her royal face. "I would have understood, and I would have killed you for it."

Her promise sent a chill running down my spine. Looking into her frozen gold eyes, I didn't doubt it at all. Dawn was a creature of incredible cunning and minimal mercy. If we had crossed her, she would not have hesitated to cut us down.

"What interesting possibilities that would have opened up for you," cruel Dawn commented, fluttering her eyelashes at me. I felt Ash go stiff next to me, and I was very careful not to move. If Ash had been executed, my deal with the Dandelion Court would have been out of balance. The fate of my soul had been riding on my decision in more ways than one.

A terrified thought slowly wormed its way to the front of my consciousness, from the plotting back of my mind. In her own way, Dawn had offered to be my partner when her mother made me a contestant on the Fae equivalent of a dating show. I had chosen Ash, Dawn had become Queen, and I assumed that had been the end of it.

If something were to happen to Ash, I would have to be betrothed to another member of the family to maintain my portion of the bargain. Two of the remaining sisters were both in golden collars, which left only one eligible member of the family.

The Queen herself.

But that is a level of hubris that is out of control even for me. The idea that Dawn would be willing to murder her sister in order to force me to marry her was preposterous. Dawn wasn't just out of my league, she was playing a different game. What with her mind, wealth, and beauty, she could have her pick of the stars. Why in the world would she set her sights on me?

As much as I wanted to dismiss the theory as complete insanity, I couldn't quite do it. A new fear moved into my already crowded brain and made itself at home. Maybe I was being paranoid, and she just wanted to know if we were loyal. But I knew better than most that the Fae never have just one goal with their plans.

DEEPLY DISTURBED, I led our party of intrigue
and murder plots out of the construction office and
into the rain. I didn't understand everything that had
just gone down, but I didn't have any more time to spend unraveling
those webs right now. There was still more trouble to get into.

I kicked into a jog as I water sluiced down on me. I didn't care
about getting wetter, although the October chill was starting to suck as
the sun was obscured by Downtown's tall buildings. No, I was worried
about the scene I had left behind, about abandoning Orion with Polaris. It's safer to leave fire and gasoline alone together than those two.

Crunching across the gravel, I opened the gate, leaving it for my
Fae companions to close. A terrible dread had begun to rise in my

chest. A certainty of disaster, like a shapeless premonition. I knew what was about to happen would be bad, but I didn't know specifically how.

I burst out of the alley and into a war scene. Bellerophon and a dozen of his black-clad guards surrounded Orion, who was on his feet, bloody fists held in a fighting stance. Ascalon lay discarded on the street.

The lesser Nephilim swarmed the Hunter, swords and knives flashing. Orion twisted around one woman's strike, spinning into a roundhouse kick that sent another assailant flying. Still they pressed their attack, unafraid of the Constellation. A snarl of fury rose in my chest. The Hunter would teach them another deadly lesson before the day was done.

The blazing sword in my hand pulsed in echoed anger, reminding me of a horrible fact. Last time Bellerophon and his thugs jumped Orion, he'd had his sword. But he didn't have it now.

I did.

For the first time in living memory, the Hunter was toothless, and the scavengers had come for the weakened alpha. My legs pumped as I broke into a full sprint, rushing to my friend's aid. I felt like the second-to-last runner in an Olympic relay race. All I had to do was pass the baton to the anchor and watch him fly.

"Matt!" Alex shouted in warning as I charged toward the brawl. My head snapped to the left, and I slid to a stop. The younger Nephilim was on his knees at the feet of the North and South Stars, a horrified expression on his face. Sagittarius the Archer held a wickedly curved knife to his throat. The Constellation gave me a cruel smile and a wink as she saw my despair.

She wouldn't dare. She had already paid the price for crossing the Hunter once this weekend. She wouldn't *dare* kill his protégé, legal or not. Anger filled me as I took a threatening step toward her. The blazing sword in my hand vibrated in furious approval.

"Careful, boy," Polaris drawled, glancing over at me with a delighted smile. "You're still a Guest." His gaze flicked down to the badge hanging around my neck that proclaimed me a member of the Faerie delegation.

The North Star's warning stopped me cold.

If I barreled in to help my friend, I would be starting something bigger than just me picking a fight. It would be a declaration of war on behalf of the Dandelion Court. Slowly, I turned to look back at the four Fae standing behind me. Ash shot me a heartbroken expression but did not move. My gaze flicked to Dawn, pleading. The Queen of All Fae gave me a small frown but shook her head slowly. The alliance between the Dandelion Court and the Hunt didn't encompass protection against the Constellation Congregation, only dragons.

There was no way Dawn would risk crossing the leadership for fear of being tossed right back out. Plus, if they were expelled from the Congregation again, my eligibility for an Impossible Task went out the window. Which would permanently close the door on that loophole, however improbable it currently looked.

The trap for the Hunter had been well laid.

Heart racing, I swung my head back to the elder Nephilim watching their guards assault Orion. Defanged though the Hunter might be, he was making them work for it. He had knocked someone's sword out of their hand and now wielded the normal blade, driving back his attackers. A mean grin spread across my face to see the immortals scatter before my mentor.

"Are you really going to let this happen?" I shouted at Octantis, hoping I could convince the South Star to be the voice of reason. She had been on our side against the dragons, why would she turn on Orion now?

"The Hunter violated the Guest rules," she answered, her blindfolded eyes not turning away from the battle occurring before us. "He knew the laws and broke them anyway."

"They were murdering mortals!"

"Who were not Guests. Doyle and his dragons did not harm a single mortal within the halls of our convention. Orion slew a *Guest*." Her head turned to take in the scaled corpse of the dragon down the street. "Dragon-slaying has always had its price."

Suddenly I felt like an idiot. I hadn't been leading Doyle away from the convention center; he had very carefully attacked people *near* it, but not in it. As far as the law of the Congregation was concerned, Orion was the aggressor and murderer.

A loophole occurred to me, and I tensed my body, preparing to throw the sword to him like the world's deadliest football. I drew my arm back, ready, when a harsh sound stopped me. I looked down to see Polaris wagging his finger at me.

"No helping," he chided. His black eyes danced with gloating mirth. I realized this had been his plan all along. He had used Orion to get rid of the dragon problem but forced the Hunter into a position where he could be disposed of too. I resisted the urge to throw the sword at the ancient Nephilim to see what happened.

Helpless, I stood on the sidelines and watched with Alex as our protector was hemmed in. He might be the greatest living warrior, but even he couldn't stand up to the swarm surrounding him. It was only a matter of time before they overwhelmed him.

A Congregation guard caught him with a slash to his Achilles' heel. Orion let out a grunt and staggered to the side, his stolen sword red with Nephilim blood. He blocked another blow, but a second guard tackled him from the side while his sword was tangled, carrying him to the ground.

My heart skipped a beat as Orion slammed to the asphalt. Half a dozen of the guards dogpiled on the Hunter, holding him down. Bellerophon circled behind the pile kicking at Orion with steel-toed boots.

I called myself a traitor, coward, and a thousand worse things as I watched. But my hands were tied as surely as if I was wearing the manacles they forced around Orion's wrists. The Hunter was bleeding from a cut over his eye, but he tossed me a tight smile over the heads of the lesser Nephilim who dragged him to his feet.

They dragged him to the North and South Stars, forcing him to kneel before them. Polaris and Octantis looked down on him, their faces as different as their directions. Polaris wore a savage smile: Seeing Orion in chains was a victory for him. Octantis's face, by contrast, was as still as a frozen pond as she gazed down on her nephew in judgment.

"Well, what are you waiting for?" Polaris demanded, looking at his counterpart. "Pronounce the justice of the Congregation." Octantis frowned but did as he asked.

"Orion Dragon Slayer, for breaking the peace of the Constellation Convention and murdering a Guest of the Congregation, I judge you." The entire street was silent, waiting for Octantis's pronouncement. I briefly forgot how to breathe.

"I sentence you to five centuries of solitary confinement in Tartarus." I crumpled to my knees alongside my companions as despair claimed me. Even if I got my soul back, I would never see my friend again. An emptiness bloomed in my chest, spreading across my body until I was completely numb.

This couldn't be happening.

This couldn't be how it ended.

Orion smiled faintly, his teeth bright red with blood from a cut on the inside of his lip. At least I hoped that's why they were covered in blood. The time was nothing to an immortal like him. He would come out the other side the same age.

"That's it?" Polaris turned on his counterpart with a furious growl. "Playing favorites, are we, Justice?"

"*Furthermore,*" Octantis continued, as if she had not been interrupted, "an eye has been exchanged for an eye." Horror filled me as I realized where she was going. "As such, I decree the Dragon Constellation's scales have been balanced. He shall be released from Tartarus during the next open cycle."

Orion's unbothered expression crumpled into one of despair at her decree. After everything we had gone through, everything we had accomplished, we had failed. Draco, the dragon god, was free. Polaris spun, staring at his fellow Nephilim with shock on his face.

"Are you mad?" he half whispered, his face going pale. For the first time, I thought I saw a glimmer of fear in the ancient man's eyes. It occurred to me that up until this moment, the North Star had managed position himself perfectly. He hadn't really wanted the Dragon Dons to free their master, but he was enough of a coward to be a pushover when they came knocking. When the dust settled from this showdown, both Orion and Draco were supposed to be in chains, and he would be free to rule as he wished. Octantis releasing the god stopped him from sticking his landing.

Draco would emerge from his imprisonment to find one of his trusted lieutenants dead at the hand of the Constellation Congregation and who did Polaris have on hand to stand up to the monster? Sagittarius? Bellerophon?

Good luck with that.

"I am just. Did you forget that?" The South Star's voice was as cold as a headman's axe.

The falling rain was the only sound for a few long moments. If the cause hadn't been so horrible, I would have gotten a lot of pleasure out of the terrified expression on the North Star's face. "What of the former squire?" Polaris asked, nudging Alex with a foot. "What judgment do you declare for him?"

"As you pointed out, he was not a Guest."

Polaris rolled his eyes but didn't protest. He gave Sagittarius a sharp nod, and she begrudgingly withdrew her knife from hovering above his neck. Alex rose to his feet, a murderous chill in his blue eyes as he looked at the Archer.

"Try it, pup," Sagittarius teased, the curved knife twirling in her left hand.

"Alex," Orion grunted, the iron of his warning overcoming the pain in his voice. My friend didn't look away, but walked toward me, body stiff as a board. I rose to meet him, and we stood side by side as the best of us was chained and taken away. My heart broke in the way it only can for brothers and blood oaths. The lesser Nephilim crowded around the Hunter, their swords drawn. Even bound and disarmed, they still feared the Hunter.

Despite Orion's warning, I still felt like a pot of water at 211 degrees, just a hairbreadth away from boiling over in rage. My hand squeezed the hilt of my sword so tightly that it started to go numb. But I listened to my teacher, and I stood there and watched them go, feeling more damned than I ever had before.

"What about Doyle?" I demanded, remembering Alex telling me how big a deal secrecy was. "He exposed himself to the mortals. How many saw him in his unchained form and will tell the whole world? The damage he has done to this Congregation is incalculable—"

"Did you not sense the veil that was drawn over this place while he flew?" Polaris asked mildly, having gotten some of his fear under control. "No one outside of it saw him, and no one who was inside it will be believed. This will be remembered as another tragedy performed by humans."

"I dunno, I think the giant dragon carcass might be a clue," I replied caustically.

"Will it?" the North Star murmured in a haughty tone. Something in his voice made me look back at Doyle's mountainous body. With disgust I realized that it was beginning to liquefy. His forelegs were turning into a horrifying black paste as if dissolved by an acid. If that continued, there would be no dragon to find.

"All great works require sacrifice," I murmured, remembering Doyle's words to Samael. The Don had known he was dead the moment he took the serum. It had always been meant for Draco, but he had been boxed into a corner.

One of the Congregation guards made a move to collect the lance, but I stopped him with a growl. I raised the burning blade in a challenge, and he took a step backward.

"Lay off it, mortal," Polaris sighed in a bored tone.

"The Dandelion Court has a prior claim to Ascalon," I said, refusing to back down. Some frantic, panicked part of me thought that if I couldn't save my friend, at least I could save one of his weapons. It wasn't the same, but it was all I had.

Polaris eyed me and glanced over at my shoulder where Dawn still lurked. He gave the guard a dismissive flick of his hand, shooing him from the lance on the ground. "Might I recommend keeping it in a vault?" he drawled. "It could be dangerous in the wrong hands."

"I know just where to put it," Alex muttered from my side.

"I can think of a couple places I'd like to stick it," I agreed, glaring at the North Star.

Polaris didn't deign to respond to our insults. He shook his head and turned away, following his hounds that were dragging the Hunter to be imprisoned. Alex took an angry step after the North Star. I reached out and grabbed my friend by the shoulder, realizing with dread that it was just the two of us now.

"Not yet," I muttered under my breath.

"Not yet," Alex agreed after a long moment. Our oath of vengeance needed no more words. Bound by blood, honor, and loyalty, it might as well have been carved in stone. No matter what else happened, I had one burning item on my bucket list before the Devil came to claim my soul.

The Constellation Congregation retreated, and we let them go. In the distance, sirens sounded as the mortals began to close in on a situation they could never understand. I wondered if Richter would give me partial credit for trying to warn him about this.

Ash walked past me, brushing me with her fingertips in a gesture of comfort as she scooped up Ascalon from where it burned on the pavement. She tossed the long weapon over her shoulder like a continental soldier and marched back toward her sister.

I stood watching them lead my friend away, feeling hollow. Despite the small victories at the convention, it was hard to imagine how this weekend could have gone worse. The Hunt had been disbanded; Draco was going to be freed and our friend locked away in his place.

Orion vanishing around the corner in chains felt like seeing the sun set below the horizon, dropping my world into darkness. I didn't know when there would be light again.

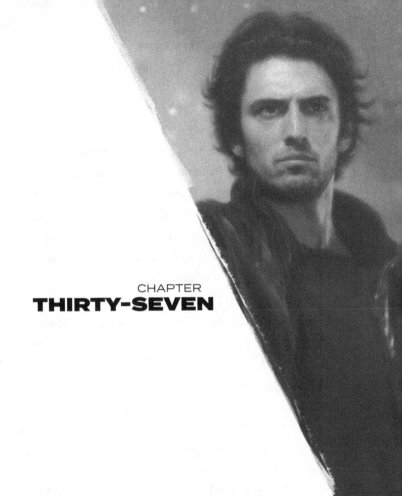

LEFT TO OUR own, empty devices, Alex and I trudged through the pouring rain to the parking structure that the faithful minivan was sheltering in. The blazing sword in my hand got a few strange looks, but people assumed it was a very impressive costume piece and let me be.

We suffered in silence during our walk. The rain made normal conversation almost impossible, and neither of us had anything we wanted to say loudly. The sky's fury echoed throughout the multi-floored structure like a dull roar as we walked down the row to where we had parked.

The spot by the van was empty now. Orion's bike lay somewhere near the body of Doyle. We should probably do something about that, although by the time he was free of Tartarus's grasp it would be a rusted antique.

Alex opened the back, and I gingerly placed the sword down. Part of me was afraid its flames would spread, setting Alex's car ablaze, but the fire seemed to know friend from foe—or in this case, interior upholstery from foe. Orion hadn't given me the sheath for the blade, so I would have to figure out a better way to store it while it waited for his return. I had a feeling it would survive the ravages of time much easier than the bike would.

With a sigh, I tossed the rest of my weapons in the back and slammed the rear door down. I needed a hot shower, a dozen ibuprofen, and a fifth of anything, and then I was gonna sleep for a week.

As I walked to the front of the van, I got an itchy feeling on the back of my neck, like I was being watched. I glanced around the parking garage but didn't see anyone or anything out of the ordinary—except for an unusually high concentration of black SUVs parked around us. Someone was trying to be clever but wasn't very good at it. Gee, I wonder who that could be.

"Hello?" I called out in an inviting manner. "We promise not to bite."

"Who are you talking to—" Alex began but was interrupted by half a dozen clicks as doors opened around us. FBI agents in black windbreakers surged out of the cars with pistols drawn, like ants pouring out of a disturbed nest. Several officers in SWAT gear trained submachine guns on me as they surrounded us.

I spotted the bulk of former Detective Jones moving next to former Detective Rodgers off to the side. They'd even brought the rookies. Special Agent Richter, my least favorite Fed, marched up to me, cold fury on his face.

"Going somewhere?" he demanded, fists clenched by his side.

"Home, mostly," I replied with a shrug. I knew I probably should be more careful with a dozen guns pointing at me, but when you've survived a dragon's flames, it's hard to keep your sense of danger sharp.

"We had a deal," he snarled, stepping closer, hands reaching for a pair of cuffs on his belt. *That* got my attention. I had some extra-strong feelings about anyone getting put in chains and led away right now. "I gave you a chance to do the right thing. Now dozens are dead, and you were involved in some sort of terrorist attack—"

"I told you there was an attack coming." I snapped, my anger finally beginning to boil over. "I called you, and I told you exactly what would happen, and you laughed at me." Jones and Rodgers exchanged meaningful glances in the back. The last thing I needed was the two of them on my case anymore.

"You also said the attack would be *tonight*," Richter snarled, spittle flecking out of his lips. "You purposely gave me the wrong info—"

"The timelines changed, but if you hadn't told me not to call you, I could have updated you."

"Or you're a part of this whole thing and gave us a bad tip on purpose!"

"You call yourself the Supernatural Division of the FBI, but you have no idea what's out there, do you? You have no idea what is coming for us."

"And what is coming for us?" The agent's voice was low and cold.

"Monsters," I declared as seriously as I could, trying to force my honesty through his thick skull.

The assembled agents around the parking garage all chuckled. A younger, less tired version of me would have been embarrassed to have all those eyes on me, laughing. But I had almost died too many times today to have much shame anymore.

"The members of the human population that have evolved to have more capability than the normally accepted range are not monsters. Sometimes they do monstrous things, but they are still just men,"

Richter informed me with the tone of a babysitter lecturing a particularly imaginative ward.

"Idiot," Alex muttered behind me.

"The tragedy that occurred today was the work of men, and seeing as you both are men who I know were involved, we'll be taking you with us." Richter glared at us as he drew his handcuffs from his belt and took another step toward me. I noted with a sense of distaste that the Feds might have no idea how the supernatural worked, but they knew to use a much more intense version of handcuffs.

"You have no idea what happened today, but if you push me, I can show you another tragedy," I threatened, summoning the last of Willow's borrowed flames. I took some satisfaction from the shocked look on Richter's face when he saw my hands catch on fire.

A dozen more clicks sounded as another set of car doors opened. I guess my fire had summoned the reinforcements. Men in black masks and armor poured out of five different-looking cars scattered along the aisle. Startled FBI agents spun, aiming their weapons at the interlopers. The masked men opened fire, their strange-looking guns hissing with the sound of compressed air as they shot darts into the ambushed Feds.

A black and green feathered dart slammed into Richter's neck, its long silver body gleaming in the low light. The man's eyes had enough time to widen before they rolled into the back of his head, and his knees went weak. With a series of thuds that sounded like an entire flock of birds falling from the sky, the agents fell bonelessly to the floor.

Jones was the last to collapse, his hand clapped to the dart sticking out of his chest. His extra mass must have taken a little longer to process the toxin. He glared at me with distrusting eyes as he went down. I thought I felt a faint vibration in the floor when he crashed into it.

Slowly, Alex and I raised our hands. Willow's flames vanished as the last of their supply ran dry. The dart-shooters lowered their weapons, standing at attention with military precision. One of them power-walked to the side of a beat-up sprinter van and slid the door open, revealing a pudgy older man in a tweed suit, who looked like he'd be more at home in a library than a shootout.

Feeling a little belligerent, I lowered my hands. Lazarus gave us both a genial smile and stepped down from the van, using one of his guard's arms for support. With the steady click of his cane, he crossed the parking lot to stand in front of me, towering over Special Agent Richter's still form.

"He dead?" I asked, nodding down at the Fed.

"Merely sleeping. Killing government agents creates more paperwork than it saves, in my experience." I have long known Lazarus is more than he appears to be, but for some reason, that cold math terrified me in a way Richter never could.

"It seems you are in need of some help," the tweed-suited monster continued, glancing around the scattered unconscious forms of law enforcement with an expression of mild curiosity. "I am prepared to offer you that help, in exchange for a favor." I've spent too much time with the Fae; that word is downright triggering for me now.

"No thanks," I replied immediately. "I got enough debts to last me a lifetime."

"I'm afraid I must insist." Lazarus leaned on his cane and stared at me, amused. "What other option do you have? The Hunter has been caged; your enemies will come for you now. An unchained dragon has been slain. The Dons will not be satisfied until they collect both your heads. Polaris will certainly not protect you either."

"And you can?" Alex challenged, arms folded.

"Protect you? No, I cannot do that. But I can hide you."

"Thanks, but we'll take our chances," I told him.

"You forget when these mortal agents wake, they will hunt you down and drag you to some off-the-books black site to interrogate you as terrorists. I'm sure they will be easy to convince that you had nothing to do with the men who attacked them. Perhaps I can at least help make that go away." Lazarus smirked as he saw the realization dawn on both our faces.

Richter would never believe in dragons. He certainly would never believe we were innocent after his entire squad was tranqed by masked gunmen. There was nothing we could possibly say to convince him otherwise.

"Besides, it may let you help your sister." Well, that was all he really had to say, wasn't it? I don't know why he bothered with all the other noise.

"What kind of favor?" I asked, narrowing my eyes.

A small smile played across the old's man face. He knew he had me.

"The deadly kind," he said.

DEATH TAX
BOOK FOUR OF THE DEBT COLLECTION:

Scan the QR Code below, or go to: andrewgivler.com/books

Thanks for reading Star Summit!

I hope you enjoyed it. If you did as always, please leave a review on Amazon, Goodreads, and anywhere else that you review books. It helps new readers find the series, and me pay my bills!

If you want to keep up with me, go to: andrewgivler.com/links or scan this (different) QR code on your phone!

ACKNOWLEDGEMENTS

Man, this is sometimes the hardest part of the book to write. So many people helped me get this book to the finish line and my biggest fear is I will forget one of them. Despite this being my third book, we had a lot of hurdles to overcome, and as always, I could never have pulled this off on my own.

To my new editing team, Laura and Taya, thank you so much for being willing to step into the middle of a series, and being so game to dig in and help me make this book solid. It's always a lot of extra work to catch up on a project part-way through and I'm very grateful for both of your efforts.

A huge thank you to the Alpha Readers, Aki, Caleb, and Molly. As always, they tolerate a sloppy mess in the hopes of helping me make something worthwhile out of it. Also, I would be remiss in not mentioning Austin and Rich from 2ToRamble (Go check out their podcast) who read a very early draft, identified a major weakness in the story and told me they didn't like it. It's only mild hyperbole to say they helped save this book.

To my excellent beta readers: Alex, Casey, Chrissy, Chris, Galen, Seb, and as always –Taylor thanks for being my sanity checks and helping me bring this sucker in for a landing.

Chris McGrath killed it with this cover, but you already knew that. Likewise, Shawn T. King's designs for this book are gorgeous.

To my author mentors, Seth Ring, Jamie Castle, James Hunter, and Bryce O'Connor, thanks for putting up with my endless questions and for answering ALL of my texts. (Except for Bryce who is the world's worst texter.)

Also, thanks Mom and Dad for everything.

I can't wait for you guys to read Death Tax.